ALSO BY BRUCE STERLING

The Artificial Kid

The Difference Engine (with William Gibson)

Distraction

Globalhead

A Good Old-Fashioned Future

The Hacker Crackdown

Heavy Weather

Holy Fire

Islands in the Net

Schismatrix

Tomorrow Now

Zeitgeist

THE ZENITH ANGLE

THE ZENITH ANGLE

Bruce Sterling

 BALLANTINE BOOKS • NEW YORK

A Del Rey® Book
Published by The Random House Publishing Group

www.delreydigital.com

Library of Congress Cataloging-in-Publication Data is available from the publisher upon request.

ISBN 0-345-46061-8

Book design by Susan Turner

Manufactured in the United States of America

First Edition: May 2004

10 9 8 7 6 5 4 3 2 1

ZENITH ANGLE:
*a measured angle between the sky directly overhead
and any object seen in the sky.*

THE ZENITH ANGLE

PROLOGUE

The Most Important Man in the World put his pants on one leg at a time. Then he put on his boots and his Stetson.

He checked the cabin's rusty mirror. The Most Important Man in the World looked pretty good in his cowboy hat. His haunted burnt-out eyes, his white stubble, and his lined sunken cheeks . . . wearing a cowboy hat changed all those things. In his Stetson, Tom DeFanti looked downright weather-beaten. Rugged. Solid. He was a man of the earth.

The little cabin was stark, lonely, old, and simple. It lacked running water, wiring, and a toilet. It required this mountain cabin and the 16,812 acres of Pinecrest Ranch to free Tom DeFanti from his monuments. His cable franchises. His newspapers. His Web sites. His news magazine. His Internet fiber-optic backbone. His international charitable foundation. His monuments loomed over him like so many tombstones.

Then there were his other, less mentionable monuments. They orbited high overhead, watching the globe around the clock.

DeFanti carefully buttoned his thick flannel shirt. September light was fading in the small glass panes.

Though he had been raised like an ugly swan by a working-class Italian family, Thomas DeFanti had always wanted and expected to become a very important man. However, DeFanti had never expected to become as incredibly rich as he was in the autumn of 1999. His holdings had blown up like a mushroom cloud, due to the Internet boom. This brought new attention to DeFanti that he didn't much like. It brought new expectations that he didn't know how to fulfill. Life for the very rich was always strange, and often dangerous.

The man who had built this old Colorado cabin had also been a very rich man. DeFanti had studied him closely. He was grateful for the dead man's useful lessons in how to get by.

The dead man had once been a very important Chicago banker. In 1911 he'd built the Colorado cabin, a tiny shelter for his astronomical observatory. The cabin was a quiet place, a safe place. The banker's ghost still hung there under the close black rafters, in a vapor of horse sweat, brandy, and fine cigars. Just like Tom DeFanti, the dead man had slept in that narrow, no-nonsense iron bed, its frame as solid as a torture rack. There was no room in that bed for his fireball society wife. The dead man's demanding rich kids were also three days away by a good long train ride. As for the dead man's lawyers, accountants, vice presidents, and stockholders, they might as well be stuck up on the Moon.

Here in the mountains of Pinecrest, the world had to let a man live. Clear air, elk, forests, red granite, fine fishing, good shooting. And the telescope, of course. Telescopes justified everything, for both Tom DeFanti and his dear friend and mentor, the dead banker. Telescopes brought both of them perspective, and solace, and a true kind of happiness. Telescopes, long nights left alone, and those sweet, dark, endless skies.

The cabin's stone hearth held a fragrant tang of pine ashes. In an old cedar chest, the dead banker had carefully hidden the sacred books of his boyhood. They were a boy's turn-of-the-century reading, adventure stories about industry and engineering, bought for a nickel each from the newsstands of boomtown Chicago. *Steam Man of the Plains* by "NoName," and about three dozen others. On overcast nights when the seeing was bad, DeFanti had read the flaking novelettes by lantern light. They were simple, good stories. Lots of manly action.

DeFanti removed the cowboy hat and splashed at his face from the tin bowl and white pitcher. He yanked open a rustic wooden drawer and thumbed through his private galaxy of pills. What would it be tonight? Prozac yes, aspirin yes, Viagra no thank you. Gingko yes. Valium yes, half a Valium, just to take some of the edge off. Plus yohimbe and vitamin A: they were good for his night vision.

DeFanti knocked his pills back with sips from a steaming coffee thermos. He gnawed at buffalo jerky to settle the drugs in his gut. DeFanti had discovered bison meat in his pursuit of a heart-healthy diet. Bison meat was the very best meat in America. Tom DeFanti now owned over four thousand bison.

DeFanti unlatched the cabin's door and left, carrying his fringed rawhide jacket. There was no sign of civilization, not a glimmer of light, not a telephone pole. One exception: far below in a stony bowl of hills, faint amber glows flicked on at the ranch's main hacienda. Over at the sprawling Pinecrest headquarters, Wife Number Four and her ranch staff were hosting a happy crowd of German cowboy tourists. The Germans had paid fifteen hundred dollars each to shoot a Pinecrest bull bison with their choice of Colt six-shooters or historical buffalo rifles.

DeFanti's fourth wife was an energetic young woman from Taipei. She was from a prominent Chinese family, spoke six languages, and had very strong working habits. Wife Number Four never slept in the astronomy cabin's iron bed. DeFanti did his best to keep her busy.

In the thin chill air of evening, DeFanti quickly missed his felt Stetson. He was too stubborn to climb back downhill for it. Besides, the cold dry breeze had chased off the smoke from the wildfires in the huge federal park to the east. It was the best observing he'd enjoyed all week.

Colorado's Continental Divide scraped at the fading orange sky. That colossal glow could restore any man's soul, if he still owned one. A crowd of man-made satellites was busily climbing from the planet's shadow. And if the zenith angle was exactly right, then the solar panels on a passing satellite might gleam down at the Earth for a few precious instants: a flare five times brighter than Venus.

DeFanti had extremely personal and very complicated feelings about satellites. Especially Iridium satellites, though spy satellites had always been his premier line of work. He had wanted in on the Iridium project so very badly. He had violently hated the engineers and financiers who had somehow launched a major global satellite communications network without him. And then he'd been astounded to see the whole enterprise simply fold up and collapse.

These wonderful Iridium satellites, dozens of high-tech metal birds each the size of a bus, beautifully designed, working perfectly and just as planned, costing more per pound than solid gold: they were glories of technology with no business model. The engineers had built them, and yet no one had come. Earthly cell phones were so much quicker, cheaper, smaller. The bankrupted satellites were doomed to be de-orbited and flung, one by one, into the black, chilly depths of the Atlantic Ocean.

This awful fate made the Iridium satellites very precious to DeFanti. The Most Important Man in the World had known some failures of his own, true agonies of the spirit. He never gloated at the wreckage of anybody else's grand ambitions. He had learned to watch such things with care, searching for men with drive who had the guts to survive the midnight of the soul. Such men were useful.

A long feathery brushstroke in the west touched his steadily darkening sky. DeFanti scowled. That mark was a jet's contrail, and by its angle across the heavens, DeFanti knew at once that the jet was headed for the Pinecrest private airstrip.

DeFanti wheeled his heavy spotter's binoculars on their black metal stand. The intruder, gleaming in fading sunlight high above the Rockies, was a sleek white Boeing Business Jet. It could jump the Pacific in two hops.

The Dot-Commie had returned.

Moments later, the jet roared overhead, shattering his serenity. The Dot-Commie had sent him some e-mail, DeFanti knew that, but the kid and his latest screaming crisis had somehow slipped De-Fanti's mind. The Dot-Commie always had dozens of irons in the fire. No e-biz fad ever escaped his notice.

DeFanti had five adult children. He got it about the nineties generation, as far as anyone did. But the Dot-Commie was special even by those weird standards, he was like . . . DeFanti rubbed his grizzled chin. The yohimbe was coming on, with a ticklish mental itch.

DeFanti knew that the Dot-Commie, for better or worse, was his spiritual heir. DeFanti's two sons wanted nothing to do with their father's empire. And properly so, because his sons, like their mothers, just didn't have what that took. The Dot-Commie took after DeFanti, though. The Dot-Commie always took plenty.

The Dot-Commie was entirely at home with DeFanti's many holdings. The cable, the cell phones, the Taiwanese chip fabricators, the Houston aerospace companies, the federally subsidized fiber-optic Internet supercomputers . . . Not only was the Dot-Commie at ease with all this high technology, he was downright nostalgic about it.

The jet slid behind a sharp ridge of pines. It missed the approach on DeFanti's short mountain runway, roared up gushing smoke, then circled and tried again. So much for clear skies. Was the kid letting his latest girlfriend pilot the thing? Why had DeFanti ever agreed to have a runway installed here in the first place?

Surely it would take the Dot-Commie a good long while to find him, up here in the cabin. Maybe Wife Number Four would politely force the kid to shower, shave, eat, and possibly even sleep. Maybe the German tourists would force him to drink a round of German beers.

DeFanti opened his laptop and checked its heavy-duty battery. He loaded the latest orbits for passing spacecraft. Tom DeFanti had always been very keen about the role of computers in outer space. He had shared those professional interests with the NORAD Space Defense Operations Center, and the National Security Agency, and the National Reconnaissance Office. With the CIA Office of Imagery Analysis. With the Consolidated Space Operations Center, at Colorado Springs. With the Air Force, and with the Space Force, and with the Navy's FLTSAT-COM, and with the National Photographic Interpretation Center. With aerospace engineering labs in Houston. With R&D labs in Northern Virginia. With camera labs in Rochester, New York. With antenna labs in Boulder, Colorado. And with Communists.

One glorious day during perestroika 1988, Tom DeFanti had found that he was helping American and Soviet space spies to share some very intimate notes. Long before the Hubble Space Telescope had ever appeared to scan the distant galaxies, Cold War spy satellites had carried giant telescopes into orbit. Those orbiting telescopes always looked down.

Through persistence and competence, Tom DeFanti had become the planet's go-to guy for "national technical means of verification." Not because DeFanti himself was a spy, although passing those notes at a disarmament conference certainly made him into one. No: it was because Tom DeFanti was basically running the spy-sat business. He was carrying the technical torch for the world's most secret industry. A very secret industry, nothing at all like normal astronomy, and not very much like normal computers, but an industry that combined both. It was quite a big, advanced, very high-tech industry. A big, dark, powerful industry. Tom DeFanti was the man within private enterprise who was most advancing that industry. He was building satellite hardware for gigantic spaceborne spy cameras. He was financing analysis software for huge torrents of visual data.

That made him an important man. Him, Tom DeFanti: a frantic business hustler who had stuck together a Houston aerospace company on a wing, a prayer, and some very quiet yachts packed with bales of Acapulco gold. He'd done some crazy things, for some desperate reasons. But he'd always had one business goal in mind: his own personal charge card for the Deep Black. Because the Deep Black budget for spy satellites was twice the size of the CIA's budget. And the Congress never ran any audits there.

The spy-sat community never advertised in *Aviation Week*. Once you became a trusted Deep Black supplier, though, you were a made man. If you could deliver their hardware on time, quietly, and within specs, you were a miracle for them. You were a major asset and to hell with the so-called budget. Six-thousand-dollar hammers; only to be expected. Ten-thousand-dollar toilet seats; go enjoy yourself.

To launder his Deep Black money, to try to make his own taxes make sense, DeFanti had started a cable company, and then a microwave phone network. He'd never guessed that cable TV would spread like crabgrass, or that cell phones would web Planet Earth with their white roadside antennas.

Time passed. Tom DeFanti grew older in his boardrooms. The wives cycled through his bedrooms, and his kids grew up and left. The Space Age gently faded into the yellowing pages of *Life* magazine. By the 1990s, aerospace jobs were fading away by double-digit percentages, while the Cyberspace Age exploded in the NASDAQ and a million Web sites. Business and the profit motive ruled the heavens and the earth.

But now, breaking his thoughts, here came the ugly racket of a trail bike. It was, of course, the Dot-Commie. The Dot-Commie was making a beeline for DeFanti's hidden cabin. He must have ridden the motorbike straight down his jet's embarkation stairs.

The Dot-Commie waved cheerfully as his bike veered wildly up the stony, darkening slope. The Dot-Commie wore a tartan shirt, jeans, boots, and an Australian outback hat. He looked both rugged and tidy. Jet lag never bothered the Dot-Commie. He ate like a weasel and he slept like a tomcat.

The Dot-Commie pulled up with a squeal of brand-new brakes. He hunted for the off switch on his spotless Japanese toy. Despite his fondness for fancy transportation, the Dot-Commie was no man of action. He tended toward pallor and plumpness. He would have shuddered at a horse.

The kid leaned the spotless bike against the gray wooden hulk of the dead man's abandoned observatory. The dead banker's old telescope had long since gone blind. His doors to the zenith had rusted shut on their iron pulleys and chains. The place had been used as a hay barn for decades. DeFanti had never altered the dead man's observatory, he had always just let it be. Now that the red Kawasaki trail bike leaned against its patient sides, he realized how much he loved that old building. What an affront that was.

"*Komban-wa*, Chairman-san!" said the Dot-Commie.

The Dot-Commie had a nice tapered chin and a smooth, tall genius forehead. He was the ladies' man version of a geek. Determined to avoid the kid's eager handshake, DeFanti absently patted the barrel of his faithful old Questar. The gingko was hitting his brain with a hot quiet rush now. The Dot-Commie had something big on his mind, and it would be complicated. It would be way too complicated. The Dot-Commie's personal schemes always included lots of extra gears and switches, just for their geeky coolness.

"So, kid, how'd it go across the big water?"

"Oh, Tom, in Tokyo, they are So Over. They just don't Get It." The Dot-Commie removed his Australian hat. His hair looked like a nice toupee on a solid stone egg. He flipped the hat and tossed it over. "This is for you, Tom."

DeFanti caught the hat, startled. "I don't need this," he lied.

"I bought it for you in Sydney. It's brand-new. It's fully adjustable, see? You just pull that little tab in the back."

DeFanti groaned in disbelief. Then he settled the kid's body-heated hatband around his own chilled scalp. The hat felt pretty good, really. The hat felt great. DeFanti always wore a hat when observing. Mountain nights were bitterly cold.

"Cell phones, the Japanese get," said the Dot-Commie. He opened his black laptop bag. "Cameras and faxes and stereos, the Japanese get. E-commerce, that stuff the Japanese never get." From an interior pocket of the bag he removed a two-ounce plastic windbreaker. He peeled it open with the delicacy of a man folding an origami crane.

"I saw the Super-Kamiokande," the Dot-Commie announced. "That was this trip's high point. That neutrino observatory. Tom, it's all you said it was, and it's more. It is insanely great."

"So, what, they gave you the lunch tour? Take this hat back."

"The name of DeFanti-san opens every door in astronomy! They loved me at Kamiokande. Keep the hat, Tom. The acolyte wears no hat when the Master lacks a hat." The Dot-Commie tunneled into his plastic windbreaker. It featured a snug little drawstring hood. He yanked the hood over his big egg head and grinned winningly. He looked like a plastic elf.

"At Kamiokande, they're underground and galactic at the same time!" the Dot-Commie crowed, dancing in place a little to shake off the cold. "About a billion photon tubes down there. They catch neutrinos inside giant tubs of water. The Japanese are underground, underwater, and observing the galaxy. All at the same time!"

"That scheme works out for them, does it?"

"They get major results!" The Dot-Commie dug into his magic black bag and retrieved his gleaming silver laptop. "So, which is bigger, DeFanti-sensei? The universe, or the screen that shows us the universe?"

"It's all about the screens now, kid."

"You bet, Ascended Master! You are beyond Zen!"

DeFanti chewed mournfully at his grizzled lower lip. "Quit bragging. It's more of the same, that's all. That LINEAR nonsense. And

NEAT, and LONEOS, and SPACEWATCH. Shipping astronomy on Internet routers. Why in hell did I ever pay for those things?"

"They can search every pixel in the sky, Tom."

DeFanti ignored him. "Nowadays, an amateur couldn't spot a fresh comet to save his life! Those stupid scanning machines will always beat him to that. God damn it, I always wanted to bag my own comet. Always. 'Comet DeFanti'!"

DeFanti put his twitching eyelid to the chilly rubber eyepiece of his Questar. He knew very well that the sky was being mapped with ruthless digital detail. That wasn't the part that scared him. No, the scary part was what space telescopes had done to the Earth. Pinecrest Ranch was easily visible from space. Any passing cosmonaut could see the place with the naked eye. The National Reconnaissance Office, as a meaningful gesture to a favorite supplier, had sent DeFanti a digital map of his whole Colorado spread.

The NRO had given Pinecrest Ranch the same loving attention that they gave to the garish palaces of Saddam Hussein. All the NRO data was stuffed inside DeFanti's laptop now. It wasn't just a flat simple map, oh, no. It was an interactive, topographic, 3-D computer model map, military-style, just like the Delta Force studied before they parachuted into some hellhole in the middle of nowhere. Tom DeFanti could ride across his Colorado spread with a mouse instead of a horse. He dreaded the day when he would really prefer life that way.

The Dot-Commie turned with solemn interest to DeFanti's second telescope. "So, Tom, what's with the tarp on this cool new hardware?"

DeFanti felt a pill-driven mental pang. He scratched below the hat brim. "I don't much care for that one, kid."

"Why not?"

"Because it auto-aligns to the zenith angle. It's got a forty-thousand-object stellar database built in. That's not a telescope. That thing's a damn Nintendo."

"Nintendo, the Japanese get! So, mind if I boot this baby up? Looks like terrific seeing up here tonight. The clarity of those skies!"

DeFanti clenched his chilly, wrinkled hands. "Yeah, except for your jet trail! That's a cloud of burning kerosene! You add that filth to the smog from the drought, and those wildfires on federal land . . . What has a man got to do?"

The Dot-Commie touched a fat black switch on the base of the telescope. The digital instrument perked up with an instant click and an obedient hum. "Wow, sweet! So, Tom, what's on our viewing agenda tonight?"

DeFanti glanced at the screen of his laptop. "An Iridium will flash at 9:17. There's a wonky old Soviet booster I've been keeping an eye on—pretty soon, it burns out big time. And after midnight, they're parking a MAGNUM/VORTEX in its graveyard orbit. We might catch a little glimpse of that, if we're lucky." He looked up. "Were you ever cleared for that one? MAGNUM/VORTEX?"

"Oh, sure. I'm cleared. I'm Mr. Cleared. We got some time to kill, huh? Can I show you something, Tom? It's important." The Dot-Commie deftly spun his laptop and confronted DeFanti with the glowing screen.

It was a long, dense computer image, all colored nodes and knobs. It looked like a galaxy, or maybe a globular cluster, violently ripped to shreds.

"Okay, so you're showing this to me."

"Tom, this is your intranet's traceroute map."

"And?"

The Dot-Commie sighed and changed gears. "Okay. The board of directors. Our latest member. That guy named Derek Vandeveer."

DeFanti said nothing. He'd been having a whole lot of trouble re-membering proper names lately. Not even the ginkgo helped him.

"The big blond guy. Beard. Glasses. Shy, endearing type. Stares into space a lot. Doodles whenever other people talk to him. Every-body calls him 'Van.' "

" 'Van.' Yeah, I know Van. The big geek."

"That's our man. Dr. Derek Vandeveer, star computer scientist, widely noted security expert. Van was a Stanford professor. He's the

VP for research at Mondiale. Van won the Turing Prize in 1994. The Vandeveer Algorithm was named after Van. Okay? We recruited Van, we put Van on our board. Because Van is our token super-geek. And Derek Vandeveer just made this map that I'm showing you."

"I knew that crazy bastard would be trouble. Is that what this is all about? This little visit of yours tonight?"

"Tom, I love it here in Colorado. I love satellites, I love an Iridium flashing. But yes, Tom. This is an emergency."

DeFanti levered the scope aside. "All right, then spill it."

"Corporate networks are complex and dynamically changing. We've got supply-chain and legacy partnerships, mergers and acquisitions activity, and a lot of staff turnover. The people come and go, and the deals come and go. But the machines just sit there. They're getting more and more cluttered as time goes on. It's the nervous system of the enterprise, that network and all its connections, and it's a living, growing thing, Tom. It's like it's got its own agenda."

"Yeah. I know that. Its agenda is to break our budget."

"Well, we didn't keep up with it properly. We let our corporate intranet grow just like the Internet grows, like a briar patch. So check out all these unauthorized connections into our enterprise network. Look at these bad links that Van found. He's outlined them for us in red here. They're mostly free connections that our people gave out for handshakes and goodwill, back when the Net was still new. This is a very interesting business structure that Van has revealed to us here, Tom. I don't think anybody has ever mapped your business activities to quite this level of detail."

DeFanti pulled down on the brim of his new hat. "Am I supposed to like this? I don't like it."

"Neither do I. Tom, you divested Pacific Data a good six years ago. But there are still IP host links in our system that date back to 1993. They still tie into Net machines that are running your news magazine's online presence, and running your charity foundation . . . Tom, your nonprofit people are *incredible*. Those clowns give away Internet access to *everybody they know*. Worldwide. They are tied into Russians, Czechs and Germans, the U.N., Gorbachev's foundations, Jimmy Carter's charities . . . They are tied into *Greenpeace*, Tom. We've got Exorbital and its deep-black projects tied into a network that is also open to Greenpeace. If the NSA ever gets wind of that, they'll go ballistic."

DeFanti peered at the densely crowded screen. "So, this yellow yarn-ball here. Which one is that?"

"That yellow one is Visual Research Labs. That's a spin-off, too. VRL is owned by the French now. But Vandeveer's global IP trace-route mapping has opened up VRL like a can of tuna fish. We could stroll through every machine they've got. Because VRL may be based in Paris now, but they're still running their graphics code off our Sun workstations in San Diego. Not one cent do they pay us for that service, either. They're freeloading on us!"

DeFanti said nothing. He hated virtual reality people. They were chock-full of crazy hype. They always had weird hair and peculiar shoes. And the French virtual reality crowd was, of course, much worse.

"We never knew the French were still hanging around in there, until Vandeveer started looking. Nobody ever asked our permission to come and go. It's just the old-school Net. They just linked up to us, and whenever they moved, nobody ever unplugged them."

"So who is carrying the damn flag here, them or us?"

"That's the big question, and so far, luckily, it's still us. In hacker-speak, we 'own' them. I mean, I'm no Derek Vandeveer. I don't hack, I'm a conceptualist. But with this traceroute map in my hands, yeah, basically I *am* their Internet. With a little work, I could pose as their system administrators, and download every confidential file they've got. And if they catch on to this bad-security situation, then that's much worse, of course. Because then they would 'own' us."

"I get it now. Cut to the chase. Who knows about this mess?"

"I do. And Derek Vandeveer. And now you, Mr. Chairman."

"Let me drive." DeFanti took the Dot-Commie's laptop. He spooled across the clustered tangle of Net connections. Vandeveer's map was the size of a bathroom carpet: tens of thousands of machines, spreading from busy hubs and linked into long, snaky webs. The networks were neatly labeled with pop-up company names and numeric IP addresses. DeFanti's Internet backbone company ran straight through the body of it, like the cloudy spine of the Milky Way.

The Internet backbone business was never an outfit that DeFanti had taken seriously. Running the Internet was a high-tech hobby for computer geeks. It was a favor he'd done to put a nice smile on the face of the National Science Foundation. But by now, 1999, in terms of market cap, it was by far the biggest part of DeFanti's empire. It had never, ever cleared one dime of profit, but the day-traders had it figured for the next Ford or General Motors. They were insane. The whole world had gone crazy.

DeFanti owned a cable company that owned movie studios. He owned a big, solemn news magazine that could make or break presidents. But in cyberspace and according to the NASDAQ, this makeshift wad of broadband fiber optics was bigger than Godzilla. And if the market believed it, well, then such was reality.

Everything on Vandeveer's map was piled up on DeFanti's backbone. Even long-forgotten outfits, like Wife Number Three's little leather-goods store, a toy he'd bought the woman to keep her out of trouble. Here was his older son's ridiculous adventure-canoeing outfit, making some bucks off the yuppie Green idiots who loved malarial jungles in Borneo. Everything.

"This son of a bitch knows more about us than we do about ourselves! How the hell did he find the time to draw all this?"

"He didn't draw it at all. That map graphs all those connections on the fly."

"Nobody can do that."

"Vandeveer does it. Van wrote that graphics program himself."

"Who is this guy? He's a menace! Where did you find him?"

The Dot-Commie was hurt. "We're a gifted generation, all right? Van was my roommate once." The Dot-Commie brandished his MIT

Beaver graduation ring. "I hooked Van up with his girlfriend—his wife, that is. Mrs. Vandeveer. Dr. Vandeveer that is, because Dottie has a Ph.D., too." The Dot-Commie smiled in the bluish light of the laptop. "They're very sweet people."

"Do we have anything useful on this guy? Like a leash, for instance?"

"Tom, please! Van is *on our board.* Van gets big comps and preferred stock. That's a very sweet deal for a little guy like him. He never does board work for anyone else. He joined us as a personal favor."

"Okay, so you kissed this hacker on the lips. And for that he gives us *this*?"

"We need this! This is what he does! Van would never cross us. Van's a straight-arrow R&D type. He's the classic white-hat hacker."

DeFanti scrolled across the tangle with angry flicks of his thumb. The map was a marvel. Not a marvel for himself, though. It was a marvel for federal investigators, industrial competitors, or divorce lawyers. It had unbuckled DeFanti's pants and dropped them round his ankles. And not just his own pants, either. "Beelzebub.darpa.mil." What clown was naming their servers over there?

The Dot-Commie's sleek face took on a gloomy look of serious adult concern. "Van has done us a big favor here, Tom. With this traceroute map, we can secure our infrastructure, plug our leaks, and eliminate a host of wasteful redundancies."

"What exactly is he trying to sell us?"

"Van's got nothing to do with selling. His R&D lab at Mondiale has a twenty-million-dollar budget and they let him do whatever he wants. He invented this! Tom, this is a unique competitive advantage for our outfit."

DeFanti set the laptop aside. "Okay, so give me the deliverable. What specific action are you recommending?"

"Okay then!" The Dot-Commie straightened alertly. "Cleaning up our own house, that comes first. That's a major capital expenditure, I admit that. But we have to do that, because living that loose is risky and just bad for business.

"Once we clean up and button ourselves down with a decent security policy, then we've got the whip hand over all those old-school hacker slobs. We can make real money there. We'll make our money by revealing this bad news to all these other people who were once linked to us. Their networks are buck-naked. We know that, and they don't know that yet. How much is that worth, Tom? You tell me."

DeFanti grunted. "That won't make us popular."

"I'm figuring this turns into a nice little sideline business all along our supply chain. Every outfit that you ever M&A'd or divested since the birth of the Internet. Every address squatter, every Internet freeloader . . . They've gotta pay us. That's only right. And, Tom, it's incredible how much just plain *junk* we're still running. Computers that we own and operate that *nobody ever looks at.* We plugged 'em in long ago and we forgot 'em. We need to yank them out of the garages and just dump them. The software they are running is years old and it's never been patched. They're very dangerous."

"Without this Vandeveer guy, this so-called threat wouldn't even exist."

"Obscurity is never security, Tom."

"It sure as hell is if no one ever looks."

"Machines will look. In cyberspace, everything looks. They'll program some net-bots to look. It's just a matter of time, that's all. We're stuck now between the old crappy Internet anarchy model, and a serious, big-time commercial industry. The only responsible course is to take appropriate steps. Before it comes apart on us, right at the seams."

DeFanti sighed. "Have you budgeted this?"

"No. I didn't. I really wanted to. I e-mailed our CIO. With a screaming yellow zonker red alert. The CIO told me to grow up and come back in ten years. That attitude won't do, Tom. That guy's due for retirement right now. Not ten years from now."

DeFanti struggled to remember the name of the Chief Information Officer. He knew the guy's face. He had a thick brown beard and he wore bad waistcoats that his wife stitched for him. DeFanti had rescued him from the financial wreckage of a dying mainframe company, and he was very loyal. He was seasoned, reliable, and lacking in ambition, everything the Dot-Commie was not. Small wonder the kid wanted his scalp.

"So what do I do for another CIO? Are you telling me you want that job?"

"Of course I don't want that job. But I'll tell you another thing, Tom. Van's connection map here is already out-of-date. Because my own network people have already cleaned house on my holding company, my Bangalore suppliers, those Chinese rocket people, and all of my e-commerce interests. Those are just baby companies, obviously. They're fresh start-ups and they don't have your legacy problems. But I don't want 'em stuck in that briar patch with all those open back doors and those misconfigured routers. That is just unacceptable."

"What is it you really want from me, kid? You want me to fire my CIO? That makes you happy?"

"No, Tom. That's not enough. You've got to fire the CIO, and the system administrators, and the whole crowd of good-old-boys who make such a habit of ignoring computer security. We need to run the networks in a better, more solid way now. Vandeveer doesn't know this, but he's given me a new management tool. We can replace all these high-salary geeks with some young engineers from India who will follow secure procedures, and work on a B-1HB visa for one-fourth their salary. That's what this traceroute map is telling me, Tom. Because that is this industry's future."

DeFanti's laptop broke the silence with a pinging sound. "Well, here we go then," DeFanti said.

"The Iridium flash already? That's great."

DeFanti glanced into his laptop and rattled off coordinates.

"How do I input those over here?" said the Dot-Commie, at his scope.

"Do it manually."

"Do I *look* like I do things manually?"

DeFanti stepped across and aligned the bigger telescope as well as his own. The two of them pressed their heads to their cold rubber eyepieces.

"Been to Sri Lanka lately?" DeFanti said.

"Nope. Should I go there? The jet's all warmed up."

"I sent e-mail to Dr. Clarke there. The 'Father of the Communications Satellite.' "

The Dot-Commie jerked erect from his eyescope. He was stunned. "Arthur C. Clarke? *The* Arthur C. Clarke?"

"Yes, and Dr. Clarke answered me. He was very polite."

"Tom, that is *fantastic*. What an honor! I saw *2001* when I was three years old."

They shut their glowing laptops to help their eyes adjust to night vision. "Are you seeing that haze up there?" DeFanti asked.

"It's pretty clear tonight, Tom. It is truly tremendous out here. What a treat."

"That's wildfire smog. Two years of drought in Colorado. Fires and fire alerts everywhere. The sons of bitches lit up that public park like Coney Island. There are state and county dark-sky ordinances, but they're feds, so they just ignore us. 'Sue us,' that's their attitude. A bunch of arrogant, wise-ass, brass-bottomed jacks-in-office . . ."

"I saw a flash!" the Dot-Commie yelped.

DeFanti switched eyes at his rubber eyepiece. No use. You had to be there just at the instant.

"It was like the flash off a rearview mirror," the Dot-Commie reported. "Metallic. Brief, yet intense."

"Back in the good old Wild West days, the U.S. Cavalry used heliographs," DeFanti said as he fruitlessly searched his patch of sky. There could be three, or even four flashes if the bird's attitude-control was going. But he was seeing nothing but stars.

"The Cavalry once sent a flash of sunlight off a mirror that was visible for ninety miles. The British Army used signal mirrors in Afghanistan. Can you imagine that? An army fighting with mirrors in Afghanistan."

"Afghanistan's not a consumer market," said the Dot-Commie. "Will there be more glints?"

"Maybe," said DeFanti. They waited. "No," he said finally. He straightened his aching back.

The Dot-Commie opened his laptop, woke the screen, and punched at keys. "So what do you make of our problem, Tom? I know it's a lot of money. But we can do that. We've got loads of market money now. Buckets."

"Okay, straight from the gut, kid. Here's the deal. You can't turn an enterprise around on the word of one guy from R&D. It doesn't matter if he's brilliant or even if he's technically correct. The middle-level people just won't go for that politically."

"Truth and technology will win over bull and bureaucracy, Tom. That's the story of the New Economy."

"No, kid, the truth does not win. For a couple of quarters the truth gets somewhere maybe. If everybody's real excited. But never in the long run, never." DeFanti shrugged. "The common wisdom always wins. Consensus, perception management, and the word on The Street. The markets, kid, the machine. The markets will go ape if we get all sweaty about some obscure security problem and start firing our established personnel. That move is panicky. It's just not professional."

"You're not Getting It here, Tom."

"Kid, I knew you would tell me that. I'm not so old that I'm blind and deaf yet. I know that it's a dangerous situation. It's dangerous like mixing Deep Black intelligence and also owning the media. But I do that anyway, because dangerous is what pays. Dangerous has got a high rate of return. Robert Maxwell mixed spies and media just like I did, and he jumped off his own yacht and he drowned. I knew that guy, Robert Maxwell. I knew him personally. I even knew his yacht."

"So we just drown our problem, that's your solution? What about Vandeveer? He's on the board."

"I've got nothing against Vandeveer. I'm glad that guy's inside our tent. You keep him in the dark and feed him lots of gold. I want him kept real happy. Him and the wife—Ditsy?"

"Dottie."

"Right. Nice, sweet, technical-weirdo people. I'll give 'em the personal gold star. The big chairman pat on the back. Very apprecia- tive. All the proper steps. All expenses paid trip to Finland for him and the missus and kids. We need some guy like him to go winkle out those little Finnish cell phone sons of bitches—what was their name again?"

"Nokia."

"Yeah, them. Nokia. God, I hate those people. A full report to the board about those instant-messaging apps. Six months, eight months, whatever. Keep him busy for us."

The Dot-Commie rustled in the darkness turning back to his telescope. "Van is plenty busy already. He's a VP for Mondiale. Van hates junkets, he only likes big toys. Fancy router hardware for his lab, that's what Van wants out of his life. I can shut Vandeveer up and I can sit on him if you want, there's no problem there. But I've got to tell you something, Tom: you're making a major mistake. We're in a high-tech revolution right now, the biggest thing since the invention of fire. If it's even halfway possible, then it's gonna happen."

"I know that you think that. But you're wrong."

"Okay," said the Dot-Commie. "If that's your full, considered judgment, I guess that's it, then."

"That's it, kid. So give me your fallback position."

The Dot-Commie pulled the thin plastic hood from his head. A dark night wind had come up and he smelled of hair gel and sweat. "Okay. Vandeveer wants to install some honeypot sites for network intruders. That way, if we are penetrated, at least we can trap the hackers."

"It's good to hear he's got some common sense. And that costs us?"

"Not much. Peanuts. He'd do it for us as a favor. He builds them for the FBI all the time."

DeFanti rubbed his stubbled chin. "This guy is a Bureau consul- tant, too?"

"Van lives on Internet time. He's thirty years old and he's got *stu-*

dents who are in the FBI." The Dot-Commie abandoned his telescope and turned his pale face to the zenith. "Well, I'm glad we hashed that issue out, at least. It's a load off my mind. My God, Tom, just look at all those stars. They've got *colors*. Look at that detail. You never see that near a city anymore. Nowhere in this world."

"This is the last place in the continental USA where a man can see truly black skies."

"You ever get the aurora borealis down here? I see them on over-the-pole flights. I see fantastic things, unbelievable."

"No. I don't." DeFanti paused. "What the hell is all that?"

"What? Point."

DeFanti raised his arm.

"I'd be guessing Cassiopeia, right?"

"No, I mean that flickering up there. That flickering looks auroral."

The Dot-Commie's voice dropped an octave. "You say, there's some 'flickering,' Tom?"

"There's *rotation*. And it's red . . ."

DeFanti began to tremble. It was some kind of object . . . It was round . . . it had thickness and depth, and it spun and it sparkled . . . He was witnessing a cataclysm in his beloved sky. It was a Flying Object, floating in the sky, an impossible creature of red dancing light.

"Look up there at that damn thing," he croaked.

"I'm not getting this, Tom. What exactly do you see up there?"

"It's flying and it's made out of lights. And it's *big!*"

"You're serious about this?"

"It's *getting closer!* Look at it!" DeFanti flinched and ducked. "Look out!"

"I'd *love* to see it, Tom. What are you talking about?"

"It tried to hurt us!" DeFanti shouted. "Now it's really moving! Oh, my God, look at the *speed* of that thing!" Awe, terror, wonder fought within DeFanti. Good Lord, to have *seen* a UFO, to know that the real world really held such things, not any joke, not a dream, *space travelers,* that alien spacecraft were true and real, just like hammers and hamburgers were real . . .

But that would burst the limits of the world. It meant total loss of control.

The Dot-Commie cleared his throat politely. "Tom, did you say this thing is 'made out of lights'? I only ask because, well, there are often good explanations for unusual visual phenomena."

"You can't see it at all? Look, it's wheeling around! It's coming back right at us!"

"No, Tom, I don't see it. I do see that it's getting a little hazier up there, as you said. So maybe it's just car headlights, Tom. It's reflections off low clouds."

"Kid, that thing is *flying.* I see a flying object!"

"Car headlights can fly. Their lights move up and down on hillsides. Wait, Tom! I've got it! It's those giant windmills."

"What?"

"It's flickering, right? They're setting up megawatt windmills down in the valley now. Those windmills are huge. Light could flicker off their giant blades."

"Are you crazy? It's a flying saucer! I can see it."

"Okay," the Dot-Commie said calmly. "Okay, I guess you're right. So then, it's got to be an artifact."

"An *alien* artifact?"

"No, an artifact of your perceptions."

"You're telling me that I'm a lunatic."

"No, Tom. I'm telling you that you're shaking like a leaf, and you're saying things that make no sense to me, and I can't see any reason why you should do that. And that's got me very, very concerned. This UFO you're witnessing, is it still up there?"

Of course the UFO was still up there. It wasn't there like a piece of aircraft metal—it was there like a terrifying bloody haze, occult, supernatural. "Yeah. It's still there. It's hovering. I think it's watching us."

"Tom, I never thought I would have to use this with you. But I learned this in the chill-out tent at Burning Man. Tell that thing to move, Tom. Give it an order, out loud. Speak right to it. Because if it's all in your head, then it'll do whatever you say."

"That proves I'm crazy."

"You're the boss, Tom. Tell that thing where to get off."

DeFanti craned his neck and stared. He was encountering a UFO. He didn't have many choices. "Move left!"

In all its uncanny majesty, the intruder slowly did as he said. It crawled across the zenith like a jellyfish.

"Move north!" DeFanti screamed.

The disc flickered in and out across a screen of distant stars.

DeFanti broke into sobs. The Dot-Commie put both his hands on the trembling rawhide fringes of DeFanti's shoulders. "Tom, let's go inside now, all right? It's just no good out here."

DeFanti's teeth were chattering. Cold tears ran down his face. "Help me."

"We've got to talk about the medications, Tom."

"I need something bad . . . I need . . . I need a cigarette."

"Back to the ranch house, okay? Can you ride the back of my bike? You're really shaky! Hey whoa! Let me help you up!"

CHAPTER ONE

With eager screams of hunger, little Ted Vandeveer drove his parents from their bed.

Dottie slipped a rubber-coated spoon between the infant's lips. Baby Ted blew out his chubby cheeks. Porridge spurted across the table.

Dottie scanned the mess. Her eyelids flicked upward meaningfully.

"Where's the au pair?" Van hedged.

"She didn't come in last night."

Van rose from his white plastic chair, and fetched a white paper towel. With the wisdom of experience, Van tore off a second towel for Ted to use as backup. Van still felt giddy inside his mansion's bright new kitchen. The new kitchen featured deep steel sinks, thick red granite counters, and a chromed fridge the size of a bank vault. When he'd signed up for a house renovation, Van hadn't known that New Jersey contractors were so enthusiastic.

At least, Van thought, Dottie approved of the changes in their house. The mansion's original kitchen had been a nightmare straight out of H. P. Lovecraft. Dottie's new kitchen was now the only place in the Vandeveer home where the plumbing worked properly.

On a corner of the new stove, a small TV played WNBC out of New York City. Van had hooked the set to a pair of rabbit ears. The township of Merwinster, New Jersey, lacked cable television. This was a serious blow to the Vandeveers, who were dedicated fans of *Babylon 5*, *Red Dwarf*, and *The X-Files*. But Mondiale was the little town's biggest employer, and Mondiale was in the broadband Internet business. Mondiale despised all cable TV outfits.

Van toweled up the baby's spew. Baby Ted enjoyed this fatherly attention. He kicked his chubby feet and emitted a joyous string of syllables.

"He said 'dada,' " Van remarked.

Dottie yawned and stirred the baby's porridge, propping her head on one slender hand. "Oh, Derek, he's just babbling."

Van said nothing. As a telecom expert, Van knew definitely that his son's vocalizations had contained the phonemes "dada." Technically speaking, Van was absolutely correct. However, he had learned never to argue with Dottie about such things.

Van dropped the dirty towel into a shiny kick-top wastebasket. He sat again in his plastic picnic chair, which popped and squeaked under his bulk. Van accepted this embarrassment quietly. He knew that it was all his own fault. He, Dr. Derek Vandeveer, famous computer scientist, owned a decaying Victorian mansion that had no proper furniture.

Historical Merwinster, New Jersey, was a gabled, colonial village, woody and surrounded by horse farms. It also boasted the third-biggest clump of fiber optics on America's Eastern Seaboard. Merwinster was a superb place for advancing high-tech research. Van routinely put in sixty-hour weeks inside the Mondiale R&D lab, so he was forced to live in the town.

Dr. Dottie Vandeveer spent her days in Boston, at the Smithsonian Astrophysics Lab. Van had bought the two of them a house in Merwinster because it seemed wrong to Van for his baby, their new third party, to have no home. Besides, Van had to do something practical with his money. Van was making money, and not just a lot of money. Van was the VP for Research and Development at Mondiale. Van was making a weird amount of money.

The TV muttered through a headache commercial, obscuring baby Ted's eager slurps from Dottie's rubber spoon. Van tapped at his trusty ThinkPad and checked the titles of the 117 pieces of e-mail piled up for him behind Mondiale's corporate firewall. With an effort, Van decided to ignore his e-mail, at least until noon. Because Dottie was home with him. Dottie was sleeping with him, and lavishing her sweet attentions on him. Dottie was cooking and cleaning and changing diapers. Dottie was wandering from room to dark decaying room inside the Vandeveer mansion, and wrinkling her brow with a judgmental, wifely look. Today, furnishing the house had priority.

So far, in his rare moments outside of the Mondiale science lab, Van had managed to buy a crib, a playpen, a feeding chair, a Spanish leather couch, a polished walnut table for the breakfast nook, a forty-six-inch flat-screen digital TV with DVD and VCR, and a nice solid marital bed. Van had also installed a sleek, modern Danish bedroom suite upstairs, for Helga the au pair girl. Helga the au pair girl was Swedish and nineteen. Helga had the best-furnished room in the Vandeveer mansion, but she almost never slept in.

According to Dottie, when she and Helga were alone together in Boston, the girl was always gentle, very sweet to the baby, and was never into any trouble with men. But in quiet little Merwinster, Helga went nuts. Helga was hell on wheels with the local computer nerds. She was a man-eater. The geeks were falling for blond Swedish Helga like bowling pins. Van sometimes wondered if he should charge them lane fees.

Dottie put the baby's yellow goop aside and got up to make toast and eggs. Van took rare pleasure in watching Dottie cooking for him. Dottie was not a natural cook. However, she had memorized an efficient routine for the creation of breakfast. Dottie fetched the brown eggs out of their recycled-paper carton and cracked them on the edge of the white blue-striped bowl, hitting the same spot on the rim, precisely, perfectly, every single time.

This sight touched something in Van that he lacked all words for. There was something silent and dark and colossal about the love he had for Dottie, like lake water moving under ice. The pleasure of watching her cooking was much like the secret pleasure he took in watching Dottie dress in the morning. Van loved to watch her, nude, tousled, and bleary, daintily attacking all her feminine rituals until she had fully assembled her public Dottieness. Watching Dottie dressing touched him even more than watching Dottie undressing.

Baby Ted was eleven months old. Ted had some major abandonment issues. Deprived of his mommy and his rubber spoon, Ted jacked his chubby knees in his high chair, with a wild, itchy look. Van watched his baby son intensely. The baby was of deep interest to Van. With his shock of fine fluffy hair and his bulging potbelly, baby Ted looked very much like Van's father-in-law, a solemn electrical engineer who had made a small fortune inventing specialized actuators.

Baby Ted packed a scream that could pierce like an ice pick. However, Ted changed his mind about howling for his mother. Instead, he picked intently at four loose Cheerios with his thumb and forefinger. Van sensed that picking up and eating a Cheerio was a major achievement for Ted. It was the baby equivalent of an adult landing a job.

Van ran his fingers through his thick sandy beard, still wet from the morning shower. He set his ThinkPad firmly aside to confront an unsteady heap of magazines. Junk-mail catalog people had gotten wind of Van's huge paycheck. For them, a computer geek with a new house and new baby was a gold mine.

Van didn't enjoy shopping, generally. Van enjoyed mathematics, tech hardware, cool sci-fi movies, his wife's company, and bowling. However, shopping had one great advantage for Van. Shopping made Van stop thinking about Nash equilibria and latency functions. Van had been thinking about these two computer-science issues for three months, seriously. Then for two weeks very seriously, and then for the last six days very, *very* seriously. So seriously that even Dottie became invisible to him. So seriously that sometimes Van had trouble walking.

However, Van's network-latency analysis had been successfully completed and written up. The white paper would be widely admired by key members of the IEEE, and cordially ignored by the Mondiale board of directors. So Van had given himself some time off.

Dottie, slim and delicious and barefoot, was silently reading the instructions that came with her new toaster oven. Dottie always read all the instructions for everything. Dottie always studied all the safety disclaimers and even the shrink-wrap contracts on software.

Back at MIT, classmates at the lab had teased Dottie about her compulsive habits. Van, however, had noticed that Dottie never made the dumb beginner's mistakes that everybody else made. Dottie was pleased to have this quality of hers recognized and admired. Eventually Dottie wrote her own vows and then married him.

Van leafed through slick colorful pages and discovered a Fortebraccio task lamp. The designer lamp looked both spoonlike and medical. It had the robust, optimistic feeling of a vintage Gene Roddenberry *Star Trek* episode. It rocked totally.

Van ripped the lamp's page from the catalog, and dumped the rest into the recycling bin at his elbow. Van's next catalog was chockfull of chairs. Van, his attention fully snagged now, settled deeply into the problem at hand. He was sitting uncomfortably in a lousy plastic picnic chair, one of a set of six that he had bought on a hasty lunch break at the nearest Home Depot. That situation just wouldn't do.

Dottie repeated herself. "Derek! You want seven-grain bread or whole wheat?"

Van came to with a start. "Which loaf has more in the queue?"

"Uhm, the whole wheat loaf has more slices left."

"Give me the other one." Logically, that bread was bound to taste better.

As a serious programmer, Van used an Aeron chair at his work. The Aeron was in some sense the ultimate programmer's working chair. The Aeron was the only chair that a hard-core hacker lifestyle required. Van hunched his thick shoulders thoughtfully. Yet, a family home did require some domestic chairs. For instance, an Aeron lacked the proper parameters for breakfast use. Spattered baby food would stick inside the Aeron's nylon mesh.

Van winced at the memory of the three FBI guys who had shown up at his Merwinster mansion, seeking his computer security advice. The FBI G-men had been forced to sit in Van's white plastic picnic chairs. The Bureau guys hadn't said a word about the plastic chairs—they just drank their instant coffee and took thorough notes on yellow legal pads—but they got that dismissive FBI look in their eyes. They were reclassifying him as a mere informant rather than a fully qualified expert. That wouldn't do, either.

Dottie didn't know about the FBI and their discreet visits to the house. Van hadn't told Dottie about the FBI, for he knew she wouldn't approve. The interested parties from the Treasury Department and the U.S. Navy Office of Special Investigations had also escaped Dottie's notice.

This was some catalog. It had chairs made of black leather and bent chrome tubing. Chairs like baseball mitts. Chairs like bent martini glasses. Chairs cut from single sheets of pale, ripply plywood.

Dottie slid a breakfast plate before him. Dottie's new toaster oven had browned Van's toast to absolute perfection. Van had never before witnessed such perfect toast. It lacked the crude striping effect that toast got from the cheap hot wires in everyday toasters.

"Derek, can you open this?"

Van put his manly grip to an imported black jar of English jam. The enameled lid popped off with a hollow smack. There was a rush of aroma so intense that Van felt five years old. This was very good jam. This black British jam had such royal Buckingham Palace authority that Van wanted to jump right up and salute.

"Honey, this stuff is some jam."

"It's blackberry!" Dottie sang out from behind her copper frying pan. "It's your favorite!"

Even the baby was astounded by the wondrous smell of the jam. Ted's round blue eyes went tense. "Dada!" he said.

"He said 'dada' again." Van spread the happy black jam across his perfect toast.

Ted slapped his spit-shiny mitts on his feeding tray. "Dada!" he screeched. "Dada!"

Dottie stared at her son in awe and delight. "Derek, he *did* say it!"

She rushed over to praise and caress the baby. Baby Ted grinned up at her. "Dada," he confided. Ted was always good-natured about his mother. He did his best to mellow her out.

Van watched the two of them carrying on. Life was very good for the Dada today. Van wolfed down all eight pieces of his toast. This was a caviar among blackberry jams. "Where on earth did you find this stuff, Dots?"

"Off the Internet."

"That'll work. Can you get a case discount?"

"You want more?"

"You bet. Point, click, and ship."

Van leaned back and slid his toast-crumbed plate aside, increasingly pleased with the universe. Dottie sidled over, bearing a plate of fluffy scrambled eggs. Van lifted his fork, but then his gaze collided with yet another catalog chair. The spectacle unhinged him.

"Holy gosh, Dottie! Look at this thing. Now that's a chair!"

"It looks like a spider."

"No, it's like an elk! Look at those legs!"

"The legs, that's the most spidery part."

"It's made out of *cast magnesium!*"

Dottie took away Van's jar of jam. "Paging Stanley Kubrick."

No way, thought Van. Kubrick's movie *2001* was all 1968! Now that it really was 2001, all that futuristic stuff was completely old-fashioned. Van sampled his scrambled eggs. They were very tasty indeed. "Magnesium! Wow, no one in the world can tool that stuff, and now it's in chairs!"

Dottie set her own plate down, with dabs of food on it that would scarcely feed a sparrow. She heaved the restless baby from his high chair and propped him on her slender thigh. Ted was a big kid and Dottie was a small woman. Ted flopped back and forth, flinging his solid head at her like a stray cannonball. "How much does it cost?" she said practically.

"Six hundred. Plus shipping."

"Six hundred dollars for one chair, Derek?"

"But it's magnesium *and* polycarbonate!" Van argued. "They only weigh seven kilograms! You can stack them."

Dottie examined the catalog page, fork halfway to her tender mouth. "But this chair doesn't even have a real back."

"It's got a back!" Van protested. "That thing that grows out of its arms, that is its back, see? I bet it's a lot more fun to sit in than it looks."

Dottie poured Van fresh coffee as Ted yanked at her pageboy brown hair.

"You don't like it," Van realized mournfully.

"That's a very interesting chair, honey, but it's just not very normal."

"We'll be the first on the block to have one."

Dottie only sighed.

Van stared at the awesome chair, trying not to be surly. Six hundred dollars meant nothing much to him. Obviously Mondiale's stock wasn't at the insanely stellar heights it had been when he had bought the mansion, but any guy who bought his wife emeralds for their anniversary wasn't going to whine about a magnesium chair.

Van couldn't bear to turn the catalog page. The astonishing chair was already part of his self-image. The chair gave him the same overwhelming feeling he had about computers: that they were *tools.* They were *serious work tools.* Only lamers ever flinched at buying work tools. If you were hard-core you just *went out and got them.*

"This is a Victorian house," Dottie offered softly. "That chair just doesn't fit in here. It's . . . well, it's just too far-out."

Dottie took the catalog from him and carefully read all the fine print.

"That chair is not that weird," Van muttered. "It's the whole world that's weird now. When the going gets weird, the weird turn pro." He picked up his wireless laptop. "I'm going to Google the guys who made it."

"You really want this thing, don't you?"

"Yeah, I want ten or twelve of them."

"Derek, that's seventy-two hundred dollars for chairs. That's not good sense." Dottie sighed. "Tony Carew keeps saying that we should diversify our investments. Because the market is so down this season."

"Okay, fine, fine, we're not stock freaks like Tony is, but folks still need wires and bits." Van shrugged. Van owned Mondiale stock because he put his own money where he himself worked. His work was the one thing in the world that Van fully understood. Whenever it came to the future, Van would firmly bet on himself. That had certainly worked out for him so far.

Dottie smoothed the glossy magazine page. "Derek, my grant expires this semester. That's not good. I've got everything publishable that I'm going to get out of that cluster survey. The peer review people are saying we need better instrumentation." She wiped at Ted's spit-shiny chin with Van's spare paper towel.

Van struggled to pay attention to her words. Dottie's lab work meant everything to her. She had been working for four solid years on her globular cluster study. Dottie had colleagues in Boston depending on her. Dottie had grad students to feed.

"Derek, it just didn't break wide open the way I hoped it would. That happens sometimes in science, you know. You can have a great idea, and you can put a lot of work into the hypothesis, but maybe your results just don't pan out."

"People love your dark energy nucleation theory," Van said supportively.

"I've been thinking of spending more time here at home."

Van's heart leapt. "Yeah?"

"Teddy's going to walk soon. And he's talking now, listen to him." Dottie stroked the baby's wispy hair as Ted's jolting head banged at her shoulder. "A little boy needs a normal life in some kind of normal house."

Van was shocked to realize how much this idea meant to him. Dottie, living with him and Ted, every single day. He felt stunned by the prospect. "Wow, being normal would be so fantastic."

Dottie winced. "Well, Helga is never around here for us when we need her. I think maybe I made a mistake there."

"We could put out an APB for her." Van smiled. "Aw, don't feel bad, honey. We can make do."

"I should do better," she muttered. "I just don't look after you and Teddie the way that I should."

Dottie was plunging into one of her guilty funks. The oncoming crisis was written all over her. Pretty soon she would start lamenting about her mother.

Dottie only allowed herself these painful fits of insecurity when she was really, really happy. It had taken Van ten years of marriage to figure that out, but now he understood it. She was spoiling their perfect day because she had to. It was her secret promise to an ugly, scary world that she would never enjoy her life too much.

Normally this behavior on her part upset Van, but today he felt so good that he found it comical. "Look, honey, so what if you got some bad news from your lab? What's the worst thing that can come out of all that? Come on, we're rich!"

"Honey bear," Dottie said, looking shyly at the spotless tabletop, "you work too hard. Even when you're not in your office, you let those computer cops push you around all the time." She picked up the other catalog again. "This funny chair you like so much? It's waterproof. And we do need some kind of porch chair. So get this one, and you can keep it outside. Okay?"

"Two?"

Her mouth twitched. "One, Derek."

"Okay then!" One chair, just as a starter. One chair would be his proof-of-concept. Van beamed at her.

The television grew more insistent. Dottie glanced over her shoulder at it. "Oh, my goodness! What a terrible accident."

"Huh." Van stared at the smoldering hole in the skyscraper. "Wow."

"That's New York, isn't it?"

"Yeah. Boy, you sure don't see that all the time." Van could have walked to the little TV in three strides, but on principle, he spent thirty seconds to locate its remote control. It was hiding in a heap of catalogs.

Van turned up the TV's volume. An announcer was filling dead air. Some big jet had collided with the World Trade Center.

Van scowled. "Hey, that place has the worst luck in the world."

Dottie looked puzzled and upset. Even Ted looked morose.

"I mean that crowd of bad guys with the big truck bomb," Van explained. "They tried to blow that place up once."

Dottie winced. It was not her kind of topic.

Van fetched up his ThinkPad from the floor. He figured he had better surf some Web news. These local TV guys had a lousy news budget.

Covertly, Van examined his e-mail. Thirty-four messages had arrived for him in the past two minutes. Van flicked through the titles. Security freaks from the cyberwar crowd. Discussion groups, Web updates. They were watching TV right at their computers, and instantly, they had gone nuts. Van was embarrassed to think that he knew so many of these people. It was even worse that so many of them had his e-mail address.

Van examined the television again. That television scene looked plenty bad. Van was no great expert on avionic systems, but he knew what any system-reliability expert would know about such things. He knew that it was very, very unlikely that FAA air traffic control at Kennedy and LaGuardia would ever let a jet aircraft just wander accidentally into a downtown New York skyscraper. New York City had a very heavy concentration of TRACONs and flow control units. So that couldn't be a conventional safety failure.

However. An unconventional failure, that was another story. An ugly story. Van had once spent a long, itchy three-day weekend with FEMA in Washington, watching information-warfare people describing the truly awful things that might be done by "adversaries" who "owned" federal air traffic control systems.

Since there really was no such thing in the world as "information warfare," information-warfare people were the weirdest people Van knew. Their tactics and enemies were all imaginary. There was a definite dark-fantasy element to these cyberwar characters. They were like a black flock of the crows of doom, haunting an orc battlefield out of Tolkien's *Lord of the Rings*. Van was reluctant to pay them any serious attention, because he suffered enough real-world security problems from hacker kids and viruses.

Van did recall one soundbite, however. A bespectacled infowar geek, all wound up and full of ghoulish relish, describing how every aircraft in the skies of America would "become a flying bomb."

Air traffic control was a major federal computer system. It was one of the biggest and oldest. Repeated attempts to fix it had failed. The guys in the FAA used simple, old-fashioned computers dating to the 1970s. They used them because they were much more reliable than any of the modern ones. FAA guys had very dark jokes about computers crashing. For them, a computer crashing meant an aircraft crashing. It meant "a midair passenger exchange." It meant "aluminum rain."

Now, Van realized, he was watching "aluminum rain" on New York's biggest skyscraper.

There was no way this was going to do. Not at all.

Van drew a slow breath. There was a bad scene on the TV, but he was prepared for it. He had been here before, in his imagination. In 1999, Mondiale had spent over 130 million dollars chasing down Y2K bugs, with many firm assurances from security experts that the planet would fall apart, otherwise. Van had believed it, too. He'd felt pretty bad about that belief, later. When computers hadn't crashed worldwide and the world hadn't transformed itself overnight into a dark *Mad Max* wasteland, that had been a personal humiliation for Van.

At least the Y2K money had really helped a big crowd of old programmers who had never saved up for retirement.

Van's New Year's resolution for the year 2001 had been to never panic over vaporware again. So Van stilled his beating heart as the blasted skyscraper burned fantastically on his television. He was living way ahead of the curve here. He was already thinking in tenth gear. Calm down, he thought. Chill out. Be rational.

Nothing really important was going to happen unless his phone rang. Some flurry of e-mail from his most paranoid and suspicious acquaintances, that did not mean a thing. Internet lists were no more than water coolers, nothing more than a place for loudmouths to shoot off. His home phone number was extremely private. If that phone rang, then that would mean big trouble.

If the phone did not ring, then he was much better off not saying anything to Dottie. Let her be happy. Let Ted be happy. Please, God, let everyone just be happy. Look at that sun at the window, that oak tree out in the lawn. It was such a nice day.

Uh-oh. There went the other one.

CHAPTER TWO

Air traffic had shut down. Van was living in a world without airplanes. His Frequent Flyer cards were useless plastic.

Van finally understood why he had bought himself a Range Rover Sport Utility Vehicle.

Van climbed into the Rover, parked at curbside as usual, for his Victorian mansion had no garage. He drove a few hundred yards from the village, parked in the colossal lot that had taken over a former horse farm, and walked through Mondiale's brown Plexiglas entranceway. Then he raided his lab for equipment. His coworkers asked him no questions about why he wanted so much hardware, or where he was going with it. At Mondiale's R&D lab, Van's friendliness to federal agents had never gone unnoticed.

The mood at the lab was shattered and jittery. Mondiale had lost a branch office inside the World Trade Center. While most of the Mondiale staff had retreated from the burning building in good order, two fatalities had been entombed in the giant disaster site. To have dead colleagues horribly killed by terrorists, that was very bad news, but the physical damage to Mondiale's telecom system was a stunning calamity. When Manhattan's two tallest buildings collapsed, New York's microwave capacity had been gutted.

Wrist-thick fiber-optic cables, safely buried deep in the WTC's subway, had been snapped, burned, and drowned. Bursting debris from the falling towers had crushed a telephone switching station in another building a block away. With cell-phone relays buried in the rubble, only one call in twenty was connecting. The landline networks were overwhelmed, with call volumes off the scale.

Cops, feds, journalists, even professional system administrators, were reduced to using Blackberry pagers. New York's telecom companies were howling for hardware, manpower, and emergency permissions from the FCC. They were struggling with closed bridges and streets thick with ash and debris.

It was the worst emergency of Van's career. It wasn't just a question of his company taking it on the chin. Feds wanted his advice, by e-mail, fax, and phone. Lots of feds wanted him. Law enforcement, military, infrastructure protection. Feds were calling him from agencies he had never heard of, and Van had heard of plenty. Van's future was swinging like a broken window in those smoking, ash-laden winds.

Van was not panicking. He felt grim confidence that he could manage. Cops were dead, firemen were dead, but Van was not dead and he was in no mood to play dead, either. He understood that his life had been profoundly changed, and that from now on his services would be needed in new ways. Everything would be different, harder, uglier, tougher, and more dangerous. He just needed a few good, solid ideas about that situation, that was all. He needed some genuine wisdom, from someone that he trusted. He needed a point of view that was solid and simple, that would settle him down.

So, for very powerful, very personal reasons, Van had to travel right away from Merwinster, New Jersey, to Burbank, California.

Dottie understood this need of his. She never asked for many words from him. As foul black clouds spread across the television screen, Dottie went into a trance of efficiency. Her bright eyes went keen and hard behind her little round glasses. She packed up the baby, and herself. She even managed to find Helga the au pair.

Van packed three PCs, a laptop, a printer, three toolboxes, eight car batteries, five cell phones, and a satellite dish. Van's car was a sixty-thousand-dollar truck with fifty-eight cubic feet of cargo space. This was the Range Rover's finest hour. He also removed the rearmost seats and packed the futon from his office, for the sake of catnaps. No matter what Van was going to be doing, he was sure he would be doing it around the clock.

Van wasn't keen on lugging Helga all the way to California. Helga was nineteen years old, and pretty, and a foreigner. For Helga, the United States was one big Disney World where sweet older men showered her with gifts. Real terrorism made Helga really terrified. Helga sobbed miserably as she climbed aboard the Range Rover. She couldn't stop weeping.

Van was an excellent driver. Dottie was a careful, methodical driver. Helga was a lousy teenage driver who lacked even an international driver's license. But Van made Helga drive the Rover anyway. The work made her stop sniffling.

As the miles rolled beneath the Range Rover's Michelins, Dottie comforted baby Ted and tried to doze, saving up for her time at the wheel. Dottie wasn't allowed much sleep. Time and again her Motorola tri-band sprang to shrill, bleeping life. Dottie's astrophysicists in Boston regarded Dottie as their den mom. Dottie was the only one in the lab who knew where they kept the whiteboard markers and the Coffee-mate.

Van had never overheard Dottie dealing at such intimate length with her colleagues. During their married life, she had usually spared him this ordeal. Van was guiltily aware that he had never been a good

faculty spouse for Dottie. They had a two-career marriage where neither party self-sacrificed. They were hugely respectful of each other's
gifts and ambitions, so whenever somebody's personal sacrifice became absolutely necessary, they would hire somebody else to do it,
and pay them a salary.

On I-470 near Columbus, Ohio, Van's third phone rang. Of the
five he had packed, the batteries had already died in two.

"Vandeveer."

"Van, that was not a hack attack." This was a familiar voice for
Van. A growl, really. Orson Welles with a Texas accent. A man who
weighed three hundred pounds and always talked straight from the
gut.

Van knew Jeb's voice well, but there was a new quality in it since
those towers had gone down.

"How do you know that?" Van said, scowling as he sat cross-
legged on his folded futon. "Did they check the avionics boxes?"

"Al Qaeda can't hack avionics. They're too dumb for that. That
was a Moslem suicide attack. The biggest one ever."

Van considered this. Moslem fanatical terrorists, crashing American jets into giant skyscrapers, with themselves still aboard. This was
absurd to him. It was a nutty thriller-fantasy straight out of Hollywood blockbusters. If Jeb said it was true, though, then Van was willing to accept it as the working hypothesis. Jeb had the best contacts
in the business.

Van cleared his throat. "So how did they do that?"

"They used box cutters to seize the cockpit. We think they
trained their kamikaze pilots on flight simulators."

"So they knocked down two skyscrapers with razor blades? And
the Pentagon, too?"

"That's the story, Van."

"What is with these guys?" Van barked. "They have got to die!"

"You haven't heard the good part yet. The fourth plane missed the
White House. That was their last target: economic, military, and finally political. They missed the White House because the passengers

attacked them inside the fourth plane. Their families got through to them on cell phones." Jeb lowered his growl. "That is gonna be the *future* of this story, Van. It's phones versus razors. It's our networks versus their death cult. For as long as that takes."

Van was in a rage. His ears thumped with each heartbeat. "It's a real good thing they like dying, then."

"Van, I need you on my team. Has anyone else called you?"

"Oh, yeah, lots," Van blurted. Jeb had called first, it was true, but since then he had heard from the Bureau. The Commerce Department. The CIRC. The OMB. Several Air Force outfits he had never heard of. Even the Bureau of Weights and Measures.

"Lotta headhunters out there all of a sudden," Jeb agreed cordially. "But where were they when the screen was blank, huh?"

Van said nothing. Jeb had been the very first cop to take serious, practical notice of Van's talents. The state and local cyber-cops in California were so hip that they ran their own user's groups. Silicon Valley cops met a lot of white-hat hacker kids, and tended to think they were cute. But when Van had encountered Jeb, Van's life had changed overnight. Young Derek Vandeveer, a dewy-eyed comp-sci student with an intellectual interest in security issues, had suddenly met the maven's maven.

Jeb had collared Van and dragged him right behind the curtains. Suddenly there were special, classified courses for Van in FLETC and Quantico, with behind-the-scenes briefings from panting, sweaty computer emergency-response teams. Jeb had shown Van the ropes, put him in the know, enrolled him in the big-time show. He'd shown Van the realities of federal information technology: awesome levels of screwup that only a superpower could create or afford. "Situation Normal: All Fouled Up." If a SNAFU remained a superpower, it was due to guys like Jeb.

"In my outfit," Jeb promised, "we actually know what we're doing. That's what's so different and refreshing about us at the CCIAB."

"Jeb, I've got to talk to a consultant about all this."

Van glanced up guiltily at the passenger seat. To judge by that stricken look in her eyes, Dottie knew very well what he was doing. Dottie knew about Jeb and Jeb's world. But Dottie was not his "consultant." Dottie was just his collateral damage. Dottie had the look of a woman in a *Titanic* lifeboat, watching the black icy water come up over the bows at the man she had left behind. Van had never been able to hide anything important from Dottie. He had married a woman with an IQ of 155.

And besides, New York was on fire.

"I knew your father, Van," Jeb said. "We never had to ask him twice."

"I told you I needed seventy-two hours to make up my mind."

"You just call me whenever you reach a decision, Van. I'll be here in the Beltway." Jeb clicked off.

As he labored on his computers in the back of the truck, Van thought darkly of the various times in his life when he should have felt terrorized. Basically, there weren't any. He'd had some strange experiences, here and there. Van could rightly say that he had been blooded out in the field. He was a civilian computer expert from a large, aggressive corporation. He'd taken part in five hacker raids with joint federal-state investigation teams. American computer cops often took large crowds with them when they raided computer hackers. This made it clear to the other, more everyday cops that kids sitting alone in their bedrooms really were committing crimes. So Van had been there when muscled Secret Service guys in their tasseled shoes and Kevlar armor were stomping from attic to basement, menacing Mom and Dad with drawn guns.

Mom and Dad were always pretty terrified by this. Van just concentrated on the bagging-and-tagging, hauling Junior's piece-of-junk hotrod PC out to the white Chevy vans. Van rather liked that part of the assignment. Especially that look on the face of the code kid when he realized that he knew nothing about the people who really owned and ran the Internet.

The hacking scene was pretty brainy as crime scenes went, but it did have down-and-dirty sides. Hacker kids were an ankle-biting nuisance, but the scene also featured ugly grown-ups who stole real money. Van's counsel had often been sought in such matters. Van knew more than anyone should know about the bad programming habits of Russian bank hackers. Vietnamese computer-chip theft rings were certainly no shrinking violets. A crime family of crazy, shotgun-toting hillbillies in West Virginia had preyed on Mondiale for years, stealing mile after mile of copper telephone cable and selling it for junk.

The thought of their criminal lives and attitudes gave Van a metallic tang in his mouth. Van had never spent much brainpower on ethics, law, or philosophy, but Van could taste evil. Cops knew this about him. Cops regarded Van as a stand-up guy. Cops bought him beer. They respected the difficult things that he told them about network security and computer forensics, and they took the technical steps that he recommended. Van's software and his advice worked out pretty well for cops. Arrests and convictions followed, and cops liked that a lot.

Since cops were underfoot and on the phone so much, Van had taught himself to speak the language of cops. He kind of liked the way that cops cut the crap. When people became cops, certain delicate, fussy, annoying parts of them got scraped off. Van understood this much more keenly after the events of September 11, 2001. The size and scale of what had happened . . . it had freed him from some complicated doubts and hesitations.

Van was not saying much about these new perceptions. He was trying to figure out his proper place in the world to come.

He stared at his wife as she cradled her infant and her phone with the same overloaded arm, the kid's noggin nudging her glasses up her cheek. Van was dragging his wife across America, from sea to shining sea, and Dottie could not tell her friends why she had left, or where she was going, or what it was all about.

Because it was secret.

Dottie understood about secret lives, because she had married a

Vandeveer. She had met Van's father, mother, and even his grandfather, and got along with them better than Van did. The women in the Vandeveer family always caught on about the nature of government secrecy, even when their men never said much.

But in the ten years of their marriage, Dottie had never had to deal hands-on with any serious secrecy, not like this. Cops, Dottie could handle: she was always very polite to cops. Dottie never cheated on taxes or broke any traffic laws. For her own peace of mind, Dottie had read the statute books of both Massachusetts and New Jersey.

Spies were more secret than cops. Sometimes the spook world did lean in on Van. Spooks were getting very into cyber-security and infowar. The NSA had always been into computers, and the rest of the spook crowd were finding that world to be more and more sexy. Van had never looked for any spooks voluntarily. But people he knew intimately had lived in that secret world. They had been transformed à la *Buffy the Vampire Slayer.* Cops changed, but spooks really changed. Spooks could be totally alone, at home, asleep in some warm, dark room, and cold, curling dry-ice fumes would pour out from under their sheets.

Government secrecy was already changing Dottie, right before Van's eyes.

Van had a dark, interior, cavernous feeling, as if his life had crumbled at a touch. He stared at the passing Ohio landscape, annoyed to find it so Ohio-like. He badly missed his e-mail. There was no e-mail available to him inside the Rover. Once he got them both online again, Van figured, he could send Dottie a nice reassuring note. He loved Dottie, but he and Dottie always got along best by e-mail. E-mail was how he had first asked her out. E-mail was how they carried out their professional lives and coordinated their schedules. They often sent each other e-mail over the breakfast table when they were living inside the same house. They'd decided to have a child by e-mail. They'd been talking over e-mail about having another one.

Van stubbornly assembled his hardware in the back of the truck, using racks and plastic cable ties. With the rear seats hauled out and left behind in New Jersey, the Range Rover was cozy for him, about the size and shape of a grad student's office cubicle. With the ongoing network crisis in Manhattan's pipes and antennas, Van figured that no one would notice his physical absence from Mondiale's Merwinster offices. Not as long as he stayed on the Internet around the clock.

Van's life's work was software. Although he had seen it done, he would never splice a cable down a manhole. In smoldering Manhattan, Mondiale was trying to call-forward thousands of local numbers, porting them from a smashed and charred facility into underused third-party switching stations in Queens and Hackensack. The FCC was freaking out, so it was willing to let this strange experiment happen.

Van knew that Mondiale's routing algorithms for "local number portability" were not going to scale up. Van knew that the porting code would break. It would break in some interesting ways. He might understand how it had broken, and where. He might figure out how to patch it. That would be nontrivial programming under tremendous time pressure, the kind that very few people could do. It was the most useful emergency service he could offer to his company.

But to be available to his stricken coworkers, Van needed fast, efficient Internet access, all across America. This sounded pretty simple. But it wasn't simple. It was impossible. Most of the East Coast was okay for high-speed Net access, except for lower Manhattan, which was on fire now. If Van phoned ahead and called in some favors, he could drive in to campuses and computer centers, to hook up on the superfast Internet2 grid. Van was a regular veteran at the Joint Techs conference, the cabal of geeks and wonks who were building the Next Generation Internet. The sysadmins of Internet2 were very much Van's kind of people.

Van had taught at Stanford before Mondiale had made him their world-beating business offer, so the West Coast was even friendlier to Van and his digital needs. There were also big islands of advanced technical sanity in places like Austin, Texas, and Madison, Wisconsin. But out here in Range Rover land, the Internet was a shambles. Van was rolling across America with two women and a baby, and the United States was huge. Van flew across America quite commonly, but he'd never rolled across it before. The USA had cyber-free boondocks that Van had never imagined were there.

Cell phones worked for data delivery—sort of. Dottie was fitfully hooking her Motorola into her laptop, using power from the Rover's cigarette lighter. That might do for the occasional brief e-mail, but that certainly wasn't Van's idea of access. For Van, cell phones were like breath mints. Even on America's major interstates, which were spiked with cell-phone towers from coast to coast, those breath mints had big holes in the middle. Any dip in the highway could drop you right out of a download.

Wireless laptops running on Wi-Fi worked only in Wi-Fi hot spots a hundred yards across.

That left Van only one way to angle it: the zenith angle. Satellites, straight overhead. Internet access direct from Space, the Final Frontier. Van had never before used a satellite Internet service. He certainly knew that such things existed, but he lacked any reason to mess with them. Van had broadband Internet2 in his office and two T-1 trunk lines into his house.

He needed to be practical, though. Outer space would just have to do.

Dottie understood this, so she let him work. Dottie needed serious Net access even worse than Van did. Astrophysicists were the world's heaviest users of scientific broadband. When an astrophysicist wanted to "send a file," that meant some colossal mountain of data that would simulate the entire atmosphere of the gas-giant Jupiter. Astronomers had such ferocious need for bandwidth that they were up for any scheme that might get it for them, no matter how far-fetched. They even hooked millions of PCs together, in giant volunteer networks, that combed the galaxy around the clock for alien radio signals.

Van was doing his best for the two of them. It was a family matter and a question of professional pride. Through misplaced company loyalty, Van had hastily found and grabbed one of Mondiale's
"Cosmoband" Internet satellite rigs. Since the Cosmoband product
was commercially available and sold off-the-shelf to Mondiale's customers, Van had assumed he would just hook up the dish and get
going.

But Mondiale had told the world an evil lie.

Van's PCs worked. His Ethernet worked, after some effort. The
batteries worked, until they ran out. The Cosmoband satellite rig was
an alien from outer space.

Like most commercial space companies, Cosmoband was battered and humbled. To the awful surprise of its starry-eyed investors,
Cosmoband had lost hundreds of millions of dollars. Cosmoband's
little fleet of leftover satellites were scraping the bottom of the cosmic
barrel, haunting the niche markets, doing automatic meter-reading
and freight-truck asset tracking.

The crippled Cosmoband had been snapped up in one of
Mondiale's legendary acquisition frenzies. This treatment only
added to Cosmoband's troubles. Mondiale's brass ignored the company, because it lacked any go-go stock-booming growth rates. All
the original Cosmoband rocket engineers had run away. Cosmoband's remaining people were a rabble of cheap hucksters. They offered their so-called Interplanetary Internet in tiny back-page ads
in *Popular Mechanics* and *Scientific American.*

They had no service guarantees. No service person anywhere
ever answered Cosmoband's phones. And their klutzy old software
didn't mesh with Microsoft's new releases.

Van wanted to punch a big metal hole through the top of the
Rover, to install the Cosmoband dish on a truck mount. Dottie, who
loved the truck, hated this idea, and worse yet, to do this was no use.
No satellite dish ever worked on a car or truck that was moving. The
least little bump or pothole always knocked satellite dishes right off
their signal.

Marveling at this gross stupidity, Van studied his blurry satellite documentation, badly printed in distant Korea. Baby Ted filled his diapers and shrieked until the Rover's walls rang with his rage. No one had explained to poor Ted why he had to spend forty-four hours and thirty-nine minutes strapped into a crashproofed car seat. Ted had turned from yuppie puppy into a mobile papoose in bondage. Ted was into a straight-out raw deal.

At a darkened roadside stop near Springfield, Missouri, Dottie pumped gas, her delicate hands clutching the ridged nozzle and heaving Arab oil into the Range Rover's 24.6-gallon belly. Van was alarmed to find himself actually setting foot in the state of Missouri. He'd flown over the state dozens of times and had never touched Missouri in his life. But Missouri had Coca-Cola and gasoline. Missouri had a stop-and-go mart with a nice clear view of the southern horizon. The mart had heavy-duty power plugs on its outside walls. No one was watching them to see if somebody borrowed a lot of electricity. So Missouri would do.

Yawning Helga, the peevish baby, and a frowning Dottie vanished in search of bathrooms, beef jerky, and Hershey bars. Van parked the Rover in a grimy corner of the tarmac, next to a dripping drain hole and a rusty Dumpster. He plugged in. Then he hauled out his big plastic satellite dish and a tangle of multicolored cables. He set up under moth-clouded streetlights.

Passersby honked at him. The skeptical people of Missouri were laughing at him and his weird satellite gizmo. Cosmoband's mobile Internet dish looked like a half-melted white surfboard welded to a chrome bar stool. Van was a grown man with a beard and a bad temper, wrestling a *Star Wars* Storm Trooper contraption.

Shaking with road jitters, Van booted the ground-control positioner. The Cosmoband receiver whined and labored grumpily. Then, with dim, mechanical reluctance, it connected.

The dish's target was dusty, old-fashioned, and underused. It was one-fifth the size of Van's Range Rover. And it was orbiting twenty-three thousand miles above the Earth.

Van triumphantly sucked e-mail from the sky.

Dottie appeared. "Honey bear, you want a Slurpee or something?"

"Nope."

She examined the cables. "Can I log on now?"

"Yep. Right through the LAN."

A smile broke. "That's great, Derek!"

As the Rover rolled on, Van read all his mail. Then they stopped the truck again, he hauled the dish out, and grabbed fresh work out of a sequence of Mondiale internal Web sites. He struggled with Mondiale's broken router code. He spewed more mail back into the sky. Then he did this again. And again. He did it under the stars, and at dawn. Then he slept on the futon. Then he did it again.

When they reached Burbank, Van was driving the Rover, the only one left awake. He was six hours ahead of schedule. They had crossed four time zones and broken speed laws in eight states.

CHAPTER THREE

Except for his bone-weariness and persistent itches inside his stale clothes, Van had no problem driving around Burbank. He had spent a lot of time in Burbank with his grandfather, in summers and on holidays.

For a time, during his marriage to Grandmother Number Two, Elmer "Chuck" Vandeveer had owned a weekend ranch up in the hills, not far from the Ronald Reagan spread. The times spent on the ranch were Van's happiest childhood memories. He had much enjoyed falling off horses, setting fire to bales of hay, and shooting rats and rabbits there.

Grandpa Chuck was one of the world's top aerodynamicists. As a jet designer, he tackled his toy ranch as a make-or-break project:

feverishly digging post holes, efficiently splitting firewood. Even Grandpa's relaxation was high performance. Grandpa's only true home, the place where he logged all his overtime, the source of his deepest passions in life, was a windowless, two-story concrete bunker, near the Burbank airport. It had lead-lined rooms for antisurveillance. It was frequented by the Air Force elite and the CIA.

Grandpa belonged to the Lockheed Skunk Works.

The city of Burbank had exploded since Van's childhood in the 1970s, eating every orange grove and rolling up the hills. The palmy streets near the airport were still vaguely familiar to him. Van sensed that he himself had transformed even more radically than the town of Burbank. From a little kid with a popsicle stick, a stammer, bad allergies, and a plastic *Star Wars* X-wing fighter, into a big, quiet, bearded geek with black glasses, smelling of sweat.

Something wasn't adding up here. Van thumbed at the Rover's GPS, alarmed. He had input the proper street address, but he didn't recognize the neighborhood at all. This was not his grandfather's elder-care facility.

Van had rarely seen his grandfather during the long hectic frenzy of the dot-com boom. Since he'd left Stanford, he'd scarcely seen his grandfather at all. Old folks' homes were far from cheerful places. Phone calls, e-mail, digital Christmas cards, and digital photos of the baby. That was pretty much it between himself and his grandpa Chuck. But now the GPS had guided him to a completely unknown destination. It appeared to be a private home, a cheap stucco duplex.

Worse yet, it was only 6:17 in the morning, local California time. Van pulled to the overgrown grassy curb and stopped the Rover. He got out, and gently shut the solid door, with care for his sleeping brood. When he stretched, his cramped spine popped loudly in three places. Carpal tunnel twinged in his overworked wrists.

Feeling lost and absurd, Van approached the front door. Duplex A belonged to "C. Chang," while Duplex B listed a "J. Srinivasan." Van had rushed headlong to California to find his grandfather mysteriously replaced by two immigrant families. And he had no other address for Elmer Vandeveer.

Van dismally pondered his next move. It was past eight o'clock on the East Coast. He might call his mother in Georgia, and ask her if she knew anything about his grandfather's strange disappearance. Van's mother was long-divorced from his father. She had settled down with a gentlemanly Southern dentist, who spared her the impossible treatment she had gotten from Van's father.

Van had never liked explaining difficult things to his mother, on the phone or off of it. Van and his mother were from two very different worlds. Van's world was serious and technical, while her world was just plain messy. Even though his mother meant well and tried to listen, she always ended up taking offense.

For Van to call his own father was completely out of the question. Van never knew his father's phone number, or even if his father had a home or a phone. Not only did they not talk, they had nothing to say to each other.

Van certainly wasn't going to call the local cops in Burbank and ask around for Missing Persons. The cops would page the NCIC database, and even twenty years into retirement, a top-secret engineer who built spy planes was not the kind of guy who ought to just go missing. That situation could get ugly fast.

Van might, conceivably, ask Jeb for help. In the world of federal databases, Jeb knew everybody who was anybody. Jeb had been there on the ground floor, literally laying the pipes. But Jeb would be ticked-off that his star recruit had lost his own grandfather—and lacked the smarts to find him.

Van decided to case the joint. That was risky and probably dumb, but at least it was practical. It didn't feel much worse than raiding some teenage hacker punk's house as the family snoozed. It was dawn, birds were twittering, and the place looked quiet and sleepy.

Van opened a rusty wrought-iron gate thick with bougainvillea. He tiptoed warily down a narrow, weedy brick path, clustered with wet pink blooms. Was there one loose doorknob around here, maybe? Just one window left open to the California breezes? Any open entrance around here? Any system vulnerability where a nearsighted computer scientist, six feet one and putting on weight, might illegally break-and-enter the home of some total strangers? Had he gone completely insane? What the hell was he thinking here? At any moment Van expected the white flick of a motion-sensor light. The frenzied barking of a Doberman. The cocking of a shotgun.

Van peeked warily through a barred window and around an untucked curtain. The Srinivasan home featured brightly patterned carpets, a sandalwood screen, a wicker couch with thick colorful pillows, and a silent TV. Dusty yellow garlands hung around a dead man's framed portrait on the far wall.

Battling his sense of despair, Van cleaned his glasses on his shirttail. Then he sidled around the house.

He heard a voice.

Van edged closer and peered through another window, this one damp and grimy, with rusting iron bars and a warped sill of cheap aluminum. He had found a kid's room, a boy's, to judge by the cheery sports wallpaper and the sky-blue ceiling. The ceiling was hung with a dozen dusty airplane models, dangling on stout black threads. They were World War II fighters: a snarling P-51 Mustang, a Messerschmidt with the Iron Cross, a red-dotted Zero.

A kid's wooden desk had a full set of modeling tools. Testor's enamels, brushes, tweezers, a big square magnifying-glass lamp, and a very odd kind of glue gun. A half-completed model was pinched by alligator clips in a jointed metal armature.

The voice came from a gumdrop-colored Macintosh computer. Van disliked Macintoshes. First, because they were cute toys for artists rather than serious computers. Second, the female Macintosh voice that read error messages aloud sounded eerily like Dottie's voice. Not Dottie's normal voice, but the voice Dottie used when she was really upset with him. When Dottie was being very, very clear with him about something.

The Macintosh was reading a text file aloud. The bedroom's faded walls, wallpapered in yellow race cars, were piled with battered white filing boxes. Many of the boxes had ruptured, spilling thick heaps of blue-stenciled engineering paper.

Van's grandfather, wearing ratty pink slippers and a pale blue terry-cloth bathrobe, came shuffling from the open door of the bathroom. He settled himself with painful care on a plain metal stool in front of the desk. Then he clicked at his candy-colored one-button Macintosh mouse.

"Step one," the Mac said in its female voice. "Attach C-1, Instrument Panel F, and C-2, Instrument Panel R, to A-1, fuselage top."

Van's grandfather raised the arm of the lamp and made its beam hover over the desk. It threw thick shadows over the model's jigsaw bits of gray plastic.

Van tapped at the window.

It was no use. The old man was hard of hearing. His eyes were going, too. His hair was gone, a few untrimmed snowy wisps. The muscle had shrunk from his spindly legs. His once-thick neck was bent and baggy, and his face, once so round, so red and beefy, was pale and creased and liver-spotted. Van was gazing through the window into a time machine. It promised him a painful future of bypass surgery, of bellyaches and Rogaine.

Van reached into his cargo pants and found his laser pointer. He beamed the laser's red dot through the window.

The old man caught on. He rose from the metal stool and teetered to the iron-barred window. Van waved at him.

Grandpa Chuck turned down the cheap window latch and tugged at the dew-spotted frame. The window was jammed. Van got a purchase on it with the screwdriver blade of his Swiss Army knife. The window jerked open an inch and a half. They gazed at each other through the bars.

"How are you, son?" said the old man.

"I'm fine, Grandpa. You?"

"Not too good, not too bad." Van's grandfather scowled. His

scowl was scary. He had been an important man, once. A man who gave orders and had them obeyed.

"I know why you're here, son," the old man said, his pale eyes slitting under pouchy lids. "It's about those Boeings. The ones that hit those skyscrapers."

"That's right," Van admitted.

"So the CIA wants you back now, Robbie? I always said those spooks would have to come running back to you, didn't I?"

"I'm not Robbie," Van blurted. "Robbie's my dad. It's me, Van. I mean, it's Derek."

The old man's face gaped. "Little Derek? Robbie's little Derek? Derek the computer kid?"

"Yeah, Grandpa. The feds are all over me. They want me to take a job in Washington."

Grandpa lifted a liver-spotted hand and smoothed the remains of his hair. "Well, you'd better come in here, then."

Van shook the iron bars. They had been poorly installed, tucked into the stucco with cheap Phillips-head screws. Five minutes with a power tool would have them all down.

"Did you ring the doorbell?" the old man said patiently. "Mrs. Srinivasan should be making her congee now."

Surprised, Van retreated. He brushed dew from the hems of his pants and rang the doorbell to Duplex B. It was answered by a stout older lady in a Hawaiian blouse, purple slacks, and rubber zoris.

"Oh," Mrs. Srinivasan said, looking him up and down. "You must be Chuck's boy. I've heard so much about you."

"I'm his grandson."

"You look just like him."

"Could I talk to Dr. Vandeveer? It's urgent."

She opened the door politely. Van stepped inside. A glossy Hindu calendar with a technicolor goddess flapped gently on the wall. The place smelled of cone incense, Lipton tea, and tandoori.

"Sorry to be so, uh, soon," Van said.

"He's no trouble, darling," Mrs. Srinivasan said cheerily, leading Van down a scruffy, beige-carpeted hall. "We keep him in my son's old room. He wanders a little. He wanders a lot, don't you know."

"I heard about that."

"Sometimes he is also very stubborn, your grandfather."

Van nodded. "Yeah."

"Please don't let him smoke." Mrs. Srinivasan pulled a house key from a chain in her hefty bodice. She unlocked the door.

His grandfather's cell smelled like a plastics refinery. He'd been using hot glue on his airplane models, something pungent. Worse yet, he'd somehow managed to set fire to his mattress. The narrow wooden bed frame had a long scorched scar under the wrinkled sheets.

Van hugged his grandfather. The old man was stooped and bony, with the empty flabbiness of old age.

"Little Derek," he said.

"I brought my son here, Grandpa Chuck. Your great-grandson, Ted. Ted's out there in a truck."

"Oh, wow." The old man stared at him peaceably.

"Grandpa, I think I need your advice."

"My advice, huh? Okey-doke!" The old man sat on his metal stool, and with a careful, visible effort, he crossed his legs. "Shoot!"

"So, did you see what just went down in New York? And the Pentagon?"

"I saw the President's speech on the TV," said the old man, growing livelier. "That kid is all right! He's not like his dad. Old George Bush, he used to come out to Area 51 when we were launching Blackbirds. Back when George was Company. 'Fifty thousand dollars an hour,' George Bush would say. No vision thing! He was a bean-counter! Anywhere on earth, any Sunday, a Blackbird could bring back pictures! High detail, too, shots the size of bedsheets!"

"Great."

"We never lost a pilot."

"Right."

"First ten pilots inside the Blackbird, nine of them became Air Force generals!"

"Right, Grandpa."

"Surveillance shots straight from Eastman Kodak, the size of dang tabletops! With a handful of planes. Every one of 'em hand-made in Burbank!"

Van had no reply to offer. An ugly thrill of weariness shot through him. He sat on the old man's reeking bed. It scrunched and shot a cloud of dust into a beam of morning sunlight.

"Made out of *titanium*!" The old man brandished his glue gun. It was big, hollow, and shiny, with fins like a Flash Gordon ray gun.

Van sat up. "Titanium, huh?"

Van's grandfather quickly hid the titanium gun inside his desk. He forgot to unplug it, though, so the bright red cord simply trailed from the desk to the wall, an obvious trip hazard. "Robbie, if I say anything I'm not supposed to say, you just forget that. All right? You can just forget about all of it." He waved a hand at the crumbling boxes on his walls. "Don't look at all this."

Van looked. "What?"

"They ordered us to *destroy all the documents*. They ordered us to *break all our tools*." The pain was still fresh in the old man's eyes. "That was the worst part, Robbie: when the politicians make you break your dang tools." He looked at the slumping wall of boxes. "The D-21, that's what this is. A cruise missile we built in 1963. Well, ol' Kelly Johnson had all these boxes stored in his garage in Alameda. He was supposed to burn 'em all. Burn every blueprint! But in Alameda? There woulda been an *air quality report*!" The old man chuckled wheezily. "Couldn't break those federal rules and regulations now, could he? The EPA wouldn't like the *smoke*! They'da sent ol' Kelly straight to Leavenworth! Ha ha ha!"

"Why did they break your tools?" Van coaxed.

"So we couldn't pull the D-21 back out of mothballs when the White House changed hands. Breaking the tools, son, that's the only way to kill a secret federal program and keep it dead. We built 'em a cruise missile twenty-five years before its time. Fifty Lockheed engineers and about a hundred union guys in our machine shop. We made that bird with our own hands. We fired it over Red China four times. At Mach 3. The Chinese never knew a dang thing about that."

"Did it work?"

"Radar signature the size of a Ping-Pong ball . . ." The old man lost interest suddenly. He groped at his bathrobe for a missing shirt pocket. Van recognized the gesture. He was missing his lighter, and his cigarettes. They'd made him stop smoking twenty years ago.

"They make you burn everything," he groused, still patting at himself. "Then they give you a secret medal for doing that. What's the name of that new cartoon? That comic strip? That good one. The one with all the engineers in it."

Enlightenment dawned. "You mean 'Dilbert'?"

"That's right, that's the one!" The old man rose and teetered to the tiny closet. He opened the warped veneer door with a squeak and picked at a loose heap of uniformly colored golf shirts. None of them had any cigarette pockets in them. "Good old Dilbert. Well, in the Skunk Works, nobody ever had to be the Dilbert. Because Kelly Johnson wouldn't suffer a damn fool around for seven seconds. Whenever Kelly lowered the boom, the Air Force brass ran back to NORAD to cry in their three-percent beer."

Grandpa Chuck chose a shirt and a loose, baggy pair of elastic sweatpants. Then he carefully sat on the narrow, stinking bed. He went through the extensive effort of pulling his baggy pants on, one leg at a time. His knees trembled pitifully. His back was very stiff. Van wanted to help his grandfather put his pants on, but there was something far too intimate about that.

"Grandpa, the feds want me for some kind of cyber Skunk Works. It's really small. It's secret. It's elite."

"Do they have a decent R&D budget?"

"Well, yeah, that's what they tell me."

"Take that job," his grandfather said. He tugged the stretchy waistband up over his bony hips. "Son, you never know what you can accomplish until you're in a Skunk Works. You pull that off right, and a Skunk Works makes big things happen. Big new things, son, genuine breakthroughs in engineering. Things competitors wouldn't believe. Things the *Congress* wouldn't believe." The old man dropped his bathrobe and fingered his golf shirt, sitting there bare-chested. "The enemy believes it, though. The enemy, they pretty much always believe it. They even believed in Star Wars!"

Van had never directly worked for the federal government. Occasional consulting as a favor to Jeb and his friends, sure, but no official title, and certainly no money ever changing hands. To get himself full-time, paying federal work, there were legendary ethics hassles. And the feds didn't pay well. If he went to work for Jeb, Dottie and he would lose a whole lot of money. "I'd have to leave my day job. Mondiale is a great company. They're building the future."

"Son, can you do this job your country is asking you to do?"

Van considered this. It surprised him that his grandfather would doubt his competence. He wasn't cocksure about dealing with Washington insiders, but he knew for a fact that he had few rivals in his own line of work. "Yeah, I can do it. If anybody can."

"Who's your boss? Is he decent?"

"Well, it's this new board for the, uh, National Security Council. There's a bunch of NSC Advisers, and one other guy. That's the guy who wants me on board."

"You're working *direct for the President*?"

"I guess so. Sort of." Van blinked. "It's software."

The old man closed his dropped jaw. "You'll grow into this, son! It'll broaden you! You *need* some broadening. Computer people get way too specialized." The old man laced his veiny hands in a big knuckly knot. "No man should ever get too specialized." He took a breath, gazed at the wall with a fixed expression, and recited something.

" 'A human being should be able to change a diaper, plan an invasion, butcher a hog, design a building, write a sonnet, set a bone, comfort the dying, take orders, give orders, solve equations, pitch manure, program a computer, cook a tasty meal, fight efficiently, die gallantly. Specialization is for insects.' "

"Who said all that?" said Van, impressed.

"A great American writer. Robert A. Heinlein." The old man looked watery-eyed at his glowing Macintosh. "Are there any Heinlein e-books these days? Something this machine can read out loud to me? I can't handle that fine print anymore."

"I'll get some for you, Grandpa," Van promised.

"I tried to make Kelly Johnson read himself some Heinlein, but Kelly never read a novel after those Tom Swift books of his. *Tom Swift and His Airplane.*" The old man snorted. "Kelly Johnson decided to build airplanes when he was twelve years old."

Twelve years old, mused Van. For him, that meant 1981. He had been eleven when his father brought home the Commodore Vic-20. He'd been twelve when he rebuilt it.

"Son," his grandfather rasped, "if you'll be working for the feds, you do need some advice. Yes, you surely do. And I can tell you something real useful. That is, how to run a Skunk Works. Once you do that right, you can't ever forget." The old man was brightening. He looked many years younger now. "The right way is one way that gets results. Are you listening to me, son?"

Van nodded soberly.

"These are simple things. They're the principles. You gotta listen, that's number one. It's more important to listen to your own people than it is to tell 'em what to do. Decide, that's number two. Make your management decisions whenever they're needed. You can figure out later whether they were right or wrong. And believe. Don't ever try to build a project that you can't believe in. Because otherwise, when they cut your funding—and they will cut it—you won't be able to tell 'em with a straight face why they should go straight to hell."

Van felt grateful. "Oh, yeah. This is the right stuff."

"Son, government programs are just like people. They get slow as they get older. They get very stuck in their ways. That just won't do for a Skunk Works. You've got to be quick, you've got to be quiet, and you've got to be on time. You had your three principles, and those are your three rules."

"Okay."

"When I tell you 'quick,' that means small. Small teams, the best people, very restricted. Ten or twenty percent of the people that normal outfits would use. No long reports, ever. Never read a long report, and if a guy writes you one, fire him. No long meetings. You want to keep 'em all working close together, no distractions, focused on the project all the time. Everybody stays hands-on with the tools, everybody stays close to the aircraft. Stick with the machine, never back off. That's how you get results quick."

"Should I record all this?"

"Just *pay attention,* dang it! It took good men a lifetime to figure this stuff out!" The old man was breathing harder. "When I say 'quiet,' that means no talking. You don't brag about what you're doing. Ever. You just do it, and you never demand any credit. If nobody ever knows who you are, then nobody knows what you did. Except for the enemy, of course." The old man cackled and coughed. "Every day, Russki spy-sats counted every car in our parking lots! Those spies in Moscow, they knew a lot more about my work than my own family ever did."

There was a painful silence. This was by far the longest, frankest talk Van had ever had with his grandfather about work. Of course, he'd always known that his grandfather built jets, but a fine haze of Vandeveer family silence had always hung over the details.

Van examined the yellow wallpaper. It was cracking and peeling in spots.

"My second wife knew quite a lot about my work," the old man said defensively. "Because Angela was my secretary. So was my third wife. Well, Doris was not a secretary exactly. Doris was a headhunter from Northrop." The old man sighed. "I should never have jumped over to Northrop, but Ben Rich had the top job at the Skunk Works sewn up, and I just couldn't stand to work on civilian subsonics."

"Give me the 'on time' part," Van prompted.

"That was it! Right! You got to be on time! You got to do it when there are stars in their eyes about it! Before they get all bureaucratic, and start counting every nickel and dime! Timing is the hardest part, son: you gotta know when good enough will do. You gotta know when to quit."

The old man tunneled his bony arms through his golf shirt. Static left the remnants of his hair like a windblown thistle. "Me, I got out. I got out at last. I should have got out earlier."

"Why, Grandpa?"

"Because of the Grease Machine." The old man made a bitter, money-pinching gesture. "The Grease Machine never needs maintenance, son. That Japanese Minister and his crooked payoffs . . . Lockheed was never the same. A Skunk Works is finished, once the Grease Machine takes over. Once the money beats the engineering, that's the end of it, son. Once the money beats the engineering, it's all just chrome and tail fins, after that."

Van felt a pang at the depth of his grandfather's sorrow. He'd been all of seven years old during the Lockheed bribery scandal. Except for family reasons, Van would have known and cared nothing about it. It was just some obscure scandal from the Watergate era.

In his later life, though, the subject had come up once. That was when a Japanese guy from DoCoMo had tried to explain to him why Japan was in so much trouble. Why Japan, with the world's best engineers and hottest products, had fallen into a hole. In the eighties they were on their way to running the world. In the nineties they were going nowhere.

Somehow Van had always just known that defense contracting was a crooked business. How could anybody have any illusions there to get disillusioned about? Luckily, he himself was from the world of computers and telecommunications. A very different world.

"Well . . ." that old man said. "That's it, son. That's all you need to know. Now you can go home and fix yourself a drink."

Van's grandfather wandered restlessly back to his worktable, and discovered the red wire of his glue gun, hanging from the drawer. Surprised, he pulled the shiny gun out and set it carefully on the desktop.

"Now don't you look at this," he said.

"Grandpa, I've seen a hot-glue gun."

"Not as hot as this one, kiddo. The boys in Burbank made me this when we got the Blackbird shaped and annealed. Titanium was Blackbird skin, it'll take Mach 3 when the shockwave's hot enough to melt lead!" He brandished the ray gun. "Here, let me turn this on."

Van noted with alarm that the cheap wall socket was discolored and half-molten.

"You shouldn't be melting any lead in here, Grandpa."

"Oh, I can melt any kind of solder in this gun, no problem." His grandfather began searching through the dusty junk in a desk drawer.

"Grandpa, let me have that thing."

"This gun's too old for you. The boys made this for me back in '63. Chuck Vandeveer's Buck Rogers ray-blaster!" He smiled in delight. "That was a dang good joke, too. They were such great, funny guys."

"Grandpa, I'll buy you a fresh glue gun at Home Depot."

"But you can't have this gun. This one's mine. You really need this solder gun, boy? Why?"

Van had no good reason to offer.

The old man narrowed his eyes. "You can't tell me, huh? It's classified? It's electronics."

"Oh, uhm, yeah."

"Lotta hard soldering work in electronics. Vacuum tubes and such."

"Sure," Van said gratefully. "Yeah."

"You keep it then, Derek, son. You can keep it as long as you need it."

"Thanks a lot." Van hastily unplugged the glue gun. Then he ripped some Velcro loose and stuffed the dangerous contraption into his baggiest cargo pocket. At least now the place wouldn't burn down. He waved his free hand at the walls. "Grandpa, how did you get in this place?"

"I'm hiding out here, that's how! After I broke out of that damn nuthouse!" Grandpa Chuck tapped the thin skin on his skull. "Old Kelly, he never knew when to leave when the time was right! Hardening of the arteries up here, that was Kelly Johnson's problem . . . I used to see ol' Kelly laid up in his hospital bed, all crippled-up and cussing-out Allen Dulles, when Dulles was already dead . . . His mind went! Now my boy Srini, though . . . He's just this young kid, Srini, but he's a good engineer, one of my best . . . He fixed up this computer for me, to read things out loud for me . . . A lotta contract work now, he's a busy boy . . . This was his room."

"He sure likes planes," Van observed.

"I pay his mom room and board, you know. His mom, she's a widow now. Family values, that's a good deal." The old man turned back to his desk. He looked with resigned confusion on the clutter of small plastic parts. "Now this here was the P-38 Lightning. Kelly Johnson's first classic design. America killed Admiral Yamamoto with those P-38s." He tapped the plastic fuselage with a mechanical pencil. "So much for your Pearl Harbor, huh, Admiral? Welcome to hell!"

One of Van's phones rang. He pulled it from a hip pocket. "Vandeveer."

"Where are we?" came a plaintive cry. "Where are you?" It was Helga.

"We're here now. We're in Burbank."

"But there's no one in the street! I looked everywhere! I'm scared. Why don't these phones work better? I forget which big numbers to dial first."

"I'll come get you," Van promised.

"Is Disneyland in this town?"

"I'll just come get you, Helga."

Van opened the bedroom door to leave. Surprised, his grandfather came after him in a shuffling old man's hustle.

The old man swung his arms. "I never got to work on the Lightning. That was before my time. But that's your future, boy! That Pearl Harbor business!" He bared his irregular teeth. "Dang, I'm hungry."

Once in the hall, Grandpa Chuck briskly turned the wrong way and hastened to an outside door. He clawed at the round brass doorknob, his fingers slipping. The doorknob clicked, but the door was firmly locked at the top with a cheap brass bolt. Grandpa Chuck never looked up at the bolt. He never thought to do it. He just pawed at the round brass knob, muttering in frustration, while Van stared at him in dismay.

The old man gave up at last, and tried to look jaunty. "How's about some breakfast, son?"

Van followed his barefoot grandfather into the kitchen. Mrs. Srinivasan was there, quiet and polite. She fetched the old man a box of bran flakes, some whole milk, an indestructible metal bowl with a big wooden spoon. The old man sat at the corner of the Formica table, scowling at her. "Television," he snapped. She obediently clicked the set on.

Van left Mrs. Srinivasan's duplex and fetched Helga from the street. Helga was overjoyed to see him. She chattered at him nervously. Van put up with this. Helga was tall, shapely, and gushy. Van knew that for some men she had a lot of sex appeal, but he had never understood why. She was not his type at all and he had never felt even a twinge of chemistry. Van was pleased that Helga was good with infants, but basically he felt about Helga the way he might feel about a tame llama.

Inside the duplex, Mrs. Srinivasan and Helga stared at each other as if they had come not from Sweden and India, but from Venus and Jupiter. They both seemed like decent women to Van, or at least okay women, but they couldn't get the remotest grip on one another. They kept addressing each other through Van: "Ask your blond girl if she wants to sit down," "Ask the nice lady if she has a real bathroom here, you know, with a toilet." Irritated, the old man turned up his morning cable news show. The TV blared war and terror, headache pills and paper towels, suicide and revenge.

Mrs. Srinivasan's phone rang. It was her neighbor, Mr. Chang. Mr. Chang was surprised at all the morning ruckus. He wanted to make sure that she wasn't being robbed. Mrs. Srinivasan was an Indian widow with an elderly man in her care. She seemed very reliant on Mr. Chang, who was the retired owner of a Chinese grocery.

There was nothing for it but to have Mr. Chang come right over. He did. He was small and gray-haired and bent, with pants belted high above his waist. Mr. Chang examined the visitors. He sat on Mrs. Srinivasan's lavishly pillowed wicker couch, and rolled himself a cigarette. Mr. Chang put such luscious handiwork into this that it was clear that smoking was his full-time occupation.

Mrs. Srinivasan set out green tea.

Another of Van's cell phones rang. Dottie had awoken inside the truck. She arrived with the baby. The arrival of little Ted broke Grandpa Chuck's foul mood. Van helped Grandpa Chuck to the wicker couch and put Ted on his bony knee. The two of them together looked postcard-cute. Even Mr. Chang was forced to smile. Van felt stunned. His grandfather and his son looked eerily alike, same round faces, same blinky, distracted stares.

Dottie plucked Ted free from the old man before Ted's uneasiness could grow into sobs. Using her baby as a wedge, Dottie swiftly broke the ice between Helga and Mrs. Srinivasan. Soon the three women were clucking over Ted in a happy international hen party. Van's stomach rumbled and his mood darkened. Van realized that he was starving.

Clearly Mrs. Srinivasan lacked the provisions to feed this sudden crowd of adults.

"Kentucky Fried Chicken?" Van hypothesized.

His insight met with swift approval. Mrs. Srinivasan was vegetarian, but not on special occasions. For Mr. Chang, Kentucky Fried Chicken was the height of luxury from the Red Chinese cultural thaw. Helga loved American fast food. Grandpa and Ted could suck on the crusts.

Van left in the Rover and fetched a big family bucket of extra crispy. Driving the Rover again, even for a few more blocks, was like having sunburned skin rubbed.

When Van returned to the duplex, two more strangers had arrived. One was a middle-aged, olive-skinned woman, in a tailored black pants suit and a hooded khaki jacket. The other was an older, distinguished man, in designer jeans, with a gold earring and graying blond ponytail.

The man was his father.

A sudden hush fell. "Is that Kentucky Fried Chicken?" his father said at last.

"Uh, yeah, Dad."

"For breakfast?"

"Yep." Van set the cardboard bucket down defiantly.

His father took a breath and emitted a quotation. " 'Let me prescribe the diet of the country; I do not care who makes its laws.' "

Van felt a familiar despair. Why was his father always like this? Why didn't he just say whatever he meant directly? Why did he have to dig into his big, 1968-hippie head, and come up with some kind of weird, senseless, semipolitical quotation? Van's dad was a former Rhodes scholar. He was ruinously gifted. Van's father was literally the only human being in the world who spoke both Afghan Pashtun and African Bantu dialects. He was also the only man Van knew who carried on conversations, in real life, using semicolons that you could actually hear.

Van looked at his father glumly. His father looked bad: piratical, slick, and never to be trusted. But he didn't look quite so bad as he normally did. He was, for instance, sober.

His father offered Van a brisk, cheery "Your dad is here, all is well" smile, a smile as thin, flimsy, and phony as individually wrapped lunch meat baloney. How had his father found out that Van was in California? How had he shown up here at this building? Without a word, a phone call, an e-mail, or a whisper of permission! The guy was impossible.

"It's more of an early lunch," Dottie offered kindly. In the rare moments when her erratic father-in-law drifted into her life, Dottie loved to play the peacemaker.

"This smells good!" declared Helga, eagerly helping herself to the chicken bucket. Then everyone went for the chow in a merry outburst of chattering, except for Van, who had lost his appetite. To cover his pain and confusion, he gave an extra-crispy thigh to his grandfather, who seemed lost in the crowd now, tired and bewildered, forgotten.

Van could not understand why his painful personal problems were suddenly the business of Swedes, Indians, and Chinese. They seemed pretty pleased with the fast food he had brought them, but how could such a thing have ever happened?

"Son, this is Rachel Weissman," his father said, introducing the latest girlfriend.

"Hi," Van told her reluctantly.

Rachel half curtseyed to grab up her chicken from the cardboard bucket. There was something very wrong with her hip.

"Where are you from, Rachel?" Dottie asked her.

"I'm from Bogota," Rachel lied. "I work in oil."

"Rachel and I have a beautiful residencia north of the city," his father aided and abetted.

Dottie blinked at them. "So you're really at home in Colombia now, Robert? To stay?"

"It's never like it sounds in the media. 'Nature gives to every time and season some beauties of its own.'" Van's father gave Rachel a warm, protective look. Rachel was in even worse trouble than Van had imagined.

Rachel was obviously Jewish, but she wasn't Colombian, Van concluded. His father looked much more Colombian than Rachel did, despite his blondness and his hefty bulk. Van's father was solid as a bear, but even before he had joined the CIA, there had always been something spacey and strange about him. When they'd finally shunted him into Counter-Narcotics, that dead end of any intelligence career, that was when his pride had broken down.

During the eighties, Afghanistan had cheered him up for a while. He'd shaped up physically, patched up the marriage, and even taken Van camping and fishing in the California mountains. But in Angola, he'd done something indescribable. Generally the CIA never gave its top agents Third World assignments that risked malaria and guaranteed diarrhea, but Van's father was a charmer. He had a genius for working himself into situations where he was unwelcome, unneeded, unwanted, and way too smart for the job.

In Angola, Van's father had crossed some line, into some mess he just couldn't mentally manage. Something oily and permanent had stuck to him for good in Angola. He'd returned from Angola with unblinking eyes like two saucers, quoting more poetry than ever before . . . Nightmare episodes in Van's adolescence, when his mother would scream in betrayed anguish, and his father would storm into his home office, to snort cocaine and translate Walt Whitman into African dialects. Those were the moments when Van would quietly shut his bedroom door, warm up the modem, and vanish deep, deep, deep into his computer. In some sense, Van had never come out.

Dottie was doing all the talking for the group. Her lips were moving rapidly as Van stood there, moored in his silent crisis. For the first time Van realized what Dottie was actually saying. She had had a lot of time to think in the car, and she had bravely made up her mind about something. Dottie was talking about quitting her lab post in Boston and taking up an entirely different job.

"So it's the perfect time for me to undertake a transition, if Derek is also switching careers," she confided to everyone.

"Mmm-hmmm." His father nodded unhelpfully.

"I do have a standing offer. Because Tony Carew . . . have you ever heard of Tony Carew? Tony is the only friend of ours who's really famous. The Davos Forum, the Renaissance Weekend . . ."

"I've certainly heard of those," said Rachel, looking interested for the first time.

"Oh, I see," said his father. "So then, Derek. Tony must be that good friend of yours who works for Thomas DeFanti."

Van saw that a response was required of him. "Sort of."

Rachel bored right in. "Have you ever met Thomas DeFanti, Dr. Vandeveer?"

"Yes," Van and Dottie chorused. They both always answered to "Dr. Vandeveer."

"That'll be my new research post in Colorado," Dottie said. "With one of Thomas DeFanti's foundations. He's always been a very big supporter of astronomy."

This whole business was very like Dottie, Van thought sadly. If he chose to mess up their fragile, tender status quo, then she would not fight with him about it. No, she would cooperate fully, by messing up their lives even faster. Would Dottie really move all the way from Boston to the Rocky Mountains while he'd be moving from New Jersey to Washington, and working for Jeb's outfit? There would be nothing left of their life together.

Well, there would be e-mail.

Helga happily chowed down on her chicken wing. Helga didn't realize it yet, but soon, very soon, Van would have to fire her. He didn't have any place to keep her. Her nicely furnished suite in Merwinster would be history.

Van pulled a chunk of chicken from the bucket and jammed it in his mouth.

He gnawed silently as the rest of them chattered happily. Then Van dumped his bare chicken bone and went out to the Rover. He beeped it open and fetched the Iridium phone. It was heavy and shaped like a brick. Van hadn't yet had a chance to try out an Iridium phone. The phones were clumsy, expensive, and didn't work indoors. The Iridium satellite network had gone broke—but at the last minute, the new post-bankruptcy owners had been rescued by the

U.S. Defense Department. The U.S. military had suddenly realized that it might be pretty handy to have phones that worked off-road in places like Afghanistan. Now Van would take the plunge for the first time as well. A fatal announcement like accepting Jeb's job was worth the ridiculous Iridium charge of two dollars a minute.

His father hastened after him. He had a bleak, naked look on his face. "I know that they want you in Washington, son! But you don't have to go through with that. There's no need for it!"

Van shrugged sheepishly. A teenager's gesture.

"Think about it. What are you going to get out of this? Do you want a Christmas card from Henry Kissinger? Son, I *know* people from al Qaeda. I've met them. They don't matter in this world. The only way they can matter is to kill themselves inside our jets and buildings. Al Qaeda can't build anything. They can't invent anything. But you can, son. You're a builder, you're an innovator. People like you are making people like them matter less every day."

"Look, Dad, I write software, okay? Don't get all philosophical. I'm never going to shoot anybody. But computer security matters." Van sighed miserably. "That scene is just so bad. You don't know what it's like to run those networks. Nobody knows who hasn't done it. It's a much, much bigger mess in there than any normal person imagines. It's been neglected way too long."

Van's grandfather appeared at the door of the duplex. No one had been watching over him. He took off down the sidewalk at a brisk walk.

"Every big outfit gets like that, son," his father insisted. "If he wasn't in jail now, I'd take you to meet Aldrich Ames. That son of a bitch is the poster boy for the crisis inside the Company." His father groaned. "He sold out every asset we had inside Russia. And no one in the Congress even noticed that Ames did that, ever! We had brave people dying who were never missed."

"Dad, the Internet gets kicked flat by teenagers in Canada. That just won't do."

The two of them apprehended his grandfather. "I'm going out for some Marlboros," the old man protested.

"I want you to have a happy life, son," his father insisted, taking a firm grip on his grandfather's bony upper arm. "You have everything, Derek. You're a big success, you're enjoying your life. She's a sweet girl who loves you, that's a wonderful baby. Do you know what you're risking there? You'll never get that back."

"I don't get off that easy, Dad. They need me. Because they know I can help. Everybody else has screwed it up."

"Derek, if you work inside the Beltway, the people who screw things up are gonna become your best friends. They're going to be your best war buddies. You're gonna encounter people worse than you can imagine, with problems that don't bear thinking about. There's no reason for someone like you to become one of them."

"No, there's a very good reason, Dad. I know I can make a difference, so I have to try. If nobody ever tries to fix the world of the Internet, the future will just turn into . . ."

Van broke off. This was a very long speech for him, and his father wasn't getting it at all. He realized that his father thought of him as a soft, dreamy person, from a lucky generation, leading a charmed life. Van didn't know whether to feel rage or pity, so he felt what he always felt with his father: gloomy confusion.

He began to shout. "The Internet turns into hell! Some awful, total mess! Where every single decent company goes broke. Viruses and worms breaking everything. Lawsuits everywhere you look. Where crazy people from the very worst places on earth try to rip you off with bank frauds and drugs and filthy pictures . . ."

His father looked at him with alarm. His grandfather was totally bewildered by Van's outburst. Van sounded wild and crazy, even to himself. Why let on about the nightmare cyber-scenario? He should never have opened his mouth, he thought. He was crushing their cherished, old-fashioned ideals.

There were horrors in the world beyond their understanding.

CHAPTER FOUR

The American agents inside Chechnya were rapidly improving their disguises. The Americans would never seem at home in the Caucasus, though. They didn't have lice, nor did they stink.

The Colonel was sharing a rocky, blasted ledge with the American agent called Kickoff. The two of them were very close, so close as to be quite intimate. Kickoff wore a black fur hat and crumpled Soviet combat fatigues. To that extent, Kickoff looked normal for Chechnya. Yet his teeth were white and perfect beneath his salt-and-pepper beard, and his skin was uncannily clean. Silky mountain-climbing underwear kept his precious American body toasty from wrist to ankles. Kickoff wore strong, beautifully knitted socks. He even wore sock *liners*. Thin, magical membranes that kept the painful rot of trench foot away. They were like condoms for his feet.

The Colonel himself stank badly of sweat, fear, boredom, vodka, and strong cigarettes. But his personal reek was lost in the awesome stench from a dead donkey's rotting haunch and fetlock. Endless skirmishes had been fought over this vulnerable run of the Chechnyan pipeline. The shallow little cave the Colonel shared with Kickoff was a well-known bandit lair. It was routinely scourged by passing federal helicopters. Every once in a while the lightning-sticks would blow a smuggler's donkey apart.

Tonight he and Kickoff would be killing bandits. Not all of them, of course. Just enough to prove a concept to Kickoff's employers. There were not enough soldiers in all the world to guard all the world's pipelines from all the world's thieves, saboteurs, and vandals. That task would have to be automated somehow, for those pipelines were the arteries of all the world's machines. Like clouding mosquitoes, human bandits had learned to pierce those pipes and drink deep. So, in return, the threatened machines would have to learn to seek, hunt, and kill.

Kickoff handed the Colonel his heavy, brick-shaped satellite phone.

"Hello again, Alexei," said the phone in Russian.

"Hi sexy," said the Colonel, his morale improving at once. It no longer seemed odd to the Colonel that he talked on a satellite telephone to a distant woman in Bethesda, Maryland, merely in order to communicate with Kickoff. Kickoff knew no more than a dozen words of Russian. Yet Kickoff was a practical man. If he couldn't haul his translator into a killing zone, he would simply phone her.

"We've grown so intimate in such a short time, my dear," the Colonel said into the phone. "Yet I understand we'll be parting soon."

"I'm sad about that, too. But it's the nature of their business, dear Alexei."

Kickoff zippered open his dappled weapons bag. He produced a marvelous, long-barreled sniper rifle, made of carbon fiber, polished fiberglass, and dense white plastic. He then seized the phone and barked into it.

The Colonel accepted the phone once again.

"That was a whole lot of stupid technical crap about his big gun," the woman said. "Are you interested in that? Should I bother?"

Kickoff was ex-American military—he had a soldier's eyes—but he was officially a civilian consultant. This was the first time the Colonel had ever seen Kickoff handle a weapon. Kickoff's lethal machine was a Western .50-caliber rifle, privately produced. Pampered special-ops gangs carried toys of that sort when, unlike Russian troops in Chechnya, they were not killing Moslem terrorists in the mud and blood every single day.

"Darling, I'm interested if you're interested. You tell me all about it. Just how wonderful is Kickoff's big gun?"

"Oh, in bed, I suppose you mean. Well, he's wonderful in bed," said the woman coolly. She was an American, and completely lost to modesty. The Colonel liked her very much for this. It was so refreshing.

"He's in good condition, with a handsome face," the Colonel told her. "Such good teeth Kickoff has."

"His name is not 'Kickoff.' His name is Michael Hickok."

The Colonel mulled over this correction. "Hickok, Kickoff." For the life of him, he couldn't hear any difference there. And why would that matter anyway, when they never spoke except through her, their translator? Women had such odd priorities.

"Does he love you at all?" the Colonel asked. "Does that matter to him?"

"Not one bit does he love me." She was bitter. "He doesn't even know what that means. 'Have a nice day,' that is what he tells me. Oh, and he buys me cheap, sexy underwear."

"My dear, how is it that we human beings forgot how to love? How did the world even come to such a state?" said the Colonel, warming to his theme. "Since this may be my last chance to ask you, may I seek your customary good advice in an intimate matter? I must decide what to do about Natalya."

"You shouldn't even ask me about that, Alexei. I never have any luck."

"If I leave Natalya here, the bandits kill her for being my mistress. If I take her home to Petersburg, the mafia kills her because she is dark. If we stay here in the Caucasus, then they kill both of us, eventually. And then there's my wife, of course. What on earth is to be done?"

"All right, I'll tell you. Get some money and leave Russia. My mother emigrated to New York in 1978. So my dear mother is finally free of Russia, and I, her only beloved daughter, now I have hopeless affairs with crazy American mercenaries."

The woman sighed in pain from the far side of the world. "At least 'Executive Solutions' got me this great translator job. They've got medical, dental, everything. I could get liposuction."

Kickoff brusquely seized the phone again.

"Now he wants you to look through his big rifle's telescope," the woman reported. "He's also angry that you spend so much time talking to me, while you hardly say one single word to him."

"That's because you are so wise and charming, while he is merely a professional killer. Can we discuss something truly important now? My Natalya is the only happy woman in Chechnya. That is the truth. There is something so profoundly erotic about surrendering yourself to a deadly enemy . . . Natalya has a holy, abject quality, very feminine . . . It's as if she absorbs me . . . I'm bewildered by it, it's a spiritual calamity . . . I used to rage at her, helplessly, confusedly . . . I love her so much that I can't even drink anymore . . ."

Kickoff gestured impatiently at the enormous rifle. Wearied by his duty, the Colonel lowered himself to his elbows and obediently gazed through the black rubber-cupped eyepiece.

He had seen night-vision goggles before. Alfa troops had them. But never a device like this. This was fantastic. The rifle's scope opened up the Chechen evening like the eye of an owl.

Now Kickoff was growling into the phone at the embittered woman in America. The American's corporate sponsors had sent Kickoff here with a huge stack of war toys and no language skills. Kickoff had ventured into the wilds of Chechnya with three little toy robot airplanes, six videocameras, a hundred delicate wind gauges, satellite phones, solar panels, a shatterproof military computer in a camouflaged gunmetal case . . . Kickoff bore a stack of cash, and many discreet documents issued by various oligarchs and moguls. Tyumen Oil and ConocoPhilips, LUKoil and ExxonMobil, Sibneft, Halliburton and ChevronTexaco. The signature of Igor Yusufov of the Energy Ministry was much in evidence in Kickoff's papers. Alexei Kuznetsov, Thomas DeFanti, Mikhail Khodorkovsky. There was even an importation permit signed by no less a man than Vladimir Putin.

It was not that Kickoff knew these important men personally, or that they would ever need to know him. However, they seemed to feel some need for the services Kickoff provided. When Kickoff declared that was he not a spy, but an American working legally on contract from civilian companies, he was probably telling the truth.

The Colonel shifted Kickoff's weapon on its bipod and trailed the eerie scope across the wrecked and glowing landscape. Repeated bombings had reduced the local storage tanks to fragments of riveted steel. Spindly trees, ten years old, grew from the tortured heaps of black tarmac and bad concrete. The hotter surfaces glowed vividly in the scope's computer lens. It looked uncanny, surgical, as if the veins of the earth had opened and bled.

Why was such visual poetry restricted to the mundane work of shooting pipeline thieves?

The Colonel daintily twiddled a diopter. The crescent Moon grew huge in the rifle's crosshairs, blooming in a square rush of pixels. Now the Moon looked big and cheese-orange, like a rind of fancy pizza from Moscow's finest Pizza Hut. Machine analysis worked its magic inside the rifle's optics. The blazing crescent of the Moon toned down, down, and the vast dark plain between the lunar horns emerged in the Colonel's vision. This was, thought the Colonel with holy awe, the Moon shining gently back at him in light reflected from the Earth.

A small red glow winked at him within a lunar crater. The Colonel was pleased; the way that red light splashed brought the Moon's rounded qualities into startling life. A moment later it occurred to the Colonel that there should not be any lights visible on the Moon. There should be no lights on the Moon at all. After all, it was the Moon.

A second red light splashed and flickered, this time within another crater. The Colonel pulled his eye from the rubber lens cup and stared at the Moon bare-eyed. To his human gaze, the Moon was a small, distant crescent. The red light was far too faint to see with the naked eye . . . But no, this was an infrared scope. He was seeing *heat* on the Moon, not light.

His wondering eye sought the rifle yet again. The red spark was playing steadily, frolicking across the Moon's surface, a shimmer and a glow.

The Colonel grabbed the phone. "Please tell Kickoff that I just saw something bizarre on the Moon. Volcanoes, I think."

"What? I can't translate that."

"Lunar volcanoes! Red eruptions on the Moon! I saw them through the sighting-scope on his rifle."

She laughed. "Oh, that? You mean that digital thing? That thing is *digital*, Alexei."

Excited tension drained swiftly from the Colonel's neck. Of course. Just a fault inside the stupid equipment. Were there really space aliens up there, live volcanoes on the holy Moon—or just a pixel or two, turned red inside some screen? What foolishness.

Kickoff tugged at the Colonel's sleeve. Kickoff gestured at his laptop. His tiny airplanes, hidden in the night sky, were sending him fresh pictures.

A Toyota pickup truck, spanking-new and doubtless Saudi-supplied, was working its way up the gorge.

The Colonel held up his leather-gloved fingers: two. There would be two trucks, for there always were. There would also be bandits on foot to escort them, with rifles and walkie-talkies.

Kickoff shook his head and made a throat-cutting gesture. Kickoff didn't care to wait for the chance of bagging both the trucks. That was not necessary to Kickoff's technical purposes. His assignment, it seemed, was merely to field-test the equipment and the support system. Kickoff gently plugged a small video wire and jack into the side of the rifle's scope. He blew dust from a flat plastic wafer and inserted a fresh, spotless disk from a jewellike case. Then he urged the Colonel on.

The Colonel nodded and bent to his labors. The first .50-caliber round, a thumb-sized lozenge of spinning steel, flew through the Toyota's hood and completely through its engine block. As the truck lurched to a stop, the Colonel put two more rounds through the exploding glass and metal of the cab. The spidery white gun kicked very gently on its bipod. There was a high-pitched hiss of escaping gas. And yet, no burst of visible fire from the long black barrel. The rifle was gentle, surgical. The rifle almost fired itself.

A glowing human figure burst free of the shattered truck, and the Colonel missed him as he fled. The fourth round struck him true, though. The oil thief tumbled instantly into two hot glowing pieces: a ruptured carcass, and a severed, spinning arm.

The Colonel sought the phone. "Tell him that we need to leave this cave now. There will be other bandits. They are never afraid of us, and they will want this weapon very badly."

Kickoff listened politely to the anxious squeak from the phone. He made an air-circling gesture.

The Colonel leaned in toward the mouthpiece. "I don't care how many toy airplanes he has, or what they can see. We're in the dark, next to bandits on foot, moving under cover. They will fire rockets on us from far up the slope, above the cave. Oh, and tell him it's a lovely gun."

Kickoff listened to the reply and made an extensive prepared speech.

"Alexei, he says to thank you for the compliment. He also says he's coming home to see me." She was excited.

"And he's taking our satellite phone away, my dear?"

"Of course he's taking our phone. But he's not taking that gun, Alexei. He's not supposed to carry it inside America. He says that you should keep it. He says he knows a good soldier can use a good gun. He wants you to know that he appreciates you."

"He's a generous man with a gift, your big friend here." Kickoff was giving a soldier a fine weapon, instead of some mere sordid bribe of dollars. That was very tactful of the American. The Colonel was touched. A handsome gift like this was a clear hint that the two of them would meet again in the future. That seemed probable enough. There certainly wasn't likely to be any shortage of oil thieves.

"Trust me, Alexei, he didn't pay for that gun himself."

"Oh, no. Of course Kickoff didn't pay for it." Yet others would. A fancy rifle like this was worth a great deal of money. Especially in the right set of wrong hands. The Colonel winced a little at that thought. Young Russian troopers, bewildered, conscripted, doomed, their flesh flying apart under those silent ferocious impacts . . . But only one side in Chechnya was awash in cash. That was not his own side. His side was merely a national army, not a global conspiracy. His side was always broke.

The thought didn't bear contemplation. And yet, and yet, Natalya. Yes, if fate demanded it, he could do a thing like that for Natalya's sake. Because love conquered all.

CHAPTER FIVE

Tall yellow cranes were digging black wreckage from the Pentagon. American flags the size of basketball courts covered the walls of federal offices, Old Glory the Battle Flag as a kind of angry wallpaper. Truck bomb barriers, strangely disguised as concrete flower pots, bloomed right, left, and center. The streets around the White House had become empty asphalt malls, where jittery tourists lurked in ones and twos.

The newly formed Coordination of Critical Information Assurance Board met in the Old Executive Building, under the sponsorship of the Vice President. The badly overcrowded conference room had leather club chairs, steel coffee urns, lots of dented mahogany, and an ancient oil painting of an elder statesman named John C. Calhoun. Mr. Calhoun didn't look happy. Neither did the crowd.

If Van didn't know all the faces, he knew the institutions. Every major federal bureaucracy had some kind of stake in computer security work. The Justice Department with the FBI, the Treasury with their Secret Service. The Department of Defense had a Defense Information Systems Agency. The Air Force was high-flying and enthusiastic, while the Navy worked to keep up steam. The Commerce Department, the National Institute of Standards and Technology. NASA was there. The Computer Emergency Response Team, the Federal Law Enforcement Training Center. Even one lonely computer whiz from the Railroad Retirement Board.

The National Security Council, Van's new employer, had sent out the invitations. This was their first big dance. If this shindig worked out, then a lot of things might work out. If this didn't work, then Van had just blown his career for a swift bureaucratic fiasco.

With a thirty-year career in computer crimebusting, Jeb was a living dinosaur of computer security. Jeb had trained a lot of the people in this conference room, and most of them owed him favors. Van had a gold-star reputation as a coder, but was a personal stranger to most of these people. Most of them were strangers to one another.

This was the cyber-version of a larger story happening all over the federal government, from Pennsylvania Avenue, to Quantico, to Fort Meade, to Pentagon City. Since 9/11, all federal security agencies had been suffering a scary process that they called "melting stovepipes." People who had spent their whole lives inside narrow institutional channels were forced to network with other feds that they'd never met.

Who were these strangers from distant, scary wings of the U.S. government? Were they rivals? Allies? Neutrals? No one even knew. The new Homeland Security empire was going to eat up any number of proud, independent agencies. Some said six, some said twelve, and some said twenty-two. This meant that no one's turf was safe anymore.

It also meant something more promising, though. It meant opportunity: the biggest federal re-org in forty years. It meant that the right bunch of computer-security geeks, in the right place with the right tools and attitude, might break out from obscurity. Bold nerds from some mainframe garage in the Commerce Department might end up giving marching orders to the Secret Service.

Jeb was the kind of man that computer people naturally turned to in a crisis. Jeb rather resembled Jabba the Hutt, if *Star Wars* characters had been cops from Texas. Jeb's mood, always dark and cynical, had ratcheted up several notches to grimly militant. Jeb had the rigid-eyed stare of a man who was summing up his life's work and laying it right on the line. Jeb had shaved his cherished beard, revealing a nest of pale double chins. Jeb had even found somebody in Washington willing to cut him an enormous blue serge suit.

Van had never seen Jeb answer to "Dr. Jeremijenko" before. Jeb Jeremijenko didn't even have a real doctorate. No one ever used his unspellable last name. Jeb had learned his computer security as a street cop who had stumbled over a UNIVAC in Houston in the 1960s.

Banging a mahogany table with the meaty flat of his hand, Jeb hushed the chaos in the room. By getting together in this very, very quiet way, Jeb bellowed, they could get some useful progress made in the stupefying mess that was federal computer-security policy. In other words, they could finally settle down and cut the crap.

No one objected to Jeb's frank assessment of the work at hand. American federal agencies had owned and used computers longer than anybody else in the world. That was bad news rather than good, for it meant that the federal government had the world's oldest, creakiest, cruftiest, most messed-up systems. Everybody who knew anything about the reality behind the scenes knew that it was awful. Computer security was obscure, ultra-technical, underfunded. It was scattered and amateurish. There was nobody in charge. There were no firm policies and no accountability. And the budgets? Laughable!

However: after September 11, a day of reckoning had finally arrived. Jeb knew it. The crowd knew it. Congress knew it. Anybody who watched the news or read the papers knew it. The old lazy, scatterbrained ways just weren't going to cut it anymore.

Every great crisis was also a great opportunity for people with the guts to dare and win. Now, Jeb declared, was the vital moment to level with each other, get a strong sense of the will and abilities of the computer-security community, and to really clear the air for solid, effective action.

Van knew that this sermon of Jeb's meant big trouble. Jeb was positioning the CCIAB to become a kamikaze high-tech outfit that played fast and loose with the old rules. Van was okay with that risk. Realistically, there wasn't any other choice. If he, Derek R. Vandeveer, was ever going to become an effective federal security official, then Washington was going to have to ditch old rules by the bucketful.

Some busybody think-tanker from the Competitive Enterprise Institute went trolling for Van: "Does our Stanford professor concur with Dr. Jeremijenko's unorthodox approach?"

"Be quiet!" Van roared back. "Be quick! And be on time." Nobody had any idea what Van meant by this, but the startled conference room went silent for twenty-five seconds.

Nobody else asked Van another question, which was great. Van hated meetings. He never did at all well in them. He knew that he was there as a potted plant for Jeb to exhibit: one bona fide, certified computer genius, pulled in from the best R&D lab in a top company. It made no sense for him to try to out-politic federal bureaucrats.

Van had invented a solid program for his new career. Since he had to be a potted plant anyway, he'd be a cactus. Think tough, look tough, talk tough. Real security pros were never chatty, chummy guys.

Van listened awhile, glaring at people at random, while caressing the keys of his laptop. Then he lost interest. They were obviously blue-skying it, these people. They weren't making progress; they were sounding each other out and trying to cover their butts. They clearly had no idea what the hell was really going on. They were scared for themselves and their futures. They were politicking. Because this was Washington. There was nothing Van could do but put up with that.

After two agonizing hours, Jeb confronted the subject of the CCIAB's own hardware. The mood in the room shifted instantly.

Everyone in the room, without exception, was very interested in the subject of computer hardware. Obviously, an outfit whose business was coordinating computer security for the rest of the federal government would need an internal system that was top-end, heavy-duty, and very impressive indeed.

At this point, Van, who had been feeling sorry for himself and was badly missing his infant son, perked up a little.

As a professional computer researcher, Van secretly hated computer security. It was boring and beneath his true talents. Making him work on security was like asking a top Olympic cyclist to make bicycle locks and bicycle chains.

Nevertheless, this was now his duty. Plus, Van kind of liked the idea of building a genuinely advanced, secure system, from the ground up, from sound theory and practice rather than implementation hacks, and without any absurd interference by stupid market vendors. If he got to do that job by himself, that would be pretty okay. Van knew he could do it, it was honest work if dull, and at least he could set a good example.

Now he had to tell a room full of people how this was going to work. Van struggled with his stage fright. Stage fright was a very old demon for Van. He knew how to beat it, though: he beat his demon with confidence tricks.

Like pretending that they were just another Stanford undergraduate class. But they sure as hell weren't. Or pretending they were all wearing red underwear. Beltway bandits in expensive suits were not exactly a red underwear crowd.

He could reach into his shoulder bag, and stick 'em up with his grandfather's ray gun. A titanium ray gun! Leveled right at their heads! The very last thing in the world they would ever expect!

That thought did it for Van. He was just fine now. Van opened his laptop. "Well," he told them, "Jeb says we should be frank."

He threw up a colorful PowerPoint screen to keep them happy. Then he read aloud from his script. "As this shows you, today's security industry will tell you certain very predictable things. They will tell you that a federal agency needs to buy their products. Secure servers, secure routers, firewalls, crypto, authentication, all brand-new out of the box . . . That is the conventional wisdom."

Van switched PowerPoint screens, to a nicer one with a lot of colored bars and arrows. "But even for us, a small coordinating bureau, those purchases would set us back sixteen million dollars. We don't have that money."

Another screen. "In the CCIAB, we can't wait the standard eight months to install conventional secure equipment. We need to be up and running, effective yesterday. We can't afford the time and money for security products. But we do have to meet a very serious security need. You reconcile those two vectors, and that means only one thing."

Van switched screens. This new screen took a while to refresh. To his vast relief, PowerPoint did not crash. "We have to create a brand-new breakthrough system. Thinking way outside the box. Really quickly, really quietly, using about one-tenth the number of normal staffers. With radically innovative hardware and code."

The room had a holy hush over it. They were totally with him. Jeb was beaming in the PowerPoint screen glow.

"In the CCIAB, we do have one great advantage. We don't need to rely on anybody's lame industry vendors, because, in the CCIAB, we actually understand code. So we can build, and we will build, our own Grendel supercluster. Grendels are made from obsolete PCs, but clustered in parallel without any von Neumann bottlenecks."

Another nice screen.

"For about a hundred grand, we will own a new federal system with more raw computational power than the entire Commerce Department. And, in the short term, that system will be very, very secure. Because no hacker anywhere has invented or found any security holes for Grendel distributed supercomputation code. There are maybe ten guys in the whole world who understand that code. They are all loyal American computer-science academics, and they are all real, real busy."

A hand went up. It was a late arrival, a skinny younger guy with a battered laptop on his knees. "May I ask a question, sir?"

"What?"

"You, Dr. Derek Vandeveer, you're one of those ten guys?"

"Yeah. And I know the other nine. Who are you?"

"Well, I'm a Web journalist, and—"

"Meeting adjourned!" Jeb bellowed, lurching to his feet.

Van was lying in bed, staring at the ceiling, and thinking hard about streams. Van had always wanted to do something useful and important with streams, because streams were inherently superior to the conventional structure of files. Van was planning to implement distributed streams within the Grendel. That was overkill, really. There wasn't a kode-kid, cracker, hacktivist, or even intelligence agency in the whole world that could break into a Grendel. But a Grendel running *streams*—man, that would be beyond all coolness.

Blinking occasionally, Van thought about streams. He thought about streams seriously, and then, very, very seriously. Eventually, Van became aware that someone was pounding on his apartment door.

Surprised, he sat up and pulled on his pants.

Van had rented his Washington apartment point-and-click off a real-estate Web site. Van had been in a big hurry to find a place in Washington, and the street was close enough to a telecom central station to get himself an ADSL line. The rooms had looked okay in the GIF file. In real life, the apartment was tiny and reeked of insecticide. Van's apartment had ugly walls of exposed yellow brick, a lot of peeling Formica, and a foul layer of oily grime on the kitchen walls and ceiling. The toilet wobbled in the bathroom.

The Web site hadn't talked at all about the neighborhood, either. Van's neighborhood was sinister. Van now kept his grandfather's ray gun handy beside the door. The people who knocked on Van's door usually wanted to sell him crack cocaine, or themselves.

Van removed his glasses and placed his right eye to the peephole.

Out in the dim, ratty hallway stood a skinny girl with a big nose, dark eyes too close together, and black, frizzy hair. She wore a strange little frock of greenish-looking, all-organic, undyed cotton, and carried a shapeless fabric purse. She looked like a Girl Scout who'd sold all her cookies and taken up panhandling.

Van undid three large brass locks and opened the door on a length of steel chain.

"Dr. Vandeveer?"

"Huh?"

"I'm your new secretary. Can I come in?"

Van considered this. It was unexpected. "Can I see some ID first?"

The woman showed him a plastic-coated mag-stripe card with an embedded photo. The card had a nice red lanyard. The card identified her as "Fawn Glickleister, Executive Assistant, CCIAB Technical Services."

"Huh," Van said.

Fawn held up a different badge, still in fresh shrink-wrap. "I brought your badge, too, uhm, Derek. These badges are new. You haven't been to work in three days."

"I *am* working," Van insisted, stung. "I just can't do any meetings with anybody right now."

"Can I come in please? It's kind of scary out here!"

Van undid his rattling chain.

Fawn came inside. She studied the big plastic weight-lifting bench, which dominated Van's small apartment. The grimy wall behind the bench was covered with posters of Full-Contact Karate champions, guys with staring eyes, flying sweat, and feet swathed in red plastic gauntlets. "Is all this yours?"

"I just moved in." The apartment's previous tenant had abandoned everything he owned, including his thong underwear, his girlie mags, and his size-twelve kung-fu shoes. Van was pretty sure the guy had gotten shot or arrested. No one seemed to know or care about that.

"Wow," Fawn marveled, "that is one really cool chair!"

The magnesium chair was the only piece of furniture that Van had managed to bring from Merwinster. He'd grabbed the chair on impulse and thrown it into the Range Rover. His plan was to junk everything in the Washington apartment and replace it all—the Korean landlord said that would be just fine—but he had lacked the time.

Fawn Glickleister was definitely older than twelve. She was older than Helga, Van's sad little fired au pair, but she was as restless as a sixth-grader. Her lips were badly chapped and her brown eyes looked red and puffy. She had a high, squeaky voice. "This chair doesn't outgas any toxins, does it?"

Van stared at her. "How could magnesium outgas?"

Fawn sat down daintily. "Wow, it's a lot more comfortable than it looks!" She pulled a thick pair of wireless specs from her canvas purse.

An ominous silence fell as she looked around the apartment.

"Can I tell you something, Derek? It's even scarier in here than it is out in the hall. Are you sure you're a computer geek? I know a whole lot of nerds, and most of them aren't, like, weight-lifting, scary karate guys in the ghetto. Hey, wow, what happened to that kitchen?"

"You just sit in that chair for a sec," Van commanded. He opened the door, stepped into the gloomy hall, and slammed the door behind him.

"Jeb," said the phone.

"Jeb, what the hell is it with this girl you just gave me? She's twelve years old, Jeb. She looks like a Muppet."

"That would be Fawn Glickleister."

"I know her name. If I need help, I know where to get it."

"Glickleister!" Jeb insisted. "She's not twelve, she's twenty-six. She's Glickleister's daughter."

Recognition dawned. "*The* Glickleister? Hyman Glickleister?"

"Do you know any *other* Glickleisters?"

Van took a breath. Hyman Glickleister. Legendary computer visionary. ARPANET. Packet-switching guru. A man thirty years ahead of his time. Glickleister had spent the last fifteen years of his life in a wheelchair, dying of some obscure neuromuscular disease, and that had only made him concentrate more fiercely. Van had been crushed when Glickleister had died. It was as if some vast blazing bonfire had gone out. There ought to be bronze statues to Glickleister in front of every router station in the world.

Van mulled it over, shaken. So weird to think that Hyman Glickleister had actually reproduced. Some woman had married Glickleister and borne Glickleister's child. Once would pretty much do it for that activity, Van guessed glumly.

"Okay, so she's his kid," he admitted. Fawn looked just like Glickleister.

Jeb was eager to soft-pedal the situation. "Now, Van, you taught at Stanford. You get it about today's young people. Fawn is bright, she's a quick study. You can mellow her out."

Jeb was old-fashioned. He still thought that college students were wild, crazy kids. Van's students at Stanford had been sober workaholic Indian and Chinese software engineers with astronomical SATs. "Jeb, I don't want her. I don't like her."

"Then I can get you another secretary. Some old lady from the Defense Department with her hair in a bun and a pencil through it. And you know what she's going to do to you, Van? She's going to tape all your phone calls to Monica Lewinsky, and she'll betray you to some political operative. People do that kind of thing in this town. I'm trying to protect you here, Van. We raging supergeeks don't have a lot of friends inside the Beltway. You're my Deputy Director for Technical Services. You're my top boy and I want to kiss you, but somebody has got to answer your phone. Because you don't do that. So Fawn will. Because Fawn is one of us. Fawn was born one of us. We can trust her."

This was a crushing speech, but Van resisted mulishly. "How about Jimmie Matson from Mondiale? He was my executive assistant in the lab. Jimmie can get it done. He's great."

"You recommended Jimmie Matson to me already. We did a

background check. Jimmie Matson is a gay guy with a substance problem."

"Jimmie is gay?" Van was stunned.

"And he's on dope. This isn't the private sector, Van. Fawn passed a security clearance with flying colors. Glickleister's daughter is more secure than you are. Lots more secure."

Van's phone beeped with an incoming call. Van decided to take it because he was losing his argument with Jeb so badly. "I'll get back to you," he said.

The other call was Dottie.

"Hi!" he said, startled and pleased. "Are you in Washington?"

"I'm in Colorado," Dottie told him. "Are you being mean to Fawn?"

"Honey, I'm not being mean."

"Fawn can cook," Dottie coaxed. "She cooks Szechuan. Fawn found me on Google and we talked over all your problems. She's very sweet."

"I don't have any problems. I don't need a secretary or a cook. Besides, the class 'secretary' is not congruent with the class 'cook.' "

Dottie's voice sharpened and lifted half an octave. "Derek, what did you eat tonight?"

"A TV dinner," Van lied, caught out. He hadn't thought to eat at all. He had been thinking very seriously.

"What kind of TV dinner?"

"A Salisbury steak," Van blurted hastily. And it was true. He actually had eaten a Salisbury steak TV dinner. He had forgotten about doing that, so he had lied to Dottie by accident.

Twenty minutes after Grendel first went up, the system received its first hacker attack. It was a port scan, and of course it got nowhere. A Grendel running streams didn't have any "ports." Van had installed emulators that vaguely resembled ports, in the way a Venus-flytrap resembled a nice little red flower.

Triggered by this assault, Van's pager went off, vibrating his right knee in the cargo pants. Van had guzzled so much coffee during the past twenty-four hours that at first he thought the jittery vibration was happening inside his own leg. Van fetched out the pager and then logged on, wondering. An attack within twenty minutes? How was that even possible?

He watched the intruder fanatically typing. Then he called Jeb. "Jeb, come over here right now. You have got to see this."

"I'm having a dogfight with the Air Force, Van."

"To hell with the Air Force, come look."

By the time Jeb arrived in Van's office, the would-be intruder had already filled five screens with gibberish and back spaces.

Van paged the terminal, up and down silently, through the long list of line commands.

"Is that who I think it is?"

Jeb's froggy eyes bulged. "It is! It's him! This is kind of an honor, really."

Fawn left her desk, where she had been cleaning up spam while listening to a book on tape. Fawn favored the fictional works of someone named Kathy Acker. Since wearing earphones at work seemed to calm Fawn down some, Van overlooked her strange habits.

"What is it?" Fawn said, chewing the end of a Sharpie.

" 'It' is The Weevil," said Jeb solemnly. "Look at that guy. He is going through all top twenty of the biggest vulnerabilities for Windows systems. And he'll do each one of them ten times."

"But we'd be crazy to be running a Windows server," Fawn objected. "Big Bill's got more holes than baby Swiss cheese."

"The Weevil is crazy," Jeb said. "He doesn't even know what Windows is. He doesn't know what UNIX is, either. But when he runs out of all of the Windows holes he knows, then he'll start in with his complete list of UNIX vulnerabilities."

"I heard The Weevil used an Apple hole once," Van offered.

"Probably an accident."

"What does he do once he's inside the system?" said Fawn.

Jeb shrugged. "He gets root."

"But what does he do when he gets root?"

"He makes himself superuser, covers up the intrusion in the logs, and looks for some other machine to get root on."

"Oh." Fawn scratched the side of her nose with her pen. "He's one of those, huh?"

"The Weevil is *the* one of those. He doesn't know any programming. He'll never know. He only wants to knows holes and vulnerabilities. He collects them for their own sake. He has long lists of them. And he tries them all, cookbook style. Manually! Look at him backspacing there."

"Wow."

"Twenty-four, thirty-six hours straight sometimes. Day after day. Weeks. From his laptop in the toilet," said Jeb. "Did you ever *see* The Weevil, Van? He's been raided about thirty times."

"I saw a pic of him," Van said. And of The Weevil's den, or whatever one called that impossible, filthy hole where The Weevil lived. At the FCIC Reunion in Phoenix in '96, they'd had a slide projector. They ran some slides of The Weevil's raid photos during their beer bust. Van could still remember those computer cops howling.

"I met him once," said Jeb, wincing at the memory. "In a halfway house in Tacoma. I just had to go see The Weevil. I mean, this was the bad guy who took control of over four thousand computers. Mostly federal. One by one. By hand. Even back then, he had carpal tunnel so incredibly bad . . ." Jeb paused thoughtfully. "I think they call that 'degenerative osteoarthritis,' really. Hands like two big hockey gloves."

"No," said Fawn.

"Yes, Fawn." Jeb offered Fawn a gentle smile. That fatherly expression looked strange on Jeb's big face, but Jeb had known Hyman Glickleister really well.

Fawn's penny loafer scuffed the federal shag carpet in her doubt. "Really?"

"Yeah, Fawn, really. I'm not kidding."

Fawn believed him. "So, uh, what do we do about a guy like that?"

"Well, he's mentally ill. The FBI profiled him as extreme obsessive-compulsive, and . . ." A summary thought struggled to burst out of Jeb. "This is the face of our enemy," he said at last. "I mean, he's not al Qaeda, but he's truly of that kind. There is just no reasoning with this guy. There's no possible diplomacy we can use with him. There's no compromise or common sense. We can't scare him off, or buy him off, or give him anything that he wants. He's got a value system so totally alien to ours that he's like a *Star Trek* Borg."

Van tugged at his beard, hard enough to pluck a whisker. "How does The Weevil even know we're here? The only feed upstream of us is the NSA!"

"Man, I sure don't like *that*," Jeb said.

Van watched the screen. The Weevil was an awful typist. Small children typed better than The Weevil. He was, Van realized, using two fingers. Maybe two stumps.

Van had had two hours' sleep and three pots of coffee, getting the alpha rollout of the Grendel system in shape. The project was turning out better than Van had imagined. In fact, it was working out in a rather interesting fashion. It was elegant and he was proud of it. Working with Grendel was worthy of his talents. The work was consuming him.

Van was living alone. He was under great pressure to perform. He was sore all over from lifting weights every night, so as to collapse and get some sleep in his cold, lonely, lumpy bed.

Then, as Grendel's very first "guest," way before any legitimate user ever logged on to admire Van's handiwork, here he was already, instantly, this . . . creature. Of course The Weevil wasn't getting anywhere against Van's secure system. It was like watching a termite trying to chew through a concrete block. But, as long as it just kept chewing, chewing . . .

"We've got to get rid of this guy," he realized.

"He'll never get inside Grendel." Jeb shrugged. "He's a lunatic."

Van lowered his voice. "We have got to get rid of him *just because he is him and we are us.*"

"Good people have already tried that," said Jeb. "Any district attorney takes just one look at The Weevil. It's like: you want me to put THAT in front a jury? It's almost blind! It has no hands! It can't even talk. It's never held a job in its life. It has no life. I'm not even sure it can read."

"How does he eat?" said Fawn.

"He's got some kind of family in Canada. They send him cash, I think. They're okay people, that's what I always heard. They're just really happy that The Weevil lives far away."

Van pulled off his glasses. "The Weevil is *Canadian*? He's a *foreign national*? I never knew that."

"Yeah. So?"

"Oh, man! That's it! Game over! Illegal combatant! Enemy of humanity! Into the razor wire! Guantanamo Bay, Jeb. Into the steel cage."

"Take it easy, Van."

Van stabbed at the screen with a finger. "Jeb, *look* at this! He's *attacking the National Security Council*! You know, *us*!"

"Huh." Jeb cleared his throat. "Well, you've definitely got a point there."

"This is his last hacker 'sploit! He is *over*! We *own* him now!"

"Van, the NSC isn't supposed to directly involve itself in operational activities in the field. And we're just a board of the NSC. We're a policy coordination group."

Van boiled over. "This punk-ass chump is screwing with us, and you're going to let him *walk*? He's notorious! Everybody in our business knows who he is! Are we wimps in this outfit, are we the *victims*? Give me his address! He lives in Oregon, right? I'll drive over there right now! I'll kick his door in and kick his ass myself . . ."

Van let his voice trail off. Fawn and Jeb were staring at him. They had both gone pale.

"I'm overdoing it," he realized.

"Uh, yeah," said Fawn.

Van touched the monitor gently. "But, Jeb, you know, this is my baby here."

Jeb took a while to nod. "Maybe I shouldn't be saying this. But I do get it, Van. You've got the right gut instinct about this issue. We need to take some steps. I'm gonna keep you in the loop here."

"Okay."

"We need you here with this new Grendel system, Van. We can't have you leaving us to run any field assignments."

Now it was Van's turn to stare. Jeb really believed that he, Derek Vandeveer, would lock and load, drive across America, and physically raid some bad guy. Take him down. Maybe shoot him.

Van watched more tortured letters wriggle across the screen. He would do it, too, Van thought, in a stunning leap of self-knowledge. He was aching to go shoot The Weevil. He would sleep better for doing it.

Where was Dottie, where was Ted? Where was his bed, his home? He was in a bad way.

"I'm thinking visa problems," rumbled Jeb, thunder gathering in his face. "Emigration violation. I'm thinking 'cyberterrorism.' I'm thinking a personal call to John Ashcroft and a serious ton of bricks."

"Did they even pass that statute yet?" said Fawn.

"Patriot Act? Honey, they're gonna pass all kinds of stuff."

Van's apartment in Washington was grimy and dangerous. His NSC office in Washington was makeshift and dull. But Van's second office, four hours away from Washington in a place they called the "Vault," was so awful that he almost liked it. It quickly became his favorite place of work.

On CNN and MSNBC, the Vault was always known as the "Undisclosed Location." Dick Cheney was supposedly in there a whole lot. In point of fact Van had never seen the Vice President wandering around the Vault, but the Vault had an interesting crowd.

Someone with a very odd checklist had tried to figure out what kind of people would be necessary to run the United States of America if Washington was destroyed in a terrorist nuclear attack. That was the big concept behind the Vault: the lively possibility that D.C. might turn, without any warning, into a weapon-of-mass-destruction field of black slag.

Washington would be instant rubble. Then five minutes, maybe six minutes later, the Vault would come online. The survivors stashed away in the Vault would become the American post-nuclear government.

The community in the Vault kept bubbling, in constant turnaround. Nobody really wanted to stay in the eerie Vault. They all much preferred to lead real lives, even at the risk of getting killed by nukes, sarin, or anthrax. So the Vault was a very mix-and-match place. It was the Melting Stovepipes business all over again, only to a factor of ten.

The inhabitants of the Vault all slept in similar steel bunks. They had the same military card tables and folding steel chairs. You never knew, day to day, who your new neighbors would be. Federal Emergency Management Agency, Army Corps of Engineers, U.S. Postal Service even . . . They'd show up with plastic-coated briefing books and bewildered expressions, to spend two weeks hiding underground.

The Vault had been built in 1962, in a nation still queasy from the Cuban Missile Crisis. It stayed secret because it had been built quietly, in a big hurry, by a very small group of top-notch fallout-shelter contractors. The Vault was located in the Alleghenies, just over the border of West Virginia. It had a rather delightful and well-equipped hotel sitting on top of it, to camouflage it from the Russkies and the American press. The Vault had successfully stayed unknown to the world for forty solid years. The West Virginians who ran the hotel were a clannish lot. They had never breathed a word about the giant warren lurking beneath them.

The Vault had huge steel blast doors and its own coal-fired power plant. The coal plant doubled as the Vault's crematorium, in case anyone died of A-bomb radiation injuries. All the telephones were red plastic with rotary dials, straight off the set of Kubrick's *Dr. Strangelove.* The biggest open space in the Vault was a small gym, so the last men on earth wouldn't go completely bats with jail fever.

Van spent a lot of time in the Vault's gym. He'd become a workout addict in the grim celibacy of Dottie's absence. His neglected hacker's body yelled out for attention: decent food, sex, sleep, a long vacation. None of those things were remotely available to Van. Ferocious exercise was pretty much it.

That attitude fit the military tone inside the Vault, though. These guys brought heavy private burdens to their fifty-pound barbells and Nautilus racks. Every Vault rat had to be emotionally troubled. The whole point of being in the Vault was that everything you knew might be blasted to ashes overnight.

There was even one big, doomed soul in the Vault's gym who lifted his weights with a security briefcase permanently tethered to his wrist. This top-secret courier never said a word to anyone, but he was a hard guy to miss. Tall, dark, silent, chiseled-looking, very buff.

Van took an interest in this mysterious stranger. Day after day passed, but no one ever set the courier free of his burden. The chained briefcase was waterproof and apparently blastproof. The guy even showered with it. Van, of course, never asked him about the briefcase. There was something way too personal about that subject.

The Vault was a barracks, and had stark, simple, military routines. The cafeteria line fed everyone three times a day, on big community tables. All the federal foodstuffs had tough-guy military nicknames, like "elephant scabs" for the veal parmigiana and "bug juice" for the orangeade. When the lights went out at night, nobody stayed up to party. The Vault went as black as a tomb.

Van and his CCIAB people became extremely popular in the Vault. Within two days, Van had installed securely encrypted broadband Wi-Fi. Thanks to Van and his fellow cyberwarriors, even the most bored, lonely Vaultie, stuck in a sealed cell with a cheap khaki blanket and a laptop, could securely surf news portals. Van expected someone in authority to complain about all this free Internet access from within a secure facility, but no one ever complained. They just accepted Internet access as a modern force of nature.

Van lived much better inside the Vault than he did in his Washington apartment. The Vault was cramped, stony, and smelly, but at least he was fed and watered regularly. Van felt safe from the outside world.

Most other federal employees in the Vault sheepishly feared an apocalypse that would destroy everything they knew. Van, however, was getting one. Van's world was literally being destroyed, in newspapers, magazines, and television, day after day.

It was hard to believe—Van would never have imagined it—but Mondiale, the mighty Mondiale, was dot-bombing. Mondiale was coming apart at the seams. This brave, heroic, visionary, cutting-edge company—the bear market was beating it to death like a cheap piñata.

This made no sense at all. Mondiale was not some flimsy e-commerce Web site with a make-believe business model. Mondiale was the necessary basis of modern civilization. Mondiale was a telecommunications giant that owned real property: cables, microwave relay towers, optical switching stations, long-distance voice franchises, big chunks of regional local loop, and even satellites.

Mondiale was a highly profitable business that was laying fiber-optic pipe around the planet, uniting the world in efficient globalized prosperity. Mondiale was the future. It was insane to think that a society in an Information Age was not going to need Mondiale and its skills and capacities.

But the world had stopped believing in that. The Bubble was the Terror, just like that. And the stock had cratered. Van's own holdings, his fortune, his net worth, were nose-diving day by day, relentlessly. Van was helpless. There was nothing he could do to escape the collapse and save himself. As a federal employee, he had placed his holdings into a blind trust.

Doing this had never bothered him. He had never been the kind of guy with any time to dabble and meddle in stocks. Of course he knew people who lived that life—one of them, Tony Carew, was his best friend. Knowing Tony well, Van had always known better than to try to outhustle the IPO hustlers on Wall Street. Van didn't mind putting his Mondiale holdings into a locked federal box. Van had confidently figured he would just leave his stock there, as a classic, sensible, long-term investor, until the big emergency was over, and Mondiale took him back.

But Mondiale was eaten by the Terror. Everything that the common wisdom had urged Mondiale to do had turned, overnight, into poison. Everything Van had discovered and assembled for them— golden vistas of research potential, a host of raw possibilities, shining ways forward . . . nothingness. Vaporware. The abyss.

It felt very good to work inside solid bombproof concrete, then.

Van was wiped out, but not quite totally. As the Deputy Director of Technical Services for an NSC board, Van had a federal salary, paid promptly every month. Van was paid about as much as a senior FBI agent, which was to say, he was paid peanuts. FBI agents never made a dime until they quit the FBI. Former FBI agents could do pretty well, when they went to work as well-paid private security people. Former FBI guys commonly went to work for big, serious-minded, major commercial outfits. Like Mondiale.

Even Tony Carew, the proverbial dot-com rich kid, had hit hard times. Tony never said a word about red-hot market opportunities anymore. Tony was fiddling with science projects in Colorado, he was angling for high-tech defense work. Tony had lost more money than Van knew how to count. And he still had to live out there.

Inside the Vault, though, a guy could get along on powdered eggs and grits. Creditors would never find you there. You didn't have to watch financial news on TV or glimpse the stocks in a newspaper. The Vault had hot macaroni and cheese. The Vault had dry yellow cake. There was no beer or alcohol of any kind allowed. There was grape juice.

That was what there was. That was all there was. That was the

Policy, and it was the federal government. You didn't have to think about it.

It got worse. Federal procurement systems were notoriously sluggish. When he and Jeb had gone over the stats for the Grendel system, they had discovered that it would take eight times longer to pay for Grendel than it would to simply build it themselves. They could wait for a procurement check to be cut, but by that time, they would have lost the critical first-mover advantage that had led them to plan a Grendel in the first place.

So Van had paid for Grendel's hardware himself.

Van still knew that this was the sensible choice. He knew that the baby CCIAB would quickly die if they didn't prove their serious chops as go-to technical people. Jeb had promised that the feds would be good for Van's money sooner or later. As the legendary Admiral Grace Hopper had often told Jeb, it was always easier to apologize to a bureaucracy than it was to get permission. Jeb did not have the necessary money, himself. Jeb had spent most of the last twenty years as a federal law-enforcement instructor.

So, Van personally tasked Fawn with buying 350 used PCs on eBay. As a bridge loan for the CCIAB, Van sold his Range Rover. The Range Rover was in big trouble parked in his Washington neighborhood anyway. It was smarter to sell his truck than to have it carjacked.

Ironically, after selling his Rover, Van had no problem at all requisitioning a posh federal limo. In fact, the black limo driver was a neighbor of his. So Van slithered around Washington in a bombproof stretch limousine with smoked windows, a vehicle often used by the Secretary of State. Then he went home to sleep in a slum.

Fawn was a practiced eBay hand. Fawn bought most of her clothes there, from tiny New Age retailers who made anti-allergenic clothing. Now Fawn bought herself a set of fake eBay IDs for "security reasons." Soon she was elbow-deep in a web of electronic transactions that Van had no time or energy to oversee.

The 350 used PCs showed up very quickly. Most of their hard

disks were crammed with pirate software, viruses, and pornography, but that posed no problems. Van stuck the 350 PC motherboards into hand-welded frames. He installed a completely new operating system that turned them all into small components of a monster system. Grendel was installed in a spare Internet rack in the bowels of the Vault, directly connected to all-powerful servers in the NSA's Fort Meade.

Days later, Van's office furniture arrived. Van hadn't asked for new furniture—he had been working off metal folding chairs—but Fawn took matters into her own hands. She bought a discontinued office suite from a defunct dot-com and boldly had it crated and shipped to the Vault's secret mail drop in West Virginia.

The CCIAB's cheerless chunk of bunker blossomed with leopard-dotted Leap Chairs and strange, hexagonal, filmy office sets, featuring spandex light shades and tiltable desks.

Fawn's flamboyant gear was a major hit within the Vault. Such comforts were unheard-of in federal employment. Envious Defense Department drones would come by just to steal Fawn's golden paper clips and her teakwood thumbtacks.

The CCIAB won a lasting nickname: "Those Cyberwar People."

Once again, Van expected someone to lower the boom on them for being too bold, but nobody ever lowered the boom on small boards of advisers that worked for the National Security Council. Except for the President himself, there just wasn't anybody in the federal government with direct authority to fuss at the CCIAB. Even the President himself would have to create a Special Review Board just to review his special boards, and in times of war, that was out of the question.

The CCIAB was not really a federal agency. Like the National Security Council itself, it was a small, make-do work gang of close colleagues that was trying to steer huge federal bureaucracies into the latest and trendiest policy directions. Like a president, the CCIAB was just a temporary passerby in the federal system. Except for Fawn herself, who had had no job when she begged Jeb for a favor, there was no such thing as a career CCIAB person. Every bureaucrat in the CCIAB was seconded-over from other careers in other bureaucracies. Karl Bowen, their top policy analyst, came from Los Alamos National Lab. Brian Coon, their chief investigator, was from the Office of Criminal Investigations of the IRS. Herbert Howland, the public relations guy, was from the Navy Broadcasting Service. And so forth.

Jeb's game plan for the CCIAB was to create a realistic policy for National Cyber-Security that the President, Secretary of State, DoD, CIA, NSA, and Joint Chiefs of Staff could all sign off on. The pitifully vulnerable federal computers had to become less sleazy and less easy. Through their own good example, sheer panic, and grim threats, the CCIAB would beat, beat, beat the bureaucrats into line. Whatever could budge would be made to budge. And the devil take the rest.

During the Christmas season, the political pace slowed down. Vital people simply vanished from Washington. Contacts did not answer e-mail. Van was glad for the chance to concentrate. His emptied head was buzzing with hot new technical ideas.

Back in his Washington apartment, Van was waiting for his latest batch of code to compile. Living in a high-crime area had brought Van useful insights about real-world security. In real life, if you had a solid wall, then you could lock the door. If one lock wasn't enough, it helped to install five or six locks.

But computer networks didn't have walls. So the "firewall" metaphor was just that, a metaphor.

A far more fertile approach would be a computational *immune system*. After all, the vast majority of serious computer attacks were not carried out by outside hackers. Hackers did not "break in" through anything that could "break." Most real-life computer acts-of-evil were carried out by crooked insiders already *within* the firewall. Thieves or double agents, people who knew the system already. Usually, they knew very well what they wanted to corrupt, erase, alter, or illicitly copy.

So a better security model would not "lock" or "wall away" anything. Instead, it would scan constantly for evil processes inside the machine. It would hunt for bad acts inside the system, in the way that the bloodstream fights germs.

This was an exciting new paradigm. It offered fruitful ways forward that resolved a host of the day's knottiest security challenges. The concept was a generation ahead of its time. Maybe two generations, given the awful state of the computer market.

All the more vital, then, that the CCIAB should pioneer a serious breakthrough like that. They could run it within the Vault, an ideal place to start a working demo for a core audience. A streaming distributed supercomputer, on broadband wireless, featuring a pilot, alpha-rollout immune system.

This inspiration set Van's brain afire. It was fantastic. And it was really likely to work, too, that was the best part. The CCIAB didn't have a whole lot of money, but they did have the attention of the top experts in the field. There was no competition in creating computer immune systems. There were no stovepipes. There were no established industry vendors trying to protect market share.

So they could farm the project out just like Open Source, develop it quickly, quietly, in closed modules, on a need-to-know basis. So while Jeb was struggling with the state of federal security in his political, bureaucratic way, he, Van, would be literally building and assembling the future of computer security. Hands-on. The real deal. Proof-of-concept. Wow.

Van's son flickered onto his laptop screen, the size of a postage stamp. Ted's creche in distant Colorado featured a webcam. Both Van and Dottie commonly watched Ted's webcam during their workdays, though nothing much ever happened there. The day care was run by a bouncy, well-scrubbed Buddhist feminist from Boulder, a thirty-something woman in braids, who wore denim overalls and a head kerchief. She commonly sat cross-legged in her Timberland boots as her little charges crawled all over her. Sometimes she read them non-gender-specific fairy tales. Ted seemed to find this treatment more or less okay. He definitely looked a little bewildered sometimes.

Sometimes Van would touch his son's flickering image on the screen and murmur a few words. He couldn't help himself.

On the day after Christmas, Van squinted through the peephole of the apartment door and was stunned to see Tony Carew.

Van undid three locks and two chains. Tony slipped inside, with a final wary glance down the gloomy hall. Tony wore a pale, tailored trench coat, a spotless snap-brimmed hat. He looked very Washington. He'd never looked that way before, but he sure looked it now.

"Van, you're a hard guy to find. Don't you answer your phone?"

"No. Not anymore."

Tony confronted the apartment. He summed it up and dismissed it in disbelief. "Is this a safehouse? If so, it's not very safe. I brought a bodyguard and a chauffeur to this part of town. I'm really afraid somebody's going to hurt them out there."

Tony put his black shoulder bag on Van's peeling Formica counter. He unzipped it and displayed a newly purchased bottle of brandy and Benedictine, still in a paper sack. The B&B bottle was two bottles really, double-necked and welded together. Glass twins in green and yellow.

In their teenage undergraduate days, Van and Tony had considered brandy with Benedictine to be the height of sophisticated drinking. It was, of course, illegal for them to be drinking at all, and doubly illegal to do it on campus, which made a doubled form of booze even tastier, somehow. They each had elaborate theories on the exact proportions of brandy and Benedictine necessary to get properly hammered.

The sight of the two crooked bottles gave Van a warm nostalgic glow. There had been such innocent joy in his life then. Tony had been such good fun. Tony Carew was the guy who had found Van the best fun he had ever had: a serious girlfriend.

Van had never before had a roommate who could match him in intelligence. And it hadn't hurt Van's feelings any that Tony was witty, fast-talking, and great around girls.

Tony took off his brand-new hat and placed it on top of his bag, so that his hat would not have to touch the disgusting countertop. "I don't suppose there's such a thing as a 'snifter' around here."

Van fetched them a couple of jumbo disposable foam cups. He'd been meaning to buy himself some glassware, but had never found the chance.

Tony set to work to open the bottles. Van checked the Casio strapped to his wrist. It was only 6:00 P.M. "Are you drinking, Tony?"

"How could I not?" Tony said. "I just came back from a rotten little holiday emergency in the bowels of the FCC."

"Oh."

"No, Van, it's even worse than that. I strongly advise you to join me immediately in a heavy boozing session."

"All right." Van knew that Tony had a point. He knew it all too well.

Tony poured their potions. He clowned around with the flimsy cups, acting drunk already. Tony wasn't genuinely wasted yet—Van pretty well knew what Tony looked like under those conditions—but Tony definitely had that first, lit-up look.

Tony had brought a burden with him. It couldn't be just the awesome, industry-smashing train wreck in federal telecommunications policy. Tony would not have come here personally just for that.

Tony's priorities shifted around some, but Tony was always Tony. Tony Carew was into money, women, technology, and status games. Tony Carew was a very charming guy. He was fluent and persuasive. Van had never competed with Tony in those aspects of life. That was why Tony trusted him.

Like most overachievers, Tony had personal burdens that weighed on him like anvils. But Tony's idea of burdens—the big money, the fast women, the struggle for status—those things fell on Van like a light refreshing rain. From their first day as friends, Van had been able to drink in Tony's problems. Van didn't judge Tony, he didn't scold. He couldn't even say that he sympathized. He needed Tony to trust him, somehow. He needed to be trusted with those things.

Van offered Tony the magnesium chair and sat on the weight-lifting bench.

Tony stroked the shining chair. With Tony inside it, it was a throne. "Wow! You should get a dozen of these. They stack!"

"Great idea." Van tilted his flimsy white cup and sipped his B&B. Instantly, its familiar velvety burn made him feel nineteen years old.

Tony studied the apartment's bare walls. Van had managed to rid himself of the kung-fu posters, along with all the previous tenant's possessions. He had kept the weight-lifting set, though. The weights were his consolation prize.

"Van, couldn't the NSC get you a furnished apartment?"

"It *was* furnished, Tony. I threw everything out."

Tony's eyes narrowed. "So you swept it all for bugs, huh? Yeah, I've seen that done before. Man, that really wrecks the place."

Van shrugged.

"Van, I can't believe they made you into a fed. I know you've got the right family background there, but that line of work doesn't seem much like you."

"Times change."

"But why are they wasting your valuable time? Why you? You're the computer-science gold standard, man. Can't they FedEx their little password crypto puzzles over to Merwinster? You've got a decent place up there."

"I'm selling my house."

"No way! It can't be!" Tony blinked. "Mondiale is cratering that hard? Mondiale, too?"

Van nodded. "On a federal salary, I can't pay the real-estate taxes on that place. I'll be lucky to sell it. I wish I knew who could buy it. The whole town's been turned inside out."

Tony's face fell. Tony was a rich kid from a wealthy family, but the money issue between them had never much bothered Van. Dottie's dad was also pretty well-to-do, and Dottie was just fine. "I knew your scene up there had a serious downturn, but . . . Did you tell that to Dottie?"

"She can do math."

"You didn't tell her, then."

Van said nothing. He and his wife kept separate bank accounts. When Van's salary and stock had begun skyrocketing with the Internet boom, that didn't seem the proper time to confront Dottie with some strange demand that they change their usual financial arrangements. That was too much like one of those creepy post-nuptial agreements. Van was never going to dump Dottie Vandeveer for some puff-headed trophy wife. Mondiale's other VPs might like to pull such stunts, but those clowns were just money people.

"You been out to see her lately, Van?"

"Not lately. We called at Christmas. Talked a lot."

"Seen her ever? Since she moved to the Facility?"

"Well, no. We're both working like crazy."

Now Tony was truly shocked. "Look, Van. Maybe I shouldn't comment here. But I've known Dottie even longer than I've known you. I've seen her in Colorado, I dunno, five times in the past two months. And you can't fly out there to the site? You married her, fella. What is the problem?"

"We trade e-mail every day."

Tony topped up Van's foam cup, a pitying look on his face. "My man, look at this dark place you're in. You really sleep in here? Are you a fifth-level federal Dungeons and Dragons troll? Are you a kobold now? Are you Gollum? She's never seen you in this awful place, am I right?"

Van nodded.

"Well, thank God for that." Tony sighed. "I'd better cut to the chase right away. It's up to me to take you two in hand. Van, she is sensitive. She is lonely and vulnerable. She'll never call you first. She has that kind of proud shyness that really bright women get. She would rather be shot first. You've got to tell her that you want to see her. You've got to insist, Van."

Van blinked. He lowered his voice. "Well, man, it's kind of hard to just go and do that . . ."

Tony touched the vest of virgin wool within his trench coat. "Van, was I right before? Ten years ago, I told you all this. Word for word. I *made* you call Dottie. I practically *beat you* into making that first call. Was I right?"

The brandy was hitting Van now. There was a hot rush to his bearded cheeks. "Yeah, Tony. Yeah, you did that for me. Yeah, you were right."

"So. What is your deliverable, then?"

"Well," said Van, "I guess maybe . . . There is this big conference coming up for the CCIAB, out at this big farm retreat in Virginia . . ."

"Which one? Coulfax? Erlette House?"

"Erlette House, yeah, that's the place."

"Oh, yeah. That would be perfect. CIA, DoD, Bell Labs, DARPA, they all do big seminars there. The food is fantastic, beautiful land-scaping, ponds, swans, arbors, flower gardens, man, the wine cellar's two hundred years old! Erlette House is where every undersecretary takes the sexy intern." Tony laughed. "End of your problem, my man."

Van sat up straighter. That did sound pretty good, really. The Er-lette House event wasn't till early spring, but by March the CCIAB would be delivering its recommendations. And he, Van, would be leaving the little board for some heavy-duty, long-term, permanent federal post. Or else contemplating sudden unemployment. Either way he should have Dottie with him. To celebrate with him, or com-miserate, or . . . No, just to be together. He owed her that.

"You're gonna thank me," Tony promised.

"I'm thanking you already."

"You should fly to Colorado to see her as soon as you can," Tony said, bearing down. "Do you have any idea what we've got going on out there? We are a world-class facility. We are bringing astronomy right into the e-world. We've got the biggest Internet2 node west of the Mississippi."

"Yeah, Dottie seems pretty pleased with the job."

"It's a great job for her. It's the future of her profession. You don't just *look* through a digital observatory, pal. Everything that it senses is archived and fully accessible on Internet2."

Van smiled. "Is this your best new toy now, Tony?"

Tony sipped his cup, raised a brow, and added more Benedictine. "You know, back in the Boom, I wondered why I spent so much time and energy on some stargazer project. That was old DeFanti's baby, and I was just his chief cook and bottlewasher. But after the hell I've been through lately—hey, now I know why he needed a real big hobby way outside the business world."

Van nodded. "The old folks get it about these ups and downs. That's part of life, that's all."

"Oh, I knew I'd see a market correction," Tony said grimly. "I never guessed I'd see anything this insanely bad."

"Don't take that to heart, Tony. Time is on your side. You'll be back. You'll be back with bells on."

This was the best thing Van could think to say, and he meant it sincerely, but he saw from Tony's wince that he had overdone it somehow. Maybe it smelled too much like pity.

"I shouldn't tell you this," Tony said, "but, you know the way router prices have crashed lately? Well, DeFanti had a standing order in to purchase those below a certain price level. Pal, we have got *unbelievable* numbers of routers in that facility. Barns full. We *are* Internet2, man, we can handle all the lambda from Juneau to Los Angeles."

"No way."

"Yes way. There's nothing new about an NSF hub being a major Internet backbone. Enron was gonna move hard into that niche, in a Bush administration. They were gonna marketize Al Gore's broadband. We were with that idea way ahead of the curve. We would have made a fortune with DeFanti's old pals from Houston. We coulda run a dozen observatories off that kind of revenue."

"How is that holding up now?"

"Oh, the price-point on routers will come back soon. It's just kind of a bridge loan to the industry, really. But in the meantime, we've got *loads* of routers. I'm thinking your Grendel thing could do with some routers. Am I right?"

"Sure it could, but, Tony, I can't buy any hardware from you."

"I could practically pay you to take 'em."

"We're friends. I'm a fed now. That's not ethical."

Tony was nettled. "Do I look five years old? How long have you been in this town? Of course I wouldn't 'sell' them to you. You wouldn't 'buy' them either. It would never show up as a financial transaction at all. You're NSC, and I'm NSF. Plus, we've got the NSA, for heaven's sake! How do you think *they* buy their hardware? They don't even damn exist."

Van shook his head. "My boss hates the NSA. They're all over our turf. They killed all the crypto initiatives. They made security bad and kept it bad, just so they could spy the easy way." Van put his cup down. "They suck."

"Yeah, sure they do, but the NSA has got black budgets that make Enron look like a bookie joint. Okay, never mind the hardware. That was one option, that's all. How about you coming out to lecture us next spring? We know how bad security is out in the networks. We're hosting the next Joint Techs conference out on DeFanti's dude ranch. Next April. Why don't you fly out there and bring us some of the noise from inside the Beltway? You always do Joint Techs, right?"

"That's true." Everybody at Joint Techs was a personal friend. That was the only way that the Secret Nerd Masters of the Internet knew how to invite you to Joint Techs in the first place. Everyone who was anyone went. "Yeah, Tony, I'd go there for you."

"You could tell Joint Techs the new party line from your boss the Jebster."

"Yeah, I'd demo Grendel for 'em."

"Oh, man. That would rock so hard. Why don't you *build* a Grendel at Joint Techs? We'll get you a truckload of crap PCs. We'll wire 'em up real time. Joint Techs will go ape."

That would definitely work, thought Van. Such a showman's stunt would never have occurred to him, but Tony was absolutely right. The guys at Joint Techs would be totally thrilled by a hands-on confrontation with k-rad streaming hardware. They would forget how to breathe.

He beamed on Tony suddenly. It was impossible not to love the guy. Van could barely remember how lousy he had felt twenty minutes ago, how grim and committed and full of fortitude. Now, with Tony in this sorry little room with him, there were suddenly some bright shining lights in his future. Days that would be full of sunshine for him. And happiness. Future days that would be *really cool*.

The guy was light and magic.

Tony silently reached to pour himself more booze. The happy moment passed quickly. There was an anvil on Tony's back.

"What are you up to, Tony? You got plans to turn it around, right?"

"Well," said Tony, who was definitely not okay, "you mustn't lose sight of the end goal, Van. After a stock market bubble, people are just as irrational as they were before. But now it's all about the terror, instead of all about the greed. They are *more* irrational now, because they can't see any future."

"You've got money troubles?"

"It's not that simple. By the way, I'm really sorry about your board of directors gig for DeFanti's holding company. You were right to resign before you turned fed, but, well, I wanted to make that thing work out a lot better for you."

"That's okay, Tony," said Van, and it was, because Van hated corporate board meetings even more than he hated federal ones. "They never got it about what I told them about real security, that was clear."

"When you're a master-of-the-universe like Tom DeFanti, some-times you just plain lose track." Tony's face twisted. "You heard all about what happened to Tom, didn't you?"

"I know that he retired. The board never talked much about that. They kept it real hush-hush."

"Oh, everyone knew Tom was getting erratic, that part was all over the media, but . . . Well, Tom finally, completely crashed. Basi-cally, Tom is a prisoner now. They wouldn't send a guy like that to just any mental clinic, you know. They *built one around him,* the way they did for Howard Hughes. Tom is delusional. They've got him trapped inside a wing of that farmhouse. The Chinese wife looks after him . . . He talks about Martians, Van."

"Oh, jeez. You mean that?"

"I know it. Tom met a UFO. Among other things. It's like the *Heaven's Gate* thing. Spaceships and Martians. He's really bent in the head. It's been a total nightmare for all the associates." Tony emptied his cup and slumped in the shining chair. "The very same powers that made Tom so great are tearing him apart. The acuity, the imagina-tion. The mental daring. I think it's the very worst tragedy that I have ever witnessed at first hand."

"My God," Van said. "I had no idea it was that bad."

"Van, listen." Tony was passionate now. "I have learned some-thing important about people who are profoundly creative. They are unbalanced. That's why they have so much to give. They *have* to give. They are fighting with some kind of black chasm inside. Great artists, great writers . . . Captains of industry, even. The top ones get much better than any human being ever needs to be. No mere re-ward could ever make anybody act to that level of performance. Be-cause it's never about the money, or even the fame. It's all about the inner terror."

"Come on, Tony."

"That is the truth, Van." He was bitter. "I have seen it happen with my own eyes."

Van rallied himself. He was feeling pretty good now, the brandy was smoothly taking hold of him, and it was time for him to exert himself for the sake of his unhappy friend. "The work is its own reward, Tony. If you do it right, it feels great. To give is good for you."

"You say that because you've got creative power, Van. You are a scientist. You're stable. You can stare deep into the screen and you really engage. I have seen you do that and it's marvelous. You get awards for it. I knew you had a gift the first time I met you. But you're not an artist. You're not a businessman, even. Because you don't have a demon. You're a nice guy."

"Tony, come on. If I don't believe in UFOs, there's no way you're gonna get me going about demons."

"Who, me? I'm just a deal maker. I'm not a creative. I'm just a glorified hustler."

Van laughed. "Tony, buck up. You do okay, man. You do great." Maybe Tony had suffered some market setbacks, but the guy had a private jet. He dated models and actresses. He spent enough on his clothes to feed a village in Kenya. Why was he carrying on like his world had ended?

And yet, Tony had always been like this. It was the other side of his charm somehow, that dark urge to put himself down.

Tony rubbed at his cheeks, the way he did as his face went numb from drink. "I do assemble my deals in rather remarkable ways, sometimes. Through pastiche and collage, basically. It's very postmodern."

" 'Postmodern'? You're drunk, Tony, cut the crap." Van rose to his feet. "You know what we should do right now? Bowling. Let's go bowling, Tony, come on."

Tony smiled. "You're still bowling? You're gonna kick my ass, man."

"No way, Tony. You are *the* bowler. You are *Mr.* Ace the Split."

"Look at your damn arms," Tony objected. "What have you been doing to yourself? You've got arms like two tree trunks."

"Two tree trunks," Van repeated carefully. As a child with a stutter, he would have found those words impossible to say. They were pretty hard for him to say right now, with that brandy hanging on his tongue. "Let's go bowl in the Pentagon. They've got some great lanes in there. I've got a Pentagon pass card."

"Now you're starting to interest me," Tony said.

"The Pentagon is full of hot chicks."

"You are plastered," Tony realized. "Did you eat anything today?"

Van shrugged. "Let's just go. This place stinks. Lemme call my limo guy."

"Never mind that, I've got a chauffeur," said Tony. He helped Van into his overcoat. The coat was West German military surplus. It was slick green nylon with elastic cuffs, some kind of a European battle-field medical thing. The coat had the many pockets Van always needed for tools, gizmos, and spare bits of hardware, even though it made him look like a secret mad surgeon. Normal people skittered away when they saw him on the sidewalks of Washington. This was one of the coat's major benefits, actually.

Plus, the coat was warm, and it was cold outside.

On his way out the door, Tony noticed the ray gun. He snagged it from its holster on the wall.

He sniffed the barrel. "This is a hot-glue gun."

"Yeah," said Van.

Tony rapped the hollow barrel with his knuckles. "So, you've got a Flash Gordon ray gun that melts glue? What is this, aluminum?"

"Titanium."

"I *thought* that was titanium. But, man, nobody can machine titanium. Even Steve Jobs can't machine titanium. Where on earth did you get this thing? It's insanely great!"

"I keep it to scare off the crack pushers."

Tony reverently wrapped the electrical wire around the glue gun's butt. "You wouldn't believe what I went through at the FCC today," he said. "It was truly awful. It was bloody blue ruin. But *this* thing, Van." He burst into whoops of laughter as he put the gun back in the wall holster. "You, my man. You have just made my year!"

Tony really did have a chauffeur, and he really did have a bodyguard. They were two dark, gloomy men with a silent, rent-a-cop, paid-by-the-hour look. They sat in the front of the limo, while Tony and Van sat together in the plush, upholstered back.

It had always been their principle never to mix liquor, so Tony opened the limo's bar to retrieve some Courvoisier. The bar supplied them with nifty little translucent green shot glasses.

Van downed his shot. This brandy was not just good, but superbly good. It was soul-stirring. It gave him just the jolt he needed to get to the point.

"Tony, why did you come to see me tonight?"

Tony smacked his lips and poured himself a second one. "Hey, I was in town, man! Tomorrow—well, maybe two days from now, counting the dateline—I'll be back in India. At a New Year's party at a mountain resort, with a very beautiful woman. I should tell you all about dating Anjali, my man. Anjali Devgan, from Bollywood. You would find this story very, very revelatory."

"That must be pretty hot."

"It is a different world over there. It is an entirely different erotic universe. That woman has ruined me. She has. She is fantastic. Anjali has made me into some kind of centuries-eaten male statue from the temples of Khajuraho. She and I are like water and fire. There are sexual clashes that yaks can hear in Nepal."

"What can I really do for you, Tony?"

"Nothing, my man! I swear I'm beyond all help!"

"Just tell it to me, all right? This is Van here."

Tony checked the bulletproof glass between themselves and the driver's compartment. "Okay . . . but I *really* shouldn't tell you this."

"Right." Van started to relax a little. Here it came, then.

"I didn't want to tell you. You're forcing it out of me."

"Right, Tony."

"I shouldn't tell you this because there is money in it. A lot of money. And I've got a lot to gain by that, so I am not an objective witness here. Bearing that in mind."

Van nodded silently.

"The KH-13," Tony said.

A spy satellite. "I've heard of it," Van said.

"It is an overengineered, sorry-ass piece of junk."

"I heard that, too."

"Two years behind schedule. Way over budget, hundreds of millions. A launch weight over seven thousand pounds, so it won't even fit in a standard Titan booster. They cheated DeFanti on that one. The KH-13 is the only U.S. spy satellite in orbit that doesn't have Tom's imaging chips. Tom got beat out in the bidding, and you know, that was a crooked deal, but that's a long story . . . The point is, they are bureaucrats. And they tried to make a new-model spy satellite. They tried to do that and they *screwed it up bad,* Van. Now, DeFanti could have pulled that stunt off, because he always had this really tight crew of top people—"

"Really quiet," said Van. "Really quick. And always on time. Top people, but maybe ten percent of the number of technicians that anybody else would use."

Tony put his shot glass on the limo's hanging board. "Yeah. I never thought of it quite that way, but yeah, that's exactly how that worked."

"So what is the problem?"

"They farmed out the new KH-13 to this bunch of crooked fat cats. So right when America really needs fresh eyes in space, we are screwed. They managed to launch exactly one KH-13, and the stupid bastard is on the blink. It is way too sophisticated and overfeatured, especially in the infrared cameras. The KH-13 is supposed to be able to spot muzzle flashes in real time from automatic weapons in terrorist training camps. That is a *crazy* thing to ask from a satellite. And whose fault is it that the project is so screwed up? It's anybody's fault! Anybody but the almighty Air Force and the NRO! They are looking for somebody to hang it on. They need a fall guy."

Why was Tony telling him this? "Tony, I'm in cyberspace, not outer space."

"There is this guy, Michael Hickok."

Van waited. Here came the rest of it, then.

"Hickok is this black-bag guy who did a lot of dirty work overseas. Chechnya, Central Asia, Kazakhstan where the launch pads are . . . Hickok's a mercenary. The guy is up for anything. He's been hired to find some political cover. So you know what the spin is now? It's all a 'software problem,' Van."

"Ah-ha." Van scowled. "Blame the coders for it. Blame the geeks."

"Hickok is going door-to-door looking for somebody to pin that satellite's problem on. Don't let that be you. Okay? Because your new outfit is getting some real credibility in the code world. That means that incompetent people will try to drop all their crap problems on you. From a great, great political height."

"Tony, we're not looking for any satellite problems at the CCIAB. Trust me here, we've got our own problems to hack and plenty of them."

"Van, look out the window, okay? This is Washington! You don't get the luxury of minding your own business in this town. The KH-13 is political. It is the kind of problem that comes looking for you."

Van thought this statement over. It had the ugly smack of authenticity.

"So here it comes, straight at me and my people, that's what you're telling me?"

Tony had turned his face to the passing streetlights. "There's not much I can do for him now, but Tom DeFanti was my people, and Tom DeFanti *was* the spy-sat business. So I *know* that problem's coming for you."

Van considered this. "But what if I can fix it?"

Tony was at a loss for words. "Okay," he said at last. "If it really *was* just a software problem, yeah, you would probably be the guy who could fix that. But that is not the problem at all. The KH-13 is a boondoggle from start to finish. The U.S. had a huge lead in spy-sats. Nobody ever figured we would really need much better ones. The spy-sat contractors had the fix in, they had themselves a sweet racket. Now they have a flying gold-plated Cadillac with an engine that is

Detroit junk. You wanna fix something? Go fix Lockheed Martin and General Dynamics."

"Okay, Tony. I hear you."

"You're a pretty good guy, Van, but you're not up for fixing the military-industrial complex. I'm not trying to tell you to rush out there with guns blazing and bring me some justice. I would never ask that of you, man. I'm just warning you to duck. That's all I have to say."

"Thanks for the heads-up, Tony. I don't forget stuff like this."

"I really shouldn't have told you that, Van. You are not properly cleared. We could go to jail for that."

Van sighed. "Tony, we're not going to jail. We are going bowling."

"Right."

"We went bowling together. That is all we did."

"Absolutely, man. Totally. Swear it in court."

"And you told me all about your hot date with this Indian actress."

"Oh, yeah, she's an actress," Tony agreed. Tony was much improved now. "But you know, Van, the actress part is kind of the least of her."

CHAPTER SIX

J eb's effort to assemble a federal security consensus had its thornier side. Washington's political establishment cared little for computers. They were completely obsessed with aircraft flight safety. To Van, this strategy made no sense. It was typical of panicky amateurs who couldn't think through security issues from a sensible engineering perspective.

Obviously, al Qaeda was not going to repeat their September 11 airplane attack. Terrorists never did that. The element of surprise was vital to them. No crew or passengers on earth would ever again surrender an airplane to attackers armed with razor blades. Not when it was obvious that everyone inside the airplane was going to die.

Logically, it was both useless and impossibly expensive to try to protect airlines from razor blades. The airlines would go broke trying that stunt. It was also beside the point. Airports everywhere were still selling liquor bottles. Any hijacker with a liquor bottle had a big glass club full of flammable liquid that could be turned into a deadly glass dagger with one good whack on a bulkhead. A fifth of Jack Daniel's made a much worse weapon than a tiny boxcutter. Where were the priorities here? Why hadn't someone thought that through?

Still, Van could understand why politicians obsessed about plummeting airplanes. A falling airplane was one of the few weapons that could kill a large crowd of politicians inside Washington.

So the CCIAB was willing to swallow that foolishness, for the sake of political need—but it got worse. If terrorists really did want to use airplanes to assault a center of government, then civilian passenger airliners were a lousy choice for that kind of attack. Civilian airliners were way too slow, too well policed, and had too many witnesses and busybodies on board. The ideal flying assassination weapon for kamikaze terrorists would be a private business jet. Their crews were small, and such jets were easy to steal from a hangar. Then the stolen jet could be packed with explosives, Oklahoma City style. It was a matter of simple physics, obvious once you worked it all out on paper. Stolen business jets were sure to hit much harder, faster, and more effectively than the September 11 passenger planes.

But while Joe and Jane Consumer were having their shoes x-rayed at the airport, nobody in federal security was doing anything useful about the stark threat posed by private jets. Private jet owners were America's richest people. Nobody in Congress dared to offend them.

American rich people were too rich to get treated like terrorists. Even though Osama bin Laden was plenty rich, and probably the world's best terrorist ever. Shoko Asahara, the nerve-gas yoga mastermind, was so rich he could afford private helicopters. If anybody was a serious terrorist security problem, it was rogue rich people.

However, this huge gap in America's air defenses hadn't escaped the attention of the Air Force Office of Experimental Avionic Research in Colorado Springs. These guys, who had the sexy military-style acronym AFOXAR, had been working on the problem with some quiet help from NASA and DARPA. Their first conversion target was the BBJ, Boeing Business Jet, the largest and therefore most dangerous aircraft of the American private jet fleet. Their scheme was to come up with a small, secret autopilot that could be quietly installed inside jets and then triggered remotely during emergencies. Then the autopilot would guide the plane and its baffled terrorists right back to earth, and the waiting arms of fully informed police.

This scheme sounded simple enough, but the devil was in the details. Remote control of flying jets posed many daunting challenges, but one of the worst was the software. Because, if some clever hacker ever took over the control system itself, then all of America's private jets could be turned instantly into remote-control flying bombs.

The AFOXAR guys had done a lot of career work on remote-controlled surveillance drones. They truly got it about air control and avionics problems, but serious network security was beyond their reach. Jeb had taken on the software problem for AFOXAR, because it was politically useful for the CCIAB to have a hand-in with homeland aircraft security. Though it made little sense from a technical perspective, it would get the attention of congressmen.

Van's Grendel project had stabilized for the time being, so Van found himself tasked with retrofitting secure spy-satellite controls for use within private jets. Van doubted that this project was likely to thrive—it would only stay sexy as long as there were headlines about hijackers—but Van was not his own boss. Besides, once he looked at the technical details, it turned out to be very interesting technical work with broad applications.

After all, spy satellites were remote-controlled flying objects. They also had some very well-tested crypto communications protocols.

Van had never expected outer space to be so rich in supersecret high technology, but in point of fact, it was fascinating.

For some forty years an incredible variety of adversaries had tried to "spoof" American satellites. To hack and "own" a supersecret American KH-11 Keyhole or Aquacade in orbit—that would be a huge accomplishment in espionage, a much bigger deal than Falcon, or Snow-man, or Jonathan Pollard. Huge enemy effort had been wasted in this. Nobody—not the Chinese, not the Russians, not even the French or the British—had ever touched America's supreme technical command of telemetry, systems acquisition, phase-locked carrier tracking loops, phase-coherent tracking, and stochastic integro-differential hybrid multichannel carriers.

Van was truly in his element with this part of his new assign-ment, and he really enjoyed his briefings. Van was way beyond a mere "Top Secret" clearance now—he had achieved ratings like "Executive Gamma" and "NKR," where his briefing material was brought to him by the hands of couriers, on flimsy, easy-burning sheets of typewrit-ten onionskin.

The grumpy, reluctant NSA and NRO techs hated telling Van anything. Their stovepipe was melting awfully. They were dropping their pants and revealing their family jewels. The NSA satellite geeks came from some strange parallel world of computation where every-thing important had been invented in the 1960s by forty thousand mathematicians under a big hill in Maryland. Van felt a strange re-spect for them—not for the modern NSA guys, who were sort of lost and snooty and owlish, but for the amazing Cold War rocket state of his grandfather's generation. A lost empire of truly macho engineer-ing, where America's best tech guys just sort of rolled up their sleeves, lit an unfiltered Camel, and detonated hydrogen bombs.

Van had lost a personal fortune while working for the CCIAB, but there was no question that he was learning incredible stuff. The NSA was a mystery even to the people who worked inside it. Their se-cret spy feats were the stuff of distant, mist-shrouded legends.

Before their first spy satellites were ever launchable, American spies had used eavesdropping balloons. They'd sprayed toxic metal clouds into the sky that reflected Soviet radio signals from far over the horizon. Fewer and fewer government veterans still remembered any of this stuff. Huge bursts of top-secret ingenuity had just plain been forgotten. It had been nailed into wooden crates and lost inside some warehouse, like the Ark of the Covenant in *Indiana Jones.*

The remote-control code that Van was now examining was a direct descendant of that mythical era. It wasn't native computer code, it was space-machine code. His own grandfather had probably had something to do with developing this stuff, as he worked on that lost 1960s cruise missile. It was a living space-age fossil. It was code built entirely for electronic spying, electronic spacecraft, and electronic Cold Warfare. It had crept into the modern cyber-world like a digital trilobite.

Still, nobody had ever broken it, because the math behind it was rock-solid. So, Van and his clients in AFOXAR now faced the serious technical challenge of repurposing this satellite control code for use in aircraft. And not normal, everyday aircraft, either. Very fast, low-flying aircraft, stolen or hijacked, skimming the hilltops to stay off Air Force radar, as they zoomed toward the White House or Capitol with a bellyfull of terrorist explosives.

The likeliest engineering solution looked like a geosynchronous aircraft-control super-satellite somehow hooked into the satellite GPS system. This was a typically bloated Pentagon-style solution that would pull down sixty billion and take a generation to design, build, and implement. Van was hoping for something much quicker and quieter that might be delivered before he died of old age.

He figured the CCIAB's best approach was to repeat a Grendel-style success. Make one working model as a proof-of-concept, and just install it somewhere in somebody's jet. The AFOXAR guys were pressuring NASA and Boeing to get them a nice handy jet they could wreck. AFOXAR guys were a small gang of young engineers that nobody had heard of, but they didn't brag much, they worked fast, and they were very can-do.

Van was in his tiny Vault office, deeply engrossed in this problem, when Fawn came swooning past his tangerine-colored cubicle divider. "Ohmigod, it's him! He's here. Elvis is here. Elvis is asking for you!"

"Who?" said Van. He was no longer even a little startled when Fawn said something apparently insane. Fawn Glickleister was not crazy. She was just so intensely bright that she cut into reality at a sharp angle.

"It's that tall dark handsome dude with that secure briefcase strapped to his arm. He's waiting out in the corridor, Van. He needs to consult with us!"

Van came to full alert. "That guy doesn't look much like Elvis."

"Well he's Southern," Fawn gushed. "He *feels* like Elvis. He's just like Bill Clinton that way. Ohmigod, he is such a dreamboat, Van. He's the hottest guy in the Vault."

"What is it with you, Fawn? Get a grip."

"Let's investigate him!"

"Show him in here." Van nodded. His code-wearied brain could use the break.

Elvis shouldered his way into Van's tight cement warren. He was wearing a black blazer and a white polo shirt and gray pants and black shoes. Elvis had changed out of his gym clothes, Van thought. This clearly implied that he could unlatch himself from that briefcase somehow.

Van offered Elvis the Leap Chair and sat on the ripply edge of his plastic computer desk. The Vault cells were so small that it was like meeting a guy inside a photography booth. "I'm Dr. Vandeveer," Van offered. "What can we do you for?"

Elvis crushed Van's hand with a Right Stuff handshake. "I'm Michael Hickok."

Van's crushed hand flew straight to his beard. He stroked it thoughtfully. Hickok didn't seem to notice his shock. After a moment, Van had steadied himself. So here he was at last then, Michael Hickok, that hustler, that ruthless mercenary, showing up at the office like a bad penny. Jeez, no wonder Hickok never took that briefcase off—he was wandering around just like that lost atomic lunatic in *Repo Man*. A cynical operator with a thirteen-billion-dollar political liability that he was trying to dump on the first available sucker.

And he'd already successfully put the charm on Van's naive young secretary. If Tony Carew hadn't bent the rules to warn him . . .

"Nice to meet you," Van lied.

"Doc, I'm told you've been cleared Executive Gamma," said Hickok.

"That's true. We do some satellite work here at the CCIAB. Communications software and protocols."

"I can't understand that sort of thing myself," drawled Hickok. "But my employers are real, real anxious to have some experts doctor their sick bird."

"I see." Van was fully prepared to lower the boom on the guy. Close up and in person, though, Hickok gave off the spooky vibe of a Delta Force karate master. It looked like he could break every object in the room with his bare feet.

Why rush anything? Van thought. Surely it would be much cagier to study Hickok's technique. Politely lure him in with a pretense of innocent cooperation. "So tell me about it."

Hickok reached into his pocket and removed a lethal-looking folding knife with a dangling set of keys. "I'll have to open this secure briefcase now."

Van glanced up. "Scram, Fawn."

Fawn's eager face fell. Fawn was not cleared Executive Gamma. "But . . ."

"Shut the door, and shut the outer door. Stand in the hall. If you see anybody strange, let me know right away."

"Yes, sir," said Fawn, who never called him "sir." She left.

Hickok opened the briefcase with a small gray key. The case held a set of common-looking Pentagon-style folders, the sort used for weapons procurement programs. Van had seen more than his share of these Pentagon folders lately. Through fifty years of military bureaucratic ritual, the Pentagon had created its own unique paperwork style, with everything initialized through chains of superior officers, and documented in quintuplicate.

Van recognized the folders he was confronting as a classic "Pearl

Harbor file." Whenever a big-ticket project went sour, paperwork escalated as the guilty parties tried to cover their asses from the investigation that they knew was coming. The folders began to bulge, dent, and rip. There was wear and tear as the evidence got tossed from hand to hand like a hot potato.

There was no way Van was going to waste his life working his way through this huge stack of self-serving gibberish. It was time to move this farce right along. "I see we have a big opportunity-cost here."

"That's the truth," said Hickok, "but my employers are willing to be more than generous with resources. That's a ten-billion-dollar project you're lookin' at there."

Van knew for a fact that the KH-13 was a thirteen-billion-dollar boondoggle that had been budgeted for eight. Van waved his hand around the junk-towering walls of his tiny office. It was densely crowded with hopeful toys of the infowar trade: solar-powered outdoor spycams, shirt-pocket-sized anthrax sniffers, biometric access gizmos that stared into eyeballs and sucked users' thumbs. Ninety percent of them were useless, but someone responsible had to look at them and throw them away. "As you can see, we have other projects here, more in line with our core tasking." Had he really just said "core tasking"? The sense of fear and threat that poured off the sinister Hickok was really jazzing him up.

"Look, doc, I wouldn't be coming here to y'all if there hadn't already been investigations," said Hickok, producing a much slimmer folder in a different shade of blue. "The bird worked fine on launch— just a few shakedown bugs. She didn't start acting serious weird till a year ago. Believe me, we had plenty of people watching her."

Van looked at the light blue folder without touching it. Something deep in him was hooked by this situation. His curiosity had been set to tingling.

Van sensed something peculiar here. Michael Hickok was a very scary guy, but he just didn't feel like a smooth political operator who was out to play pin the tail on the donkey. Hickok just didn't seem bright enough to be capable of a scheme that complicated. Maybe

Tony Carew had never personally met Michael Hickok. Just possibly, there was some big, dumb, simple mistake here. Something that had gone wrong a long time ago, that Van could put right.

"So, is the bird tumbling?"

"Nope. She's solid as a rock."

"Noisy links? Bandwidth too tight?"

Hickok shook his handsome head. "She can talk to the ground."

Van had to like a guy who called a satellite "she." "You might have some antenna obscurations. Are you getting a lot of SEU's?"

"What's that again?"

" 'Single Event Upsets.' "

"Look, doc, I can follow most of this, but I'm just a simple country boy who is ex-Air Force Special Operations Command," said Hickok. "You want a solid air-to-ground spotter link for a Predator drone in the back end of nowhere, then I am your man. Rocket science, that's a little beyond me. But I can sure see it's not beyond *you*. Let's talk some turkey here. You look to me like the kind of man who can get this job done!"

Van was flattered. Then he sensed a trap snapping shut. Oh, yeah, this was the honeypot principle at work here: no overconfident hotshot could resist a sweet appeal to his ego. It amazed Van how good it felt to be played for a real sap.

"It's not likely I'll ever repair a satellite for you," he said. "The CCIAB is a policy board."

"But there's money waitin' on the table! You could hire people! And people tell me this Grendel machine of yours is twenty years ahead of our time."

Now Van knew that he was being played for a sucker. "That may be so, but Grendel also takes a whole lot of my work time. All of it, really. I'm sorry to turn you down."

Hickok's face darkened. He was not the kind of man to take a rejection kindly. It was clear he'd had more than his share lately. "It's like that, is it?"

"Like what?" Van said.

"You can't deliver! You're one of those R&D guys, so you're always chasing the next hot biscuit. You're all velocity and no vector!"

Rage flared within Van like a match on crumpled fax paper. "Look, pal, you're coming to me, I didn't come to you. Why should I care? Take a hike."

"Why should you care? We're in a war now, Jack! I got buddies of mine freezing their ass off in the 'Stan, and you're sitting here with this faggoty dot-com stuff!" Hickok flicked a finger onto Van's halogen desk lamp with a light aluminum clink. "That is America's next-generation spy-sat, you egghead dork! It could save the lives of American soldiers out in the field! But not you, no, you're too good for that!"

With a heroic, life-changing effort, Van got his searing temper back under control. He wasn't going to punch a guest inside his own office. Besides, something deep in him told him he was confronting a very dangerous man here, somebody who could kill him easily. "Look, Mr. Hickok, if I'm not serious about this war, then what the hell am I doing in a damn secret bunker in West Virginia? You wanna tell me my job? Sit down here and start coding. See how far you get."

"That's what I'm asking from *you,* doc."

"Go to hell. The KH-13 is a sorry piece of junk. It's gonna fall out of the sky like a bank vault. You want that thing to fall on me and my people? No way. Go find some other sucker."

"Look, you don't know all that," Hickok protested, with surprising mildness. He touched his pale blue folder. "You didn't even look at the evidence here."

"I don't need to look at your evidence."

Hickok's eyes grew round and mild. "You're a scientist and you're saying that to me? Scientists are s'posed to look at the evidence. That's what I always heard."

"Well . . ." Van fell silent. He felt pinned down. No option was good in his situation suddenly. "Look, this has got nothing to do with scientific evidence. This folder here, this blue thing, this is a legal trail. I'd have to sign off on it to look at this blue folder. Then your bosses would be all over me. Right away. They'd nail me for it because I was the last guy to touch the hot potato."

Hickok narrowed his eyes. "Damn. I never thought about it that way. So that's your big problem, huh? You don't want your nose in a mousetrap."

"You bet that's my problem."

"That's right," Hickok admitted. "They'd do that kind of thing, too." It wasn't a question. It wasn't even an admission. It was a realistic assessment. "But if you really fixed this bird, doc, they wouldn't have to blame anybody."

"I'd love to fix your bird," Van told him. "I'm of a different generation than those guys who built the Space Age. We've got much better methods of computer analysis now, and I like to think that maybe I actually *could* fix the thing, if I had some time and resources. But they don't want me to fix it. They just want me to touch it." Van shrugged. "Look, I'm not putting my initials on any of that paper. That's too much to ask of me."

"I can get it about all that," said Hickok. "Everywhere I go in this world, there's some kind of hell that started long before I was ever born." Hickok had gone strangely stiff. Suppressed fury, maybe. It might even be shame. "Suppose I left this little blue folder under a bench in the gym."

Van felt his eyes widen. "That's crazy. That's an NKR document. You wouldn't do that."

"I take long showers," Hickok snarled. "You're a tough guy in the gym, right, Mr. Computer Geek? I've seen you in there. Maybe you could skip a couple of your sets on that Nautilus."

Maybe I would, thought Van, and maybe I wouldn't. And maybe he would, and maybe he wouldn't. He jumped from the edge of his worktable. "Why not right now?"

CHAPTER SEVEN

Tony Carew spent his afternoon watching his girlfriend performing in the snow. Anjali aimed to become Bollywood's Heroine Number One, outdoing Aishwarya Rai, Bipasha Basu, and the Kapoor sisters. If flesh and blood could do this, then Anjali had them to give.

Anjali lip-synched to the piercing Hindi soundtrack while whirling, fluttering, bumping, and grinding. Repeatedly, glowingly, beautifully. Take after grueling take, on a sunny midwinter day, at a nine-thousand-foot elevation.

Indian film fans loved romantic mountain scenes. So much so that the Indian movie industry had worn Switzerland out, and Tony Carew was supplying them with Colorado's mountains, instead. The audience for Bollywood movies was rather peculiar about snow. The core Indian village audience, all billion of them, regarded snow as a mythical, romantic substance, something like fairy dust or cocaine. So Hindi film actresses never wore coats or jackets while dancing in the snow. They had to perform bareheaded and bare-armed in their customary midriff-baring chiffon, brilliantly smiling and bitterly freezing. Between takes, Anjali rushed to the sidelines to drink hot goat's-milk cocoa and breathe oxygen from a black rubber mask.

Anjali's co-star, Sanjay, who was also her cousin, was the film's male lead. Being a man, whenever Sanjay was in snow, he got to wear thick boots, long trousers, and an insulated jacket. Sanjay was big, solid, deft, graceful, and wonderfully handsome. The Bombay film clan of Sanjay and Anjali had been breeding movie stars for a hundred years. In Sanjay the family had produced a huge, beautiful animal.

In Bollywood, actors weren't just movie stars—they were "heroes." Sanjay was a twenty-first-century Indian hero. Sanjay wasn't kidding about this ambition, either.

Like most film-star children, Sanjay had started his film career as a teen romance lead, but he needed those big mid-career payoffs as a tough-guy Indian action star. So, Sanjay had boldly enlisted in the Indian Army. Young Sanjay had been a soldier against Moslem terrorists, on patrol in the blood-spattered mountains of Kashmir. He had driven an Army jeep and carried a machine gun along the dangerous Indo-Pakistani Line of Control. Sanjay had won a huge amount of worshipful Indian media coverage for these patriotic publicity stunts. Pundits in the know were already talking wisely about Sanjay's future political career.

The Bharatiya Janata Party or "Indian People's Party" were Sanjay's brand of leaders. The BJP were tough, heavily armed right-wingers who had been running the Indian government since 1998. Sanjay was the BJP's kind of movie star, a modern guy with big modern Indian muscle, great Indian clothes, cool Indian moon rockets, and extremely dangerous Indian atom bombs. Sanjay's violent adventure movies always played well with these tense, nervy Indian super-patriots. Sanjay's dad, who had won huge popularity playing Shiva in a TV soap opera, was a BJP member of the Indian Parliament.

Knowing all this, Tony was very concerned about Sanjay, and not in a good way. Tony's wild romance with Anjali had gotten a lot of play in the Bollywood film press. Bollywood always publicized the love life of its film stars, and the more peculiar, the better.

Sanjay could break both of Tony's arms like matchsticks. And yet Sanjay had never said a word about the Anjali situation. Tony wasn't quite sure if this dicey situation was just a given, or completely unspeakable. Many, many things in India were both at the same time.

Tony had a lot of investments in Bangalore, and offshore outsourcing was one of his major lines of work lately. What Anjali got out of all this was less clear to Tony, but Anjali always went along for Sanjay's hunting trips, no matter where in the world he went. While she was hunting, Anjali was allowed to live without her golden saris, her heavy jewels, her movie cameras, and her greasepaint. Hunting trips were the closest thing to freedom that Anjali would ever be allowed.

Tony was also pretty sure that Anjali had been deputized by the family's women to spy on Sanjay. She always went along with the big-game hunter to make sure the family's favored son didn't do anything unpredictable and James Dean-like, such as blowing his own head off.

The sudden glamorous arrival of Indian film stars had absolutely thrilled the Indian staff at the Colorado telescope facility. The Indian staffers that Tony had hired were Bangalore software hacks, living in America on business visas. Most of the time, the Indian staffers felt very isolated in the remote Colorado mountains. Sanjay and Anjali had done wonders for their morale. Sanjay and Anjali seemed pleased to tour the wonders of the telescope and to pose for friendly snapshots with the staffers. Bombay film stars took their offshore fans very seriously.

With another day's shooting wrapped up and in the can, the film stars drove to Pinecrest to kill some elk. They took a sturdy set of nicely heated Jeep SUVs, with ruggedized tires and the standard Pinecrest luxury tourist provisions. Their driver and hunting guide was a Chinese servant who called himself "Chet." Like all of Mrs. De-Fanti's Chinese ranch staff, Chet was so tidy and reserved as to be practically invisible.

Sanjay sprawled in the Jeep's toasty passenger seat, wearing a brand-new black cowboy hat and a spotless leather jacket. Pinecrest Ranch had loaned Sanjay an enormous .338 Winchester Magnum. When he wasn't caressing the rifle, Sanjay made a lot of use of his silver hip flask. Sanjay tended to drink steadily while "hunting," also easing the tedium with high-stakes poker games and dirty songs in Hindi.

Tony and Anjali also rode in Sanjay's Jeep, sharing the backseat with Tony's smaller, very uncomfortable 30.06 rifle.

They were trailed by two other big Jeeps from the Pinecrest fleet, bristling with weapons and crammed with Sanjay's male drinking buddies from the film crew. Being from Bollywood, Sanjay never went anywhere in life without a posse of backup dancers.

The Jeep lurched over a boulder in the uphill trail, and Anjali brushed against him. "Tony," she fluted.

Tony brushed a wrinkle from his nylon jacket. "What, *sajaana?*"

"Tony, you're too quiet. What are you thinking, Tony?"

"Why, I'm thinking of you, *maahiyaa.*"

Anjali's eyelids fluttered. She was twenty-three years old and had the eyes of a Mughal concubine. Her eyes inspired in men an uncontrollable urge to shower her with jewels. "So, what, my dear, thinking what? That you miss me when I don't see you? Because I miss you so much, Tony. Morning, noon, and night." In a gesture of limpid sincerity, she placed a slender hand against her brassiere.

Tony coughed in the dry mountain air. "Baby, sweetie, honey-pie, *terii puuja karuun main to har dam.*"

Anjali broke into a musical peal of laughter. She loved it when he quoted her song lyrics. "Oh, you, you lover boy! Just shut up, *yaar!*"

The Jeep lumbered into a chilly patch of open air and twilight. The long drought had been unkind to Colorado. A local mountain, federal park territory, had snowy slopes measled all over with big seared patches of black ash.

"Your little mountains look so sad," said Sanjay. "They're not the Himalayas, dear boy."

"You're absolutely right about that," said Tony.

"And your fancy telescope is too low. Lower than India's big mountain telescope."

"Yeah, you mean that Indian Astronomical Observatory up in Hanle?"

"It's four hundred meters higher than yours."

"Two hundred meters," said Tony. "I measured it."

Sanjay turned in his seat, throwing back a leather-jacketed elbow. His gazellelike eyes were reddened with altitude and drink. "Is that a joke?"

"If you like."

"I don't like jokes."

"I don't like *you*," said Tony. Two heartbeats passed. *"Ruup aisa suhaana tera chaand bhii hai diiwaana tera."*

The Jeep erupted in laughter. Even stony Chet the driver chuckled, relieved to see that Sanjay was guffawing at Tony's wit instead of putting a bullet through somebody.

Sanjay was all chuckles now. *"Bindaas,"* he told his cousin.

Anjali lifted one dainty thumb and wiggled it enthusiastically. It was a gesture completely without any Western equivalent. *"Yehi hai* right choice!" she purred.

The Jeep's engine labored as Chet fought the slope. Anjali put her pink-nailed hand around Tony's forearm. "You're so good with him," she whispered.

"Am I good for you, precious?"

Anjali glanced toward the front seat. Sanjay was sinking into boozy indifference. Anjali drew her tapered finger down Tony's cheek and gently caught and pinched his lower lip. This was her favorite caress. Incredibly, as always, it worked on Tony. It blew every circuit in him. It plunged him instantly, wildly, uncontrollably, into the head-spinning saffron depths of the Kama Sutra.

Tony had never believed that such things were possible. When he was away from Anjali—and he spent a lot of time away from Anjali, for the sake of his sanity—he found himself incredulous that such things could ever happen between man and woman. But then she'd be back in his arm's reach, and oh, my God. It wasn't her beauty that had trapped him, or the fantastic sex, or even the looming, steadily growing danger that some angry man in her family would shoot him dead. It was the sheer sense of wonder, really. Anjali Devgan had been Miss Universe 1999. She was quite likely the most beautiful woman in the entire world.

Chet pulled the Jeep into a sloping meadow.

Sanjay drained his silver hip flask, zipped his leather jacket, shoulder-slung his heavy rifle, and bounded right out the Jeep's door. The other two vehicles pulled up and stopped, crunching through some low-hanging pine branches. Nobody looked eager to follow the great man and his gun. There had, apparently, been some unlucky incidents in the past.

These Hindi film guys were good-natured media pros. Unlike Sanjay, they were not rifle-toting assassins by conviction. The hip Bombay film dudes were mostly interested in the nifty contents of their Jeeps, which had been loaded with Teutonic thoroughness for the benefit of German hunters. Big windproof tents, portable tables and chairs, gas stoves, odd German board games, ecologically correct windup lanterns, rope, matches, cases of German beer, latrine shovels . . .

In the back of a Jeep, Anjali discovered a thin, silvery NASA space blanket. She pulled it from its plastic wrap. "How pretty."

"Yeah, baby, that's for astronauts."

With a practiced whip of her wrists, Anjali fluttered the thin silver garment through the air. Then she wrapped herself in it with a well-rehearsed, arm-twisting spin. Instant space-age sari. The film boys looked up and applauded cynically.

"It's warm," she told him, eyes glowing.

Tony nodded speechlessly. On her, it was so very hot.

Anjali shot him a come-on look that burned the marrow of his thighbones. Then she drifted off into the pines, gently trailing her silver scarf, her spotless Timberland boots flashing over the fallen trees.

With a steely effort, Tony waited until Anjali had faded from sight. Inflamed though he was, it wouldn't do to run off with Anjali in full, blatant sight of the entire crew. Anjali was a clever and practical girl. She wouldn't run much farther than earshot.

Tony fiddled unconvincingly with his rifle while the boys struggled to set up a nylon and aluminum tent. Stalking elk in Colorado snow was the last thing on the film crew's minds. As soon as they could manage, they'd be settling into those heated camp chairs to get right into the German beer and the poker cards.

Tony set about to track down his girlfriend.

Unfortunately Tony Carew was a dedicated urbanite. Once in the huge, chilly forest, he quickly lost her footprints and all trace of her. A few discreet Nelson Eddy forest love-calls got no response. When Tony searched harder, he even lost the camp and the Jeeps. How had he managed to wander off without a handheld Global Positioning System? He stumbled through the pines in increasing dismay.

He heard the repeated boom of Sanjay's rifle.

Sanjay had blown away not one, but three elk. The three huge dead animals were lying in a clearing, almost nose to tail, big heaps of bloody meat.

Tony emerged from the woods, his rifle in the crook of his arm.

"They didn't run," Sanjay told him.

"They didn't run?"

"No. What's wrong with them? They should run from me."

Tony led Sanjay across the brown, snow-choked grass to his nearest kill. An elk was a huge beast, three times the bulk of a deer. It had a lustrous sofalike hide, and a rack of antlers the size of an easy chair.

The black skin of the animal's muzzle had a scorched, cracked look. Its eyes were filmed and filthy. Caked slobber was streaked down its muzzle.

Tony switched his rifle from one arm to the other. "Nobody's been looking after these animals since the old man went wrong in the head."

Sanjay was as stupid and vain as most young actors, but he had flashes of lucidity. "These animals are sick, Tony. They are *very* sick." Sanjay tipped his black hat back and raised his elegant brows. "They are blind."

Tony nodded soberly. "Yes, they are. Do you know of a sickness called 'elk wasting'?"

"No. So this is it?"

"It's similar to Mad Cow Disease. From the same source, really. It starts in tainted food. Old DeFanti used to feed his elk cattle chow, to keep them sleek during the winter. I always warned him that the cattle chow might be tainted. But he was an old man, stubborn. Sometimes he wouldn't listen to good sense."

An ugly smile spread across Sanjay's face. "So that is your story, eh?"

"How's that?"

"I could make a film from this. I could make an epic. The story of Mad Cow Disease. The story of the West. It first came when the British slaughtered sick sheep, and fed the bone meal to innocent cows. A very wicked practice. For years they tried to conceal the sickness from those who ate the flesh of cattle."

Tony shrugged. "Well, everybody really needed the money."

"Then the sickness came to America. Not in England's cattle. In America's wild animals. 'Elk wasting,' it gets a new name here."

"Well, yes, I guess that's all true, more or less."

"And then that Western sickness struck down Tom DeFanti himself! Because the owner of this land fed his animals that evil poison. Then he ate their flesh! Now the madness is inside his own body! The world's great master of high-tech media is a sad, mad beast!"

"Don't talk that way about him." Tony tightened his grip on his rifle. "He was my guru."

"Sorry, *bhaiyya.*" Sanjay seemed touched. "Really sorry. It's just . . . that is such a wonderful script for a horror movie. Very modern. Very Ramgopal Varma."

Tony gritted his teeth. "I never told you that story, Sanjay. You never heard that story from me. Nobody ever talks about Tom that way. Nobody asks or tells."

Sanjay shrugged, and fixed Tony with his brown, lambent gaze. "The man is my host! Why would I talk against him? I ate his salt—although, thank God, I never ate his meat."

"Right."

"I've been around the world many times. I've seen stranger things than the fate of your guru. The world is strange, these days."

"Tom's life was always strange." After a moment, Tony decisively jacked a round into the chamber. "Sanjay, all these elk must be destroyed."

"What, all of them? Now? Today?"

"Yes. Because elk wasting is a contagious disease. It's an unclean herd. The Colorado tourist trade doesn't talk about it much, but for obvious reasons, they're at war with this."

Sanjay considered this for a long moment. Slushy snow fell from the height of a tree. "What a beautiful hunting trip you have offered me here in America," he said at last. "Look at the huge head on your fine beast here. What's that word?"

"Antlers."

"Antlers, yes. Fantastic antlers. Another fine trophy for my hunting club in Ootacamund."

"Let the head be, Sanjay. You don't want a taxidermist touching that brain matter."

Six more elk, stumbling together in a clump, entered the clearing. The elk had their muzzles down, as if sniffing along. They were thudding into each other's flanks as if they found comfort in it. They were graceless and dirty. Some were drooling.

Tony snapped off a shot. It was hard to miss at this range. A cow went down and lay in the grass, thrashing. The herd panicked at the sound of the shot, but they could not see to flee. They just stumbled, crashing and ripping their hides against the underbrush.

Sanjay deftly shouldered the heavy Winchester. The rifle boomed again and again and more elk buckled, jerked backward, and collapsed. When the heavy-grain bullets took them at the base of the neck, the elk went down as if guillotined. Sanjay was an excellent shot.

One surviving elk thrashed into the undergrowth. It wouldn't be hard to track. Sanjay put a final shot into a crippled cow.

He gave Tony a brotherly pat on the shoulder. "You don't worry about this, Tony. Because yes, I understand. I can help you with problems like this."

"Just as long as it's quick, Sanjay. And kept quiet."

Sanjay swung his chiseled chin in a nod. "We'll get my very best boys! And your very best guns."

CHAPTER EIGHT

The CCIAB had a difficult relationship with America's spy satellites. Spy satellites were critical infrastructure of intense and lasting importance to national security. Since the satellite programs also had a huge black budget, everybody naturally wanted in.

The little CCIAB was in no political position to make any bold grab for these crown jewels of orbiting spookdom. As Tony Carew had cynically pointed out, the likeliest role for the CCIAB here would be "fall guy."

And yet, on a stark, technical level, the KH-13 satellite was badly broken. Obviously, some really gifted technician ought to fix the thing. Nobody seemed to be getting anywhere with it. If the KH-13 failed, that would be a massive disaster. An economic, industrial, technical, and military mess. Van felt that preventing a massive disaster was probably his duty. What else was he good for? Why else had they hired him? What else was he doing in Washington?

Van knew that the CCIAB had many pressing problems on its agenda. These were serious political challenges innate to any reform in computer security: the distribution of security-certification logos, the establishment of baseline security standards, a wise judgment of the regulatory costs of compliance, the daunting difficulties of online patch distribution, the rating of potential flaws and vulnerabilities, even the awful discovery of certain flaws "too expensive to fix" . . . The list went on and on. Basically, these problems had one commonality: they couldn't be programmed away or fixed by engineers. They could only be solved through sincere, extensive, fully briefed bargaining and negotiation among the power players. That was why nothing much had ever happened to resolve those problems.

This whole situation was the very opposite of his grandfather's rules for technical progress—especially, that burning need to stay close to the machinery.

The KH-13 was machinery. Van thought that he could shine there.

Van knew that fixing a spy satellite was a long-shot. Realistically speaking, how could one computer-science professor cure an ailing multibillion-dollar spacecraft? But Van also knew that the job was not hopeless. Such things sometimes happened in real life. For instance: Richard Feynman was just a physicist. But Feynman had dropped a chunk of rubber O-ring into a glass of ice water, and he had shown the whole world, on TV, how a space shuttle could blow up.

If Van somehow solved Hickok's zillion-dollar problem, that would prove that he, Derek Vandeveer, had a top-notch, Richard Feynman kind of class.

Van had sacrificed a lot to get his role in public service. He'd given up his happy home, his family life, his civilian career, his peace of mind, and a whole, whole lot of his money. Van wanted to see real results from all that sacrifice. He wanted to do something vital.

The KH-13 was probably the grandest and most secret gizmo

that the USA possessed. If Van somehow found the KH-13's busted O-ring, then he would be giving America the ability to photograph the entire planet, in visible and infrared, day and night, digitally, repeatedly, on a three-inch scale. Yes, that really mattered.

Careful not to mention the advice he had gotten from Tony, Van broached the matter with Jeb. Jeb quickly understood the implications. Yes, it would obviously get the CCIAB a lot of kudos if they could technically outsmart the Air Force, the Space Force, the National Reconnaissance Office, NASA, and the host of federal contractors who had been working on satellites since the days of the V-2 rocket. It would make the CCIAB look like geniuses and it was just the kind of stunt that really impressed congressmen. Weighed against that was the scary prospect of getting in over their heads, then getting blamed for it.

So Jeb, in his own turn, talked the matter over with some old-school technical buddies from DARPA and the Defense Department's Office of Special Projects.

A plan emerged: a firewall strategy. Jeb would protect the CCIAB by moving Van one step out from the organization. For satellite work, Jeb had Van "loaned out" from the CCIAB to the "Transformational Communications Architecture Office." The TCAO was a joint effort of the Defense Information Systems Agency, and the Assistant Secretary of Defense for Command, Control, Communications, and Intelligence.

The "Transformational Communications Architecture Office" was an easy outfit for Van to work for, because, basically, the Office did not exist. The Office was just an empty box in one of Donald Rumsfeld's ambitious DoD "Transformation" schemes. And even the NRO and NSA were terrified of Donald Rumsfeld. Rumsfeld had once been the boss of the futurists at RAND. Rumsfeld had a horrible knack for asking simple, embarrassing questions that nobody had ever thought about before. Nobody wanted to cross him.

Rumsfeld seemed kind of okay about cyberwar issues. Whenever computer security was mentioned at National Security briefings,

Rumsfeld made some brisk notes. Tom Ridge's imaginary Homeland Security agency was badly stuck in the mud, but Jeb felt pretty cheerful about Rumsfeld's Department of Defense. Donald Rumsfeld was the closest thing the CCIAB had to a patron in the Bush cabinet.

So, like a lot of other policy players in the Bush administration, Jeb had taken to speaking in Rumsfeldese. In return for allowing Van to meddle with the KH-13 satellite, Jeb announced that it was time for Grendel, Van's "project launch," to be "spun out and delegated to a responsible agency that can add some structure." Van was not allowed to whine or moan to Jeb about this harsh decision, either. Instead, Van was told to "avoid overcontrolling" and to "ease that personality bottleneck."

It was Hickok who explained to Van what this speech meant in English. "Your boss is taking away your best toy and he's selling it out to the highest bidder, fella. Your Grendel gizmo is bait for the brass hats now, pure and simple. Jeb wants to see those big boys fighting a bidding war to take that thing over, see? That'll improve his bargaining position with them."

"But I built it," Van protested. "Plus, I paid for it all with my own checks."

"So what? You can't grow it any bigger. You don't have the money or staff around here. So don't you feel bad about that! If some major outfit takes all that hard work on for y'all, hey, that's a big victory!" Hickok beamed on him. The loss of Grendel meant that Van had time to work on Hickok's problem.

So, Van won official permission to tinker with satellites. Unofficially, this permission meant very little, because Van was already neck-deep inside the blue folder. Michael Hickok, the man who had leaked it to him, had instantly become Van's best war buddy.

The two of them were always close, because Hickok was physically chained to the KH-13's secret documents. Whenever Van examined the satellite's problems, Hickok had to be present with him in the room. Van had never gotten over the burning tingle of curiosity, the technical thrill he first felt as he leafed through the weird, forbidden schematics of the world's most advanced flying spy machine.

At first, as Van obsessed over the KH-13's malfunction reports, Hickok just idled around the CCIAB's concrete den inside the Vault. He flirted with Fawn, made cell-phone calls to a series of loose women, and paged through computer security brochures.

But Michael Hickok was a man of action. It wasn't in him to waste time. He watched Van's office routines, then he made himself useful.

Van's least favorite job was to demo security gadgets for the Vault's many cyberwar groupies. There were packs of gizmos arriving for Van every day. Dongles and decryptors. Peel-and-stick RFID labels. Teflon and Kevlar security cables. Barcodes and asset tags. Ridiculous home-made EMP blasters right out of the aluminum-foil hat set. Teensy-tiny locks on chipsets sculpted right into the microscopic silicon with ultra-high-tech MEMS techniques . . . The CCIAB had become a clearinghouse for American infowar toys.

Van spent a lot of valuable overtime reviewing and clearing peculiar gizmos for the Special Forces. The Delta Force, the Navy SEALS . . . they got to carry any kind of gadget they pleased, but they were too small to support their own R&D labs. They had to depend on the kindness of strangers.

Hickok quickly got the hang of Van's spiel to Vault visitors. It was basically the same old Frequently Asked Security Questions, over and over again. Van hated this mind-dulling routine. When ignorant people failed to read the manual and asked him stupid questions, this brought out Van's tough, potted-cactus side.

After watching Van stammer, bark, and hand-saw his way through these briefings, Hickok asserted himself and just took them over. Hickok did very well at the work. Hickok had a knack for boiling down complex technical issues to a military briefing level that career bureaucrats could understand.

With his baritone voice, his soldierly good looks, and two fists that could break solid bricks, Michael Hickok was a top-notch computer-security salesman. He was certainly the best promoter that the little CCIAB had ever had. Hickok scared the living daylights out of people. Once Hickok was through wringing them out, federal officials would leave their business cards with pale and trembling fingers, and beg for emergency help.

Van's new best pal was no computer whiz. He was a whiskey-drinking Alabama guy with a high school education. Hickok liked dirty jokes, heavy metal music, and reckless women, except on Sundays, when he was always in church. Hickok was the simplest man that Van had ever befriended. Hickok had few self-doubts. Hickok had no interest in complex ideas. Intellectual puzzles just irritated him. Van found something very refreshing about all this.

It took just one more thing to move the two of them from coworkers to comrades. That thing was gunfire. Guns were much more than just a hobby for Michael Hickok. Guns were a basis of Hickok's very life.

The two of them went out two times a week, and on Sunday evenings after Hickok's church services, drinking heavily, bowling, and firing advanced automatic weapons. They quit bowling after two Sundays, because Van was an excellent bowler and Hickok really hated getting beaten at anything. So they stopped the bowling, and cut back on the drinking. They settled on just the guns. Van was happy to learn about guns. Hickok knew plenty about them, and Van was a star student.

Van hadn't fired a weapon since he'd plonked at rabbits with a single-shot .22 on his grandfather's ranch. In Hickok's company, though, Van put on goggles and ear protectors. He roared his way through Ingrams, Uzis, and Pentagon lab models with no names at all, just acronyms. Weapons like the boxlike "OICW," the "M249 SAW," and a futuristic, four-barreled, 15mm mini-rocket launcher from the U.S. Army's Soldier Systems Center in Natick, Massachusetts.

Hickok had incredible contacts in the world of specialized weapons testing. Hickok knew gun nuts who made Charlton Heston look like Winnie the Pooh.

Van quickly discovered that guns were extremely interesting technical devices. When Van considered the many ingenious engineering problems that had been solved by master gunsmiths, he was fascinated. It didn't matter to Van that he was myopic and only a middling good shot. Van spent most of his time in the range stripping Hickok's guns down and putting them back together.

Left free to get hands-on with guns, Van learned a lot. Enough to know that he could build a gun himself, if he wanted.

If he ever built a gun, it would be a digital cybergun. It would be smart, interactive, precise, speedy. It would put every single bullet exactly where it was meant to go. It would fill up graveyards faster than the Black Death.

Van found that it refreshed his mind to tinker with lethal hardware. Guns inspired Van, they got him out of his mental box. When Van returned from the firing ranges to bend his full attention onto the KH-13 spy satellite, the satellite problem cracked around the edges. Then the problem started to yield to him.

Van tossed and turned, in eighteen-hour days, and in the depths of the night. He labored through blind alleys, made wild leaps of insight. He called in a lot of favors. He gave of his very best. He worked quietly, and he worked very quickly. And then, all in a rush, it went.

The truth was that the satellite's so-called software problems had nothing to do with the satellite's software.

The satellite's software was incredible. The code was built to mind-boggling, unheard-of security specs. It made AT&T switching station software—the most paranoid commercial code Van had ever worked on—look as loose and scattered as empty Schlitz cans at a beer bust.

The satellite's software had been assembled and vetted by three hundred humorless, white-shirt-wearing, avionics-software drones in Clear Lake City, Texas. The KH-13 had three different onboard control computers, each of them independently running 420,000 lines of code. It was belt, plus suspenders, plus a straitjacket.

Those 420,000 lines had exactly one fully documented, well-understood bug. This was totally unheard-of. The very best commercial software written to that length would have suffered about 5,000 bugs. The KH-13's software was the dullest, least creative, most focused, most disciplined software that Van had ever seen. It scared him. It was sober, detailed, frighteningly methodical. The code's design specs alone ran to thirty volumes.

Every single line of the 420,000 was completely annotated, showing every time it had ever been changed. Why, when, how, and by whom. Every change was rigorously linked to some severe dictation in the design specs. Literally everything that had ever happened to this vast program, down to the tiniest detail, was recorded in a giant master history. And since this code re-used some fully tested code from earlier spy-sats, the reports stretched back some thirty solid years.

There was something genuinely nightmarish about this KH-13 code. About its complete lack of inspiration, creativity, and cheerful hacker sloppiness. About its gray, sober, steel bank-vault qualities. Van realized with a sinking in his heart that this was the gold standard for the safety and security that he and the CCIAB were trying to impose on the daffy, geeky, loosey-goosey software world. In a cyber-secure utopia, all software would look just like this.

But the satellite's coders, for all their horrifying clerkly skills, were only part of the satellite system. The secret aerospace bureaucracy that had built the KH-13 had worked on a strict need-to-know basis. This meant that no human being had ever understood the KH-13 as a whole.

There were still big black patches in Van's knowledge, too. Any device of that size and complexity was just too vast for one human brain to hold. But Van had researched the problem with unusual methods. Van knew that he understood things about the KH-13 that were not grasped by anyone else in the world.

Van went to report his triumphant progress to Jeb. He was eager to explain his ingenious solution to someone who could fully appreciate it. Unfortunately, Jeb was not cleared for learning about the innards of spy satellites—that was one "stovepipe" that was still holding firm. So Jeb simply thanked him, congratulated him on the hard work, and gave him a new assignment.

Van was now "tasked with creating" a new, bang-up technical presentation for the forthcoming federal computer-security "Cyber-Strategy Summit" in rural Virginia. Jeb was obsessed with this conference, the golden climax of the CCIAB's policy-making efforts. It was absolutely vital, said Jeb, that "America's cyber-security community" should come out of this Virginia shindig with "some broad policy guidance and momentum on the ground."

This Virginia retreat would be the CCIAB's last best chance to gather all the major federal players, and get them to line up, see sense, split their differences, dig deep in their pockets, and all sign on together on the same policy page. Then there would be real, true change in the world. Real structure, tasking, and accountability. Finally, American computer security that knew what it was doing. Sensible. Businesslike. Orderly. Realistic.

Van had to beg permission from Jeb to report his satellite findings to some proper authority. Finding a proper authority took some time, because (as Van now realized) nobody anywhere had ever expected Hickok to find somebody who could actually solve the problem. When a good candidate was finally located inside the intricate spacewar bureaucracy, Hickok insisted on driving Van from Washington straight to Cheyenne Mountain, Colorado.

Hickok's special courier vehicle had a bulging fiberglass shell, a telescoping mast, and nineteen-inch metal racks full of command-and-control hardware. Hickok's Humvee could open links to FLTSAT-COM, MILSTAR, NAVSTAR, INTELSAT, INMARSAT, EUTELSAT, and the Pentagon's Global Common Operational Picture. On this cross-country trip, Van's e-mail arrived for him on Navy-sponsored dot-mil satellite channels designed for aircraft carriers.

Hickok's professional life was strangely familiar to Van. It was full of small elite teams. Quick, quiet black-ops soldiers who did peculiar things on very short schedules. They never bragged. The American press never printed a word about them. They were very busy guys. They were very much like top-end computer wizards, except for one thing. They were not pale, pudgy hackers wearing glasses. They were cold-eyed athletes with crazy, kick-the-door-in fitness standards.

Behind the Humvee's wheel, Hickok was an iron man. Hickok drove like a low-flying aircraft buzzing the Kuwaiti Highway of Death. Hickok's reflexes were so much keener than those of normal drivers that he whipped through traffic with race-car twitches of his fingertips. Van learned to watch the windshield as if it were the screen of a video game. It was much easier on his nerves if he pretended that the two of them could just win some extra lives.

Whenever Hickok needed a break, he retired to the Humvee's cavernous backseat. There he amused himself, munching take-out double cheeseburgers, sipping strawberry shakes, and leafing through his usual leisure reading, Christian apocalypse fiction. Hickok had no problem reading novels in a moving car, for Hickok was Air Force Special Ops. Hickok never got carsick. He had the stomach for five or six gees.

Hickok was a big devotee of a best-selling series called "Tribulation Force." In tomorrow's post-Armageddon world, the Rapture had carried off all the Believing Christians, leaving all the liberal scoffers, skeptics, and atheists to fight it out with the evil troops of the Antichrist. Hickok liked to read the most ruthless sections of the book aloud, chuckling to himself.

"Y'know," Hickok sang out suddenly.

Van gripped the Humvee's wheel. Van was dead tired, but it was a lot more relaxing to drive the Humvee than it was to watch Hickok doing it. "What is it, Mike?"

"We never really talked about that secretary of yours."

"What's Fawn done this time?"

"Did you ever clear it with her about those surgical gloves?"

"Mike, I'm just her boss, all right?"

"What is it with her allergies? The girl is allergic to everything. And what's with that talcum powder? Is that all in her head?"

It was pitiful that Hickok asked him for advice about dating geek women. Van already had a geek woman. And unlike Hickok, who was awesomely promiscuous and never thought twice about it, Van badly wanted to keep the geek woman he had. Dottie was the only woman in his life who had ever understood him.

Now that Van was out of his bunker office and with his nose out of the briefing papers, he could guiltily realize how much hell he had been through and how much harm he had done to himself. Why was he shooting the breeze with some war buddy when he was a married man?

Van knew that Dottie's love for him was large, and generous, and without conditions. But oh, how they were hampered by all those other boundaries in their lives. All those far-sighted, professional postponements, those acts of scholarly discipline, those duties and obligations. They were both so well meaning about it, and maybe that was the worst thing. It wasn't like they really meant to neglect each other. They just arranged their lives so that they always could.

They talked each other into it somehow, making nice lists in their e-mail, researching the alternatives, checking out a spreadsheet maybe, wisely agreeing on what was surely best for them in the long run.

But the long run never came around for them. They used their smarts and knowledge to lop off all time for each other. There was something inhuman about being dutiful workaholics, something that wrecked marriages, shattered families, and made a man and woman shrivel up inside. It was going to kill them both someday.

Without his wife and his child, hinges had popped loose in Van's soul. He could feel that something quiet but vital to his humanity was slowly going down the shredder.

Why was it that he could never tell Dottie these things? She never denied him things he needed—when he asked her for them. But when he was worn down like a pencil nub, he couldn't even find it in himself to ask. They were like a couple who talked in sign language, and now were losing their fingers. It just wouldn't do. No.

Cheyenne Mountain was just one stupid mountain in Colorado. But Dottie lived in the Colorado mountains now. He was going to see Dottie and try to set things straight. Van had already sent her e-mail.

It was a bright, drought-stricken day. The sun gleamed off looming slopes of bare red rock and patches of trapped snow. Cheyenne Mountain loomed so large and bald and frowning that Van had a dizzy spell.

The legendary Cheyenne space base was something of a disappointment to Van. Cheyenne Mountain commanded America's ICBMs and it had the capacity to blow up the whole world. It should have been a lot stranger than it looked. Cheyenne was basically a rather typical Air Force base, just stuffed inside a big stone bottle. No grass here, no flagpoles. Bad overhead lighting. Miles of dusty exposed plumbing and ventilation.

The entire base was supported on giant, white-painted steel springs. If half of Cheyenne Mountain vaporized in a fifty-megaton first strike, the deep bunker would just bounce on its springs a little. The machinery of America's nuclear vengeance never came unplugged.

The security people took away Van's cell phone and his Swiss Army knife. They photocopied his New Jersey driver's license and demanded his social security number. They let him keep his heavy NSC shoulder bag and his cork-lined instrument case. Without his ever-present pocketknife and pocket phone, Van felt both robbed and naked.

Hickok had secured an appointment with Major General Edwin A. Wessler. Wessler was a big cheese around the KH-13, but he was not Hickok's boss. Michael Hickok never showed up on anybody's organizational charts, so he never had any "boss." Hickok referred to the various interested parties as his "sponsors."

Major General Edwin A. Wessler turned out to be a big, bluff, balding guy with rimless glasses and a Hawaiian tan. General Wessler had just been reassigned to Cheyenne from a missile-tracking base in the mid-Pacific. Wessler was only partially moved into his new office. The place was all beige paint, gunmetal shelving, and scattered blue folders.

The screen of Wessler's new Dell showed that he was working on a PowerPoint presentation. Wessler's topic was "GEODDS, Baker-Nunn, and the ASFPC."

"GEODDS," Van muttered, rubbing his aching forehead.

"Yes, sir!" boomed General Wessler. "GEODDS can spot an orbiting object the size of a basketball!"

Van put his heavy bag and case on the floor. His back ached and his wrists were sore. The altitude was killing him. Being at high altitude deep inside a stone cave was somehow much worse.

Wessler flicked Hickok's business card with his clean, buffed fingernail. "'Executive Solutions,' so what kind of outfit is that, Master Sergeant?"

"That's a long story, sir. Ever heard of the Carlyle Group?"

"I don't need any long stories today," Wessler told him with a thin smile.

Major General Wessler had an aeronautics degree, an MBA, and had worked for both NATO and NASA. General Wessler was not just any everyday general. He was a literal rocket scientist. Wessler wore an elastic blue one-piece jumpsuit with starred shoulders and a U.S. SPACE FORCE breast patch. General Wessler looked tanned, fit, and ready to spring right aboard the next Shuttle liftoff. Even though he never did anything spacier than stare deep into a tracking screen.

Van found it rather weird to meet a no-kidding, real-life general from a "Space Force." It was weirder yet that America's Space Force had bases all around the world, with forty thousand service personnel. America's Space Force was twenty years old. Why had he never seen any Space Force soldiers in any war movies? Or TV programs, either. Not even *The X-Files.*

Van coughed on the dry mountain air. Wessler removed loose books from the metal seat of his office chair. "You'd better take a load off your feet, flatlander! I'll have an orderly bring you a Pepsi!"

Van hated Pepsis, but he sat down gratefully. He focused his aching eyes on Wessler's stack of brand-new books. The titles were *War at the Top of the World, Tournament of Shadows,* and *The Prize: The Epic Quest for Oil, Money and Power.* Their pages were thick with fresh yellow Post-it notes.

Wessler barked orders into a bright red desk phone.

"I brought you something good here, sir," offered Hickok. "It sure wasn't easy finding it. I had to kiss me a whole lot of frogs. But, sir, I believe this approach might work out!"

Wessler lowered his brows in a scowl. He had about a mile and a half of shining bald forehead. "Why'd you leave the Air Force, Mr. Hickok?"

Hickok was startled. "Well, it just seemed like the right time for me to move on, sir."

"Don't hand me that crap! Why'd we lose an airman like you? And now you're here telling me you think you know how to manage a satellite, Master Sergeant? What on earth is that all about?"

"Well, sir," said Hickok, standing straighter, "if you want the truth about why I left the Force, it just got too obvious who was calling the shots there in Kosovo. It was the damn United Nations!"

Wessler didn't take that remark at all well. Van was very alarmed. They'd agreed earlier that Hickok would do the talking, because Space Force was a branch of the Air Force, while Hickok was Special Ops, also Air Force. Two wings of the Air Force trying to fly together, how hard could that be?

"Mr. Hickok may be a civilian now, sir," Van spoke up. "But I'm NSC."

"That's not what your card says, Dr. Vandeveer! This card says you are DoD!" Wessler read it carefully. " 'Transformational Communications Architecture Office, Department of Defense.' " Wessler's glasses gleamed fiercely. "That outfit doesn't even exist! It's nothing but a press release!"

"Well, we're way ahead of the curve," Van mumbled.

Van was saved by the arrival of a young airman with a Pepsi. The drink came in a sixteen-ounce plastic Los Angeles Lakers cup.

"Sir," Hickok told the general, "that big space re-org at the Pentagon is not the lookout of me and the computer doc here. So there's no need to bring up the subject of 'space transformation.' If you'll just hear us out a minute . . . We came a long way, and well, we've got some good ideas."

Wessler hitched up the elastic belt of his blue jumpsuit and sat by his computer. "I'm listening."

Hickok shot Van an urgent look. Startled, Van put his Pepsi on the floor.

"Well," Van blurted, "uh, sir, when I first saw those SEU reports, I had it figured for thermal failure. Some kind of heat load. But of course, this bird is the most advanced infrared spotter we have. So if there's anything it would spot, it would certainly be heat."

"They tell me you're a programmer."

"That's right."

"Cut to the chase! What's gone wrong with the bird's software?"

"Nothing," Van said, lunging for his cold-sweating Pepsi. "It's the hardware. First, I had to correlate those reported anomalies with its orbital position."

Wessler stared at him. "You tracked the bird's zenith angles?"

"Well, yes."

"That is the one thing no one is supposed to know! The orbital periodicity, that is the most jealously guarded secret we have! If the adversary learns that, then he can do denial and deception!"

"It wasn't that hard to figure out," Van said. Other national governments already knew about the KH-13. It was the business of their intelligence services to figure such things out. So Van had used

French commercial SPOT satellite photos, easily purchased through the Internet. Using these photos, Van had watched Indian scientists at various Indian nuclear weapons centers busily moving their cars and trucks to baffle the KH-13. The Indians were doing their usual denial and deception efforts against the new American spy satellite, trying to disguise the feverish activity in and out of their nuclear weapons centers. Given the Indians' keen awareness of the KH-13's orbit, it was easy for Van to download a PC simulator program from Dottie's astrophysics lab, and deduce the satellite's orbit by himself. Dottie was happy to help him find the right program, and she had never suspected a thing.

"The KH-13 is in a standard American spy-sat LEO/POLAR orbit," Van said. "Apogee 256, perigee 530 . . ."

"Never mind that."

Van nodded hastily. "So, once I had the orbital periodicity, then I could see these damage episodes are far from random. They only occur when the bird is transiting from the highly charged polar regions into the mid-latitudes."

This news put General Wessler right off his feed. Wessler started fiddling nervously with the track-wheel in his mouse. "So, what do you mean to say? That it's surface-charging? That there's an arc discharge?"

"Well, that's part of it," Van said. "I had to look at SD-SURF."

"Space Debris-Surfaces, yes, we ran that diagnostic almost a year ago."

"Yeah, you always run that program," Van told him. "But SD-SURF was written in FORTRAN way back in 1983. So SD-SURF treats the spacecraft's surface contours as a faceted geometry. That simulation's not entirely accurate, because you get these peaks and waves of flux and probability surfaces that are artifacts produced by granularity in the model. That's due to the way the subroutine interrogates the ballistic limit surface . . ." Van's voice trailed off. Hickok and Wessler were both staring at him blankly. He had completely lost them.

Van cleared his dry throat. "So, anyway, I rewrote SD-SURF and sent it to some friends of mine over at NCAR."

"Do you mean NCAR up in Boulder? Those Atmospheric Research guys?"

"Yeah. Yes, sir."

"But NCAR is a civilian agency! They're not cleared for any of this at all!"

"SD-SURF is not a secret. SD-SURF is public domain. It's free for download off a NASA Web site."

Wessler made a quick note on a Post-it. "We'll have to see about that right away."

"So, uhm, I had NCAR run my improved version of SD-SURF on their weather-simulation supercomputers. And while I was at it, I also had them search their files for space weather. Solar discharges, photoelectron flux, the works. Everything."

Wessler narrowed his eyes. "Oh, ho."

"There was no correlation," Van said. "Not at first. To maintain my confidentiality, I told my friend at NCAR to search *everything*. So he also ran through all of NOAA's *conventional* weather records. And there, a strong correlation turned up. There is a direct relationship between these, uh, damage episodes and storm fronts moving across the western USA."

"You mean the weather on the ground."

Van nodded. He hated talking this much. It was making his head ache.

"Dr. Vandeveer, can I remind you of something? That bird is two hundred fifty miles up!"

"I know that, General. But there's a lot we don't know about the upper thermosphere. My friend at NCAR put me in touch with a friend of his at NOAA who's a world expert on sprites and elves."

Wessler tugged at his ear. " 'Elves'?"

"Sprites and elves. Sprites and elves are huge discharges from the tops of thunderclouds," Van said. "Nothing like lightning. They go *up.* They are very big. Colossal. The Shuttle has photographed them from orbit." Van paused. "Show him those elf and sprite pics, Mike."

As Hickok busied himself unlatching the case from his wrist, Van forced a swallow of Pepsi. It tasted even worse than he remembered.

Wessler examined the set of glossy NASA printouts. "So, Dr. Vandeveer, you're telling me my satellite was attacked by elves."

"That's just one hypothesis," Van said. "But I can tell you, as a fact, that there has never been a damage episode that wasn't correlated with a storm front. When I searched those storm records, that's when I realized that there haven't been just four episodes, as your reports say. There were seven episodes, including three weaker storms with three much weaker attacks. The very worst came with the most violent storm last winter. December 17. Those onboard power anomalies."

"That was really bad," Wessler said gloomily. "We really thought we'd lost her that time." The elf pictures had shaken Wessler. Van had felt the very same way when he had seen them. It was truly bizarre to realize that the Earth's upper atmosphere had some gigantic blistering explosions that no one but pilots and astronauts ever saw. Sprites and elves, "Transient Discharge Phenomena." Sprites and elves sounded almost crazier than UFOs, but they were very real. Every bit as real as the northern lights.

"That December event," Van said. "Some very similar power surges happened to the Hubble, before the Shuttle crew fixed its Kapton sleeves. The power surges mean that the solar panels were vibrating on their bistems." Van bucked his hands back and forth. "It means that something almost tore the wings off your spacecraft."

Van put his Pepsi down. He felt drained. But Wessler had a face like a cross-examining attorney. "We used to have those 'episodes,' as you say. But now we have ongoing operational anomalies. What do you make of that?"

Van could handle that question. "That's BUMPER, your space-junk debris collision program. I looked at BUMPER, too. BUMPER has an unexamined assumption in its design specs. BUMPER assumes that debris cannot intercept a spacecraft from more than ten degrees above or below a plane tangent to the Earth normal."

Wessler scratched the back of his neck. "Of course. Otherwise that debris would fall right into the Earth's atmosphere and burn up immediately."

"No," said Van. "Not if the debris were coming *off of the spacecraft itself.* Not big chunks of space junk, not yet. But a fine haze of debris. Ionized. Ablated. Particles and ejecta from violent surface shocks. You would get a dielectric constant on the spacecraft that would reattract those contaminants and precipitate them onto specific areas of the hull."

"You see, it's just like a microwave oven, sir," Hickok broke in helpfully. "You can't ever get smoke in outer space because there's no air up there, but if it got blasted by an elf or sprite or like that, then there would be gas and dust. Kinda like a hot cloud of grease."

"I know what the man's talking about," Wessler said tautly.

Hickok shrugged. "Well then, you sure got me beat."

"I understand it, but there's no reason for me to believe it," Wessler said. "Why do I have to believe in elves, all of a sudden?"

"I don't know," Van said. "There wasn't time to fully examine that question. But I do have a working fix for your satellite's problem."

"This is where Dr. Vandeveer and I part company, sir," Hickok said eagerly. "Because I *do* know! And it's no damn little elves, either. We are *under attack,* sir! This is *spacewar!*"

"What?" said Wessler. "How? Who? The Russians?"

"Well, why not the Russians?" said Hickok. "I've met some Russians, sir. I know they're up for anything."

"The Russians can't launch anything at us! I have personally seen their space centers. The Russian space centers are totally broke! They can't pay their own power bills."

Hickok bored in. "The Red Chinese are building rockets, sir! They can lift big payloads! I reckon they're sandbagging us."

Wessler raised his brows. "What do you make of that concept, Dr. Vandeveer?"

"I don't believe in sandbagging attacks," Van said. "Sand is not an effective space weapon. Fine debris like sand would ionize quickly, then it would fall out of orbit. Besides, a cloud of sand from a Chinese rocket would injure other spacecraft, and we haven't seen any signs of that." Van pulled at his beard. "Have we seen other signs of that, General?"

Wessler closed his lips tightly. He had nothing to offer on that topic.

Van tried to smile at him. "Let's all be reasonable here. We don't have to bring any elves, UFOs, or Communists into this." He cleared his throat. "Let's just say . . . cause or causes unknown. Then we can focus on patching this problem you have."

Wessler's face set like stone. Van knew that it was time to move right along in a hurry. "Can you help me with my case here, Mike?"

Hickok opened the cork-lined instrument box. Van removed the extra foam-rubber padding. He was very relieved to see that his breadboarding had survived the rough trip from Washington. Van had had to leave his grandfather's big solder gun back inside Hickok's Humvee. Van had gotten so used to using the ray gun for work that he didn't think he could manage any more with a normal soldering tool.

Van sensed that this demonstration was his last chance. "Like I said, about that space dust," he said. "I've got a friend in Los Alamos National Lab who models particle action in dielectric fields."

"You seem to have a whole lot of unnamed friends, Dr. Vandeveer."

Van's temper sharpened. "General, in the President's National Security Council, we don't exactly lack for helpful contacts."

Wessler heaved aside a stack of folders on his desk to make extra room for Van's box. "Please. Do help yourself."

Van took a deep breath. "Ionized dust seeks equilibrium, to balance that electric charge. So the dust will settle wherever the fields on the spacecraft guide it." Van removed an extremely secret printout from the case. He ran his finger across the schematics. "That means you're getting a cloud of filth on the KH-13's sensor booms, the edges of the chassis, and especially right about here. This highly charged area, just at the rim of the Mylar insulation. There's a big component there, under the skin of the hull. It's an MIL-STD-1541, Taiwanese capacitor. Just like this component in this case."

Wessler gazed into the box. "Where did you get that thing?"

"They're pretty standard. My secretary bought it off eBay." Van sighed. "Ideally, I would have liked three milspec control-CDUs in this experiment as well, but that is way beyond my salary." Van touched a switch. "Okay, General, I think we're ready to roll now. I want you to watch this voltmeter here. Mike, fire the model up."

Hickok put his hand to a gray plastic crank. There was a faint crackle.

"See that needle bouncing?" Van said. "Now look at these SEU records. Bang, bang, beat, beat, blip. Same series, same surges, same rates of decline. That's it, General. This is your bug, that's your ongoing operational anomaly. It's a hardware glitch, and it's in this capacitor. It's got so much dirt on top of it that it is overheating."

"You're telling me there's too much dirt on it," Wessler said. "But you can't tell me *why* there is any dust in the first place."

"No, sir, I can't tell you that. But I can tell you how to fix it. You need to spin the spacecraft."

"Spin it," said Wessler.

"Spin it on the longitudinal axis. That'll fling the loose dust off, and whenever these, uh, episodes happen again . . . well, spinning will spread the stresses evenly across the whole spacecraft. So you won't get that pitting, that, uhm, that sputtering . . ." Van was losing it. Those words he'd just said, "ongoing operational anomaly." That was a regular tongue twister. "You tell him, Mike."

"The bird spins like a chicken on a spit, sir. Won't blacken all on one side, turns golden brown, like."

"But the whole point of a satellite is to have a steady, fixed camera!"

"No," said Van. "The whole point is steady, fixed *images*. You can compute the fixed images from a spinning satellite camera."

"That's impossible."

"No. It can be done." Astronomers could help a lot with orbiting camera images. Van hadn't breathed a word to Dottie about it, but he knew it could be made to happen.

"It's like Hollywood special effects, sir," said Hickok proudly. "We'll just fix it up in post-production. Like *Jurassic Park!*"

Wessler rose from his desk and put both his hands in his blue jumpsuit pockets. He had the look of a man who badly needed a drink.

"You will lose two, three percent of acuity if you spin the camera," Van admitted. "But you've already lost that much acuity to that so-called CCD fogging. That is not a CCD problem at all, by the way. That is dirt being blasted off your spacecraft and settling on your lens."

Wessler was still pacing. "We don't have the fuel to spin that bird. We're not made out of hydrazine up there."

"That's right. You'll also lose fifteen months off the expected nine-year life. But at that rate of damage . . . the satellite won't live two years."

"Our bird is under attack!" said Hickok, passionately jumping to his feet. "There is something up there, sir! I don't know how it got up there, but it can't be any accident that we have this problem during a War on Terror. Some evildoer is screwing with us, sir. I just know that."

Wessler sat down again. "I don't get a briefing like this every day."

"No," Van agreed.

"Where the hell did they dig you up, Dr. Vandeveer? You're a hell of a guy, and I've never even heard of you."

"MIT," Van said. "Stanford. And Mondiale."

Wessler stared as if a toad had jumped from Van's tongue. "You're from *Mondiale?*"

"I'm from Mondiale's R&D lab," Van said hastily. "I quit to work for the government."

"I can't believe this!" Wessler shouted, standing up again. "You crazy sons of bitches, my *mother* owned Mondiale stock! You're a *phone company*! How did you lose ninety percent of your stock value? You people are completely crooked!"

A moan slipped out of Van. "The whole industry is hurting . . ."

"I can't go to my best people and tell them to screw up our satellite on the say-so of some goofball from Mondiale!"

"I know that," Van blurted, waving his hands in panic, "I know that the company hurt a lot of people. But you don't have to take my word for this! That's not a problem, not at all! I don't want any credit for this, no, no! You just have to *look* at it. That's all. Look at the bird. See how bad off it is. Shocked or burned. Like that!"

"How?"

"You can send up the Shuttle."

"Do you know the price of a Shuttle flight? And the scheduling? Those old birds are falling to pieces!"

"Train the Hubble on it. Search it for burn marks."

"Civilian telescopes are not our department."

"Just look at it, that's all," Van begged. "Do it from the ground."

"No! Observatories are *strictly forbidden* to image American spy-sats. I certainly wouldn't want them getting started! Besides, they lack that technical capacity."

Van had nothing left to say. His wife's new adaptive-optic telescope would certainly have that capacity. But it was two years away from coming online. By then, it would be no use.

Hickok stared down at Van, expecting some final wizard miracle from him, but Van realized that he was beaten. He couldn't believe that Mondiale had brought his whole scheme crashing down. But that made a horrible sense, for in the last few months Mondiale had screwed up everything in Van's life. The big shots who had hired him away from Stanford were about to do a perp-walk, in handcuffs, in front of cameras. Guilty of stock fraud. Failures. Disasters. Deceivers. From leaders of a revolution, they had turned into liars and cheats.

Van had done his best, but he had blown it.

"What the hell's going on here?" said Hickok loudly. "I got your problem fixed, General! And you won't even *look*?"

"This guy is from Mondiale!"

"Like Lockheed's better? That bird could save the life of Special Forces spotters in Afghanistan! You're telling me, what, that's too much work for you? Use a KH-11!"

"That's completely outside normal channels."

"You're gonna let our adversaries destroy our best surveillance asset while you sit here like some jackass?"

Wessler turned beet-red. "Mr. Hickok, you can't push around a Space Force officer by yelling a bunch of saucer-nut crap. We are the *only* force on earth that has military space capacity. There *is* no one else. That's not even remotely possible."

"Who cares what your fat-cat industry vendors think is possible? That bird is dying up there! I busted my ass, I got you a genuine gold-plated computer genius here! He can fix the damn thing! If you don't fix it, then you, *you,* are betraying our men out in the field."

Wessler's throat was moving. Van realized that Wessler was silently counting to ten. Van had never seen a grown man in uniform do that before. It was very frightening. Finally Wessler spoke. "I believe I've given you two dilettantes all the time that you need."

"That does it," Hickok announced. "I quit!" He took a key from his pocket and undid his wrist-cuff. Then he tossed the briefcase on a metal chair. "This turkey of yours is dead meat! I want no part of this! You useless sumnabitches couldn't run a model rocket show!"

Wessler looked at him, his reddened face flickering through rage, disgust, and pity. "Master Sergeant, I really don't believe this is your game."

Hickok leveled a throat-cutting stare at him. "Oh, so it's a game to you, is it? You can't get your big square head around an asymmetric threat, General! No wonder they hit the damn Pentagon out of a clear blue sky. I'd rather dig ditches in Lebanon than hang out with you pie-eating game-boys. Jesus Christ."

"Mike," Van said.

"What?"

"Let's go now, Mike. All right? We'll just go."

CHAPTER NINE

Hickok wasn't the kind of guy to silently nurse his grudges. His first stop outside the Cheyenne base was to pick up two fifths of Jack Daniel's.

Van drove the Humvee as Hickok slurped his bourbon and griped. In going to visit Dottie, Van was borrowing Hickok's courier truck.

The failure gnawed at Van. He was right, he knew he was right. Why hadn't that worked? Why hadn't he been more convincing?

Two reasons, really. The first was painful and personal. He, Dr. Derek Vandeveer, was a geek. He was a classic, bearded-weirdo, introspective nerd. Oh, yes, he could hold his own when people came to him with technical problems. But he didn't have the grit that it took to really kick ass and take names. He should have had that kind of quality. He had nobody to blame for his weakness but himself. His grandfather would have broken that stupid Air Force general like a matchstick.

Almost. He'd been so close. If not for that ugly Mondiale business . . . but that shouldn't have mattered. Or, at least, Mondiale was only one aspect of a much deeper crisis. He should never have sold out to private industry in the first place. At Stanford, at MIT, people had high standards. People had intellectual rigor. At Mondiale, nobody cared at all about principles. The method at Mondiale was to build a prototype in R&D. Then throw it over the wall to marketing and product development. That was what Van had just tried to do with this military professional. And it just hadn't worked.

Van fiercely gripped the Humvee's padded steering wheel. He was driving a vehicle the size of a living room, through dense Colorado commuter traffic, on snowy, hairpin mountain turns. White-line fever had him totally keyed-up.

Phantoms of shame and guilt danced on the snowy road ahead of him. Not only was he not a true leader, he was not truly a scientist, either. That was the tragic core of the whole ugly mess. Computer science was a fraud. It always had been. It was the only branch of science ever named after a gadget. He and his colleagues were basically no better than gizmo freaks. Now physics, now that was true science. Nobody ever called physics "lever science" or "billiard ball science."

The fatal error in computer science was that it modeled complex systems without truly understanding them. Computers simulated complexity. You might know more or less what was likely to happen. But the causes remained unclear. When a hard-headed, practical man like General Wessler asked him "why," all that Van could do was helplessly wave his hands.

He could have become a mathematician. He knew he had some skill there. Math would have been a much better choice for an ugly man who was shy and retiring. It was only personal weakness that had made him give in to the lure of computers. They called it "software engineering," but that wasn't engineering, either. If he'd been a true engineer like his grandfather, he would never have gone to the

Space Force with such a cheap, lousy hack. He had brought them a half-baked notion. A hack was something rough-and-ready, tacked onto the end of a legacy system that was too huge, complicated, and overwhelming to fix. That was why he'd failed and been kicked out in disgrace.

Jeb had given him the very same siren song. "This time, we'll really straighten it all out." No. No one could ever promise that about computers, because that was never the truth. It didn't matter how good you were, how smart you were. Nobody ever "fixed" computers. You just threw the old computer out and got another one. Any genuine reform was impossible. The only thing you could do was layer some fresh mud on top of the cracks.

That, or just give up. Go into hiding, just hide from the burning shame. Yes, he, Derek Ronald Vandeveer, was a phony-baloney security expert for an agency that didn't even exist. But it wasn't like he could return to his previous life. What had happened to Mondiale and their competitors . . . that wasn't a "bubble." That was a train wreck on top of an avalanche. He, Derek Vandeveer, was part of the worst destruction of wealth in human history. Men he knew and trusted, corporate visionaries building a new and better electro-world, were out on bail. The very guys who used to drop by his lab in Merwinster in their pressed slacks and cashmere sweaters, to ooh and ahhh at the prototypes. Their second homes were auctioned off by bailiffs. Their trophy wives had vanished off the fashion pages into dry-out tanks.

Why had he ever, ever believed in that crap? As a last, fatal bottom line, what kind of terrible verdict was that on his own integrity and good judgment? He'd been in the lab blowing money entrusted to his company by widows and orphans. By the mothers of Space Force generals.

What possible right did he have to thrust himself into public policy? What was he doing here now? A full nightmare awareness struck Van. An awful vision of the hordes of the cheated, the deceived, and the damaged. Millions of normal people across America, across the whole world, who had no awareness of what he had done to them, what he was trying to save them from . . .

Remember that hot stock that you bet on, Mr. and Mrs. America? All those nerds you trusted to bring you a New Economy? Well, they're driving massive trucks in Colorado. Lost, alone. With drunken ex-soldiers. In a War on Terror. Cursing, bewildered, frustrated, violent.

In his panicky haste to flee Cheyenne Mountain, Van had abandoned his cell phone and even his beloved Swiss Army knife. His pockets were truly empty now. Nobody would even talk to him. He was doomed. The CCIAB was doomed. The satellite was doomed. Maybe even America was doomed.

"You're sure as hell not saying much," said Hickok.

"I screwed up bad, Mike. I should have nailed that. That should have worked."

"You're the one bitching? I don't even have a job now!" Hickok flung his empty whiskey bottle out the Humvee's window, with an overhand Molotov lob. Then he cracked the seal on a second. "You've got a wife and a kid, fella! All I got in my life is this truck and some Dixie Chicks tapes."

"You want a job, Mike?"

"That wouldn't hurt me," said Hickok. "What, a job with your outfit, you mean?" The idea amused him. "You're gonna turn me into a true-blue cyberwar freak, Dr. Professor?"

"Yeah, Mike. You're hired. Come by my office when you get back to D.C."

Hickok peered at the fine print on the whiskey label. "I think maybe I'll drive back straight through Tennessee. Tennessee makes the best damn liquor in this whole wide world!"

Dottie's telescope needed black skies. Black skies in America were few and far between. There were some strange and spooky places in the backwoods of Colorado. Mountain people always lived free. The

nooks and crannies of the Rocky Mountains had Space Force generals, and ancient hippies, and silver miners, and jack Mormons.

"Out here in God's country, we got ourselves some dropouts!"
crowed Hickok, drunkenly pounding his leg with his rocklike fist.
"The real off-the-grid people! Polygamists. Unabomber types. And
there's survivalists!"

During the Y2K panics of 1999, Van had come to know quite a lot
about survivalists. And what he knew, Van didn't like. Survivalists
were people of bad faith. Their faith was that civilization would
break down, and ought to break down, and deserved to break down.
That no one in charge should ever be trusted. That all authorities
were useless, deluded, or evil.

The survivalist faith was to abandon everyone and everything.
Go into hiding. Buy lots and lots of gas masks. Cement. Water filters.
Sacks of grain. Bars of gold.

"Mike, do you know any of those survivalist types?"

Hickok's lids fluttered. He sat up in the Humvee's backseat. "You
bet I do! Us 'snake-eaters' can live right off the land! Escape and eva-
sion under the stars! Cover your face up with dang mud! I used to
train around these parts. If I recall myself correctly, there should be a
roadside depot yonder. Sell you most anything you need to know!"

Van soon found Hickok's depot. The place didn't look like much.
A big red barn. He wanted to press right on and get to Dottie's place.
Then he saw a glowing yellow roadside sign standing next to some
rusty gas pumps. The sign was measled with shotgun pellets. KNIVES
AMMO, it bragged. GUNS GUNS GUNS.

"Whoa," said Van, hitting the brake.

Van arrived late at his destination, pitched out at the end of a two-
lane road. The drunken Hickok wheeled his Humvee and roared
back down the mountainside. He'd said something about a girl waiting in Fort Collins, but Van was not convinced of it. With that brief-

case finally off his wrist, Hickok had the look of a man aiming for a major-league bender.

Van was left standing alone in a cold Colorado night, under two pools of amber light that fell from curving, snake-shaped poles. Observatories hated light pollution. So these Martian-looking light poles carried weird LED panels that shed a very thin gleam. Reading by their light was like wading underwater in a hookah.

Van set down his brand-new survivalist backpack and stared up at a beautifully painted sign. ALFRED A. GRIFFITH INTERNATIONAL ASTRONOMICAL FACILITY, it announced. This big sign—it was a dignified metal billboard, really—carried eye-squinting little logos for a whole swarm of federal sponsors and private contractors. NATIONAL SCIENCE FOUNDATION. AURA. NOAO. NASA. NORTHRUP GRUMMAN OPTICAL SYSTEMS DIVISION. CANADIAN SPACE AGENCY / AGENCE SPATIALLE CANADIENNE. MAX PLANCK INSTITUT FUR EXTRATERRESTRISCHE PHYSIK. Warning: This Is a U.S. Interior Department Endangered Species Refugium.

To Van's right, to his left, stretched a galvanized twelve-foot steel elk fence. It was topped with nasty whorls of razor wire.

Too bad nobody had included a doorbell here.

There was no way for Van to enter Dottie's facility. It was very clear that nobody ever showed up here who wasn't fully expected. The fences were too tall and sharp to climb. The gates looked built to resist a headlong charge by angry buffalo. There was no intercom and no guard on duty.

Van had no cell phone.

The winter night was getting colder.

Van opened his pack and pulled out his laptop. Another tough break: there was no wireless signal for his laptop's Wi-Fi card, either.

As Van was accustoming himself to complete defeat, the overhead light poles winked out. How very bright a million stars were in the mountains, suddenly.

Van opened his laptop. The federal dot-pdf on his screen was horribly titled "Draft Reporting Instructions for the Government Information Security Reform Act and Updated Guidance on Security Plans of Action and Milestones." Van did not have to read any more of this awful document, though. Instead, his computer was going to give him enough light and heat to survive the night.

Van dug in his pack and wrapped himself in a four-dollar NASA surplus astronaut blanket. He chewed a brick of indestructible NASA-surplus spaghetti. He warmed his hands on the hot battery of his laptop. He'd been in a paranoid mood, back at the survival store.

Hooded in his windproof blanket like a silver garbage bag, Van sat on his bulletproof backpack and confronted the glow on his screen. What did it matter if he was alone, cold, lonely, and humiliated on the end of the road? Van had a lot of important office work on his lap. Many unread reports, many policy statements, and important federal white papers. Requests for commentary. Invitations to important seminars. He could achieve a lot while freezing in a wilderness.

The air was thin up here, and it got colder yet. Van rearranged and color-coded his many, many files and folders. As he typed, his fingers turned blue.

After an hour and forty-two minutes, the black gates spontaneously opened. Van was forced to scramble out of the way or be crushed. A slab-sided white panel truck barreled through.

Before the gates could swing shut, Van grabbed up his pack and hustled inside.

Van trudged uphill in cold and darkness, under starlight, with his eyes gone big as an owl's. It was a very steep climb. For all his hard work in the gym, the hike had Van huffing, wheezing, and rubbing his thighs. When he plodded his way over a crest, Van could see, lit up like toy ballerinas, a distant nest of gently whirring rotors. Wind power, renewable energy. Out here, those pretty dancing windmills wouldn't smudge their perfect skies with smoke.

A deer stared at Van fearlessly and went back to raiding the bushes. The road lifted suddenly. Van found himself walking on an echoing metal bridge. More amber lights loomed ahead. Here was a parking lot, all of it up on pillars. It was filled with silent electric vans and logo-covered golf carts.

Van had found Dottie's research complex. The pictures she had sent him didn't do the place justice. It was a whole lot odder than it looked in the brochures. The place was like a Silicon Valley health spa built for mountain hobbits.

The complex rose right up a mountain slope, all twinklingly underlit with tiny amber lights. The offices were made of cedar, granite, glass, and aluminum. Lots of perforated grating, pillared balconies, and shiny steel handrails. All these buildings were poised on the mountainside on daintily curved metal feet. Endangered species could frolic right under their floors. Roof gutters caught all the snow and rain and fed it into big cisterns.

It looked amazingly pretty, like something out of a kid's encyclopedia. For some touchy enviro-fanatical reason, nobody had been allowed to dig anywhere, to break the tender mountain soil. So all the Facility's water, sewer, and electrical were neatly suspended on pylons, like an Alaska pipeline for toilets. The place was overrun with fat, silver-wrapped pipes. It looked like it had been designed by Super Mario.

Van huffed to catch his breath, then clomped straight up a set of toothy aluminum stairs. He opened a double-paned glass door. He walked down a hall floor lined with dark cork.

He knocked at Room A37.

The door was opened by an old woman wearing rimless bifocals, a colored head scarf, and a lumpy, hand-knitted sweater.

"Sorry," Van muttered, "wrong room."

"You must be the husband," said the gypsy woman.

"Uhm, yeah."

"You're late. Dottie had to go. Why didn't you call?"

Van made a beeline for Dottie's bedside phone. "I'll call her right now."

"Don't do that. She's on television."

"At night?" Van said.

"Of course at night! It's a telescope!"

The talking woke Ted. Ted was sleeping in a plastic crib at the foot of Dottie's bed. Ted hustled sideways on his Disney-cartoon sheets and peered through his bars. He saw Van and shrieked.

Van advanced on his son and picked him up.

Ted had become huge. Ted's noggin was thick with brand-new blond hair. Ted seemed to have added a full fifty percent to his body mass. When Ted struggled, he really meant it now. In Van's long absence, Ted's marshmallow baby body had turned into muscle. The boy looked ready to jump into his own clothes, grab up his cup and rattle, and get himself a day job.

"It's me, your dada," Van bargained.

"NOOOOOO!" Ted thrashed his thick legs as if jumping hurdles. He was wearing a long-sleeved red flannel onesie suitable for chilly nights. Ted looked like an infant lumberjack. "NOOooooOOOOO, no, Mama!" His diapers stank.

"I'll tell Dottie you are finally here," said the unknown babysitter. She vanished out the door.

Van set Ted down on the chilly floor as he hunted down a pack of diapers. Van hadn't changed a diaper in ages, but it wasn't a skill one forgot. Ted resented this brutal procedure. He gave Van a look of bitter, jaded suspicion.

"It's all right, Ted," Van lied. He buttoned Ted back up and set him on his pudgy feet. With a determined scowl, Ted gripped the edge of his mother's bed and sidled away from Van.

For the first time in his life, Van had some insight into what had gone wrong with his own father. It was guilt. That was why the guy had finally crumbled. Because of burning guilt, dirty guilt, painful, humiliating, fully deserved guilt. There were bad acts in a man's life that could never, ever be repaired.

Van sat on Dottie's bed, which was narrow and hard. Dottie's high-tech eco-room was creeping him out. This was like the home of some alternate Dottie from a bad *Star Trek* episode. Dottie's tight, virginal sheets had tiny blue flowers. Dottie had a small, oval-shaped, Energy Star fridge. She had a hot plate and a pretty teapot on top of her bamboo clothes drawer.

Dottie's computer desk was ergonomic and very disturbing. It had many adjustable plastic cranks and was made of swoopy red plastic lozenges. The desk had one special kidney-shaped shelf way up on a tall metal arm. The shelf was poised at a weird, unlikely, Dr. Seuss angle. The tall shelf held one empty, dusty little flower vase.

This was a room that was silently screaming for a man's disturbing touch. This room really needed its hair mussed. It was all Van could do not to start hitting things with a bat.

"Ted, son, how do you live here?"

Ted replied with bitter whimpering.

Van persisted. "Hey, Edward."

Ted turned his small face toward Van, but he was openly skeptical.

Van zipped open his backpack. "You wanna see something really cool? I'm gonna show you my ray gun!"

Feet skidded down the hall. Dottie had a new haircut and had put on five or ten pounds. Van stood up. Dottie zipped across the room and gave him a kiss. It was a nice, solid "I am your wife, here are my lips" kind of kiss.

"A long trip, honey bear?"

The feel of her soft arms around his neck was saving Van's life. Loneliness drained out of him like poison. "This place is the middle of nowhere!"

Dottie nodded, blue eyes bright. "It is! It is. But no one ever leaves us." She shrugged out of her padded jacket.

"Why not?"

"Because the catering is too good! There's Indian food, Chinese food, they had a barbecue chef in today . . . We ate wild elk!"

The sight of Dottie meant so much to him that he felt faint. "You look great, honey."

"This is my TV outfit." Dottie went to the cubbyhole bathroom and flicked on its fluorescent, eco-correct lightbulb. "There was a crew in tonight from Australian television. I seem to be the big PR person around here now . . . It turned out that I'm pretty good at that. This is not the biggest adaptive telescope in the world, but you know, it really looks great on TV."

"No kidding."

"This is the only telescope facility ever designed by a major modern architect. Did you see all that fiber-optic out there? We got really big pipes here!"

Van sighed. It was hard for him to rally any enthusiasm for another Internet money hole. After the stock crash, Mondiale was doing a scary reassessment of the company's physical assets. Internet routers were in such oversupply that they were worth only twenty-five cents on the dollar. No wonder Tony had stuck some surplus Net hardware up here in the high backwoods. All out of sight, out of mind.

Dottie found a heavy quilt. "It gets so cold up here," she said. "They don't like us running the electric heaters . . ." She lifted Ted and put him back into his crib. Ted looked relieved and interested. Ted hadn't seen his parents together in several baby eons, but his mom was happy, and the routine was jogging his memory.

For the first time, Ted offered Van a smile. Van put a hand on his son's face and looked deep into his eyes. It was like gazing through a powerful mirror straight into the youth of the universe.

"Derek, look, this thermostat has a power meter built right into it, isn't this great? They're in all the rooms."

"Why won't they let you heat the place? We're way up in the hills!"

"Astronomers get used to that." Dottie tucked Ted into a spotless blanket. "It's a very nice place up here, honey. We get health care. We get paid vacations . . . There's horseback riding. We got workout rooms and massage . . . We get big-screen movies. We get *Bollywood* movies."

"And you watch that stuff on purpose?"

"Bollywood movies are great. *Fiza*, that's such a wonderful film. It's all about a Moslem girl from Bombay whose brother is a mujahideen terrorist." Dottie's voice fell. "I cried and cried."

Dottie had been crying and crying, thought Van with a pang. She was being so bright and sweet to him. Two minutes together, and it was as if they had never parted at all. But he knew she had suffered. He had suffered. He had suffered so much he had no idea what to do with his feelings.

He hauled Ted back out of his crib and set him on his knee. He couldn't keep his hands off the kid. Ted was such a lively presence that holding him was like licking a fresh battery. "So, who was that babysitter who was here?"

"That's Dr. Ludewig. She used to run a radio telescope in Denmark. We get a lot of visiting scholars from overseas here. This place, it's a lot like Cerre Tololo in Chile. For colleagues in Europe and Asia, we're such a big deal." Dottie turned to him. "I'm gonna get some great publications out of all this."

"I thought you were still two years away from your 'first light.' "

"Sure, we are, but running the telescope is just part of our action." Dottie was always completely serious whenever she discussed her career. "It's all about leveraging digital instruments with the Net. We're building the world's biggest star archives here. Lots bigger than MAST or HEASARC. They're already using us for their backups and mirror-sites, because our bandwidth is so hot. We're the only physical backbone that NSFnet has crossing the Continental Divide. We've got tremendous pipes, stacks of equipment, machines we haven't even unwrapped yet. Racks and racks of numerical simulators. It was 'pre-owned' by the feds, but we're astronomers, so that doesn't matter to us. We're like kids in a candy store."

This was a billionaire federal contractor at work, thought Van, with a potent mix of private and public money. It had to get like this, when fewer and fewer ultra-rich people controlled bigger and bigger chunks of America's economy. Peel a few labels off, and the government's suppliers and buyers turn out to be the very same guy.

Van understood that well now, because he watched the federal government's "Industrial Base Management" happening every day. Van himself was both Mondiale R&D and CCIAB Tech Support. He was knee-deep in the system, too.

Jeb called it "the Smoking Room." Step one: get those heavy operators into the smoke-filled room. Step two: close all the doors and windows. Step three: pick only the contractors who are willing to play the game. When you leave government, then they'll hire you. You'll be them, and they'll be you. The Smoking Room had a built-in revolving door.

"Yesterday's Technology at Tomorrow's Prices." That was how the National Reconnaissance Office had gotten itself a marble office complex and the best cafeteria in Washington—even though, officially, nobody had ever heard of the National Reconnaissance Office. They ran satellites. They were real. Real, real secret.

The Smoking Room. The Grease Machine. The military-industrial complication. Van's head was swimming. "Mmmm."

Dottie was concerned. "Is it your altitude sickness?"

"Yeah, honey. Sorry." He hated disappointing her.

"Sweetie, you just relax awhile now." She took Ted away from him and put the baby back in his crib. Then she fluffed up a pillow, flopped Van on the bed, and pulled his shoes off. "It's so late. Did you eat anything? You know what? I have some really good Chardonnay. That'll fix you up."

Van had to laugh. It was doing him such good to hear her rattle on. "How good is it?"

"It'll relax you, you'll fall right asleep." Her blue eyes were full of wifely promise. "Tomorrow, though, we'll do everything."

Van accepted a glass. Van didn't much care for sweet, girly chardonnays, but this one was good enough to get him up on his elbow. "Wow, honey, this stuff's great."

"I can afford it," she told him. "They pay us a lot and there's nothing to spend money on up here. Housing is free. All our meals are catered. We even get dental."

"Wow."

She sat on the bed demurely and looked down at him with a tender smile. "You know why it's like that around here? Because it's still the 1990s up here, that's why. When DeFanti set this all up years ago, he thought it would be really hard to get any top technical people to live way up here. After all, we don't even get to have cars . . . So he budgeted us for big dot-com-style perks. Tony would change all that if he could—that guy is such a cheapskate—but that's the way De-Fanti angled things with the feds. So it's just stuck in cement. Nobody's got the authority to change any of it."

"I thought Tom DeFanti went nuts."

"He did, but that doesn't matter now. This telescope is supposed to be his monument. He really, seriously wanted it to last for a hundred years. DeFanti was always kind of strange that way, but . . . Derek, this is such a good place. This is just what life was like when people just like us were really happy. The work is challenging. We get creative freedom. They really pay us. It's a beautiful little campus. The food is fantastic, there's all kinds of cool hardware, there's day care . . . I love it up here."

"That's great."

Her smooth brow wrinkled. "Whenever I go out of town, to Boulder or Denver, then I see how bad it's getting outside. People out there are crazy now. Everyone is completely terrified."

"It's not that bad," Van lied.

"Yes, it is."

"Yeah, Dottie, you're right, it is that bad."

There wasn't much more to say on that topic. It was too depressing. Dottie arranged the sheets and quilt around him. "Honey, this bed is too small for us. Tomorrow we'll go down to DeFanti's ranch. I made us reservations. They've got cottages and a hot tub! Is your head any better now?"

"Yeah." A drink always helped Van with his altitude sickness. Alcohol flushed open important blood vessels inside his skull. Van sat up and pulled his pants off. He'd bought new slacks in order to confront General Wessler, hoping to look more professional. As he dropped them to his ankles, his brand-new knife fell out of his pocket.

Helpfully, Dottie scooped it up. "Is this a new gadget, honey?" It was a fist-sized lozenge the color of soot. She picked at its thumb lever, and a black, razor-sharp serrated blade slid out.

Dottie dropped the knife, scarring the floor. Startled words tumbled out of her. "Oh, honey, this is like some awful thing that people would like murder somebody with!"

"It's a hunting knife," Van lied, plucking it up. "Tony always talks about the great hunting up here in the mountains." Hickok had talked him into buying a tactical SWAT knife at the survival store. The knife was blacker than a Gothic ninja. It featured a carbon-fiber handle and a titanium carbonitride blade finish.

"You got that thing for Tony?"

Van closed the knife and hid it at the bottom of his pack. Van had never mentioned the existence of Michael Hickok to Dottie, because every single thing regarding the KH-13 was so entirely off-limits. A brilliant lie burst out of him. "Nowadays, they never let this kind of thing on airplanes. But I came here by car, so, you know, I'm just holding it." He sipped more wine.

Dottie's sweet face clouded. "Why would he want that ugly thing from you? What is wrong with that man? Nothing ever satisfies him!"

Van blinked. "What's so wrong with Tony?"

"Oh, nothing. Nothing at all, I guess. Except for his nineteen-year-old girlfriend! Derek, he is *buying* that woman. This Indian movie starlet, this creature with snaky black hair who hangs all over him and has eyes like two headlamps. Does that sound healthy to you?"

Van knew very well that Tony's girlfriend Anjali was twenty-three, but seeing Dottie's reaction, he wisely held his tongue about it. "Boy, that's a big shame."

"I worry so much about Tony. In all the years I've known him, he has never had one stable, adult relationship. That woman is taking advantage of him, I just know it. He is completely besotted."

Van choked back the urge to snicker. "Besotted"? What kind of word was that? The last time he'd enjoyed a talk with Tony, back in Washington, Tony had been rolling his eyes like a cartoon wolf over this little Indian actress.

It was very funny to Van that Tony Carew, the poster boy for jet-setters, had finally found the one woman in the whole round world who could lead him around by the nose. An Indian movie star, of all the wild things. It was so like him. Van had been plenty curious about the girl, so he had found one of the actress's Hindi-language movies on an Indian-made DVD. Tony's sex-bomb girlfriend turned out to be this sugary, Technicolor hoochie-coochie girl who didn't even kiss her co-stars. The whole ridiculous thing gave Van a warm, bubbly, glowing feeling. Poor Tony, poor old Tony, that lucky slob.

Jeez, at an altitude like this, that Chardonnay had some kind of kick.

He patted her hand. "Precious," he said, "we should just let old Tony just be Tony. You and me, we get to be you and me. We can be happy, if they give us a chance. That's what counts."

A flush rose to her cheeks. Dottie's shoulders started to shake. Oh, for heaven's sake, she was going to cry. Van's heart smoldered guiltily within him. Well, why shouldn't she cry? She had good reasons.

He put a hand on her shoulder. "Honey, it'll be all right now. It'll be good for a while."

Dottie only sniffled all the more. Why could he never tell her the right thing? Sometimes he almost got it all straight in his head. But he had a cramp in him that would never let him give her the right words.

The baby was asleep again. They were stuck in this small cold room. Dottie was crying and his head still hurt from the thin mountain air. But at least they were alone, and no one was bothering them. Dottie's little room didn't seem so bad once Dottie was inside it. It was lots bigger than his tiny Vault office, and probably much less weird, too. Dottie was here with him, that was the point. He wasn't freezing outside the Facility's gates in the dark. He should be grateful for that. Plus, there weren't any Space Force generals around here. Life wasn't so bad, it was pretty good after all, wasn't it? Yes, life had to be good. He pulled his shirt off.

Dottie's eyes widened as she wiped away her tears. Van grinned at her. Yeah, in her absence, he'd really been hitting the gym! He'd shed a lot of flab! Thanks to those Nautilus machines, he'd never been in better shape . . .

"What happened to your *shoulder*?"

Van glanced at the fading blotch of purple and yellow. He had hammered his shoulder black-and-blue with the bouncing butt of a South African combat shotgun. The thing had a spinning drum magazine that spewed shells as if they were confetti.

Dottie touched the bruise in wonder. "Honey, you really got hurt!"

Of course the blazing shotgun had hurt him some, but it had been so exciting that he hadn't even cared. "A little accident at work," he lied. He stretched out on the taut, narrow bed.

In a moment she had slid in next to him under the heavy quilt. They never shared the same bed much as a couple. With lives in separate cities, they had never fallen into that habit, somehow. This bed was much too small. Dottie clung to him as if they were stuck on a life raft. He was too tired and winded to make love to her, but he was taking huge comfort in the heat of her skin, in the even sound of her breathing. His star girl. A gift to him from the universe. On some silent level of his soul he had felt a profound terror, a deadly conviction, that he would never hold Dottie again.

Dottie pillowed her head on his arm, locked a leg around him, and fell fast asleep. The room was very dim. He could barely make out the sweet line of her nose, her cheekbone.

How frail the world was.

He'd never known, until he stepped behind the curtain of power, that civilization was mostly a matter of keeping up appearances. Up at the very top of the power elite, in the little counsels and committees of the great and the good, even the people who happened to be scientists and engineers had to become witch doctors. Yes, he was a politician now, too. To run the world, you had to find it in yourself to grit your teeth and just fake it. Just stare them down, never back off.

That was where he'd blown it with the General. He hadn't come to that man with a warrior's air of command-and-control. "The aura of inevitability."

Van closed his burning eyes. Tomorrow, just for once, he had nothing to do but to be together with his wife and child. Why should that seem like such a fantastic privilege to him now? Because he had volunteered for all this. He had willingly turned himself into a weapon.

Van hovered at the brink of sleep, his chest heaving at the thin air. The shining image of his grandfather's gun occurred to him. The gun pressed against his mind's eye, heavy with dream-importance. The ray gun had run out of solder as he worked on his doomed KH-13 presentation. That's when he had opened it up, removing four tiny steel screws, and discovered that the engineers of the Skunk Works had built a fake jet engine inside there. When he'd popped off the butt of the ray gun, he was looking right up the round model rocket rump of an SR-71 Blackbird. To make the gun work, you had to shove solder wire up the jet's exhaust, round as a gun barrel. That was true geek humor. Very crew cut and bow tie, very 1960s styling. No wonder his grandfather had always treasured the thing.

Wine and weariness came down on him and pressed him flat.

At 3:00 A.M. the baby's screams woke them. "Oh, Derek," she said, muddled and confused, "I always let Ted sleep in here with me."

There was nothing for it but to jam lonely Ted into the bed with the two of them. The sleepy and irritable Ted wriggled like a flannel otter, wedging his body between his parents and hacking for space with knees and heels. Van, who had been hovering at the edge of altitude suffocation, came wide awake.

Van climbed out of the bed, then put all his clothes on, because the room was icy. He wrapped his shoulders in Ted's abandoned blanket, sat at the desk, and woke Dottie's laptop from its sleep.

Dottie's room might be neater than a convent, but he had never seen Dottie's computer in such an awful mess. It horrified him to realize that Dottie Vandeveer, his very own wife, was using Windows Outlook Express on broadband without any security enhancements. She'd customized all her icons, too. They were not her usual dainty stars and comets, but icons that a Goth chick would have gone for: bats, UFO aliens, witches' cauldrons. Important files were scattered all over her screen, most of them named with doubled exclamation points!! and shouting CAPITAL LETTERS. Van was staring straight into an X ray of his wife's unconscious mind. The news here was not good.

Van had finally reached some kind of peak event in his marriage: he was sending his wife e-mail from her own machine.

Dear Dottie, I never told you how hard this new life would be for both of us

No, that wasn't it at all, that way was just no good. His words vanished into the left-moving vacuum of her DELETE key.

Dearest Dottie, I can't tell you why this hasn't worked out as I hoped

Dottie, I'm not allowed to say just what

Dear Dorothy

There was a sudden electric snapping. Power failure. All the lights went out.

Van groped his way back toward the bed in pitch-blackness, and he lay down fully clothed.

CHAPTER
TEN

PINECREST RANCH, COLORADO, FEBRUARY 2002

Dottie prodded him flirtatiously with her bare toes. "Well, hero, now you know what you were fighting for!"

Van nodded, breathing hot steam. He balanced his cold German beer on the edge of the hot tub. To judge by his surroundings, he was fighting for the right of eccentric rich guys to buy the whole planet.

Thomas DeFanti's "cottage" had once been a pioneer Colorado farmstead, all hard rock and tough gray timber. Then some pet architect had transformed the place into a billionaire's secret love nest. It was all done-up inside in black-and-chrome, high 1980s style. It was like Hugh Hefner seducing *The Unsinkable Molly Brown*.

Pinecrest Ranch, to judge by what Van had seen of it, was a mix of Hong Kong and Hollywood Western. Mrs. DeFanti, the zillionaire's fourth or fifth wife, was the guardian of the old man and his big spread. Mrs. DeFanti was turning his Ponderosa into a bonsai Chinese ranchero. She was dusting the buffalo, she was grooming the antelope . . . She was a chip mogul's daughter from Taiwan, and she was re-creating Colorado as a Pacific Rim luxury spa.

Guest meals were served up in the main ranch house, in a sunny conservatory with a stunning mountain view. Van had started his day with Russian eggs Benedict with spinach and caviar, plus pineapple juice and an inch-thick buffalo breakfast steak. His altitude sickness was banished. The protein, vitamins, and half a gallon of Jamaican Blue Mountain coffee had definitely gotten his motor running.

Dottie, who was off the pill, had surprised him with a condom, which they promptly broke. Van was shocked to see her shrug off this mishap, and even laugh about it. She was in a mood he had never seen.

The cottage's hot tub was like a little amphitheater, surrounded by black solar-water heaters. The tub gave off a volcanic Jacuzzi sizzling in the crisp winter air. Van had never made love in a hot tub before. As the pulsing currents beat and sizzled against his naked flesh, he got it about the appeal there. It was like having more sex without even needing to move.

Dottie sampled her glass of white wine, and tucked her cold hand back in the hot water. "Honey, that was too long apart, okay? I don't wanna be a computer-security widow."

"We can meet again at that big to-do in Virginia. And after that, Tony has invited me to a Joint Techs conference up here."

Unhappiness crossed her face. He'd given her the wrong answer. She didn't want him to just make some dates.

He couldn't tell her the simple thing that she needed to hear. Even though he knew what that was, more or less. It was something like: "Honey, I missed you just as much as you missed me." But that wasn't quite true, and he knew it.

Those months apart had brought him an ugly self-wisdom, Van thought as his floating feet bobbed in the sizzling water. There was something wrong with him as a man, a husband, a father, and a human being. He was the only child of a troubled marriage. He came from a line of people who were way too bright. He had an ability to concentrate and work creatively, and he also had a thorny, geeky isolation.

And those were not two different things. They were the very same thing. Beneath his shell, his personal armor, he had a vast, galactic gulf of need. It was huge and ruthless, like an autism. It would never be filled. And that wasn't her fault at all, for a thousand loving Dotties couldn't fill it. His heart of hearts lived there in a gulf of darkness, and his love for her was like one single glowing star.

If he'd been a poet he could have told her that in some nice way, but Van had never in his life packed a thought like that into words. He might have made a start at saying it—but there was worse. In her absence from his life, in the icy vacuum where her warmth had once consoled him, there was a new and powerful emotion growing inside him. As Van floated there at ease under the big winter sky, looked after, fed, watered, loved, now he could see that feeling, now he could finally put a name to what was going on inside of him. It was rage. He could see that rage within himself as if watching it through a telescope. It was black and hard and dense, like a neutron star.

He was someone who read manuals, wore glasses, and typed on a keyboard. About the most violent thing he ever did in his cyber-warrior life was to look for a buffer overflow. But rage was growing in him, because rage was a native part of his soul. Rage grew there in the entirely natural way that grief would grow in a widower.

Van had nothing to say to her about this. He couldn't any more wrap his tongue around that than he could lick broken glass.

Dottie looked over his shoulder. Then she found her glasses, put them on, and stared.

Van found his specs as well. Two men were approaching their cottage on horseback. The first was a young Chinese servant. Van wanted to think of this Chinese kid as a "staffer," but Mrs. DeFanti's Chinese underlings were most definitely "servants." They were around all the time, thoughtful, watching and attentive, but barely there. They made the most self-effacing British butler seem like a brass band.

The second man was also humble and ghostlike, but in a very different way. His padded jacket, his tartan shirt, his felt cowboy hat, they were perched on his quiet flesh like the clothes on a cowboy paper doll.

The two horses plodded by gently, long heads down, on some very private go-round. Van and Dottie sank deep into the hot water. The servant ignored them serenely, as if two naked lovers in a tub were no more than two pinecones. The old man's gaze fell on them and lingered. He had eyes in a waking dream. They seemed to stare across a thousand light-years.

The horses plodded on and carried their human cargo into the pine trees.

"I should have stood right up and waved," Dottie said.

Van laughed, startled.

She swam over and wrapped her chunky little body around him.

"We don't have many illusions about that old man," she told him, her lips an inch from his neck. "At the Facility, nobody does. When he was between marriages, he used to go to astronomy seminars and hit on all the women. Oh, boy, the stories you used to hear whenever Tom DeFanti was on the prowl."

"How do you know all that? Aren't you a little young for that old guy?"

"There aren't that many women in astronomy, honey. Word always gets around."

Van gave her a smile. Somehow, it all made sense.

"I got myself one of the cute guys," she told him, rubbing his collarbone. "Everybody knows."

Van kept his smile up, but the sight of Tom DeFanti had given him a real turn. Van had met a lot of odd and remarkable people lately. He had met the President of the United States. He'd met the Secretary of Defense, the National Security Adviser, and the Attorney General. Once, at an industry junket, he had had a long chat by an elevator with both Bill Gates and Warren Buffett, who were riding up to the penthouse together to drink beer and play poker. Bill Gates had noticed Van's name badge. He had said something nice about how "hard-core" Van might get, working at Microsoft Research in Redmond.

Maybe if Bill Gates had caught it in the neck from some huge Enron scandal. If Bill Gates had suffered a total mental breakdown. If Bill Gates was shambling around like some kind of snake-bitten ghost. Then maybe Bill Gates would be as scary as Tom DeFanti had just been.

The world's rich people were all getting spookier. During the Bubble, there had never been so many truly wacky people who were just totally, crazily loaded with cash. Up at the very top, they stopped counting their money and they wanted to act just like governments. George Soros had his agents all over Eastern Europe. Ross Perot wanted to be President, and Ken Lay . . . they'd all lost the idea that there was any kind of limit to what money could do to the world. Even Osama bin Laden was a rich guy. It was like they were all staring straight into the sun.

"Honey," she said.

"What?"

"Try to relax, okay? I'm Facility staff, I rented this place. We get to do that with Pinecrest, it's, like, an understanding. They won't do anything. It's all just fine here."

"Right," he said.

"What do you want to do today, honey? We have our own day just for once, we can do anything we like. Hiking, or horseback riding . . ."

"No."

"We could go back inside and try out that big waterbed."

Van finished his beer. The pores had opened up all over him. He was never going to get any cleaner. All the lovemaking had reset Van's erotic dials to zero. He didn't want to stay around this place anymore. He was ready to put some clothes on and get something serious accomplished. "I've got a great idea," he told her. "Why don't we go see your work?"

"Okay. After lunch."

"Let's go."

"Derek, we're having shrimp bisque at the ranch house. With blackened tuna. Plus sautéed morels in truffle oil."

Well then. Maybe Dottie's plans would be pretty much okay.

After a sumptuous meal, while his gut was stuffed, his head was logy, and his temples were thudding with coffee, they returned to the Facility. Dottie took an electric cart up the mountain. It was icy, windy, and the air was impossibly thin, but there was a fantastic view. It was the basic business of observatories to have a fantastic view. This one was colossal.

Sex, food, and coffee had whipped his altitude sickness. With a sidelong grin at Dottie, Van left her and hauled himself hand-over-heel up the broken slope of a granite crag.

He needed to get up there in order to soak it all in. That massive sky. The upended bones of the Rockies were laced with racing clouds and their slope-sliding shadows. Wrinkled peaks dusted with white ice. The long run of green pines. Ancient brown landslides, with old miners' roads crumbled and vanishing. The blackened scars of small forest fires. From the Observatory, the Facility was entirely lost inside its trees: just an aerial, the crisp white rim of a satellite dish.

Hovering above the postcard scene was an airborne silver blob. It was an aerostat, on a long striped mooring line.

Van had noticed the airship at once, and Dottie had told him about it. This shiny ship was NORAD-surplus, some experimental barrage-balloon radar scheme that the military had never successfully put into operation. DeFanti had reworked the blimp scheme, trying to commercialize it, to repurpose satellite communications, just for local neighborhoods.

This wild notion had never caught on in the bigger world outside, but around here in the mountains, a little blimp with telecom aboard did make sense.

Pinecrest Ranch, the Facility, and all the smaller local ranches nearby were isolated. They were in a land of dark skies, in a federal area zoned for radio research since the 1940s. Antennas and cable TV were forbidden. So, if the weather permitted, then they could get some connectivity off a floating baby satellite, a cute little Mylar airship. It was technically sweet. A silvery floating jewel for the twenty-first century. A bold proof-of-concept. It was just the touch that this landscape needed.

Van's shame and despair had left him. In this huge American sky and these mountains, he found himself light-headed with a golden sense of the world's possibilities. He *did* like it up here, being with Dottie. It was great. If the stupid war would only end, and if he blew off a few personal bad habits, yeah, he could make a go of it, living up here. The mountains of the West would become his home. He could go native. He'd get barrel-chested, and tanned, with boot calluses on his soft hacker feet.

His son would grow up as a mountain boy. Ted would be a skier and a climber. He and Ted would be mountain rockhounds together. He'd get a rifle and a fly-fishing rod. He and Ted would hunt and hike and fish every weekend. Tents and campfires at night, maps and compasses. He would look the kid right in the face and tell him wise, fatherly things about the world. He would make up for everything he was failing to do, failing to give.

Dottie waved at him from below the crag, her words to him lost in the keen wind. Van climbed down to rejoin her. Dottie looked strange to him after his reverie. This dainty woman with straight brown hair and unplucked eyebrows, those lips that never wore lipstick. A thick denim shirt and jeans. She was the most precious thing in the world to him.

The telescope's round barn was big, but smaller than it looked in its publicity. The dome featured clamshell doors that opened to the zenith. The observatory rotated neatly on gimbals to track the moving sky. The structure had a strangely sleek, sporting-shoe look. It was like a gigantic shopping-mall kiosk.

Inside it was still and warm, for the walls were very thick, protecting their precious instrument like a foam cooler full of premium beer.

As an astrophysicist's husband, Van had visited more observatories than any man should ever have to. Van was used to the look of serious scientific instruments. He had never seen a telescope half this pretty. Big professional telescopes always looked frazzled, stuck-together, and one of a kind. Here, though, Van knew at once that he was standing in the presence of an old man's darling.

This telescope was polished and elegant, bejeweled with buttons, plugs, and switches, like a trophy wife at a Nobel Prize party. It—she—was five stories high. A towering complex of struts had delicately tapered arms painted in designer enamel. Her bottom was a great big mirror bowl of glassy blue hexagons in a green plastic case. All the joins and seams were suspiciously perfect. This telescope was like the Hubble's sexier little sister.

The objective of an "adaptive telescope" was to remove the twinkle from the stars. The instrument did that by reshaping the telescope's mirrors in real time, computer-corrected, flexing in subtle response, just as the atmosphere moved. This very cool idea had clearly caught DeFanti's technical fancy.

But—Van wondered—was it really necessary to neatly countersink all the bolts? Why was the scope's outer casing snapped together so seamlessly, like some bride in a posh limousine? Then there was the wiring. This telescope had a haywire Medusa wealth of wiring. She was screaming her torrid romance with the Internet.

In the mighty effort to bring her online, it looked like the local techs had subjected her to major cosmetic surgery, maybe two or three times. Every glass hexagon drooled out a black Niagara of electronic actuators. There were rafts and banks of fiber-optic lambda just lying there, seemingly abandoned. This baby had enough wiring for a Swiss atom-smasher. No wonder they loved her on TV.

"She's real cute," Van said aloud. His voice echoed from the vault. They were alone with this towering instrument, two human beings reduced to the size of Rocky Mountain marmots. Just this sleeping Bride of Science, her control consoles, a scattering of office chairs and wire-bound manuals, some dirty coffee cups and sleeping bags. Scientist clutter.

"They had real trouble with the original design," Dottie admitted. "Architects have such big egos. He didn't want any bunch of geeks telling him that ugly things work better sometimes." Dottie spread her hands. "So we're not Keck II or Mauna Loa, okay? But those materials are top-notch, really built to last. As for our bandwidth, well . . . This will be Internet2's only live cyber-observatory. Everything streaming in real time right over the NSF backbone. Tom DeFanti wanted every kid in every inner-city school to see the whole universe. If they couldn't see their sky any more because of all that city glare, well, he'd just give them the universe, free, by the Info Superhighway. And if Al Gore was President now . . . well, he probably could have got a lot of federal money for doing that."

"What gives with the bad wire job?"

"Oh, well, we call that our Bhopal problem. See, when the original contractors left, Tony hired all these cut-rate Indian engineers . . . They keep coming in here, running expensive tests, putting it online, taking it down again, and rewiring it . . . Nobody ever tried this before, they're fiddling with it day and night . . . He's not the world's greatest project manager, Tony."

"I never had Tony figured for that line of work."

"Getting this thing built, that was Tony's first big success for Tom DeFanti. It was practically impossible to build any telescope this close to federal parkland with all those regulations and endangered species rules, but . . . well, here it is, Tony arranged all that. Tony always hooks things up in such a clever, Tony-like way."

"Like he hooked up you and me," Van said.

She looked at him innocently. "What, honey?"

Van pretended interest in the complicated bulk of a diachronic beam-splitter. He had almost put his foot in it, right there. "Oh, yeah, Tony used to talk to me a lot about how he got on DeFanti's good side. This scope meant a lot to him."

"I found out how he managed all this, you know." She was proud. "See, Tony made good friends with all the people who really hated the project. They were mostly these hippie Green characters from Boulder, real not-in-my-backyard people. So Tony went to them, and he attended their meetings, and he gave them some of DeFanti's money, and he said to them, well, we'll just build it all Green! Everything Green! All renewable energy, everything recyclable, all local materials, and very organic. That was a lot less expensive than fighting their lawsuits. So, I live in, like, a real showpiece for Green construction methods. Most telescope facilities are like Sherpa camps compared to this place. Green people used to come up here in busloads just to gawk at us."

There was something else weighing on Dottie's mind. He could see it was something important. "So then what?" Van said.

Dottie shrugged. "So then, I guess they just got bored with us after a while. I mean, we're just a bunch of astronomers. Besides, our telescope isn't even up and running yet. We don't even have a proper PR department to do public outreach. I mean, I *am* the PR department now, basically. That's me."

"It's all right now? Those Greenies don't bug you anymore?"

"Oh, DeFanti gave them so much money that they put him on their board. They've got some really nice offices in Boulder now that were built by this same guy. He's a really famous Green architect now. They, like, love him in Holland."

Insight came to Van in a rush. Tony Carew had gamed the poor bastards. Tony had been their ruin. Because once upon a time, his enemy had been quick, and quiet, and probably always on time. A small, dangerous gang of Green fanatics. But with a warm smile and a big checkbook, Tony had lured them into the system. He made them get official and slow and bureaucratic, so that all these wild-eyed yarn-hat tree-huggers had to put on suits and ties, and play their office game, and totally lose their edge. Nothing left of their wild spirit now but their name and maybe their old logo . . .

Was Tony that smart? Yes, of course Tony was that smart. If Tony had the opportunity, if he found a way to angle it just right . . .

"What was Tony's angle in all this?" Van said.

"Well, DeFanti was just so thrilled. It was Tony's idea to name this place after DeFanti's real father, 'Alfred A. Griffith,' some totally obscure guy who died when DeFanti was seven. That was the best thing that ever happened to us astronomers. Tom DeFanti got this big reputation as this steward of the land . . . That was eight or nine years ago now. A major project like this takes a long time."

"Where were Tony's big bucks?"

"Do there have to be any big bucks? It's a telescope!"

Van tugged at his beard. "You know this is Tony Carew, right?"

Dottie winced. "Oh, honey, he's your best friend . . ."

"Yeah. I know. That's why I know all this stuff."

Dottie was hurt. She looked him in the eye and looked away. "Well, word does get around . . . I don't really know this for a fact, but . . ."

"But Tony had an angle," he said.

She lowered her voice. "Do you know about pipeline easements?"

"You mean like legal permission to lay fiber-optic? Yeah, sure."

"Well, Colorado passed a lot of Internet easements once. They were trying to wire up the rural part of the state, you know, equal access rights to the Info Superhighway, and all that. But then, a couple of years later, DeFanti got that law changed in the state legislature into *gas pipeline* easements. Just a word or two in some state committee, real quiet. Then came that big energy crunch in California. That huge natural gas shortage they had. There were some really big energy companies involved in that. Companies with really big friends."

Van grunted. The Grease Machine. Of course. There were only so many ways over the continental backbone of the Rocky Mountains. California's thirst for energy was colossal.

If you committted a corporate crime in a forest, and nobody knew it was there, was it even a crime at all? What if you turned right around and gave the cash to charity, like Carnegie did, or Rockefeller? The underprivileged kids of America, noses pressed to their computer screens so they could see their stars . . . Van paced around the telescope, silent, chin up. He stared up at every beam and bolt and crevice of the great machine. She looked so clean. So remote from earthly doings.

Van's footsteps echoed from the distant vault. This place was like an opera stage, and here, wired for sound, was the diva. Mondiale had spent billions laying fiber-optic easements across America. Out here, DeFanti found a quiet way to cross the Rocky Mountains, sliding through the wilderness, with a giant firehose of natural gas. Gas pipelines were notorious for exploding. Gas pipelines were very dangerous and dirty, never the kind of thing you could build right out in the open. But that infrastructure had to get built somehow. People needed the energy. Everybody happily used the gas pipes. Nobody faced up to the consequences. So the pipes got built by quiet operators. Guys like Tony. A guy who could do a little sleight-of-hand with those telescope mirrors and the all-natural windmills. Who would ever guess that building a telescope was all about natural gas?

Was he being too cruel, too suspicious? His work had changed him. All that dirty work on computer security, stuck inside some bombproof vault. Was he a professional paranoid now? Was he a mean bastard, because he'd spent so much time thinking about terrorists and crooks? Maybe he should have more trust for the motives of big business. Like those fine people of Enron, Arthur Andersen, Global Crossing, and his own beloved Mondiale.

Van rounded the telescope. He spoke to Dottie again. "These walls were built out of hay, right? Don't you worry about that?"

"It's strawbale, honey. Strawbale is very safe. When strawbale is packed down tight and walled off like this, it can't catch fire. Straw is very light, and it's Green and organic, and it's great insulation. A telescope spins to follow the stars, you know. This whole building spins just like a top."

He smiled briefly. "Then it's great."

"Everybody asks me that question, about the straw. That's my number one Frequently Asked Question. The straw is great, honey."

Dottie drove their electric buggy back to the Facility. Van found himself tired but clearheaded. That ugly failure at Cheyenne Mountain still rankled him, but the sting was fading. Yes, everybody he knew faced a compromise or two. Real life was never made of spun sugar.

Was it so bad that he'd blown it, trying to tackle some satellite's bureaucracy? Was it that bad that his best friend politically faked people out, so that he could sell them the power and energy those very same people had to have?

Then Dottie took Van into his element. The Facility's Network Operations Center was three stories high, glass-fronted, and nestled right into a cliff.

"We never thought we'd have so much telecom equipment in here," she told him. "Our architect built this place for our public relations people. This was supposed to become their office here, a kind of big tourist attraction, but . . ."

Van was thrilled. Every Internet2 office he'd ever seen was like a tomb compared to this fantastic place. It didn't even spoil his enjoyment that all the hardware was 1990s vintage. Cisco Catalysts, Juniper T640s, Force10s, and Chiaro optical switches . . . They were up and running, too, their fans were humming busily. They were dumping the power of hundreds of toasters into the February air. Van walked past a glass library of color-coded backup tapes. He skirted open metal cabinets, draped with thick gushes of fiber-optic cable.

"Over here"—Dottie beckoned—"there are stairs."

"Just a sec," said Van. He had discovered the local network technician on duty. The guy, an Indian, was wearing a bright polyester T-shirt, sky-blue jeans, and joggers. He had a thin hipster chin beard and was leafing through a magazine called *Stardust*.

He glanced up politely as Van approached him.

"So," said Van. "How's that big Code Red attack working out for you guys?"

"Oh, sir! Do I look worried?" The tech chuckled indulgently. "We're an OpenBSD shop here!"

Van's eyebrows rose. "Good man! Well then, how about those new RPC vulns?"

"Is just not a problem at all! Using 'nfsbug' and patched it all weeks ago."

"SNMP traps?"

"Oh, no, sir, for already we installed version three! We encrypted the protocol data unit, also!"

Van gazed at his new friend in deep satisfaction. "I don't suppose you guys have agent-based packet filtering yet."

The tech put his magazine down. " 'Agent-based packet filtering'? Isn't that a *theoretical* solution to attacks?"

"Not anymore," Van told him.

"Honey," Dottie objected, walking up.

"Should I know you?" said the tech. "I know your face, I think, sir."

"I'm Derek Vandeveer." Van stuck out his hand.

"You are *Van!*" shouted the tech, vaulting from his Aeron chair. "You are the *Van!* Oh, sir! This is such an honor." He ignored Van's offered hand and lunged straight for Van's shoes. He reverently brushed Van's Rockports with his fingertips. "Oh, sir, I'll never forget your paper on traceroute mapping."

"This is Rajiv," said Dottie as Rajiv stood back up. "Rajiv gets a little enthusiastic."

Rajiv placed his palms together, beaming. "Oh, Mrs. Vandeveer, I should have known this is him, your famous husband, here at last! Oh, what a joy to meet you, sir. That work with Grendel you have been doing. There's so much to discuss!"

Dottie's face wrinkled. She was "Dr." Vandeveer. She hated being called "Mrs." Vandeveer.

Van stroked his beard. "So, uh, tell me, would you be that guy, 'Rajiv23,' who posts on Alert Consensus List?"

"Oh yes sir, that is indeed me!" cried Rajiv, thrilled to be recognized. "And what a contribution you are making on that list, sir. I forward all your notes to the Bangalore Linux Group!"

"So will you be at Joint Techs this year?"

"Oh, of course I hope so, sir."

"Then let's have a beer, dude. We'll talk!" At Dottie's insistence, Van left him.

Dottie trotted up a set of stairs to the building's third floor, Van clomping behind her. She turned and frowned down at him. "I hope you don't mind me boring you to death with my little GRAPE-6 simulators."

"Oh, don't mind that guy, honey." Van was hugely pleased with himself.

"Derek, I get maybe forty-eight hours with you, and you would have talked to that man all day."

"He doesn't kiss like you do, baby." Van gave her a sharp pat on the rump. After a moment, Dottie laughed.

Upstairs, things were much busier. Dottie greeted half-a-dozen colleagues, but after scolding him for talking to Rajiv, she was much too sheepish to chat with them about her own work. She settled in next to a console. "I guess I shouldn't show this silly little thing to 'the Van,' but I've been working on this cluster simulation for four years."

"Honey, I always love your demos. Just run it."

"These GRAPE-6's were designed for n-body problems by a Japanese physics department. GRAPE, that means 'Gravity Pipe.' "

"Boot it up, sweetie, come on."

"We're directly integrating equations of motion into model globular cluster dynamics," Dottie said smoothly. "We've had n-body codes since the sixties, but we broke loose by an order of magnitude up here. These GRAPE cards do a hundred teraflops. I've got the rest of the system modeling stellar evolution and mass transfer. Oh, and collision models. If we get a cluster core collapse, then the collision model really gets hairy."

Van silently watched a black-and-white LOADING bar crawl across Dottie's screen.

"We're down to five or six simplifying assumptions now," Dottie said, "and we're spanning fourteen orders of magnitude, from the diameter of a neutron star to the size of the cluster itself . . . Okay, wait, here we go now."

Van stared at Dottie's screen, stunned. Of course he had seen Dottie's cluster simulations before. He could remember them from grad school, as crude little X's and O's crawling sluggishly around on a plain green screen. The thing he was looking at now was busier than a swarm of bees. There were stars inside Dottie's box, millions of stars. It looked for all the world like a Hubble photo, but alive. The stars were wildly churning in balletic interactions. Plunging. Knocking into each other. Doing orbital tangos. Looping, kissing, hovering.

The round cluster of stars was seething. It was boiling away like hornets at war. It took computers to prove that a jeweled globe of stars was unstable. In any telescope, a globular cluster looked as solid as a baseball, but it was a temporary enterprise. Stars tumbled into the core. They suffered unbearable close encounters there. They got slung like shot out of their family. They flew into the awesome darkness and solitude of intergalactic space.

The sight of it set the hair up all over Van's head. What if you were *living* around a star like that, thought Van, just living on some nice, sweet little planet. What if your daylight sky was boiling with neighboring suns as big as beachballs. And then, oh, my God, what if you flew too low and too close to one. In just a few dozen human lifetimes, the constellations would warp like putty. The heavens would turn against you and your world, and would blow you away at half the speed of light. You and yours, your innocent civilization, expelled into some unbearable icy exile, never to be retrieved.

"We call this process 'evaporation,' " Dottie said. "Sooner or later, all the stars have to leave the cluster family. Let me run you this other model, the one with the galactic tidal action."

This time the unhappy cluster was taken in hand by forces beyond its ken. What could a little cluster do in the horrendous grip of a superpower galaxy? Clusters were mere golden bubbles. Galaxies were vast flat saucers, cold, spinning, implacable. The uneven force of their gravity bent and tore at the bubbles. There was a mighty tide.

Van could see it. The attraction of the galaxy was too much for the globular cluster. The stars peeled loose, they struggled toward exile, clinging fitfully to one another. They were ripped out of the cluster in long trains of refugees. Some fell into the galaxy, alien migrants falling down from high off the plane, strangers from an angelic height, doomed to meet some alien fate. The broken cluster, wrecked into mere rags of gas and dust, hung there, half obliterated . . .

"We're talking twenty orders of temporal magnitude here," Dottie told him. "Two neutron stars have a close passage in milliseconds. But the death of a globular cluster . . ."

"They die?" Van said.

"Of course they die, honey. All stars die. So do all clusters. But here"—she waved at the screen—"my clusters don't die quite properly. The universe is only thirteen billion years old, so I don't have any good observed case studies for a cluster's late-period dynamical interaction. I'm pushing at the limit of this instrument. I'm going thirty billion years into the future."

"Oh."

"I mean, those numerical errors do accumulate, when I do that."

"Oh, yeah."

"I really have to fight with that problem," Dottie said. "Thirty billion years, it'll take me quite a while to push that. A long time, maybe. Maybe the rest of my life."

Van patted her shoulder. "Baby, honey, you're doing just great!"

After a fabulous Szechuan dinner, they took Ted with them for the last night at their Pinecrest love nest. Van was no longer impressed by the place. There was something comical and squalid about this aging zillionaire's bachelor pad.

The place was not childproofed. Ted had to live inside his stroller and pen. This was not any kind of home for the three of them, a place like this. Their lives had gone wrong. His wounded pride had stopped hurting now, but he'd made some kind of serious misstep. He could feel it in his bones.

At two in the morning, Ted's whimpering woke him. Van got up and stalked across the floorboards. "We're gonna let your mom sleep this time," he told the baby. He changed Ted's diapers and stuffed him into his walker. Ted had a nifty walker that Van had shipped to him in a lonesome moment. It was made of cool cast-plastic, a toddler's bumper car.

Ted was clearly thrilled to be up with his dad after midnight inside a brightly lit bathroom. Ted's mother always made Ted sleep, but here Ted was finally getting to do what Ted most ached to do in the wee hours of the morning. Ted wanted to hurl himself around the room with a clash of plastic wheels, gurgling with glee, little arms slapping like pinwheels, a string of eager drool hanging from his chin.

Van would be back in Washington by nightfall. He would be forced to tell Jeb that his KH-13 misadventure had gone bust with the Space Force at Cheyenne Mountain. He'd wasted his time, wasted valuable resources . . . To make up for it, he'd have to work twice as hard on the Virginia summit, really dig deep into the rabbit hat . . . Van looked at himself in the mirror, leaning close to take it in without his glasses. He had been a damned fool.

He tiptoed away as Ted cooed and burbled. He silently fetched his backpack from the foot of Dottie's bed. He returned to the bathroom with the jet-black SWAT knife.

He couldn't fly back to Washington with this throat-cutting pig-sticker. Airport security would go nuts over it. But he'd bought it. It was his. It was stupid to not find some kind of use for it.

Van grabbed a thick mess of beard and had at it. The knife went through his bristles like they were cotton candy.

Six minutes later Van was looking at his bare face while Ted happily sucked on and spat a loose fistful of his beard. The SWAT knife was beyond razor-sharp. It had taken his beard off like a laser. He had thin little paper-cut nicks here and there. No wonder Hickok swore by this knife. Hickok knew his stuff about SWAT weapons. The knife was a jewel.

Van hadn't shaved his beard in years. His damp, sleek rubbery face had the pale, surprised look of a shaved head.

Next morning Dottie stared at him in astonishment. "Oh, honey," she shrieked, "Oh, look at you! Oh, honey bear, you look so young!"

This wasn't the response he'd expected. "Young"? His plan was to lose the goofy hacker beard and look more like a serious Washington professional. "Young"? What about his nose? His nose had grown three sizes overnight.

Dottie was experimentally kissing parts of his face that had not been kissed in ages. Bare skin reacted in startled pleasure.

"Oh, honey, you look so handsome this way. You look so clean. Look at Daddy, Teddie!"

Worn out by his 3:00 A.M. adventures, Ted was fast asleep.

"You like it?" Van said.

"It's different . . . Of course I like it. I married you, didn't I? Change is good sometimes."

"I don't know what they'll make of this, back at my work."

"Honey . . ." Dottie paused. "If you only knew what your face looks like, when you talk about your work now."

"What do you mean?"

"Derek, those people are *torturing* you. It just hurts me so much. I don't like these people in Washington. I don't like this administration, I don't like this stupid War on Terror . . . I can't even bear to read the newspapers now. They're not our kind of people."

"Now what?" Van said. "What do you mean?"

"Honey, you don't have to go back to them. You know? You don't have to go back to the war, honey. You can stay right here and live with me. Derek, you hate that kind of work. Security work is ugly, dirty work. Sweetheart, maybe I didn't say this before but . . . things are going *really well* for me up here. In most campuses, the astronomy people are looking at those awful new budget problems. Nobody's ever seen it that bad . . . But up here, I have only one problem. I have no Derek Vandeveer."

"Huh," said Van. "Wow."

"We won't have those huge amounts of money anymore, like we did when you were VP. But that only got us in trouble anyway. Derek, you would do great up here. They'll let you use all the network hardware. You can do all those cool, fun computer-science things you really wanted to do. Like, you can finish your paper on Ramsey theorems. No boss and no schedules, honey. You would be so *happy.*"

"Do I look so sad to you now?"

"Honey, it is written all over your face! I can *see* your face now. I haven't seen you without a beard in, what, four years? You cut it for my mother's funeral."

"Oh, yeah," said Van. "That's right."

Dottie wiped at her eyes. "People don't have to *choose* to have bad lives that we hate. You're such a wonderful person, Derek. You're a good, clean, strong person who means well and has a huge gift . . . There's nobody in that government who is a decent person like you are . . ." She was sobbing. "I want you to come and live with me, Derek. I'm so sick and tired of living alone."

Van sat on the bed. His soul was flapping like a blown sail. "Oh, Dottie."

"I have a right to you. I'm your wife. Why should we neglect each other? I want you to come live with me. We could have another baby. They didn't draft you. You're not in any uniform. Why don't you just do it?"

"I have a title," Van said. "I get paid. They trust me."

"You hate that work. It's changing you. You should see what you look like when you're trying to talk about it. Your eyes get so hard and cold. Your face gets sour . . . You look like a big dog guarding the world's last bone."

Van did not take this as an insult. He recognized the truth in what Dottie was telling him. He had the kind of face that cops often had. Cops were people who were never just freely happy to see you. Even if they were nice guys, and many cops were, they always, always had to give you that guardian look first, to size you up to see if you were dangerous, or armed, or insane. He'd seen that guard-dog look on the faces of a hundred people in the Vault, and now, yes, he had it, too. He had it because he deserved it. He had earned that face. He had it because he was one of them.

"Honey," he said, "there's a lot to what you say. I know that. But I can't just leave. There's a real big deal coming up in Virginia . . . Jeb says . . . well, Jeb says a lot of things . . . but if that all goes well, then it will all be worth it."

"What about us? I want you to live here."

"It was just a staff job," Van told her. He was really talking to himself. "I never told Jeb I'd make it my career. Even Jeb's post isn't full-time. We were just supposed to . . . paper over the cracks until we can establish solid policy guidance and add permanent structure at a federal level, hopefully cabinet level."

"Derek, I never heard you talk like that before. Not when we were happy."

"Well, that's how they have to talk." Van groaned. "Honey, I know that I'm overdoing it. I need you to tell me when I go off the rails. When you're not there for me, yeah, the inside of my head gets pretty strange."

The suite's phone rang discreetly. Van's limo had arrived.

Van dug hastily inside his survival backpack. "I'll miss my plane in Denver if I don't leave right now. But here. I need you to hold on to some things for me. Take this hunting knife. Oh, and take this ray gun."

Dottie gripped the ray gun's cord. "You really carried this thing around with you, Derek?"

"All over. I need it to solder," Van told her. "It makes a great office paperweight, too. But they're so dumb on planes now that they won't even let me take a thing that *looks* like a gun. And that bad gig I just did with the Space Force . . . well, I can't tell you about that. But I wasn't happy with that. That really backfired, it was so bad . . . It took me weeks to work on that, and I pulled in help from everyone I knew, but, yeah, you're right, Dottie. I can't fight with you about that. It would have been a hell of a lot better for everybody, everybody in the whole world, if I had just stayed here with you. Maybe watching some sci-fi on TV. Eating that venison sausage. With that cantaloupe. That stuff was great."

"They don't have any TV here."

"That would have been even better. Some Bollywood movies with the venison sausage, yeah, I want that. I do."

She threw her slender arms around him. "We had a great time, didn't we?"

"Aw, Dots, it was such a honeymoon. It was just so great. I just wanted more and more. Someday, someday real soon now."

"I'll come see you in Virginia."

"You send me some e-mail."

Van made the mistake of reading his e-mail in the Denver airport. He'd granted himself just three days out of the loop, one brief human chance to eat, and sleep, and maybe kiss his life's companion. Three days, and the CCIAB's office came right apart. It was like reaching out in a blackout to touch a spitting high-power wire.

Jeb had forwarded a first-class flame from some Pentagon rat inside the Joint Chiefs. General Wessler hadn't signed off on this bureaucratic nasty-gram himself. Wessler wasn't the kind of guy to be that dumb. Van knew that it had Wessler's fingerprints, though.

Stingingly, the complaint didn't even mention Van by name. It was all about "two self-appointed technicians from the so-called Transformational Communications Architecture Office." Van found himself described as "some know-it-all Beltway buffoon" and "that Ivy League professor in his beard and beret." A *beret,* for God's sake?

Most of the rest of Van's e-mail centered on the CCIAB's Virginia event. This was quickly taking on the proportions of a major crisis. The CCIAB was quickly running out of time and leeway.

The CCIAB might be one place where the buck stopped, but they were too small and too temporary to function in the long term. Even the National Security Council was not big enough to run the giant federal government. The NSC just talked to the people, who talked to the people, who ran the federal government. Very soon, fatally soon, the CCIAB would be facing the fate of a million other small blue-ribbon boards and small federal advisory committees. Deliver, and die.

Jeb had bet the farm on this battle in Virginia. It was going to be the CCIAB's Bull Run and Gettysburg all at once.

Strapped like a bondage victim in his narrow tourist-class seat at thirty thousand feet, Van was grim. He never asked Tony Carew for favors, but now his situation was hitting the fan. In pulling Tony, he was going to be pulling his last trump.

Tony's ever-eager answering service, a voice-mail jail full of sexy robots, told him that Tony was in Taipei. Van tugged at the aircraft's phone wire and persisted.

When Van finally managed to appear at Tony's ear, Tony was very tolerant about it. Jet lag never bothered Tony. Tony was even elated.

The reason for this soon came up. The Indian girlfriend had just fled from Tony's hotel suite. Tony was insanely thrilled by her visit. Somehow, against all odds, Tony had stolen her from her watchful family in Bombay for one secret, rapturous night, with just the two of them, and none of her relations, servants, managers, or groomers. Tony couldn't have been prouder if he had magically raised the *Titanic.*

Tony granted Van his favor without a second thought. Then he went right back to chew and jaw on his obsession.

It sure mattered a whole lot to Tony that this girlfriend of his was supposedly "the world's most beautiful woman." Van scowled. After hearing from Dottie about it, Van had changed his mind about

Tony's infatuation. Dottie was right, she was always the voice of good sense. This was not a healthy relationship for Tony, this goofy long-range romance with the constant travel. Tony needed to settle down with a woman that he could depend on.

Why was Tony missing the obvious truth about her? His girl-friend was a movie star from a foreign country. It wasn't her business to really care about Tony Carew. If he ever went broke, if he ever got sick, that little fortune hunter would be gone from his life like a shot.

Tony ranted on, tirelessly. Van finally excused himself and hung up. He waited ninety seconds, slid a different credit card through the phone, and called Michael Hickok's cell phone.

"I'm up in a plane," he told Hickok.

Hickok dropped his cell phone with a clatter. Van heard drunken giggling in the background. Hickok scrabbled the phone up. "Gimme a break. I'm with a lady friend and I'm not even wearing pants."

Over the roar of the plane's engines, the giggles sounded a lot like Fawn Glickleister. At least, Van hoped it was Fawn. It was pretty hor-rible to think that two women in the world would both giggle like that, and that Michael Hickok would sleep with both of them.

"Mike, you're a pilot, right?"

"I've got a pilot's license," Hickok said, yawning. "That don't make me Top Gun."

"Okay, you remember that AFOXAR device we were working on? The hijacker interface that overrides and controls private jets?"

"I thought you blew that off, Van. You and your big fat boss can't afford to rent any big fat private jet for your big fat shindig in Vir-ginia."

"I just found a friend who will loan me his big fat jet."

"Oh," Hickok concluded. "So that would be different."

"Now I need some guy who can fly a Boeing Business Jet, from the ground, with that little joystick."

Hickok chuckled richly. "Hey, you just found your man!"

"Can you pick me up at Dulles tonight? I've got to stop by my apartment on the way to the Vault."

"What, you mean right now? I've gotta drive some more? I just got here! I broke speed laws in fifteen states!"

"I get in at nine," Van said. "If you're still busy, bring Fawn with you."

Hickok slapped his cell phone shut with a flat plastic clack.

Van's flight arrived late due to weather. Hickok was waiting, and he stared right past him.

Van tapped Hickok's shoulder.

"Whoa! Van! Where's the beard?"

Van shrugged.

Hickok squinted. "You gotta do something serious about that long-ass hair now, Professor. You look like the jumbo version of the Little Dutch Boy."

Hickok hated leaving his Humvee parked outside Van's Washington apartment. The Humvee was a military super-jeep, but Hickok, with a Southern-boy pride in his wheels, hated the thought of its paint job ever coming to harm.

"I can't believe you live around here," Hickok groused. "There's hookers around here. There's crack gangs!"

"I'm a security expert," said Van. He avoided a splatter of vomit on his stairs.

"Like what, so that makes my car safer?"

Van pulled his keys. But the door of his apartment opened at a touch. "Oh, Lord," he blurted.

The lamp was lit. Van looked around. Nothing obvious was missing. There wasn't much in the apartment to lose.

The keyboard of his Linux machine had been pried open.

"They're still in here!" Hickok said tautly.

The door of Van's bathroom swung out. A stranger stepped out with a gun. Van was astounded. When leveled at his own chest, the black barrel of a pistol looked as cavernous as a garage.

Van had no idea who this intruder was, but he instantly recognized the handgun as a seven-shot, all-electronic, Australian-made O'Dwyer VLE. A really nice gun. A great gun. A real beauty.

How could he get killed by some device that he had once taken apart with his own hands?

"Yo, Fred!" said Hickok, his deep voice squeaking just a little. "Long time no see!"

"Reach for the sky," Fred ordered.

Hickok only laughed. "I'm not packing any heat. You're packing heat in here, Fred?"

"I'm on assignment," Fred said defensively.

"You have any idea who you're aiming to shoot here? This guy is from the National Security Council! Dr. Derek Vandeveer, this would be Mr. Federico Gonzales. Old war buddy of mine."

Gonzales scowled. "Why the hell did you have to tell this chump my name?"

"We're supposed to be all on one side in the War on Terror, aren't we? You let me know if you changed sides, Fred."

"Nope," said Fred. He kept the pistol steady, though, and he spoke from the side of his mustached lip. "You might as well come out now, kid."

A second burglar emerged from Van's bathroom. He was tall, stooped, and thin as whipcord. He wore black-rimmed glasses, and had a military haircut. The "jarhead" look. Brown fringe on top, white sidewalls all around.

The second burglar carried a black plastic impact-resistant toolbox in one big hand.

"Hey, you guys are AFOCI," Van realized, recognizing the hardware.

"No, sir, I'm William C. Wimberley."

"But that's an AFOCI toolbox," Van insisted. "I helped to vet that thing."

"Air Force Office of Cyber Investigation," Hickok clarified. "The AFOCI boys are in and out of the professor's office all the time."

"We're not AFOCI," said Gonzales. "I heard of 'em, though."

"We're Cyberspace Force," said Wimberley.

"Okay, maybe he's in Cyberspace," said Gonzales hastily. "That doesn't mean I have to be in any damn Cyberspace."

"You just installed an AFOCI keyboard bug inside my Linux box," said Van, staring at Wimberley.

"Okay, yeah, fine," Wimberley told him. "Maybe I did that. Why should you care? You would never have known about that."

"Who the hell do you think you're talking to? Of course I would have known!"

"Nobody ever looks inside their keyboards," said Wimberley with a sneer. He was very young. "Not even you, Professor. I know who I'm talking to here, okay? If I hadn't pled out, you would have testified at my trial!"

Van stared at him. Wimberley looked vaguely familiar, but only vaguely. "So what was your handle?"

"Bionic Ninja of 214."

An anklebiter. "What, you were like fifteen back then?"

"Sixteen," Wimberley said. "The Secret Service broke into my parents' house. My mom never got over that. She still takes Prozac. All just because I borrowed a little long distance from your sad-ass phone company that just lost forty-five billion dollars!"

Van took a sorrowful breath. "The Air Force didn't mind your rap sheet?"

"The modern United States military loves troubled, aggressive young men with high IQs," Wimberley told him. He had a settled voice and a lethal stare.

With an effort, Van stopped his knees from shaking. The hell of it was that Wimberley's bug would have worked. Of course Van would never have looked inside his own keyboard, and the tiny device would have been silently beaming every keystroke he made to some monitoring station blocks away.

"Look, I'm NSC, and I know something about your so-called outfit. The U.S. Space Force can't just start up a 'Cyberspace Force' on its own get-go. They've got no policy guidance from the top."

Gonzales weighed in suddenly. "The Space Force are the only service branch that can run mil-spec cyber-security," he recited. "No other military outfit has the extensive computer networks or the time-tested technical skills."

"Are you nuts?" said Van. "The Space Force is supposed to run satellites! That's got nothing to do with viruses or DOS attacks! The guys tasked with defending military systems are the Computer Network Defense Joint Task Force over at DISA."

"Who's Deeza?" said Wimberley. "I never heard of 'em."

"They've been at the job since 1998!"

Hickok was even more skeptical. "Look here, kid, there ain't no such thing as 'cyberspace'!"

"There is if we say there is," insisted Wimberley.

"But why did you come here to my place?" Van said. He was genuinely baffled.

"I hate to break the news to you, Professor, but information warfare happens inside people's computers! And you, you're trying to sabotage a mission-critical eighteen-billion-dollar satellite project! You don't think important people are gonna notice about that? We know what you're up to."

Alarmed, Van turned to Hickok. Hickok just shrugged. " 'Important people,' he says."

"You're a left-wing professor from Stanford," Wimberley amplified. "You're a peacenik."

" 'Left-wing'?" said Van, stunned. " 'Peacenik'? I just had lunch with Paul Wolfowitz!"

"Your wife is in the antiwar movement," said Wimberley. "She was Eastern Seaboard Coordinator for Physicists for Social Responsibility!"

"Dottie is from *Massachusetts*!" Van said, outraged. "They're all like that up there!"

Wimberley stared back at him. "Don't you ever Google yourself? It's written all over you. Look at that hair and those clothes."

"And that's supposed to give you some kind of right to Watergate my apartment?" Van blurted.

"Oh, yeah," said Wimberley. "It generally does."

"Nobody ever catches us," said Gonzales, shifting his shining handgun and looking at his wristwatch. "You're supposed to be way off in another state. We're supposed to be long gone from here by now."

"Yeah," said Wimberley, hefting his case. "We kinda need to be going right now."

"Hold on," said Van. "I just happen to be the Deputy Technical Director of the CCIAB."

"So what?" said Wimberley. "I never heard of them either."

"So I built you that burglar case, you sorry little punk! There's no way you're just walking out of here when you just broke into my own house and tapped my own computer with my own hardware!"

Wimberley set the heavy plastic case by his feet and folded his long, wiry arms. "What are you gonna do about it, Dr. Superspy? Call the cops on me?"

"I've got a gun right here," Gonzales bargained hopefully.

Hickok chuckled. "Aw, come on, Fred."

"If you want these cyberweapons," said Wimberley, putting his boot on the case, "then you're gonna have to *take them away from me.*"

Blood rushed hotly to Van's face. "You don't think I could do that?"

Wimberley laughed in scorn. "Let me put you in touch with reality! I'm not some make-believe warfighter, like you are. I enlisted, dude. I am tomorrow's cyber-military. You're just some flabby-ass civilian professor from some failed telecom company. Plus, you're ten years older than me. So if you attempt to confiscate my weapons here, I will kick your fat ass right up between your shoulders."

"You are out of your mind," Van told him. "You're some nutcase punk who called himself 'Bionic Ninja.' I outweigh you by fifty pounds. Plus, this is *my house!*"

Wimberley turned to Gonzales. "The hippie here is hallucinating. I think maybe you'd better just shoot these guys."

Gonzales snorted. He thumb-jacked the magazine out of his pistol and threw it to Hickok. Hickok, ever-alert, snatched the bullet clip right out of midair.

Gonzales sat down cozily in Van's magnesium chair. "Do I look that stupid?" he announced. "One bullet, two bullets, that's not even gonna slow this dude here down. Because, boys, this dude here is Air Force Special Operations, just like me. Mike Hickok and me, we are always 'The First Ones There'!"

Hickok burst into laughter. He sat on Van's stained and ragged couch, with a loud thrum of broken springs. "Aw, come on, Fred, this is D.C., man. This is some guy's apartment!"

Gonzales put both his elbows on his knees. "The way I see it, these candy-ass computer geeks have got a score to settle."

"You're right," Van said. The words startled him as they hit his own ears, but then he realized that he meant them. Rage rumbled through his chest like a rolling cannonball. He was in deadly earnest.

Hickok coughed into his fist. "Van, sit down. Let 'em both go. It's all some big mistake."

"Your friend Fred here can go if he wants," Van said. "I didn't build him that O'Dwyer pistol. That intrusion case though. That tool case is mine."

Wimberley took off his black-rimmed glasses and set them on a table at the foot of Van's lamp. "I can see that I've got to kick this guy's ass now," he announced. He put one fist inside another and loudly cracked his knuckles. "This won't take long." He looked at Hickok and Gonzales. "I just don't want to see you two snake-eater boys start crying about this, or anything."

"Are we gonna cry, Mike?" Gonzales asked Hickok.

"You ever see me cry, Fred? We were in Bosnia damn Herzegovina." Hickok's face was alight with a greed for battle. "My cybergeek is gonna wipe the floor with your cybergeek."

"No way, homey."

"Yes way. Because he is smarter, man. My computer geek is like ten times smarter than your geek."

Gonzales barked with laughter. "What the hell difference does his brain make?"

Van took his glasses off and set them aside. He tried to stare into Wimberley's eyes. Without his glasses, the enemy's eyes were two distant brown blurs.

Wimberley's first swing was a contemptuous slap. The slap was a spiritual experience. In one Zen instant, it found the black fury that lived within Van and brought it to roaring life.

Van lunged forward. The flying impact of his body knocked Wimberley straight backward and into the magnesium chair. Gonzales leapt free of it, hunched and dodging, and the beautiful chair went legs-up and buckled, with an expensive crunch.

Van was suddenly gasping for air. Something had plunged deep into his gut. It was Wimberley's boot. The kid scrambled nimbly back to his feet. Quick, hot impacts. One in the eye. One in the forehead.

Van got a clawing hand into his enemy's collar and slung him headlong into the room's single lamp. The lamp tumbled and the room went dark.

Van clenched his fists and swung at empty air. Suddenly the enemy was on his back, leaping on him from behind. Van stumbled backward, smashing his assailant against the wall. Wimberley wheezed. Van tore a choking elbow loose from his throat. Wimberley's shoes scraped the wall, and with a powerful kick, he heaved them both away. Van stumbled and tottered off balance, groping wildly. He plummeted. He crashed suddenly, blindingly, smashingly, into the sharp, rigid corner of his computer table. He felt his whole skull cave in. His mouth flooded instantly with blood.

With a bestial roar he lurched upright. Wimberley stumbled, scrambling in darkness. Van kicked his legs from under him, clamped a hand on Wimberley's scrawny neck, and smashed his head against the floor. The whole building shook. Wimberley emitted a desperate, catlike squall.

Van sank a knee into his enemy's guts and hammered his skull with a fist.

Wimberley went limp.

There was a sullen sound of liquid dripping.

The overhead light came on.

Wimberley's unconscious face was spattered in blood.

"Get up, Van, Jesus, he's out cold."

"He's bleeding," Van mumbled. A piece of his tooth fell out.

"No, man, *you* are bleeding. You are bleeding all over him. Jesus, what happened to your face?"

Van put his hand up. He could not feel the shape of his mouth. His cheek. It was all gone. There was nothing there but a nightmare patch of bloody mush.

Things were lively at the local emergency room. A man who had merely had his face smashed in had to sit down and take a number.

Van held his iced towel against the ruins of his face. He could not touch the damage there without mind-bending pain and a sense of deep, cosmic, nightmare terror. He hadn't merely lost some of his teeth. He had fractured, really smashed, the inner structure of his skull. The gaping wound wasn't about to stop bleeding. The staffers were calling around for a specialist surgeon.

The young woman sitting next to Van had red, staring eyes and dirty blond dreadlocks soaked in drying blood. Gore had soaked the shoulders of her white Guatemalan blouse. Blood had spattered her broomstick skirt.

"Hey, friend," she said to him. "What's your affinity group?"

Van moaned, his tongue thick with blood.

The girl opened a woven yarn-bag covered with leftist political buttons. She dug in her bag and retrieved a small digital videocam. "So, you were outside the World Bank with us, right? Did they come after you with those horses?"

Van said nothing.

"That's when I caught it, from the horses. I sure hope somebody puts all that up on Indymedia. Did anybody tape you? I mean, when the pigs hit you?"

Van shook his head minimally.

The bleeding girl looked around the chaos in the emergency room. It looked like a campground for derelicts. "I wonder where they put the rest of us. We can't be the only ones."

A wave of blackness coursed through the rupture in Van's head. He blinked in silent agony.

"Your eyes look nice," she told him. "You didn't get pepper-gassed."

Van nodded behind his blood-soaked towel.

"I'm gonna have to get stitches," said the bleeding girl. "They're gonna shave off my hair. But, friend, I don't feel scared anymore. I just don't feel scared of those warmongers. Because the power is in the streets now, man. I can feel the power." She squeezed Van's loose hand, warmly. "Our streets, okay, brother? Our streets! They can bust my head, they can bust your head, but they can't bust everybody's head. Pretty soon America will wake from this nightmare. The corporate media lies, man! They all *lie!*"

Van shifted his towel. Some ghastly crust parted stickily into the fabric. The icy numbness came alive with a flare of deep, burning pain.

"You know why I feel so happy now?" said the injured girl. "Because there weren't any *chemtrails* today. I checked again and again. I looked up at the sky and it was clean! No more chemicals up there! So they're just plain running out of whatever that bad stuff is, that's what I think. That poison that keeps the people so passive."

Van's eyes blurred over. He was suffering double vision. Double vision had never happened to him before. Now he understood why people talked about it so much.

"After 9/11 there weren't any jet trails up there for *three whole days,*" the girl insisted shrilly. "Not one jet trail across all of America! What does *that* tell you, huh? Wow, just *think* about what that means!"

A nurse slid her face in Van's field of view. "You're Dr. Vandeveer? Yes?" She slid a blood-pressure cuff over his arm. "We've got to move you now. I think we've found you that ambulance."

CHAPTER ELEVEN

Van was in a hospital bed, confronting his e-mail. His damaged face was hot and stretched. The flesh felt rubbery. An inflated tire, a Macy's blimp. There was a very thin strip of surgical steel, securing the ruins of his left canine and bicuspid. His aching tongue could not stay away from that wire. It was like a steel I-beam installed in his head.

Dottie had written him such a brave letter. Dottie was apologizing to him for daring to be so lonely and unhappy. She was promising to do better. She said that she was proud of him.

As sedatives coursed through his flesh, Van read his wife's electronic sentences over and over. For the first time in his life, he could literally hear Dottie's spoken voice behind her blurry pixels. Van thumbed his way back to the top of the screen again. Some indescribable comfort was seeping into him. In real life, Dottie would not have repeated the same consoling words to him, over and over again, one hundred slow, blurry times. A man in a hospital needed that.

Of course, he hadn't yet typed one word to Dottie about getting his face smashed in. What was he going to tell her? What if somebody else told her about it first?

He had just gone through a violent, crazy, amazingly painful ordeal, all for the sake of some wild notion . . . so useless, something utterly stupid . . . Van turned his aching face toward the black plastic case of spy tools.

Van's burgled apartment was not a safe place to leave a top-secret infowar tool case. So, despite the surprised protests of doctors and nurses, the hardware was still with Van. The case was locked to Van's iron hospital bed frame with a laptop security cable. Come and take it, if you dare.

Van had beaten the living daylights out of another American in order to control the tools. Van sank his swollen head into the small, sterile pillow. His face had been smashed in by a computer security policy war. Why not some kind of real shooting war, for heaven's sake? He wouldn't feel half so bad if he'd been mangled while fighting with al Qaeda.

Van slid his tongue along the luscious edge of that steel wire inside his head. He was never in his life ever going to fight al Qaeda. Van knew that perfectly well now. Cyber-security was all about computer policy. Infowar was a form of war for high-tech people sitting quietly at desks. Bin Laden didn't surf the net. Al Qaeda were Third World fanatics on low-tech bicycles who talked only to their mullahs and their cousins. Al Qaeda guys got recruited in madrassas and sent to live in Pakistani slums and Afghan villages. They were bitter, freaked-out, culture-shocked men. They existed in such a frenzy of rage and wounded pride that suicide was a blessed relief to them. Being a martyr was so much, much better than being al Qaeda that they leapt at a chance to explode themselves in the midst of much happier people. "We long for death more than you long for life." That was their bumper sticker.

Terrorists didn't fight wars. The whole point of terrorism was to kick a government so hard, in so tender and precious a spot, that the government went nuts from rage and fear. Then the machinery of civilization would pour smoke from the exhaust. It would break down. Back to the tribes and the sermons, the blessed darkness of a world without questions.

Van looked at the chained black case. So it did matter. Cyberwar had always been about Americans and what Americans chose to do with their tools. Van knew that it mattered, because all he had to do was imagine himself losing the fight. Suppose that Wimberley broke into the hospital room and tried to take the case again. Would Van lie back with a ruined smile this time, let the hardware go? No. Not at all. Van would yank the intravenous feed from his arm, jump up, and fight all over again.

After all, he had won. Maybe no one knew how, why, or what the real reasons were, but so what? The world was full of humiliating, secret battles. Van had won in front of witnesses who were used to secret fights. No substitute for victory. He was woozy and scarred in a Washington hospital, but somewhere, a rogue operative had been dragged back to some lair with the crap beaten out of him by a computer-science professor. Message sent. Let's roll.

Van rubbed one-handed at his crusty eyes. He slid sideways into a twilight sleep.

When he woke the anesthetics had faded. His broken skull smoldered like a fire in a coal mine. Every scrap of flesh, once cold and rubbery, was burning briskly.

Dr. Mukherjee was the young surgeon on the night shift who had rebuilt Van's face. Mukherjee had luminous eyes, slender wrists, and a sweet smile full of unfeigned doctorly kindness.

Mukherjee set his transparent clipboard aside. He probed the interior of Van's mouth with his white-gloved fingers. "There is no sign of infection," he reported, staring intently and feeling his way over the aching pulp. "The facial bones will knit quickly in a man who is so fit." The latex-coated fingers left Van's mouth. Mukherjee gave Van's solid left bicep a reassuring pat. "You are military, eh? A training accident."

Van grunted. His pulpy gums were blazing with pain.

Dr. Mukherjee nodded knowingly. "Demerol." Mukherjee made a note on his clipboard with the gleaming steel of a Rotring ballpoint. "Your blood pressure is too high for a young man. You should go fishing, eh? Take leave for a while. Relax."

Van moved his shoulders to suggest a shrug. He was sore from kicks and punches in his back and gut. The spreading bruises from those wallops were nothing compared to his broken head, though.

"We will discharge you tonight. The breaks were clean and the ducts were not severed. New bone will grow through the bone cement. In a month, the steel comes out. That's a walk-in procedure."

Van realized that he was being told amazingly good news. Face smashed in, yet he was out of the hospital in one day. Should he feel grateful?

"You will need tomography," said Dr. Mukherjee. "The roots of the teeth, there I cannot tell you. I'm a maxillofacial surgeon. I'm not an orthodontist."

"Mmmph."

"You need to see an orthodontist, Mr. Vandeveer. In your later life, you might spend much time with orthodontists." Dr. Mukherjee delicately turned a sheet of hospital paper. "If you were not American . . . or if you lived thirty years ago, which is to say the same thing . . . then you would have been badly disfigured last night. Yes, marked for life. Very unfortunate. But not today. No. Today you will be fully restored to quite normal appearance. They do wonderful things with teeth now. Although the lip, the lip concerns me."

Van's split and stitched upper lip no longer felt like part of him. It belonged to some distant, remote, legendary being. The Michelin Man, maybe.

"You will lisp," said Dr. Mukherjee. "For a while. You might lisp *quite* a while."

Van nodded silently.

"There will be scarring. Cosmetic surgery is a possibility. Or you might grow a beard, sir. A beard would look good on you, I think."

Fawn brought him flowers.

"Nobody knows about what happened," she assured him. "I mean, okay, Mike Hickok knows. So I know. And those two tough guys in your apartment, they must have got a real shock. Because you beat his ass up!" Fawn's eyes shone with sincere secretarial pride. "That was just so awesome. Wow! I told everybody that you fell down the stairs. Was that okay?"

Van typed and showed Fawn the screen of his laptop.

THAT SHOULD WORK

"You look better than I expected. That must really hurt a lot, though."

Van spread his hands. The pain of healing was different from the shocking, heart-thudding pain of being wounded. Pain made him simpleminded and sentimental. It made him wildly, totally impatient.

"I brought you a good book to read. I know it can get pretty boring in a hospital."

Fawn offered Van a paperback. Van took it. An embedded needle twinged in his left forearm. Fawn's book was an obscure, Czech-printed, English-language paperback edition of some plays and essays of Vaclav Havel. To judge by the smashed spine and dog-eared pages, it had spent hard time in the bottom of a student's backpack.

Somehow this ludicrously crushed and smashed book gave Van a warm, grateful feeling. This artifact was so much worse off than he was.

Fawn blinked behind her glasses. "I spent a lot of time in hospitals when I was like sixteen, seventeen. I mean, a *lot* of time. That used to drive my dad nuts. Even my mom freaked out, and she was, like, used to our health problems."

Van put Fawn's book on the steel roller-tray next to his bowl of mush.

"When I got better, I made my parents send me to Prague. Because I heard that Prague was like the coolest place to get away from your crazy parents. Well, Prague was cool, but I was never a cool person. I did make this one cool friend there though. My friend Eva. She's Czech. Eva knew my dad, so Eva was nice to me."

Van typed at his screen.

"That book's real rare here in America. All Czech stuff is small-press stuff. It's a small country."

WHAT'S IT ABOUT

Fawn ignored him. "See, here back in the USA, they always talk about Vaclav Havel like he was some kind of saint. Well, he was. He is. But my pal Eva, she's, like, personally related to Vaclav Havel. Eva had to have this saint guy as her President."

Van raised his brows, or tried to. The right brow moved. The left one was still numbed from his surgery.

"Eva told me, yeah, Vaclav Havel is like this saint, but a saint can't run a government. I mean, very first thing, the country splits in half. Havel is a terrible administrator. His health was bad, all the time. And his first wife, the First Lady everybody really liked, she died of cancer. He married the second wife and nobody could stand her, because she's, like, this hippie actress."

Van looked at her silently. Why was Fawn torturing him like this? What on earth was the woman's point?

"We've never had a really good talk like this before, you and me!" Fawn said. She removed a pair of latex gloves from her purse and found herself a tissue. "I feel like we're really communicating now!"

With a struggle, Van found his tongue. His tongue had not been directly hurt in any way that he understood, but his tongue was really sore anyway. "Thanks," he lisped. "It was good of you to come, Fawn."

Fawn's eyes briefly leaked tears. "I don't want you to worry about anything, boss. I'm taking care of all of it for you."

"Mmm-hmmm."

"I'm gonna get you your money back that you spent on Grendel. Jeb said that should be my number-one priority. And wow, the way you screwed up that requisition process, getting that money back is like a full-time job."

Van sniffed. His sinuses were a wreck.

"Jeb really admires you. I mean, for a cop, Jeb really knows a lot about computers. Jeb doesn't mind that computer geeks are kind of hopeless idealists. Jeb knows you were really the best."

I *am* the best, Van thought. Was it worth the pain to mention this out loud? No. No use in saying that at all.

"I learned so much working with you," Fawn told him gratefully. "Like, it was so cool of you not to say anything to anybody about my stupid little love affair at the office. I had to grow out of that little problem on my own. I always heard that was unprofessional, but you know, until I really did it, with a really stupid guy like Mike Hickok, I didn't know why it was stupid."

Van's heart began thudding.

"Anyway, now I'm fully briefed about that. So I've just folded that up and put that little subject away." Fawn wasn't kidding. "Van, I just got two great job offers from DARPA and Homeland Security. I can get an important, top-level staff job with a real federal bureau. They know I worked with you and Jeb, and they want me bad. You'd definitely pick DARPA if you were me, right? DARPA, they're Advanced Research Projects, and all."

Van nodded.

"That's why I'm picking Homeland Security. Security work is a good job for a single woman. Women are great about home and security issues. I kind of stink at advanced research, but home and security, that is all about attention to detail. That's where I shine."

Van closed his eyes. He opened them. Unfortunately, Fawn was still sitting there.

"I mean, like, when we started whistle-blowing at Enron—that was all us *women* in the Enron office who were doing that, you know.

We women at Enron were the only ones who were *paying attention to the details.*"

Van stared at her.

"Boy, those big cowboys in Houston sure thought they were hell on wheels. 'Fast Andy' Fastow, Ken Lay . . . They kept dividing the company into these *neat little teams,* you know, just ten percent of the normal accountants . . . Really quick responses, and all these quiet, secret offshore projects that no one ever talked about . . . I'm so lucky that Jeb found me a federal job after all that. I mean, life after working for Enron . . . I don't even *tell* people that I once worked for Enron. The weirdest part is, that was like a totally plum job, too. I mean, Enron recruited the top of the top of the class. The best of the best. I was Enron fresh out of college."

Van sucked cold air through the gap in his broken teeth.

"But thanks to you, I can make a brand-new career. In federal security, I can go just as far as my talent can take me. There's no glass ceiling there! I mean, Janet Reno was Attorney General!"

Resignedly, Van adjusted Fawn's bedside bouquet.

"Can I tell you one more thing, Van? You look so nice without that beard. You look so normal. I mean, that side of your face that isn't swollen. I like your hair that way, too. It's kind of like Sonny Bono before he became a congressman." Fawn offered him her nicest smile. Then she sneaked a look at her watch.

Van showed her his computer screen.

WHAT ABOUT THE HAVEL BOOK, THOUGH

"You can keep that."

Van typed faster. I MEAN< WHAT'S IT ABOUT< FAWN< WHY ME?

"You read it, and see if you can find that out for yourself," she said.

ERLETTE HOUSE, VIRGINIA, MARCH 2002

Erlette House was an eighteenth-century Virginia estate. It had once been a rival of Mount Vernon or Monticello. It had become a country retreat for the power elite in Washington.

Once upon some mythical time, most senators and congressmen had been land-owning squires. They felt most at their ease in the simple, warm hospitality of some big rural farm. In Erlette House, this gentlemanly fiction was still kept up. The hay fields were still raked with teams of horses, even though Erlette House had helicopter pads, a landing strip, and a computer center. Erlette House was surrounded by modern Virginia suburbs, with strip malls and glass office towers. But Erlette House was still a real country estate, sort of. It had livestock, roses, and swans.

Van, Dottie, and Ted had been assigned their own rooms in the Erlette House "Lake Cottage." This "cottage," actually a small mansion, featured stone hearths, Federal-style chairs of antique oak, primitive American art, and a four-poster bed with a lovely handmade quilt. The Lake Cottage brimmed over with old-school East Coast Establishment virtue. Every object in its rooms sat there in timeless restraint, polished by good taste, power, and heaps of old money. Except, of course, for Van's and Dottie's laptops, which were like two Martian tripods out of H. G. Wells.

Dottie collapsed on the bed. The white feather mattress dented around her like a stick-toasted marshmallow. Dottie was very prone to airsickness. Her long flight to Erlette House on Tony's jouncing private jet had badly upset her stomach. She was pale and greenish.

Van popped the lid from a cold curved bottle with an attachment of his Swiss Army cyberknife. "You want a Dramamine, sweetie?"

"I'm trying to keep one down," Dottie said in a small, pinched voice.

Van put Dottie's Perrier bottle on the bedside table. The bedside table was ancient, wobbly, and dented. The table was very old. It was some kind of eighteenth-century American furniture invention that had never quite caught on. It looked like it had been whittled into shape by Ben Franklin on a bad day.

Van sat in a shield-back mahogany chair next to Ted's space-age plastic child-carrier. Dottie's spell of weakness gave Van the tenderest and most protective kind of husbandly feeling. She had been so glad to see him, practically tumbling into his arms off the plane.

Although she knew some of the truth by now, Dottie hadn't said one word to him about his crowned teeth, his new beard, or the lisp. Actually, Dottie had said something to him about the lisp. She had said that it made him sound like Humphrey Bogart.

Van freed Ted from his plastic seating device. He put Ted on his knee. Ted was cheerful. Ted did not mind air trips at all. Ted was in top condition, as if he'd been shipped from distant Colorado in Ted-shaped foam blocks.

Ted looked thoughtfully at his stricken mom, as if logging her vulnerabilities for future exploitation.

"You should just go now, Derek," Dottie said, words muffled into the pillow. "I'm sure you and your boss have a lot to talk about here."

Van settled deeper into his chair. "I don't care," he said.

Dottie turned restlessly. "What?"

"I said I don't care, honey. This is my outfit's last big event, and I gave that job all I want to give to it. I don't want to see any of the panels here. I don't care about the speakers or the lobbyists. I don't want to schmooze . . ." Van winced. Van hated the word "schmooze," and with his scarred lip it sounded even nastier, somehow. ". . . schmooze with the presenters. I never liked to speak in public. I'm not gonna talk here. No. They got enough out of me. Enough is enough. It's all political now. We're putting on a big campaign show here. I hate this."

"Oh, honey."

"This dumb business with Tony's jet. I got hurt, and we ran out of time to do it right. It's not fully proofed and tested. That prototype would never work under real-life conditions, any more than Star Wars missile shields can work. It's vaporware. It's a hoax!"

"Oh, honey, if you worked on it, I'm sure it's not a hoax."

"Well, it's just symbolic. That's the best you can say about it. I'm a scientist! I'm a scientist, and I'm doing political spin." Van ran his hands over the lengthening bristles covering his cheeks. "Okay, maybe I have to do that. Maybe there's no choice. But that doesn't mean I've gotta do that *to you*. Never to *you*. I want to look after *you* while we're here. That's what I want, okay? And you, too, Ted. It should be about you, and me, and Ted."

Dottie scrunched herself into the pillow. "This seems like a really nice resort . . . But I feel so sick."

"Drink that Perrier."

Dottie sipped from the bottle obediently. After a moment, she burped. "Oh, God, that's just so awful."

"You'll get better," Van said knowingly. "You just rest. Ted and I will go off to the Great House for a little bit. We'll bring you back, like, a nice slice of lime and the fruit plate."

Dottie put the pillow over her face.

Van left, carrying his son on his hip. They forged across an open field, past a pergola laden with vines, across a rolling hedge, and up-hill to a pillared and porticoed historic mansion. It was a warm late March day, smelling of April. The weather was favoring them. Van put his laminated ID badge over his neck. He walked upstairs, past white pillars, carved doors, and a spiral staircase. He entered the on-going conference. The event was formally titled "The Joint Strategic Summit for Critical Cyber-Security Practice," with a hyphen. It was amazing how much discussion there had been inside the CCIAB about that stupid hyphen.

Ted was the only child-in-arms attending the Joint Strategic Summit. Ted immediately became the star of the show. Van was sur-prised by this. Van had planned to take a very low profile at the event, which was really Jeb's show all the way. But Ted, shiny-faced and glee-ful, was upstaging all the pundits, movers, and shakers. Dignified men and women with graying hair and American flag lapel pins could not keep their hands off Ted. It was as if Van had created Ted as a high-tech animatronic toddler.

Van had become used to government and industry people suck-ing up to him a little. He knew that it wasn't personal. It was his job title that got those firm handshakes, those invitations, and all that flattering mail. He was the Deputy Director for Technical Services of the Coordination of Critical Information Assurance Board. For a brief period, mostly while stuck inside a concrete vault in West Virginia, Van had been able to assess some of their stupidest ideas and technologies, and thank God, to quickly get rid of some of them.

Van offered Ted a juicy chunk of cantaloupe off a giant cut-crystal fruit plate. Ted, who had a tiny but effective set of choppers now, went after it with gusto.

Here was a familiar face. It was Pico Yang. The unusually named Pico Yang had been a Stanford colleague of Van's. He was one of the ten guys on the planet who understood Grendel's operating system. Pico had an Irish wife and four Chinese-Irish kids. Pico didn't seem much impressed by one Ted. Pico had plenty of Teds.

"You gotta tell me about this aircraft guidance demo. That sounds like a miracle."

Van leveled with him at once. "The flight OS is crap. The latency problems are nontrivial. The multipath effects killed us. It only works on line of sight. That kludge we stuck together doesn't even qualify as an alpha rollout."

Pico beamed upon him. "That's great news, Van. For one terrible moment I thought I was forty years behind."

"It's possible to build one that works. If you've got a spare fleet of satellites and sixty billion."

"California state budget," Pico said. "The school is taking it in the neck. Neutron-bomb buildings all over Silicon Valley. Worst financial crisis since World War II. You left California at a great time, Van. You wouldn't recognize us if you came back now."

"It's tough, Pico."

"Lots of states. Not just us."

"It's *real* tough."

"Plus the war. I couldn't believe it when you went into defense work, but, Van, you were way ahead of the curve. Good for you, man. Real smart move. Great job with the Grendel, too. The streams, Van. Wow. The way you handled streaming, that just knocked me out." Pico gulped heartily from a tapered glass of white wine. "That's a cute kid."

There was nothing Van could do for Pico now. Maybe earlier—
but not now. They had thrown Van out of the Vault because the
CCIAB was on the point of expiring. Leaving the Vault was like get-
ting paroled from federal prison. At the same time, though, for a
Vault rat, that message was unmistakable. Go get lost, fella. Uncle
Sam no longer needs you. You can go fry now.

There was Tony Carew over there, smiling, charming, eagerly
pressing the flesh. Tony was chatting with a circle of spellbound federal officials. Tony had crashed the big party on Van's ticket, but Tony
looked completely at ease inside Erlette House. Tony looked like he
attended Joint Strategic Summits for Critical Cyber-Security Practice
every other Tuesday.

Van turned away from Tony and Tony's eager new friends. No
one would ever cling to him like that. Van pretended to study a large
white foamboard announcing the Summit's panel topics. "The Department of Homeland Security: A Historic Creation." "National
Milestones for Proactive Software Protection." "A Robust and Re-
silient Critical Infrastructure: The National Infrastructure Assurance
Partnership." "Sharing Vulnerability Analysis Within a Competitive
Environment: The Delicate Balance." Van was not going to any of
these panels, although he personally knew the vast majority of the
panelists. Van had already skipped the event's keynote. It had been
delivered by the Secretary of Transportation.

It wasn't that these were boring topics or boring people. They
were a lot less boring than they had been made to sound. The stark
truth was that these panels had nothing to tell Van that Van didn't already know.

Now, finally, after months of ceaseless labor in the trenches, Van
really understood what he had been up against all along.

He understood all the crushing issues that had prevented decent,
well-meaning people from ever getting anything useful done in national computer security.

Problem number one: there was no such thing as a "national"
computer. At all. That was a contradiction in terms, like talking

about a black sun or a square triangle. You could put a flag decal on the side of a computer. You could hide it in a military base. You could pay for it with taxpayer money. But talking about "American" computation was like talking about "American" mathematics or "American" physics. It just didn't come with flags.

National people were the wrong people to attempt that security job. A nation, any nation, was just too small. Any cable map could show you the enormous fiber-optic pipes that circled the planet. Tycom Transatlantic, Emergia, Americas-II, Africa ONE, Southern Cross, FLAG Europe-Asia. Pipes laid across the planet's sea bottom at fantastic expense and effort. Specifically built to reach distant, extremely un-American places. Places like Santiago, Capetown, Mumbai, Perth, Shanghai, and Kuwait City. Places chock-full of alien computers owned by very un-American people.

The whole *point of the effort* was to become less American. That was why it was called Internet instead of USA-Net. It was possible to build nets inside your own nation that only your nation could use. France had tried it: Minitel. Britain had tried it: Prestel. National networks died horribly. It was like trying to build a computer net that only talked to Milwaukee.

It got worse. Even inside American national borders, you couldn't wrap computers in the red-white-and-blue. Eighty-five percent of the hardware was owned by private industry. *Multinational* private industry.

Multinational private industry that *had gone broke.*

The computer and telecom industries were on their knees. They had lost legendary, incredible, colossal amounts of money. They had lost diamond-mine, mountain-of-gold heaps of money.

They had tried to build a commercial for-profit Internet. There was nothing commercial about the Internet any more than there was anything national. That was why it was called Internet instead of Internet Inc.©™.

The Internet belonged to a world of the 1990s, a Digital Revolution. The people in the 2000s were way over the Digital Revolution.

They were deeply involved in the Digital Terror. The nervous system of global governance, education, science, culture, and e-commerce, it was all in a spasm. It had all broken down in a sudden terrible panic in the last mile. The last mile stood between those great, big, fat, global, huge, empty, terrifying fiber-optic pipes, and the planet's general population.

The Net had not just broken. It had been abandoned, cast aside in fear and dread. Because the movie companies, and the telephone companies, and the music companies had suddenly realized that their "intellectual property" would not remain their property for one pico-second, when everyday people all around the world could click, copy, and forward all their movies. All their music. All their calls home to Mom. And the people did that. The children of the Digital Revolution were a swarm of thieves. More people had used Napster than voted for the President of the United States. Nobody paid for that music.

People didn't pay. The people were free. In a world like that, there wouldn't *be* a music business. There wouldn't *be* a movie business. There would be no such thing as long-distance charges. There would be no long distances. There would be no business. Nothing but *it*, the Net. And the horror of that freedom could not be endured.

So the Information Superhighway had just *stopped*. Stopped dead with its sawhorses and construction lights still up, like an incomplete overpass. A titanic physical investment. Dark fiber. Not lit up. In receivership. Gently rotting in the mellow ground.

Business could not save itself from the situation it had eagerly brought on itself, this world of free and open access. It could not spare the effort and revenue to reinvent itself as a safe, secure, comforting, for-profit utility. There was no such thing as a computer "business," really. Racing into cyberspace was not a business enterprise, any more than the long-dead Space Race had ever been a business. Money fell out of it here and there, but that was not its point. It was a tremendous, wrenching effort in pursuit of the sublime. People aiming for the Moon, touching it for a golden moment, and being left with massive bills and rusting gantries.

There was some software business around. There was Microsoft, which was a monopoly. Microsoft was never secure, because of the hatred. Microsoft was hated everywhere, despised, mercilessly attacked. Sabotaged, tormented, humiliated. Microsoft was a *pathetically vulnerable* monopoly, because every hacker in the world who knew anything at all about computers understood how to attack Microsoft and its products.

Microsoft's operating systems had never been built to resist the focused hatred of every alienated hacker in the whole world. No single system could ever bear up under that level of focused intellectual assault. It was like trying to save Saigon when everyone in the whole world was Viet Cong. There were not just dozens of holes in Big Bill's code but *thousands* of holes. The patches of the holes wrecked the code, quite often. The patches of the holes had holes. Some of Microsoft's holes were unrepairable even in principle.

Bill had more money than anybody in the whole wide world, but Bill didn't have enough money to save himself. Except for the Microsoft operating system—a monopoly—and the Microsoft Office Suite—another monopoly—every other venture Bill had tried lost huge amounts of money. There were a couple of really pretty nice Microsoft computer games that made a little money. That was about it.

The biggest competitor that Microsoft faced wasn't even a business. It was a new and terrible thing in the world. It was Open Source, a thing that frightened Microsoft so much they regarded it as a cancer.

Open Source aimed to eat away Bill's empire and replace it with a swarming, leaderless ant pile of global hackers. And Open Source wasn't a government any more than Open Source was a business. There was no one to negotiate with. There was no one to cut a deal with. There was no one to regulate. There was no one to bomb.

You could bribe them. But you could never bribe all of them. You could sue them, arrest some of them, but that really looked stupid, and besides, they were probably living in Finland.

Everyone claimed they wanted secure computers. Everyone was terrified of the consequences of the lawlessness, which were very bad and getting steadily worse. Viruses. Worms. Scam artists. Porn. Spam. Denial-of-service attacks. Organized crime. Industrial espionage. Stalking. Money laundering. The specter of infowar attacks on natural gas pipelines, aircraft control systems, dams, water reservoirs, sewage systems, telephones, and banks. Black horses snorting and stomping in the stables of the Digital Apocalypse.

You sat people down and you explained what computer insecurity really could do to them, and they got really, really scared and upset. They wanted something done about it. Until they figured out what effective security really meant for them, what it would do to them. Then no one really wanted secure computers. No one at all.

The spies didn't want to fix the holes in computer security. Spies liked to spy on computers. Cops didn't want to fix the holes in computer security. Cops liked to wiretap computers, and to grab them, open them up, and examine them right on the spot. Customers didn't want to fix the holes in security. Customers didn't want to ride a little motor scooter weighed down with a ton and a half of cumbersome locks and chains.

Scientists understood how to lock code down, but they hated intellectual property.

The military was sincerely good at really securing computers. The military excelled at defense. But they adored attack. The American military excelled at infowar, cyberwar, and electronic warfare. They were always making up horrible new methods of breaking, smashing, subverting, and violently destroying the whole works.

Business couldn't do much about it. Business was broke, it had already died at its post.

And on the far side of the dead dot-coms, the dead pipes, there was Wi-Fi. If the Internet was the child of Cold War nuclear warfare, then Wi-Fi was the child of the Special Forces. Wi-Fi was all about little military-spec spread-spectrum radios. Secret radios. Tiny radios. The very kind of thing that Delta Force liked to carry way behind the lines of enemies (and allies).

Wi-Fi was just getting started, and when Van thought about it, it filled him with chills. Wi-Fi carried data that was *fast, cheap, anonymous, wide-open,* wireless, portable, great big bleeding menaces to data protection, to intellectual property, to information security, sold in shrink-wrap packs as if they were bubble gum . . . Wi-Fi was a *nightmare.* The stuff coming down the pike was *worse.* It was like it was evolving *on purpose to make a secure life impossible.*

Van shifted Ted from his right hip to his left. Someone tapped Van's shoulder.

It was Tony.

"Van," he said, "want to introduce you."

An older man. White mustache. Glasses. Balding. Blue shirt, brown slacks. A conference ID on his lanyard.

"Jim Cobb."

"Dr. Cobb!" said Van, almost dropping his son in astonishment.

There was no such thing as a Nobel Prize for computer science. James Cobb had won a Nobel Prize anyway. He'd had to share it with a Swedish physicist. Everybody knew that when it came to Swedes the Nobel committee had a soft spot the size of Stockholm.

"The Bell Labs Concurrent C superset," Van gushed.

Cobb smiled. "That's funny. Nobody talks about that much, these days."

"I wrote my thesis on that."

"The press always wants to talk about the photonics," said Cobb. That was what he had won his Nobel for—he and the Swede, who was his electrical engineer. "You never get the time of day for the work that you loved best."

"That superset paper in '79, that was the best," Van said, knowing that it was true.

"You know the best way to have truly great ideas?"

"How?" Van blurted eagerly. He was talking to a true-blue genius who had had at least seven genuine, world-class great ideas. A phenomenon.

"Have a hundred, and throw away ninety-eight of 'em! Haw haw haw!"

Cobb was laughing, but Van sensed in his gut that Cobb had never gotten over the anguish of it. Cobb had loved those ninety-eight lousy ideas with just the same passion as the two, or five, or seven, that had saddled him with his immortal fame.

"That way you handled synchronization conditions in Grendel," said Cobb.

"Yeah!"

"Where the capsule structure supports inheritance."

"Exactly!"

"I liked that," said Cobb. "That was cleverly handled."

Van wanted to sit on the floor. James J. Cobb had praised him. James Cobb, who knew the behavior of semiconductors down to the atomic level. A top-notch theorist with "his head right down in the bits." A true grand master from computing's heroic age.

In Bell Labs, guys like Cobb didn't even bother with the borders between disciplines. They were the wizards of the coolest, tallest ivory tower around. Guys who did physics at breakfast, electrical engineering at lunch, and programming after dinner. Bell Labs had originated the transistor, plus UNIX, C, and C++, and the Karmakar algorithm. The little R&D crowd at Mondiale could only dream of the colossal achievements at Bell Labs.

"Cute kid," Cobb told him. "Where's Mom?"

"Oh, Mom's resting awhile," Van said. "This is Ted."

"What, so you're feeding the baby, changing the diapers? You younger guys are something else." Cobb lifted a cocktail glass to his lips. Van hadn't noticed any hard liquor at the party. Everyone else was carrying wineglasses. Apparently when you were a Nobel Prize winner at Erlette House, it wasn't hard to find vermouth and olives.

"What's your latest project, Dr. Cobb?" said Van.

"A year ago," said Cobb, "February 2001, they shut down Bell Labs in Silicon Valley. First time that Bell Labs ever closed a facility."

"Right, I heard that." Bell Labs was Lucent now. And Lucent was very broke.

"Real focused on short-term research payoffs. I was working on HDTV. Not a lot going on there."

"I guess not."

"Had my own consulting company for a while, that didn't work out. Just lately it's missile defense."

Van tried not to stare. Missile defense? Star Wars? The ultimate in pseudoscience phony baloney? The great Jim Cobb reduced to working on Star Wars?

Van glumly supposed that there was money in it. A huge amount of money had been thrown away on Star Wars.

"It's not like you think," Cobb lied. He tipped his martini rim below his white mustache. "It's the Airborne Laser project. Air Force."

"Oh," Van said with a nod, "the photonic emissions."

"To tell the truth, that's not the part they have me working on."

Van lifted his brows. The Cyber-Security crowd was getting a bit liquored up and noisy. Ted squirmed vigorously in his arms.

Cobb stared emptily over Van's right shoulder. "You have to imagine," Cobb told him, "trying to stuff one hundred and eighty thousand pounds of laser equipment into one 747 cargo jet. That's the Airborne Laser. They need fourteen laser modules to shoot down missiles, and six of them already outweigh any jet's lifting capacity. Chemical laser. Huge, flying tanks of chlorine, iodine, and hydrogen peroxide. The devil's brew, that stuff. It sloshes. Oh, boy, it sloshes." Cobb leaned way back, lifting his free arm. "You are trying to aim that giant, flying chemical laser at a rising missile that is clearing a silo . . ."

"It's a death ray?"

"Lasers never work well," said Cobb, wobbling back upright. "Lasers are always underpowered. Lethality is in the kilojoule per centimeter range. You just can't do efficient optical coupling in chlorine-iodine wavelengths. There are ways to slide those pulses around, but when it comes to combining them . . ." Cobb started to hand-wave. He looked for a place to set his empty martini glass. He failed to find one. He absently tucked the narrow stem of the glass into Ted's sweaty little fist.

Suddenly Cobb was searching in his jacket. He found a business card and handed it over. Cobb's card had an old-school ARPANET address, nothing but dots and numerals.

"Mama," said Ted agreeably. Dottie had arrived. To Van's astonishment, she was wearing a short black cocktail dress. Dottie had hose and heels. She had earrings that matched her necklace.

Dottie gently relieved Ted of his empty martini glass. "I think I'd better get you a fresh one, Ted."

"This is Jim Cobb," said Van. "From Bell Labs. My wife Dottie, Dr. Cobb."

"Oh, yes, Bell Labs," said Dottie brightly. "The three-degree cosmic background radiation!"

"They thought that was pigeon crap," Cobb told her, blinking.

"I beg your pardon?"

"That microwave hiss from the birth of the universe. They thought it was pigeon droppings inside the Bell equipment. So they cleaned out the horn. Then they found out that it was the universe radiating right at us."

"That's quite a story," said Dottie.

"They were looking for crap and they found cosmic significance. The very opposite of most scientific endeavors!"

Dottie stared at Cobb. It was a rare privilege to hear Bell Labs humor, straight from the source. "My husband often speaks of you, Dr. Cobb. He's a big admirer of your work."

"Love to have you out to the BMDO," said Cobb to Van, slurring a little. "I'd show you that COEA."

Tony reappeared. Tony was escorting a woman who was almost certainly the most attractive woman at the event. She turned out to be the wife of a colonel at the Center for Strategy and Technology at the Air War College. She quickly took Cobb in hand, chatting at him amiably.

"Your AFOXAR people are still inside my damn plane," Tony told Van. "Meet me there before the demo, all right? We've got to cross some i's and dot some t's."

"Tony, I can't do anything they can't do. They're fully trained Air Force technicians."

"You and I need to talk, Van."

Van scowled. "You're not getting cold feet about this, are you?"

Dottie broke in. "He'll be there, Tony."

Tony nodded and moved on. Van looked at her, upset. "What was that about? Ted and I were just about to bring you the fruit plate."

"Honey, that was over two hours ago. I feel fine now. We have to do the banquet dinner now."

Van despaired. "Oh, honey, please don't make me do the banquet dinner."

"They got Ted his own high chair. It's all been arranged. They're seating me with the other CIA wives. I wouldn't miss this for anything." Dottie smiled. "It's important, honey. They really want you to go."

Van did not want to go to the stupid banquet even the least little bit, but without a Dottie to run away and neck with, there was no point in fleeing. At least the food was good—the food was great, in fact—and he was not required to rise and speak in public.

Van wasted many valuable moments of his life listening to tedious master-of-ceremony business. Boring crap about lost objects, departing buses, golfing opportunities . . . Then Jeb rose to speak.

It cost Van a pang to see poor Jeb walk to the podium. Jeb was actually walking rather than waddling. The poor guy had lost a whole lot of weight while running the CCIAB. Rumsfeld, who had lived to be seventy-something and was in top physical condition, had been ruthless with Jeb. Rumsfeld had sent Jeb a bullying torrent of interoffice notes, "Rumsfeld Snowflakes," demanding Bethesda checkups and heart-safe exercises.

Jeb put on his bifocals to pick through his three-by-five note-cards. Van had never seen Jeb so meek and dull and conciliatory. Jeb didn't even start his speech with his customary risqué joke.

"The President's board has accomplished, magnificently, the principal goals set for our strategy . . . Speeches, articles, and private meetings have changed the paradigm of the IT buying community. We will never return to the old, careless ways . . . The CCIAB projects already in progress will be making a smooth transfer to the Assistant Undersecretary for Infrastructure Protection in the DHS . . . Quiet but effective work is being done today by the OMB to make our federal government the smartest and the largest buyer of safely configured software and hardware . . ."

What in the name of Pete was all that about? *This* was the big show-stopper Jeb had promised? Where were the tough guys? Where were the antiterror warriors who were going to kick everybody's ass? Trained, efficient, cold-eyed operatives who would crush cyberterror without mercy? To hear Jeb talk, the whole effort had been about procurement issues.

". . . the safe computing benchmarks developed by the U.S. National Security Agency and the Center for Internet Security . . . The National Institute for Standards and Technology's Certification and Accreditation Program . . . the Undersecretary of the Information Analysis Infrastructure Protection Directorate who will oversee collection and storage of the critical infrastructure data in a database . . ."

Van's eyelids were fluttering. He looked around the conference room, past the bouquets and sweating ice pitchers. Jeb's audience was drinking Jeb in. This was *normal* speech to them. Jeb was *normalizing* the computer world. People who had been howling, paranoid prophets in the cyberwilderness two years ago were getting turned into fully vested bureaucrats. They were *real* bureaucrats, with real titles and real offices. A little slice of the funding pie there. An under-secretaryship here. Funding. Turf. Accountable responsibilities. Oh, my God.

Now Jeb was gallantly name-checking all the usual suspects within the CCIAB. "I can't say enough about the tireless efforts of Herbert Howland, our director of public relations . . . Stand up, Herbert, where are you, take a bow . . ." A pattering of applause.

Van's fingers dug tightly into the linen tablecloth. Oh, Jesus. So this was why they had insisted on his being here at the banquet. The ritual applause. Stage fright bit deeply into him. His cheek jumped. Restoring nerves were tingling in there, as they grew their way back through the bone cement in his head.

"And the CCIAB's heroic Deputy Director for Technical Services, Derek Vandeveer!"

Van forced himself to his feet. To his shock and awe, there was thunderous applause for him. The loudest applause of the night, by far. Frantic, almost. The idiots would not shut up. There was even *whistling.* The whistling was coming from Michael Hickok, who was at a table with the AFOXAR crew. Hickok went on for a good eight or nine seconds when everyone else had stopped.

Van sat down, his face flushed and blazing. What was that about? Had he really done that great a job? Impossible. That crushing humiliation with the KH-13 . . . Van looked dazedly across the room to Dottie's table. Dottie looked happy enough to burst.

When the banquet broke up, Van sought her out. "Did you hear all that clapping?" he asked her. "Was that just me?"

She jounced Ted on her hip. "Oh, honey, Ted and I were just so proud."

"Let's get out of here. That was truly weird."

"You promised Tony you'd go to the landing strip and help him with the test flight."

Van had promised Tony no such thing. "Let's go put our feet up. We'll feed the swans or something."

"Oh, no, not now. I've got to go have a drinky-winky on the big verandah with the CIA wives," said Dottie. "They're telling me all these amazing stories about the husband I never knew I had."

"They're not 'CIA wives,' honey."

"Well, that big redhead sure is. The one who's really looped. I think she knew your mom!"

CHAPTER TWELVE

Van had no alternative but to walk to Tony's jet. It was a surprisingly long way. Erlette House had actual fields out here, growing tall, peculiar, East Coast historical crops. What was that stuff over there? Flax? Hops? Hemp? He'd never seen the like.

The AFOXAR staffers, eager for publicity, had flown in an entire Joint Special Ops command post. It was pushing it more than a little to have tents, briefing boards, spotters' binoculars, laser rangefinders, and spidery spread-spectrum antennas, but AFOXAR was never going to have a better opportunity than this to advertise their services to a crowd of feds. Van offered a vague wave to Hickok, who tapped the side of his ground-contol helmet and gave a thumbs-up.

Van walked up the jet's embarkation stairs. Tony's jet was scarily big. It could have held twenty people, if someone had ripped out the love nest's white leather couches and the twenty-three-inch tiltable digital display screens.

So here he was inside a fully fueled private jet in Virginia. It really was that easy. If he knew how to fly this jet, he could be smashing into the White House in minutes. Van went up to the cockpit cabin, which had no security door. There was no pilot on duty. There was no one inside the jet but Tony Carew.

"Where's your pilot?" said Van. "AFOXAR said they'd put five or ten tech guys in here!"

Tony lifted a finger to his lips. "Shhhh!"

Van had never been inside a jet's cockpit before. The BBJ had two pilot's seats, tastily upholstered in lamb's wool, plus two black plastic yokes and six bluely glowing digital screens. Big flat planes of glass surrounded Van on three sides.

"You're the pilot, Tony?" Van said. "When did you get a pilot license?"

"Oh, come on, Van. Who needs one? John Travolta can fly one of these things. Fleabitten al Qaeda guys straight from Yemen can fly them. They're not a big deal. And whose show is this, anyhow? Is this about a bunch of punk kids from AFOXAR? Why let them hog the glory?"

Van said nothing. He wasn't thrilled at the way this was going. He scrunched himself into the copilot's seat. He was looking at a gleaming forest of switches and dials. The BBJ had a massive double-handled throttle, like a huge yellow beer tap. His seat had a flip-down pane and an overhead projector.

"I flew her over from Colorado myself," said Tony. "That was a milk run. I had to fire my pilot. I'll have to get rid of that leather decor, too. I'm selling this thing, you know. I'm selling her to the party directorate of Bharatiya Janata. In India, she's gonna be a political campaign plane."

"No kidding."

"Indians can do all kinds of cool things with jets once they're free of the good old FAA regulations. For those village voters in India, a jet like this is pure stage magic. They'll paint her green, white, and saffron. Dress her up like a sacred cow on parade. They can fill the fuel tank with luminescent sparkles and outdo the Navy Blue Angels. Her best days are all ahead of her." Tony patted the instrument panel, his face tinged with sadness in the glow of the altimeter dials.

"Why did you sell your jet?"

"Why else? I had to. In some other, better world I'm just a dashing tramp flyboy, Van. Maybe I do some milk runs from Bombay to Dubai. I fill this bird up with gold chains and bangles. I settle accounts with some *hawala* guys and then I can buy another plane. That's how they finance Bollywood movies . . . but, you know, come on. That's a mug's game, it's the smuggler's blues, right? That kind of life doesn't *push the high-tech edge.*"

Tony leaned forward in his pilot's seat. "There are only sixty-one of these babies in service in the whole world. And I have the only one that can be flown off a Web page." Tony held up a clipboard. "Really. I mean, here's tonight's little flight plan, okay? Twenty minutes, and it's almost all automated."

Van rubbed at his twitching cheek. All automated? No, not exactly. The exact situation involved Michael Hickok standing outside in the gently gathering Virginia darkness with a portable plastic gizmo frankly based on a Nintendo control joystick. Nintendo joysticks worked great, actually. They were extremely dependable interface devices.

The engines began to roar.

"Van, in politics, people need a damn show!" Tony shouted. "And that's just what we're gonna deliver. Think of the takeaway sound bite we're giving these guys! 'I went to Virginia and Derek Vandeveer grabbed a jet plane right out of the sky!' "

Van stared at him.

"You know what I like best about this remote-control rig of yours?" Tony bellowed over the engines. "That it's all *invisible*! I mean, if we didn't know better, we'd think we were haunted by spooks!"

Tony sent the plane into a taxi run. The engines drank fuel and they picked up speed in a hurry.

The jet left the tarmac. They were airborne.

"No freight load," said Tony as the roar of takeoff faded. "She's light as a feather with just you and me on board. Stop looking so freaked, Van. I'm telling you, this is totally a picnic. We could go in the back and watch stag films."

Van found his voice. "I don't think stag films will go over real well inside India."

"People are the same all over, Van. I mean, just maybe, you live in a nation of rich maharajas, influence peddlers, crooked elections, and corrupt accountants. With big software industries, and huge gaps between the superrich and the underclass. Where son follows father in political dynasties, hassled by Moslem terrorists. Is that your country? Really, pick any two."

The jet began to bank. Van sneaked a look out the flat black pane of the window. Maybe he was going to survive this.

"Let me show you something really cool here," said Tony, scrabbling under his seat. "Look, the pilot's got his own gun." He produced a snub-nosed Smith & Wesson revolver. "Boy, a pilot with a gun, that makes you feel a lot safer, right?"

"Put that away, Tony."

"It's never loaded," Tony assured him. "Bullets equal zero." He tucked the weapon back in its holster. "But they always ask me about that now. They do, I swear. I've got, like, fifteen Taiwanese chip executives in here for a dirty weekend in Bangkok, and it's like: 'Does our pilot have a pistol in the cockpit?' Like what, you Chinese businessmen are aching to polish each other off inside the fuselage? The world has gone nuts, Van. It's like we're all under a curse."

The plane bounced twice, violently. The engines whined.

"This must be the good part of tonight's show," said Tony. He took his hands from the controls. "We just got fake-hijacked in midair, right in front of your adoring crowd." For the first time, Tony clicked his seat belt.

"So," said Tony, stretching, "tell me about your next big step, career-wise."

"I don't know," Van told him. "I think I might move out to Colorado with Dottie."

Tony was astonished. "What? You're gonna waste time out there with my little telescope? Didn't you hear those clowns yelling and cheering at that banquet? Man, you can have any post you want!"

"I don't know what that was even about."

The plane went into a terrifying sideways slide. Van clutched at his armrests, heart hammering.

"Do I have to spell it out to you in words of one syllable?" Tony said, unperturbed. "I guess I do, huh? Van, you are their hero."

"Huh?"

"You're their man, Van. You're their ball-breaker, you're their kick-ass guy. What cyberwar people want more than anything in the world is a geek who is genuinely tough. Did you see any 'Cyberspace Force' people in there at that meeting? Did you wonder why not?"

The plane leveled out. Then, sickeningly, it began to climb.

Tony glanced at his clipboard. "I'm loving these AFOXAR kids. They've got brio. No, Van, the unlikely attempt of Colorado Springs to become the computer-security capital of the visible universe, whoa, that has come to sudden grief. Word got around. When I found out my pal was in a damn hospital, I made some words move around. To the President's political adviser, specifically. He's a busy guy, but he didn't mind when I gave him just a few words: 'illegal bug,' 'National Security Council,' 'rogue operation inside Washington,' some words like that. Major General Wessler has got himself a brand-new field assignment. General Wessler is going to be sucking brown dust in Mesopotamia."

The plane dipped violently. Tony whooped in glee. "And that Cyberspace Force, who had such nice brochures . . . They are not even an idea now. They are not even the idea of an idea. They are buried like Pompeii under eighteen solid meters of volcanic ash. What happened there, huh? Dr. Vandeveer happened, that's what."

"Look," Van protested, "I know that you told me to stay away from that satellite . . ."

"I know, I know, Jeb was real ambitious. You guys just couldn't stay out of the loop on the KH-13. But let me tell you how all that plays to the people at this event, Van. How it looks is, the Cyberspace Force went down and dirty on you, and the CCIAB went down and dirty right back. And there was some kind of encounter. And you came back from that, and your boss kisses you in public. And they *don't* come back, and their boss gets broken like a breadstick. So everyone claps real loud for you. They clap till their hands get sore. Because they are terrified of you, man. You are their stud cyberwar general. You are the geek who killed and ate some real military. You rock."

"That's not at all how it really was."

Tony sighed. "Who even cares? You're never going to tell them the truth about beating up some wacky little soldier inside your apartment. And neither am I, or anybody else, ever. The point is that a cyberwar needs heroes. There aren't a lot of cyber-heroes around. In fact, you're pretty much the only one in the world."

The ground was coming up outside the window. "Michael Hickok wasn't like you said he was, either, Tony. What you said about Hickok was all hype. I hired that guy."

"Van, that was okay, too. I still think that guy is evil, but if Hickok chose to jump ship and join your side, then he's smarter than I thought. Hickok is a goon, but if he's *your* goon, that's terrific. I can trust your judgment there. When it comes to cyberwar, you're the best around. Really. You just are."

Van wiped sweat from his forehead. "Tony, why are you angling this?"

"Because your scene is where the action is, brother. This event of yours has been very good to me. The Internet boom is history, but there's still money in security, and there will be a lot more once people knuckle down and shape up. Thanks to you, a ten-billion-dollar boondoggle is finally on the ropes. That KH-13 is facing cancellation.

And that is great news. It's a new day now. We're gonna put that kind of bureaucratic bloat behind us, and move right on. Nobody cares about gold-plated Cadillac satellites in a real shooting war. It's all about rapid point-and-shoot now, that's the new trend. It's all about Predators. And, Van, you and I just proved to everybody watching us that we can turn Boeing's biggest private business jet into a giant remote-control Predator. I'm a very proud and happy guy to know you, Dr. Vandeveer. This is working out brilliantly."

The jet touched down. It jounced violently and became airborne again. Luggage compartments flapped open and there was a distant crashing from the galley. Then the wheels hit with a screech.

The end of the runway rushed upon them. Straps bit into Van's chest and gut.

The jet stopped. The engines died. Hot metal cooled and ticked.

"Yahoo," Tony murmured. "Yahoo-dot-com."

Floodlights flicked over the runway. Van saw to his horror that an enthusiastic crowd was surging toward the plane. Tony laughed aloud. "Van, look at 'em! You are a movie star!"

"I'll have to give them some kind of speech," Van realized.

"Van, a great tech demo can save any situation. And you just gave them one. This is a victory speech. I'll jot you down a couple talking points."

Van was awake inside the Lake Cottage. He felt too elevated to sleep.

Dottie was sleeping in the featherbed. A tendril of brown hair was glued to her forehead with sweat. The woman should never take Dramamine and also drink white wine, thought Van kindly. It really made her manic.

So funny that Tony Carew somehow imagined that his actress girlfriend was his wild angel. That woman was playing a phony role, that was obvious. While Dottie, who had been married to him for ten years, had found her inner tigress.

Van had never imagined Dottie for a gossip, but it seemed that her work in public relations had turned her head around. In just one evening mingling with the Joint Summit crowd, Dottie had wormed out a host of inside stories that Van had never heard or even dreamed of. This stuff was all cocktail blather, obviously, but it was about *himself*.

People from outside the CCIAB had notions about him that were wildly divorced from reality. They knew that he lived in a slum, but they thought he had chosen to live there because he liked to beat up crooks. People thought he had a black belt in Tae Kwon Do. They knew for a fact that he carried a high-tech gun. He was supposed to be hacking into foreign computers every week. He was recruiting Special Forces people, breaking into terrorist facilities and installing Trojan Horses and fatal viruses. Also, supposedly, he was having an affair with Fawn.

This bizarre tittle-tattle might have upset Van, except that Jeb was catching it even worse. Jeb had a whole set of legends attached to him, like a shark followed by remora fish. Jeb had heart arrhythmias. He had advanced diabetes. He'd had a fistfight with Donald Rumsfeld and Condoleezza Rice had had to break it up (this was the best story, actually). Jeb got anxious phone calls three times a day from Larry Ellison. Jeb had a Republican Party slush fund. Jeb had hired Cuban exiles to wiretap the French Embassy. Jeb was addicted to Halcion pills. Jeb was secretly gay.

He, Derek R. Vandeveer, had become the toughest, scariest cyberwarrior in Washington. It made Van wonder if he had ever understood anything about any other human being in his life. Was he delusional? Maybe, when it came to computers, *everyone in the world* was delusional.

On a number of occasions, Van had met the President of the United States. This poor guy even had his own military acronym: POTUS. In real life, Van had met an affable Texan baseball fan in his fifties who liked nothing better than eating pretzels and watching a few innings on the ol' boob tube. He had twin teenage daughters who gave him a lot of grief. This was the President of the United States.

Somehow this was the very same guy as the remorseless military war chief who was relentlessly crushing the world's most feared and respected mountain bandits.

And now he had even met James Cobb. Van opened his laptop bag and retrieved Cobb's business card. For Van, this had been the true highlight of the Virginia Summit. It had moved him deeply that a man he had once idolized had recognized him as a colleague.

Up popped Cobb's Web site. It wasn't a site at all, just a series of retrievable files, like in the good old days when the ARPANET had been the info highway for engineers. No spam then. No porn. No commerce. No viruses. The watering hole for tech wizards. ARPA, Stanford, MIT. Bolt Beranek and Newman. UCLA, Xerox PARC, IBM, and RAND. Those were just labels really. Labels for the same few dozen tech guys, little teams of ten and twenty scientists, nice and quiet, really quick, supplying what was needed whenever the need came up . . .

All those Cobb papers from the seventies and eighties . . . In his heyday, the guy was publishing like crazy. He was throwing off ideas like a blowtorch spat out sparks. Conference proceedings on three different continents. James Cobb was literally all over the map. Not just in one discipline, either. Cobb was making connections that no one before him had ever thought to make. He was using systems analysis and information theory to slice through the rest of human knowledge like a layer cake. It was like he had three brains inside one head.

Van could still remember the mind-blown tingle he and Tony Carew had felt in their MIT dorm as they looked through Cobb's work. They would sit up together at night, getting steadily drunker on the new intellectual frontiers this guy was violently forcing open . . .

And in looking at the papers, Van realized with an adult shock that most of them had gone nowhere at all. Cobb had had a whole lot of really sexy notions that just did not play out in the real world. Van himself was older now. He could recognize the work of Cobb's youth as a young man's fancies.

Van had a further insight. It crept up on him like a kind of dread. For the first time, he recognized a kind of emotional distress in what Cobb had done. These ideas were not just freely pouring out of Jim Cobb. They had been squeezed out of him. There was something primal and animalistic about Cobb's huge burst of creativity. Maybe it had satisfied him, maybe he took pride in it, but his act of mastery had hurt him, it had cost him. James Cobb had paid a human price for his science. He had paid some pitiful, heavy dues, like a master of the blues guitar.

Van looked at his watch. It was almost 2:00 A.M. Suddenly he wanted to drop everything. He wanted to seek out Jim Cobb as he slept in his Erlette House room. He wanted to wake Cobb up, to tell him that he had achieved enlightenment. He was no longer a student. He truly *understood.* He wanted to become the man's friend.

Van looked at the computer screen, his heart thudding with inspiration. Of course he could not find Cobb's peaceful room, pound the door in, and wake him up, shouting frantically. No, that would be senseless. He would send Cobb a professional e-mail. Nothing frantic, nothing weird and geeky. The master addresses his fellow master. Very cool. Very considerate.

A technical note. That would do it. Something that he and Cobb could share together. Co-authoring a new paper, maybe. Wow. A great idea, that would be fantastic. After all, the guy had practically invited Van to help him. He could breathe fresh life into something that Cobb had left on the side of the road. It would be like a Festschrift tribute. That should be easy. There was so much there to choose from.

Van's fingers hovered over his keyboard.

Cobb, James A. (1981) ADAPTIVELY PULSED LOW-POWER EMISSIONS IN MASSIVELY PARALLEL COLLIMATION. *Prospectives in Tunable Bandgaps,* Conference of the Max Planck Society, Ringberg Castle, Germany.

He clicked on it. What was this paper, again? Doing something weird and off the wall by tuning laser bandgaps. It seemed to him that maybe Tony had spoken of it once, ages ago. Tony had always had a fondness for Cobb's wildest, most out-there notions.

Very weak photonic clusters. Digitally packetized. Reflectively collimated in real time into massively parallel beams . . .

Half an hour later, Van left Dottie sleeping in the suite and walked out under the quiet Virginia stars. He opened his cell phone.

Hickok answered at once. It was almost 3:00 A.M., but there was massive party racket in the background, and Hickok was drunk. "Hey, Van! Come on down and join us by the pool! These AFOXAR guys love you!"

"Mike, I know it's late, but I need you. Right away."

Hickok was crestfallen. His voice had sobered. "So, what, you didn't like my piloting today?"

"Mike, this is spacewar."

CHAPTER

THIRTEEN

Look, it's simple," said Hickok. "Van is the strategic leader. I am the tactical leader."

"Dr. Vandeveer's a civilian," Gonzales objected.

"Cyberwar is our brand-new kind of war, dude. I'm a civilian. You're a civilian. He's a civilian. The enemy are civilians. We're all civilians."

"I didn't even *want* to be a civilian," said Wimberley. "I got a dishonorable discharge. You know what that did to my job prospects?"

The four of them were sitting at midnight, in the mountains of Colorado, in the back of a rented camper-truck. The camper was parked off-road and hidden under a camouflage net. Van wore a black silk shirt, black cargo pants, a black leather jacket. He had a black shoulder bag, black socks, and black Rockport walking shoes. Van didn't normally dress like a New York humanities professor, but it would do. If he was caught breaking into the premises of the Alfred A. Griffith International Astronomical Facility, he had a good cover story.

After all, he was Mr. Dottie Vandeveer. He was an old college buddy of the guy who ran the place. There was nothing in Van's shoulder bag that couldn't pass close inspection. Black gloves, black woven hat—well, it got cold up here. Earpiece and mike—that was just a cell phone. Digital recorder, videocam, big deal. Laptop, he always had a laptop with him. He was a computer scientist.

The other three cyberwar infiltrators looked like the Mutant Ninja Turtles from Mars. Hickok, Gonzales, and Wimberley were impossibly scary. Van was used to it now—it had been his idea—but he could hardly bear to look at them. Their monster helmets had inbuilt night-vision goggles. They were big pointed Cyclops snouts with matching counterweights in the back. They had faceless black ski masks of fireproof Nomex. They owned the night in their shapeless black battle jackets, black combat pants, black Kevlar gloves, and black lace-up SWAT boots. They had great big black humpbacked ALICE packs.

They looked like three giant black plastic action figures. Any normal man who saw these three trolls stalking past him in darkness would assume that they were hallucinations.

The odd part was that none of it was even official U.S. military gear. It had all been bought or rented off the shelf, from various milspec commercial suppliers. None of it was even secret. Except for the loaded AFOCI burglar case that Van had brought from Washington.

"Sure you don't want to take the case with you?" Van asked Wimberley. The kid was looking shaky. "We could bungee it right to that ALICE pack."

"I don't deserve to carry it," Wimberley sniveled. "I got my ass kicked over that fair and square."

What was it gonna take to cheer this kid up? "There's fifteen grand waiting for you in a bus locker in Boulder."

"That helps," Wimberley admitted. "That's gonna help me a whole lot."

Van was spending the down payment on a house in order to invade, burgle, wiretap, and hack his wife's workplace. Van wasn't quite sure why this cyberwar operation was worth forty-five thousand dollars to him, plus the rental for the gear, the truck, and the airline tickets. Van had almost crawled out from the shadow of total financial disaster. This misadventure had put him right back in.

Not to mention that agent-running his own unapproved black-bag operation was eighteen different kinds of illegal.

It was just—he had to know. If he did not learn the whole truth about this evil weapon and its capabilities, he would never have another quiet night in his whole life.

Don't call it war. Call it science.

"This is only a recon mission," he told his three employees, for the tenth time. "No rough stuff from you tough guys. We're here to be the eyes-on-target. We infiltrate. We observe activities, intentions, and capabilities. We record and we verify. We plant remote sensors. Then we exfiltrate. Nobody sees us. Nobody hears us. Nobody gets hurt. Nobody gets shot. Because this is real, live cyberwar."

"I never pack heat," said Hickok.

"We don't get caught this time," Gonzales agreed.

"If we get caught, will the President pardon us later? Never mind, man, okay, I got no guns anyway!"

"Okay then," Van said. "Let's go ahead and roll." He tucked the headset into his right ear.

The four-man team did not have to roll very far. Following their highly detailed satellite maps, they left their rented camper and strolled through the pines to the edge of the Facility's fence. They found a ragged valley where the builders had run their fence under an old, sickly-looking box elder tree. The night was dark and gusty, with thin overcast. Wind tossed the spreading tree limbs. Box elders had weak wood. It wasn't much labor for four men to throw a grapnel rope up in the tree, time their heaves with the wind, and rip the old tree apart, nicely crushing the fence.

No alert defenders rushed over with any Jeeps and machine guns, because, after all, they were just astronomers, and it was just a tree falling in the wind. The four intruders climbed up the fallen tree limbs and over the smashed fence. Van was careful not to snag his civilian clothes.

"Loan me that oxygen mask," said Van to Hickok. "This altitude's killing me."

"Can't you carry this tank yourself?" said Hickok, rubbing under his black foam kidney-pad. "I got enough gear, that's for sure."

"No I can't carry it. An oxygen bottle looks way too much like a detonation bomb." Van huffed at the plastic mask. Relief flooded his body.

As planned, the four of them split into pairs. Gonzales and Wimberley, the B team, were tackling the Network Operation Center. Van and Hickok were going uphill to covertly inspect the Weapon of Mass Destruction.

Hickok set to work to hijack a small electric golf cart for the long ride up to the observatory. This wasn't hard. The astronomers had quite a lot of golf carts, and most of them still had keys in them.

Hickok detached his helmet mike. "You know what I miss in a cyberwar gig?" he said. "I miss the air support. No Pave Low, man. No C-130s. For Air Force Special Ops, man, that is hard."

"I was completely crazy to hire those two Cyberspace guys," Van mourned.

"No you weren't," Hickok said. "I hate to say this, but nowadays, most all the 'special' in Special Ops comes from the private sector."

"I'm crazy because there is nothing up there, Mike. I'm doing this because I am paranoid. There is no weapon up there. We're not gonna find anything. That is a half-completed telescope."

"No it isn't."

They drove the electric van silently, in darkness, slowly and without opposition, up to the site of the observatory. They manhandled the cart out of sight, down a talus of construction debris. Van threw a camouflage net over the cart. Van was new to handling camouflage nets. There was a real art to it.

Hickok produced the folding, spindly antenna of a multiband burst-radio net. He pointed it down the hill toward the Facility.

Gonzales came in at once, clear as crystal. "We got an incoming vehicle now," Gonzales reported. "A big black limousine. I'm making four—no, five occupants. Wow, this thermal imaging rocks!"

Wimberley was breathing heavily into his helmet mike. "It's quiet inside the dorms. Just a lot of sleepy astronomers. That Network Operation Center, though. A whole lotta lights on up there." They heard the whisper of his rubber-soled boots as Wimberley moved closer to his surveillance target. "I'm gonna unlimber this shotgun mike."

"That would be Carew inside that place," Van told Hickok. Hickok pulled down his Nomex mask. His face, already hard, grew harder still.

"You guys copy all that noise here?" Wimberley reported. His sensitive shotgun mike was picking up the rubbery thud and falsetto vocals of London-style Indo-disco. Bhangra music. "That's sure not like any kind of music I know. Lemme see if I can filter that noise out."

Odd digital muffling. A woman's shrill voice emerged faintly, her words strained like spaghetti in a metal colander. "You cannot talk to a lady like that, Tony! You dare not say a thing like that to me—"

Van broke in. "Wimberley?"

"Yes, sir."

"Never mind the subject's personal life. Go use your thermal imaging on the electrical station. I want to see if he is routing any wind power through those big fiber optics tonight."

Gonzales spoke up. He was calm and focused. "My limousine people are heading straight for that network center. I think we're gonna have ourselves one big party."

Van examined the big door to the observatory. It was stoutly pad-locked. It was a simple brass padlock, but there wasn't need for more security than that. This Facility was very isolated. And, after all, they were just astronomers.

Van set after the padlock with a digital pick from Hickok's utility vest. This pick was new, and British. It was the size of a large fountain pen. It used fiber optics to probe the inside of the lock, then calcu-lated the shape of the ridges on the key. When the computation was over, the butt of the pick slid out a nicely formed piece of stiff wire. It was awful what MI-5's new e-gadgets could do to the security inside conventional mechanical locks. Van really hoped it would be a good long time before normal thieves caught on to this.

Van carefully scraped the lock open. When his hands stopped trembling, he enjoyed more oxygen and had a gulp of Gatorade from Hickok's canteen. It was windy and freezing up here. He put on his gloves as well as his black hat.

Wimberley reported in. "Those generators sure give off a lot of heat! How much power is in those windmills?"

"Half a megawatt each," said Van. Wind power was intermit-tent—sometimes a little, sometimes a lot. That made wind energy particularly easy to steal. Who would notice if you shaved off some electrical power in a big storm passing through the western U.S.?

"Four people left the chauffeur behind in the limo," reported Gonzales. Gonzales was puffing a little after hefting his ninety-five pounds of rucksack cybergear uphill, at a dead run, after a moving car. The effort didn't seem to bother him much. "Subjects were two men, two women. I'm at the Network Center now, and I'm making nine people in the ground-floor room behind this wall. If this mil-limeter radar works."

"It was working okay when I left Washington," Van told him.

"Then it needs improvement," said Gonzales. "The limo has Col-orado license plates. It's registered to Pinecrest Ranch."

That was quick, thought Van. And so far, it had been really quiet. Maybe they would actually get this operation done on time.

Van pulled hard at the observatory door. The weather-stripping popped open with a hermetic smack. Van stepped inside the observatory's vault. The place was empty. It was delightfully warm.

"Real toasty in here," said Hickok. He unbuckled his helmet.

The telescope—that diva of the skies—looked pretty much like she had last time Van had seen her. There had been some additions on the ground, though. A new set of a dozen stacking, folded chairs. Coffee mugs and a big coffee decanter. A new, large designer desk— a multishelfed thing with power strips, big enough to call a console. And, standing near the door, a handsome little Japanese telescope. The little scope was some top-end toy for a rich stargazer hobbyist, sitting on a sturdy tripod.

Van walked to the big desk. It held a scattering of CDs and technical documents. He looked under it and behind it. A set of travel bags had been stowed under there.

A black fabric rifle case. The hunting sure was great around here.

Hickok rounded the giant telescope in awe, his nozzled head tilted back. "Check this thing out!"

"I've seen it," Van said.

Hickok pulled off his helmet. "I meant with these infrared scanners."

Van slipped Hickok's too-tight Kevlar helmet over his own ears. The bridge of his glasses crunched up against his nose.

Then the diva showed him her true colors.

The Lady wore a bloody crown.

A glassy ring of pulsing light. Ten thousand photo-multipliers, the sensors meant to lift the faintest glow of distant stars from the surface of the mirror. They had become a spider crown of red-glowing eyes. In the infrared of Hickok's heat detector, they winked, they twinkled. They were red-hot.

The optic pipes that carried light away could also bring light in. And the mirror that brought light down from the zenith could also shine light up into the sky.

Van gave Hickok his helmet back.

"You know what chaps my ass most?" said Hickok. "That son of a bitch had the guts to build a spacewar weapon in Colorado. Hell, that's where they *train the Air Force.*"

Gonzales reported. "The party is breaking up. I'm painting them with the spotter. You copy that now, Team A?"

Hickok opened his command-and-control laptop. The map on his screen was like a little military sandboard. Four blue triangles. A little cluster of unsuspecting red squares. "I copy, B."

Two red squares veered off from the others. A blue triangle zipped after them in pursuit. "I'm gonna move in to catch these two with my parabolic mikes," Gonzales said.

Van adjusted his earpiece.

Stolen voices swam into his head. Tony Carew.

"There were sixteen carts out here tonight," Tony remarked. "Now there are only fifteen."

"You *counted* them?" said a woman's voice.

"No, honey. I've got an eidetic memory. It's my gift."

"It's so cold and windy out here! Let's take the limo. Make those stupid Chinese take these ugly little carts."

"These delicate roads won't hold up the weight of their big limousine," said Tony. "That's why we use all these carts. Anjali, it's a sensitive matter to demonstrate the capabilities of my instrument. You don't see nice old Mr. Liang or nice old Mr. Gupta complaining about this."

"Your stupid clients don't have to wear sleeveless dresses." The cart's tires crunched. The voices faded out of range.

Gonzales came back in. "The male and female just departed in a Facility vehicle. They are riding up toward your telescope, Team A. Okay, I am painting two more groups now. I am making . . . four men in that first party. Two men, two women in the second party. Hold on here, whoa. We have got two bodyguard types inspecting the vehicles."

"Those bodyguards brought guns," said Hickok knowingly.

"We don't know that," Van protested.

"No professional would do this sort of thing without a gun," said Hickok. "I don't care if they're Chinese, Indians, or goddamned Martians."

"I'm running this operation," Van pointed out, "and I don't have a gun."

Wimberley broke in with a yelp. "Hey, I don't have a gun either! Everybody said not to bring any guns!"

Hickok sighed. "Would it break y'all's heart if I'd brung along one little Beretta in my ankle holster?"

"Hey, I can skip back to the truck and fetch us two MP5s and a Mossberg twelve-gauge," said Gonzales eagerly. "Wouldn't take me ten minutes!"

"No, no, no!" said Van. "Keep your eyes on the prize!"

"The boss man's right," said Hickok. "We came here to play cyberwar. Fred, you break into that party room and bug it. Kid, I want to see you break into that Network building. Get real busy with those desktop Tempest bugs. Me and the professor are gonna plant audio up here. Then we all retreat outside the structures. We hide out under our camou tarps. We just listen and we record. That is the Policy. We stick with the Policy."

The Policy was good and sensible. The Policy did not involve any sudden trips to an emergency room. Hickok slapped his translucent Wi-Fi bugs to various discreet surfaces. Van tuned the bugs into audio channels on his laptop. Then, with time ticking for the arrival of their guests, Van and Hickok went outside to shut and lock the observatory door.

The instant Van shut the observatory door, the audio signals from within the building completely vanished.

"I thought you said this structure was made of straw," said Hickok.

"Looks like they used some copper mesh in that straw." Sensitive instruments needed electrical shielding.

"Then if we want to overhear 'em when they're inside there, we gotta improvise," Hickok said tightly. "We gotta go back inside there and hide ourselves."

"That leaves nobody outside here to lock this door," Van pointed out. "If they find this place unlocked, then they'll know we're in there."

Hickok froze in confusion. He looked at the padlock, and then he gazed down the mountainside. "I can see those headlights coming fast." Hickok began to pray under his breath. "Lord, I, your soldier, am called upon to perform tasks in isolation, far from familiar faces and voices. With help and guidance from my God, I will never surrender, though I be the last. If I am taken, I pray that I may have the strength to spit upon my enemy . . ."

"I'm going inside," Van told him. "You run the team awhile, okay? If they catch me, I was just curious."

Van slipped inside the observatory. He ran across the floor, kicked some heavy luggage aside, and hid himself beneath the big console desk.

It took Tony some time to key his way through the jiggered lock.

Distant conversation. Van stuck an earpiece into his ear and turned down the light on his laptop screen. The audiobugs worked splendidly, sending him six different audio streams. It was like he had six ears.

"Try to be nice to Mrs. DeFanti," said Tony. "She's been through a lot of emotional pain over all this."

"Why don't you call her 'Katrina' to me?" said the actress girlfriend viciously. "It's 'Katrina' you are always calling her, so sweetly, face-to-face!"

"Honey lamb, if the former 'Li Huping' wants to be 'Katrina De-Fanti' now, why is that a problem? Give me the word, and you could be 'Angelie Carew.' That would look great on a nice new American passport."

"You are lovers with her."

"Look, she is twelve years older than I am," said Tony, pleading.

"Mrs. DeFanti is completely devoted to a much older man who is mentally ill. Katrina and I have useful talents for each other. It is very possible for an adult man and woman just to be good friends. Really, it is!"

"You are *lying*!" The actress drew a sharp breath. "Or you are abnormal."

"Okay, fine, I'm abnormal," Tony said. "I prefer 'extraordinary.' 'Brilliantly talented.' 'Fantastic.' 'A dream boyfriend.' But okay, 'abnormal' will do. Just be nice to Katrina for one evening. That's all I ask! There is a lot of money at stake. Crores and crores, and lakhs and lakhs, of rupees."

Tony's voice faded in Van's earplug. To Van's astonishment, he saw that Tony was suddenly standing right next to him, at the edge of the outsized desk. Tony set down his black shoulder bag. It brushed the edge of Van's black shoe.

Van looked up, and saw Tony's pale, strained face. But Tony did not look down. Tony's special guests were arriving.

As the observatory door yawned open, Van's earpiece caught a faint cross-talk of radio chatter. The cyberwarriors outside the observatory sounded real busy.

Tony left to face his guests. Van quickly opened Tony's shoulder bag. Tony's bag was a rat's nest. Crumpled business documents. Headache medicines. Indian gossip magazines. A laptop. A set of Bollywood DVDs.

A titanium ray gun.

Tony's customers entered the observatory for their demonstration. There was a babble of voices and the clatter of portable chairs.

Someone wandered into range of the fifth audio bug. Van turned up his audio stream.

"I can't like a man who lies to a hunting companion," said a male voice. "Yes, I might buy a jet from him, but I can never be his friend."

"I hate what he did to my husband's elk," said a woman. "He never asked my permission to blind them and scorch them with his laser beams. Those poor creatures!"

"How could poor animals hide from a reflecting balloon in the sky?" said the man. "It's just not sporting. Such an ugly business happening there, when your American plantation is so pretty and beautiful. My film crew and I, we so enjoyed our stay at Pinecrest. That suite was just like the Raffles in Singapore."

"Oh, you noticed," said the woman, pleased. "I've been to Singapore so many times."

"Look at Carew moving those chairs. Can't he let the guards do it? He's so busy, busy, busy all the time! He's like a servant!"

"They all are," said the woman thoughtfully. "Always. But I've come to like them, the Americans."

"They are lovable, in a strange way?"

"All right, I don't love them. But I love *being* American. Everyone on earth should be American. I put on my sunglasses. I go to Denver. I'm just a woman, I'm just a normal American woman. No one makes a bother of me, they just sell me whatever they have. 'Have a nice day.' "

"I also like America very much," the man confessed. "They know me too much in Bombay, Nairobi, and London. In America no one knows my face yet."

"They must have noticed that you are very, very handsome."

"Thank you so very much. But why would beauty make a man happy, Katrina? *Duty.* Duty is what makes a man happy . . ."

Van listened as Tony set to work to entertain his special guests. Tony's audience did not fully understand his American English. This forced Tony to speak very slowly. His taut, ranting voice echoed from the top of the observatory vault. "You are about to see . . . the single most astonishing . . . and significant technical development . . . in the modern Revolution in Military Affairs . . ."

The dome's great double doors opened to the black night sky. The observatory's strawbale walls spun as lightly as a carousel.

Van hastily picked up another squawking earpiece. The open roof had hit the right vector. He was getting a signal from his cyber-war team.

Wimberley's frantic voice. ". . . burst of electrical down there! When that wind picked up, they really . . ." Then Wimberley's signal vanished, and Hickok and Gonzales were still blocked out.

"Now that our roof to the stars is open, I suggest we make our Iridium calls," said Tony. "Mr. Gupta, you may call your home offices at the Research and Analysis Wing in New Delhi. And, Mr. Liang, perhaps you'll be kind enough to call the Second Department Analysis Bureau in Beijing. It's time for a joint understanding."

An icy mountain draft rushed down from the black night sky. It chilled Van's flesh as he crouched below the desk.

Overhead lights faded. New lights flashed on, stagily.

Van dared to press his belly to the floor and sneak a look around the desk. The Lady was beautifully lit now, a diva poised in creamy pools of light.

Van climbed to his feet in the thick gloom. His head pounded with the altitude. Tony and his guests were completely seduced by this gizmo. They had no idea that he was standing in a pool of darkness, watching them.

Van silently opened the fabric rifle case. He removed Tony's gun. An elk rifle. It was loaded. There was a huge brass round already in the chamber.

Van leaned his elbows on the ergonomic desk and stared down the rifle's scope. He picked their human faces out from the darkness, his crosshairs dissecting their heads. They were civilian targets. Utterly unsuspecting.

A Chinese functionary. He was an older man with thinning hair, a big gut, and a carpetbag. A younger Chinese man at his elbow, some flunky gopher and interpreter. His bodyguard had the stiff back and humorless scowl of an old-fashioned Red Army commissar.

Katrina DeFanti was a pleasant, middle-aged Chinese woman with nicely done hair and a roomy pink Chanel suit. She looked exactly like the kind of woman who should never, ever be shot at.

An Indian film star. Another Indian film star, even prettier. A much older Indian man, with an accordion-sided valise, a white Nehru jacket and whiskers. An impassive Sikh bodyguard, who looked like he was cut from solid teak.

Van had spent time in shooting ranges. He had learned a lot about rifles. He felt confident that he could put bullets into each one of them. But, as a professional cyberwarrior, he also knew that such crude behavior was counterproductive. Why had Tony bothered to hide a rifle inside this building? What on earth did he expect to gain by that pitiful tactic? For a struggle of the kind happening inside here, a simpleminded rifle was an admission of defeat. It was worse than stupid. A rifle was pure despair.

Van climbed back under the desk and returned to his surveillance duties.

"Whenever a great power achieves a spacewar capability, this creates a whole variety of remarkable technical spinoffs," Tony told his guests. "Through our methodical exploration of this weapon's capabilities, we've discovered its peripheral features. When combined with laser reflectivity from a Mylar aerostat, we can refocus effective heat beams over a seventy-five-kilometer radius. In early Star Wars parlance, that beam was known as 'The Finger of God.' Space-based lasers have never been put into practice. They are simply too heavy to launch with conventional rockets. Even airborne lasers need a chemical power plant bigger than a 747. However, this ground-based laser, combined with an airborne mirror, can dominate the horizon. It can hit settlements, moving vehicles, any target chosen."

The Chinese translator spoke up. "Mr. Liang would like to ask a question."

"Of course! Ask me whatever you like."

"Mr. Liang would like to ask a question of Mrs. DeFanti."

Tony was startled. "I, uh, yield the floor."

"Mrs. DeFanti, please tell us something. Is this strange device responsible for the many unsightly forest burns that we witnessed in your husband's rural properties?"

"Yes, Mr. Liang," said Mrs. DeFanti in English. "The laser here caused forest fires on my ranch, and elsewhere. There were a number of incidents. The laser also burned up two of the communications blimps."

"One can't expect pinpoint accuracy from an airborne blimp," Tony said. "But that's one feature only! Much more remarkable is the laser's fantastic ability to project colossal holograms. Here one combines the laser beam with an airborne chemical compound that fluoresces in infrared light. Spray that chemical across the sky, and you have psychological warfare effects previously undreamed of. Imagine the effect on the morale of enemies unprepared for an illusion of that size!"

Now it was Mr. Gupta's turn to object. "How do you place these pollutants up into the sky?"

"That's a very simple matter! Jet exhaust! Chemtrails!"

The Indian actor spoke up. "You put adulterated fuels in that jet? You never told me you had spoiled the jet's engine with contaminants."

"I didn't harm the jet," said Tony, shocked. "It's not a Space Shuttle. Boeings can burn anything."

"But it's a matter of principle," said the actor. "You did not disclose to us that you had subjected my property to unclean fuels! The Bharatiya Janata Party will have to reduce its price accordingly."

Tony was angry. "Sanjay, you're letting this go to your head! I know you've taken pilot training, and I know that's rather hard to get in America, these days. But the condition of the Boeing Business Jet is completely a side issue. I think Mr. Gupta and his superiors in New Delhi can speak for themselves."

Mr. Gupta removed his bristly ear from his brick-shaped Iridium phone. "Oh, no, no." He chuckled richly. "Sanjay Devgan is not merely our movie hero, don't you know? Inside the Research and Analysis Wing, Sanjay Devgan also happens to be *our hero*. Our brave young colleague has our fullest support!"

Mrs. DeFanti spoke up. She seemed irritated. "Gentlemen, I know you are all jet-lagged. But if you squabble in this way, we'll be up here all night. I want to see this ugly matter resolved. My husband is too troubled a man for such complex affairs. I want this situation liquidated."

Liang ran this speech through his Chinese interpreter. Then he replied. "We Chinese are not interested in some remote device in the rural mountains of America. We do have some interest in the plans and the hardware. Could you ship?"

Mrs. DeFanti grew peppery. "All right. I am merely a housewife. It's not my fault that we Chinese suffer a Two Chinas policy! I am very weary of having my family in Taiwan required to sabotage visual imaging chips, just so that major heat sources in a narrow band of laser wavelengths cannot be detected on the ground by spy satellites. It was very tiresome and difficult to get those Taiwanese chips designed, bought, and installed in American spysats, just so that this spacewar laser would not be visible. If the American spies seek other chip suppliers for their later spacecraft, then it will be senseless for any of us to build spacewar lasers at all. Your lasers would be spotted instantly by American spy satellites, and blown to shreds with American cruise missiles. So you must deal with us now, and pay us now, or else this entire laser effort is useless!"

Tony cleared his throat. "Well, as Katrina points out so aptly, there you have it. It's our way or the highway. The very good news is, we *have* successfully defeated the KH-13 satellite. Using this weapon, we burned the KH-13 so effectively that it will never be trusted again. We have proved that, with this telescope, we have a covert device which is also the world's first and only effective spacewar weapon. With this laser capability in place, we can defeat any craft that any space power ever puts into orbit."

"Into *low* orbit only," said Mr. Gupta skeptically. "You cannot damage any spacecraft in the valuable geosynchronous Arthur Clarke orbit."

"There's nothing that far out but some harmless comsats," said Tony. His wristwatch bleeped. "We need to wrap this up now all right? It's time for our product demo."

Electro-actuators kicked into life beneath the Lady's great blue mirror. The digitized mirror was clicking and flexing, moving in tiny increments of a few wavelengths of light. The digital telescope sounded like a roomful of typists.

Tony spoke again. "I didn't mean to interrupt our valuable negotiations, but it's necessary to time this demonstration with care. We are about to attack the Iridium spacecraft that is carrying your phone signals, gentlemen."

"How can you prove that?" said Sanjay.

"You'll be able to hear the attack happening in real time," Tony promised. "And so will your sponsors at home in your nations' capitals."

"You might be simply changing the phone signals inside this observatory building," said Sanjay silkily. "So that proves nothing at all."

"I was aware of that objection," said Tony. "As you all know, my personal associate inside the National Security Council is extremely well placed in American cyberwarfare circles. It will be simple for Dr. Vandeveer to get the outage reports from the Iridium's new owners. I can forward those reports directly to you. That will prove the power of my antisatellite capability."

The spies listened silently to their satellite phones.

"The Iridium satellite is not being destroyed," Mr. Gupta reported at last. "We hear only a faint crackling! We have not even lost our phone connection to New Delhi!"

"It's an overcast night," Tony explained. "The damage is mild. The ideal conditions for our laser are clear nights with a strong storm front through the local windmill farm."

"Wind there, and yet no clouds here? How often do you get those weather conditions?"

"There is very good visibility up on this mountain. After all, this is a telescope."

"Snow, rain, then they make your laser weapon quite useless?"

Tony tapped busily at his laptop for some time. Then he spoke again. "Of course it takes some time for a silent beam of light to destroy a metal satellite. We do not have enough wind power to destroy satellites instantly. Besides, it would be very foolish to detonate satellites, for then the Americans would know the truth at once. Think of this fact, though: we could attack Iridium satellites, weather permitting, very stealthily, for years. A reputation for bad technical performance would finish Iridium off for good. Then we could short their stock and buy Iridium competitors, such as Globalstar. That would be so profitable that it would easily pay for this telescope."

"Globalstar loses money already," said Mr. Gupta gloomily. "If satellite phones made money, our Indian ISRO would be launching telephone satellites! Millions of Indians have never made a phone call."

"Maybe you would do that," said Tony. "More likely, you would become a customer of Mr. Liang. China already has a financially sound commercial space-launch service."

"Why is it getting so hot in here?" said the actress suddenly. "So cold, and then so hot in here! Where is my coconut milk? Did you bring only coffee?"

"When do you begin your so-called satellite attack?" said Mr. Liang's interpreter. "Our phone line to Beijing is still working perfectly!"

"We *are* attacking that Iridium satellite," said Tony. "Right now. There is no visible beam. It is a very energy-efficient process. The adaptive beam has to penetrate miles of atmosphere with as little signal loss as possible. We don't even generate the laser pulses locally. We amplify them and collate them. We are beaming Internet traffic up into the sky, from the telescope, right now. Those Internet signals come from all over the planet."

"Don't the people miss their Internet when you throw it up into outer space?" said Sanjay.

"It's all spam."

"No."

"Yes, I am attacking a satellite with laser spam."

"No."

"We are running a major Internet backbone across the Rocky

Mountains here," said Tony patiently. "We have spam filters. Nobody ever asks where the spam goes. We beam the spam into outer space."

"You are an evil man," said Sanjay simply. "I don't like you. I never liked you."

"Why are you selling this laser weapon to us?" demanded Mr. Gupta. "Why don't you sell your weapon to the Americans? They are the ones obsessed with space violence."

"Because India and China are the planet's two emergent space powers," said Tony passionately. "China is about to launch its first manned mission. China is only the third nation on this world that is able to launch men in space. And India has an unmanned moon rocket planned for 2008. You Indians, you Chinese, you *need* this space capability to diminish America's overwhelming space power. The Americans don't need laser weapons. Not at all! If the Americans want to attack your Indian and Chinese satellites, they can *fly up with a Space Shuttle and bring them down whole in one piece.*"

There was a long silence as the listeners consulted their satellite phones.

"It makes no sense for us to purchase American weapons on American soil for use against American satellites," insisted the Chinese interpreter. "Your proposal is absurd. We do have some interest in the hardware and the technical plans. A very mild interest."

"You *don't have any choice,*" Tony shouted. He tried to calm himself. "Look at the geomilitary realities here. You are the two oldest civilizations in this world. You have a billion people each. But the Americans completely rule your air. The Americans have more advanced fighters and bombers than all other nations combined. The Americans completely rule your seas. The Americans have nine supercarrier battle groups and whole fleets of nuclear submarines. On land, the Americans have nine thousand Abrams tanks with the world's most accurate fire-control systems. Nobody else even has the *experience* of the American armies—since 1985 the Americans have been the only military that still fights genuine wars. The Americans are taking over your planet by force of arms. And now, after one terrorist incident from some small cult of fanatics, the Americans feel completely justified in attacking anyone, anywhere, at any time! And with space dominance to leverage all those other military assets, the Americans *can do that.* The Americans can strike with total speed and accuracy on every square meter of this globe! If you don't move into space warfare, your militaries will be completely irrelevant."

"No space weapon will ever harm the many American submarines," said Mr. Gupta wisely. "Nor would this one trifling weapon be of much use against the vast host of American satellites. However, I concur that this weapon has one important use. This weapon might be of great use in harming the Chinese space program. We Indians could rent this laser and attack Chinese photoreconnaissance assets. For instance, we could burn up the orbiting Tsinghua surveillance system, a considerable irritant in our Indian nuclear development efforts. May I ask my esteemed colleague Dr. Liang what he thinks of that prospect?"

Liang engaged in consultation with his interpreter and his telephone. "We Chinese would consider that a very hostile, provocative act from the Indian nation, likely to create a nuclear crisis between our two great powers."

"I fully agree with Dr. Liang. May I further ask if Dr. Liang considers it necessary to beg foreign technical assistance in order to sabotage India's peaceful space program?"

More consultation. "We Chinese are entirely aware of India's space ambitions. We Chinese feel entire confidence that indigenous Chinese space technology will conclusively prove China's superiority to India's halting efforts in this regard. 'Begging' is not necessary for us. 'Begging' is more of an Indian skill."

"May I point out to my esteemed Chinese colleague, as a matter of record, that India has an English-speaking population, vigorous democratic institutions, a market economy, and is rapidly becoming the planet's software powerhouse? May I further point out that Indian engineers are so very common in the United States that this *very space war weapon* is manned by Indian engineers? China has a manufacturing capacity that we respect—but it is Indian genius that is going to lead South Asia into the twenty-first century!"

"We are entirely aware of the bellicose Hindutva sentiments of Dr. Gupta! We are glad to consider outer space one area of peaceful competition, in which the Indian government does not feel driven to repeat the gruesome atrocities of Kashmir and Gujarat."

"My esteemed Chinese colleague should not think that the genocidal sufferings of the Tibetan people have escaped our notice—"

"Seven hundred and fifty million dollars!" Tony shouted at them.

The two fell silent.

"That's all! Just seven hundred and fifty million dollars was all it took to cripple a thirteen-billion-dollar American spacecraft," said Tony. "Can't you people see the amazing financial leverage in that? I didn't even ask you for that money in a lump sum!"

"The Indian ISRO can send a spacecraft all the way to the Moon for seven hundred and fifty million dollars," said Gupta indignantly. "That amount of money is absurd."

"No Chinese moneys will be forthcoming to you," said Liang's translator, with finality.

"We Indians could build an infernal machine like this with our own strong, skillful hands," said Gupta. "We built atomic bombs and we tested them successfully in defiance of the entire world! Let no one think we Indians lack the ability and resolution to build space weapons. We scorn to do that. That is the truth: we scorn to do any such wicked thing." Gupta rose to his feet. "These negotiations are at an end."

Van looked around the desk. It was true. Tony's guests were leaving. They simply opened the door and walked out in a body.

Tony was abandoned there with two women: Mrs. DeFanti and the little actress.

"Don't look so sad, Tony," said Mrs. DeFanti. "That was all a negotiating ploy. You are a technical genius, you have them completely dominated. Those people are mere spies, not entrepreneurs like you and Tom. What can they do but play psychological games? The Indians and Chinese can never think like Americans think. They can't treat a billion dollars like fast food. You astonished them here, Tony. Really, you amazed and impressed them very much. They'll consult with the home offices, and talk to all the elders. Then they'll come back to you."

"But I can't wait while they stall for time," Tony said hollowly. "I'm past waiting. I really need to make this sale. There's nothing else left, Katrina."

"I'm taking my limousine home," she told him. "Stop fretting, darling. You've always got a place with Tom." She kissed him on the cheek.

Mrs. DeFanti left the observatory. Tony looked hopefully at his girlfriend. "Well, honey, by pulling that sad little snit like that, those suckers missed the very best part! I guess that situation looked pretty bad, but you know, I'm not too surprised by what they did. No, I'm not. They don't appreciate me, that's all. They can't grasp the scale of my achievement here. But you know what I'm going to do now? I'm going to do the most amazing thing that any man has ever done for a woman he loved! I am going to write your name on the Moon."

Anjali Devgan didn't seem much impressed. "What does that mean?"

"You'll be able to see it happening, right through this beautiful Japanese telescope. This used to belong to Tom DeFanti, and I brought it here just for you. I am *literally* going to write your adorable name, with a laser, on the surface of this planet's satellite. A-N-J-A-L-I. That process will take about half an hour. If we get some overcast cirrus, we might drop a few pixels here and there. But, honey: it's the Moon!"

"You're writing my name on the Moon in English?"

"Why not?" Tony paused. "Honey, please don't do this to me. I don't have a font in Hindi."

"I know that Chinese woman is your lover. She kissed you on the face in front of me! She called you 'darling.' "

"I can *get* you a font in Hindi. I just can't get it tonight."

"You have no soul, Anthony Carew. You are a decadent Western intellectual. You never think of anything but your power and your money. I am sick and tired of being your concubine, Tony Carew. I don't care how many toys you give me. You are unworthy of my love. You have no home. You have no warmth of elders in your house. You cannot marry me properly as a man should marry a woman. There is no husband's mother to properly send me my sargee. You want only love without commitment, and sex without children. You have no future!"

"Honey, people in the modern world can work out little issues like this."

"I'm going home to marry Amitabh. That's what Bapuji wants from me."

"Anjali, you can't marry that guy. Amitabh? Even as Bollywood star-children go, Amitabh is as dumb as a racehorse." Tony recoiled from her scalded look. "Okay, fine! Go marry Amitabh, have his kids! I'm willing to look right past that!"

"I hate you, Tony Carew. You are evil. I should never have erred and sinned with you. My audience will forgive me my vamp roles when I give them children." Anjali looked at her jeweled watch. "I'm never going back to that ugly Chinese woman's stupid ranch house! Never! I am flying away from you in Sanjay's jet. I have a three-night engagement to dance in London. Bipasha is there, Kareena is there. I want to talk to my star sisters! They understand the sorrows of life!"

"Oh, come on, *sajaana* . . ."

"Our love affair is over, Tony. I don't love you, and I never want to see you again." She left him.

Tony stood immobile. Then he turned and ran headlong for the desk. He scrabbled at the black fabric rifle case and unzipped it. He stood the rifle on its wooden butt. Trembling all over, he jammed his chin against the muzzle.

Van stepped into the light. "I disarmed your rifle, Tony. Bullets equal zero."

Tony glared at him with red-rimmed eyes. "Oh, for God's sake. You? What good are you to me now?"

"I'm no good to you, Tony. I am the end of you, pal." Van leveled the ray gun.

"What's with the titanium toy? Am I under arrest or something?"

"No, Tony. You are not under arrest. I hacked you and I own you. You are an illegal combatant. It's the steel box in Cuba for you, you son of a bitch."

Tony made a sudden break for it. Van cut him off, grabbed his jacket, and punched him twice in the head. Then he dragged Tony bodily across the floor of the observatory. He threw Tony headlong across a tumbling heap of metal chairs. He opened a chair. He picked Tony up and sat him down.

"Now what?" said Tony, wiping his split lip. "I guess you can beat me up. What does that prove?"

"I am not beating you, Tony. I am interrogating you. Are there any other ones?"

Tony was stunned. "What?"

"Are there other laser weapons like this telescope? Anywhere on planet Earth."

"Would I *need* another one?" said Tony. He gestured wildly. "Look at her! This is the most fantastic weapon in the world! I *built a death ray,* man! I built a no-kidding, working death ray in the very same world that's got bubble gum and *Hollywood Squares* and Chee•tos! I can *fry spacecraft!*"

He drew a sobbing breath. "Okay, so they don't blow up all at once! Maybe it takes me a few months to destroy them! Sometimes the orbit isn't quite right, sometimes the weather is wrong. But I am *bigger than NASA,* dude! I could take down a Shuttle."

"You are a traitor, Tony. You wrecked a spy satellite for money. And you just outed me, to Chinese and Indian intelligence agents, as a part of your rotten conspiracy."

Tony looked up wearily. "Van, would you stop pointing that ray gun at me? That's just really geeky. The thing melts glue, all right? It's not even plugged in."

Van reached down and plugged the gun into a power strip.

Van looked up in time to see Tony nerving himself to leap on him. "Forget trying to kill me," Van said. "I led my cyberwar team here. We have surveilled and recorded everything. You're toast, Tony."

Tony laughed hollowly. "That's a good try, pal. You are a glorified computer clerk for an advisory board. Real military people are never gonna move one inch without clearance from SOCOM and the Joint Chiefs of Staff. I could be in Tahiti by the time those morons shuffle their paperwork."

Van looked at him in wonderment.

"Tony, you sold out."

"Why would you even wonder at that?" Tony said passionately. "That was the whole point of living in the 1990s! Did I ever *ask* to be born under some particular flag? I could live in Bombay. I *wanted* to live in Bombay, the action there is amazing. I could live in Shanghai! Shanghai has got skyscrapers that make New York look like a bombed-out rathole! So what if I sold out the USA—what about the USA selling *me* out? I don't even recognize this country since 9/11. It's mean! It's vindictive! It's aggressive! It's broke, that's the worst part. And it invades places! Your country is like a giant Serbia. The people who run it are moron oil company people. I'm a dot-com guy. I am thirty-two years old. I was right on top of the world. Then I went from genius, to bum, to bankrupt in eighteen months! I was right in the middle of the fastest, most potent, the best technological revolution in human history. I was making that happen, I was a true-blue revolutionary. It's been no time, Van, and I'm already history. I'm obsolete, I'm invisible. The sons of bitches vanished me. It's just like I was never there at all."

"Tony, you used me in an act of treason. I swore an oath. I'm in the government."

"What, you're wrapping yourself in the flag now? Is this Hollywood, are we cuing the violins? Me telling the Indians about you, that was just my bargaining ploy. Those Chinese didn't sign anything. It was all just an ad pitch." Tony looked at Van's face searchingly. "Come on, pal. You were never a top venture-capital guy, but you were definitely one of us. Don't you know how much you've lost already? What's left of your life?" Tony wiped at his bleeding lip. "Do you even know why I had that stupid ray gun in my stupid bag? I was going to mail it to you. From wherever. I was never gonna come back here to this creepy little version of America. I don't have to, and I don't need to. I can make another life in a better place. Let me go, Van."

"You're not going anywhere."

"Anywhere will do. I'm an inventive guy, I've got a big imagination. I'll just reinvent myself overnight, okay? It doesn't matter wherever you send me, because I'm global. I'll go live in some stupid leper camp in Thailand if you want. Then I'll bring the joy of broadband connectivity to the planet's illiterate masses. Wouldn't that make you happy?"

"How, Tony? You angle all that, and then I do what for you? What is it you want from me this time?"

"Nothing! Nothing, really! You just let me be free."

Van moved his chin in a nod. "You see that large, black creature standing in the doorway over there? Standing in the only exit? Between you and all that freedom?"

Tony glanced over his shoulder and yelped.

"That is one of my cyberwarriors, Tony. I ordered them here so that I could demolish you."

Tony stared at Van in astonishment. "What the hell are you talking about?"

"Tony, al Qaeda is only fifteen years old. American Special Ops commandos have been dying in secret wars ever since John Kennedy turned them loose in 1963. These are my guerrillas, and we just defeated you and your spacewar scheme. I need to know something now, Mr. so-called Space Warrior. Your only way out of here is through my soldier. Will you kill him?"

"Is this a trick question?"

"Yes."

"Kill him with what, exactly? You took my rifle away."

"You might use this ray gun that I am pointing at your chest, Tony. Because I put one of your rifle rounds inside of it. And then I plugged it in."

Tony looked at the ray gun skeptically. "You're kidding me. What the hell kind of weapon is that? You plug it in, you turn the heat on, and sooner or later a bullet explodes and somebody gets killed? That's your big concept here?"

"That's cyberwar, Tony."

"Look, Van, I don't want to play your weird ray gun game."

"*Now* you don't want to play it, Tony. Because I play it better than you do."

Tony bent to look up the gun's barrel. "You really put a real bullet inside that cool little toy?"

"Cyberwar is real."

The ray gun exploded: Carew catapulted backward out of his chair. A 250-grain elk cartridge was designed to take down a bull elk at four hundred yards. It ripped a hole through Carew.

Van looked down at a stinging pang in his arm. A blackened shard of metal had lodged in his flesh. There were perforations all through his black shirt. Little dust-sized bits of titanium shrapnel. He could feel the bigger ones dribbling fresh blood.

Hickok walked up from the black doorway. He leaned down without a word, grasped the shard of metal, and yanked it out of Van's arm. Van gritted his false teeth and said nothing.

"I'll get a field dressing on that wound," said Hickok, opening his pack. "I can't believe you just shot this bastard. Those Cyberspace boys are being so good down there. They didn't hurt even a fly."

"Mike, listen to me. In information warfare, a shooting never counts for much. Media is everything. We're going to vanish this guy and all his works. We're gonna break all his tools. Nothing that happened here ever really happened. So the public never learns."

"I get you, sir," Hickok said.

"Those foreign techs in the Network Operation Center? Five minutes ago they were a bunch of engineers on visas. From now on they are a covert cyberterror cell. If you have to shoot them, that's fine. If they run and hide, good luck. If Ashcroft gets them, God help them. It's time to phone in some backup."

"Hoo-ah, sir." Hickok dressed the bleeding wound in Van's arm with comradely tenderness. "Who exactly do we telephone about a situation like this?"

"That would be the Homeland Security Computer Emergency Response Team. Oh, wait, they don't exist yet. Who's closest over here? The Air Force in Colorado Springs? Phone the damn Air Force, Mike. Get me the black helicopters."

Van winced as Hickok tied off the bandage. "Demerol," Hickok said knowingly.

"Yeah, Demerol," said Van. "That's wonderful stuff."

Hickok examined the spreading stain of blood under Tony Carew's corpse. "Boss, we got ourselves a very dead rich guy here."

"I'm ahead of the curve with that. We've got to sanitize this whole area. I've got a plan."

"I knew you would have a plan, Dr. Vandeveer. Can I tell you something now? I have seen a lot of people killed. A whole lot. I stopped counting back in 1998. Nintendo wars, yeah, air strikes, yeah, collateral damage, yeah. But in all that time, I have never killed a bad guy with my own hands, no, not ever." Hickok looked Van in the eyes. "You are one tough bastard, boss. You are the true pro."

"The evildoer goes straight into his weapon of mass destruction," Van said.

"Aw, no, Van. Jesus."

"Yes. We dump his body into the telescope. We override his weapon's operating system. We turn up those laser amps to eleven. We shut the gates to heaven. We lock that door from outside. Then we vanish this terrorist. Utterly. He is less than history, he is less than ashes. He's going to vaporize. This is an airtight building made of flammable straw. When the heat and pressure builds up in there, we are going to blow this gizmo into bits."

Hickok scratched beneath his helmet. "How do we do all that, again, exactly?"

"You don't do that, Mike. I do it. You stay near here and you put it all on video."

Van drove the cart one-handed, in the dark, down the mountain slope. Van had a fully loaded elk rifle, a sling for his wounded arm, and an open laptop. Hickok had attached the oxygen mask to his face, rigging him an improvised black harness for the tank.

With fresh oxygen inside his lungs, Van literally had a second wind. Van had blown right past fear, loathing, rage, and exhaustion into a state of battlefield glory. It was two o'clock in the morning. He had killed. He had been wounded in battle. He felt not one atomic particle of remorse or doubt. His mind had never been clearer in his life.

He was exalted.

The truth was, he loved war. He had never been in war before, but now he recognized war as his home. He loved war more than he loved women, food, or sleep. He would grind his teeth when cyber-warfare was denied him. In moments of peace, he would miss his dear war gone by. He would miss it so.

Wimberley was waiting inside the operating center. He was standing over an unconscious technician. He was tapping at a mouse.

Van set his rifle aside. "So what happened to the weapon's operator here?"

"I sprayed nonlethals on his keyboard. All over his fingers, Dr. Vandeveer. That spray-on stuff is voodoo."

"Too bad. I was planning to interrogate him."

"No need for that, sir," said Wimberley. "I set Tempest bugs on his monitor. We got every screen shot. Every keystroke. I'm just resetting these system preferences so we can push this laser past the limit."

"Can we get enough wind power to surge this weapon past its red line?"

"I do think so, sir," said Wimberley. "And that power-console guy looked real surprised when I busted in there and knocked him cold."

"How'd you do that?" said Van.

"I used a chair leg, sir," said Wimberley. He stared at Van's wounded arm and tactfully said nothing.

Another Internet technician appeared at the far end of a tall set of blue cabinets. He was carrying a hunting rifle cradled in both arms.

Van made a one-handed lunge for his own rifle, but Wimberley just turned his black-helmeted head. "U.S. Cyberspace Force!" he shouted from the keyboard. "Freeze!"

The technician dropped his rifle with a panicked clatter. Van heard an exit door bang open. He heard shoes rattling down a set of stairs.

Wimberley returned to Van with the abandoned rifle. He checked the action expertly. "No round inside the chamber. Safety still on. He busted the scope when he dropped it, too." He returned to his screen. "You were right about the no-guns rule, sir. Guns, that's just not our way."

"What does a giant laser death ray run under?" said Van.

"OpenBSD. And X-Windows."

"Awesome." Van had another huff of oxygen.

"I can run this console. I'm controlling all the enemy's software. You know what, sir? I'm about to blow up a spacewar weapon. I'm gonna save an American satellite. Me. William C. Wimberley. This is the most important thing I'm ever gonna do in my whole life, and I'm only twenty-one years old." Wimberley looked at Van and blinked. "You didn't have to give me another chance, sir. I broke your head in."

Van shrugged.

"I am such a screwup. I've always been a loser. When your phone call came for me to do this, I was drunk and I was crying in my beer.

I just thought, maybe he'll give me some money. I'm a pretty smart kid, Dr. Vandeveer, but I never knew who I was, or what the hell I was doing. I'm finally gonna do something here that really, really matters."

Van nodded. He had heard about such things before, but he had never before seen it happen. He was seeing a troubled young man rehabilitated by his military service.

"The past is over and we're gonna set it on fire," Van told him, waving him on with his free left arm. "You carry on."

Van watched his laptop screen for Hickok's video surveillance.

The observatory's round wall was bulging. The building warped and began gently smoldering. It was very strange to witness a weapon being demolished on a screen, thought Van. He had just been physically inside that place. He had ordered all the buttons pushed to smash it, but the resulting mayhem could have been anywhere on the planet: North Korea, Iran, Iraq.

Plumes of red light. Boiling gas was squeezing itself through the curved doors to the heavens. As the gas hit fresh air, it caught in thin, livid flames.

There was violent flashover as all the laser-blasted fumes within the structure ignited at once. The explosion was sudden and elegant. The walls of packed hay splayed out like a giant child puffing a dandelion. The observatory blew its top. The rounded dome tumbled headlong down the mountainside, twirling like a tossed coin.

Tufts of flaming hay swirled across the blackened foundation. Bouquets of flame stuck to the molten instrument consoles. The Lady was in agony. She was blackened, on her knees. Her very bones were going. The mirror of Venus, stamped flat by the boot of Mars.

When dawn broke, the black helicopters had already been and gone. The local civilians were standing around the wreckage of their telescope. Their prized handiwork was a total, tragic loss. Some of them were spraying bits of flaming hay with fire extinguishers. Most were just wringing their hands, mourning in small groups. It was an awful thing to lose a major scientific instrument. It was a cultural calamity. Gonzales offered Van a pair of binoculars. Van refused them.

Van didn't care to look at people as the smoke rose from their hopes and dreams. One of them was almost certainly Dottie.

"You gotta try this MRE, Van," said Hickok. "A man who's lost some blood needs to eat a meal. You learn that in combat."

"Is that dogface chow?" said Wimberley, sniffing at it.

"No, man, this stuff's brand-new. It's civilian MRE. Made in Brazil! Got this sort of pork loin and pineapple thing going, these really spicy black beans . . . and it's self-heating!"

Van put the food across his knees. He used the fork left-handed. The food tasted great. In Brazil, people could really cook. Why did Brazil never have wars? he wondered. Brazil was a really big country on a big American continent. How come Brazil had no enemies? It didn't make sense.

Brazilians didn't invent much. Well, that explained it.

Van had more oxygen. His tank was low.

"Here comes the enemy plane," said Gonzales.

"Okay," said Hickok, climbing to his feet. "Now this is the part that an Air Force boy likes best."

The Indian actor was flying his newly purchased jet plane. He had just taxied off from the DeFanti airstrip. It seemed a little odd to Van that two groups of Chinese and Indian spies would fly off across the Pacific Ocean together, all polite and collegial, inside the same aircraft. But they were people of two practical nations, thought Van, and the trip here hadn't been their idea.

For a moment, Van suspected that the Boeing was out of range of the overriding radio signal. But when it came to forward air-controlling operations in the mountains, Michael Hickok knew his stuff.

The jet banked hard left and roared over them so sharply that the mountainside shook. Birds exploded from the forest.

Wimberley had taken off his helmet to eat. He jammed his hands over his ears.

Hickok caressed his joystick. The captured jet spewed black smoke and rose in a steep arc. "Looka that," crowed Hickok. "I got 'er. Boys, this is sweet."

"Okay," said Wimberley in a stunned, small voice. "You just used that black box and you pulled a jet out of the sky."

Van and Hickok exchanged wary glances. Wimberley and Gonzales had not attended the Summit in Virginia. The general public was not at all up to speed about cyberwar projects to control civilian jets.

"Yeah, I did that," Hickok told him, grinning. "Now watch me put 'er into a slow loop over the telescope ground zero there. That aircraft is chock-full of Indian and Chinese space spies. Can you imagine the nerve of those clowns? They're supposed to hate each other! Everybody knows they hate each other! But here they are, infiltrating our own country, and picking on my favorite satellite. I have got them right by the throat!"

Wimberley stared at Van. "You can really grab jets out of the sky?"

Van nodded.

"Who the hell are you?" Wimberley demanded. He was shaking. "Where did you come from? What world is this?"

"As long as he's on our side, what difference does that make?" said Hickok. "It's time to settle the hash of the Space Invaders here. Hey, Fred! Did you make that Indian Special Ops guy, that actor with the pecs and the biceps?"

"I saw him," growled Gonzales. "Those Indians sure like 'em pretty. I hate a pretty spook."

"That actor is the pilot up there. Check this out." Hickok slapped at his joystick. The jet careened violently. "He's a real hot dog, isn't he? He loves to push the envelope!"

"No need to be cornball," said Gonzales. "Special Ops are 'the Quiet Professionals.' So fly them straight out into middle of the Pacific. Fuel runs out, then they go straight into the drink. That's quick and it's quiet."

"The middle of the Pacific is way beyond radio range," said Hickok. "And that's too slow. I'm thinking a fast power dive straight onto the top of that mountain yonder."

"We are letting them go," Van told him.

"What?" Hickok demanded. "Then why did we just catch 'em?"

"We are letting them go because only punk-ass al Qaeda losers crash airplanes. We caught them to show that we can catch them. We have destroyed the space weapon here. They see that. We own them. They know that. They have no idea who we are. They only know that we are in America, and that we own them. If we kill them now, that sends a message. It says that their resistance matters, so we want to kill them. If we send them back to their bosses, then they *become* our message."

"What the heck kind of message is that?" said Hickok. "Can't we just wipe 'em out? That would do."

"That message is: Our command of technology is beyond conventional military resistance. The conventional military struggle between nations no longer matters. We are the agents from a new geopolitical arena. It's time to carry out our struggles in a new, improved way."

"What kind of cockamamie war doctrine is that?" Hickok demanded.

"It's cyberwar!" said Wimberley.

"It's information warfare," said Gonzales. "It's like media spin or something. Am I right?"

"They are human beings in there," said Van. "We need to convince them of something important right now. They need to believe that it's cyberwar or it's bloody-handed terror suicide, and those are the only kind of wars that get allowed. Now we can make that distinction clear to them. Let them fly back home, Mike."

"Okay," said Hickok. "I know that you know that. What I wanna know is—*how* do you know that?"

"I was inside that plane once," Van said. "That's how I know."

PENTAGON CITY, SEPTEMBER 2002

Van woke up. It was his birthday. He stared at the cigarette-stained ceiling. This was pretty sure to be the worst birthday of his life.

The federal refund money for the Grendel system had finally come in. That was the pool of cash that he and Dottie were both living on. This was a small miracle, and he was grateful for it, because the CCIAB no longer existed. Quick, quiet, and done with its work, it was not even a Washington memory. Just another blue-ribbon panel, offering wisdom to power. It was as if Van's labors had never been.

Van had never expected such a strange reaction from Washington's establishment. He had run a black-bag operation, shot a man, blown up a multimillion-dollar scientific instrument, and captured and released highly placed agents from two foreign intelligence agencies. Van had imagined that they might either arrest him, and put him on trial, or they would give him a secret medal. It had never occurred to Van that he would blow their minds so badly that they would do nothing at all.

The ruined observatory was, officially, the victim of an accidental fire. Officially, Tony Carew had vanished. Better yet, he had vanished in India. Strange news about Tony was all over the Bollywood film magazines. According to the tabloids, he had vanished on a hunting trip to the Himalayas. Nobody had gone to India to look for Tony. Nobody seemed to care about a ruined entrepreneur from the Bubble. He'd been a star's plaything and once she had dumped him, there was nothing left of him but a kind of black vacuum.

Derek Vandeveer was also a nonperson. Jeb had a new job handling security with eBay. Fawn had a nice federal post. Michael Hickok, as a policy, never explained to anyone what he was doing.

Van was left alone. Van's phone did not ring with eager job offers.

His e-mail bore no pleas and flattering invitations. Van wasn't looking for any job in computer security, anyway. Van wasn't exactly
looking for much of anything, really. He was searching.

He was running a small Web log. Nobody seemed to understand
Web logs yet. Van had one. It was a quiet, fast-paced Web log. He used
it to absorb and spread ideas. Van's Web log involved genuine issues.
The genuine issues were the issues that political people lacked clichés
for. Web logs interested Van. There was no money in them, yet, and
the political campaigners were just catching on. Web logs were in
combat for attention. That was the most interesting thing about
them. Combat for attention. War of ideas.

In his deep exile, Van was doing a lot of reading. His field of study
was war. He was reading Clausewitz. Clausewitz was a dolt. He was
reading Lidell-Hart. Lidell-Hart was full of himself. He was reading Miyamoto Musashi. Musashi was a New-Agey Zen mystic. He
was reading Sun Tzu. Sun Tzu had some rather interesting stuff going on.

Official Washington was avoiding Van. Van understood this. He
was no more welcome to the official power structure than Watergate
burglars and Iran-Contra conspirators. Washingtonians avoided
such people while the heat was still on them. The wheel moved
back around, eventually. Then the malefactors became talk-show
hosts.

Van was earning a little pin money by working on a rollout of
Bastille Linux. He was also drinking rather a lot. It was hard for a
warrior not to drink when he was kept away from the action. He had
discovered a fondness for big pint cans of Foster's Lager. Once he had
been bright, whimsical, inventive. Now he was dark, dangerous, inventive.

The loss of her telescope had brought Dottie's career to a shattering halt. She left Colorado and brought Ted with her to share Van's
life. The family was broke, and living in a tiny, unfurnished duplex in
Pentagon City. They had no careers, few prospects, large tax debts,
and a host of personal humiliations. They had no offices, and both

had to work underfoot in the grimy nook that called itself a living room. That was also where Ted had his playpen.

If times were hard in computer science, they were brutal in astronomy. Dottie's people were cutting budgets past the bone. Dottie's blighted résumé included a lot of public relations work for an astronomical facility that had somehow burned down its telescope. Through no fault or intention of her own, Dr. Dottie Vandeveer had wandered into a world of hurt.

Dottie looked pale and drawn lately. Her face was lined, her brown hair showing strands of gray.

Van rose from the bed. He showered, ignoring the mildew in the grout. He went into the soot-stained kitchen in a T-shirt and underwear.

The four new chairs in the kitchen had red bows on them.

"Happy birthday, honey," Dottie told him.

"Wow," Van blurted. "Magnesium chairs!"

"You like them?"

"They are the best!"

"I got them secondhand for you!" Dottie crowed. "Barely used! They were so cheap!"

Van sat in one of the metal chairs. His ass felt metallic and cold through his white cotton underwear, but the chairs had always been a lot more comfortable than they looked. "Four of them, wow!" he said loudly. He sipped his instant coffee. "That's just great! You are so good to me, babe." He nibbled some burnt toast.

Dottie perched in one of the chairs. "Derek," she said shyly.

Van looked at his wife. He knew instantly, in his gut, that Dottie was about to tell him something dreadful. She was using her kindest, sweetest voice, the kind she used when tactfully urging him toward something that would have great rusty fangs like a bear trap. Dottie looked pained and greenish—she'd hardly been eating in the mornings, maybe a sip of coffee, a nibble off a stale doughnut.

He had married a proud, shy, lonely, vulnerable young woman with an intellectual gift. And now, in his care, and due to him, she was reduced to . . . what? She was a soldier's wife, he thought. A woman who made do. He was one of the world's secret soldiers. They had become hard, gritty, wounded people with bitter lines around their mouths. What did the future offer them?

"Derek, something important has happened . . ."

Van moved to the edge of his new chair. "What?"

"You're going to have me around a whole lot. You're going to have me on your hands all the time." Dottie rubbed her forehead. "This is my birthday present for you, but you're really going to have to put up with me now, honey . . ."

What on earth was the woman rattling on about? Why didn't she cut to the chase?

"Derek, I'm pregnant."

Van absorbed this input. Where was Ted? he thought instantly. Ted really needed to hear this news. This was going to be of enormous importance to Ted.

"I know this is a bad time for us to have a baby . . . But, you know, the only job offer I've got is in Denmark . . . Oh, God, Derek, I've been so careless and stupid . . . I can't believe that happened. It just ruins everything. After all this, things are so bad for us, and now I'm pregnant." Dottie burst into sobs.

Van felt something extraordinary happening within him. A dead black crust was breaking open. He had known no word for that feeling until it began to lift away from him under tremendous internal pressure. But now he knew what that feeling had been. It was grief. It was grief.

Now the black grief was receding from him. It was blasting away from his heart at half the speed of light. Something inside him that had been tiny and sparklike and bitterly embattled was expanding like a vast red star.

He was huge inside. He glowed and burned. He had gravity.

"Baby, that is great news. You are saving our lives here."

Dottie lifted her head. Her morale was in visible ruins. "I get so sick, with that morning sickness. I get so helpless . . ."

"This is the best birthday gift I've ever had."

She blinked in disbelief. "You really think so?"

"I don't think so. I know so. Four people in our family, that is like a little squad. We'll get really quick, and stop complaining so much from now on. We'll change our lazy habits. We'll get things done whenever they need to get done."

"Derek, this will ruin our careers."

"No it won't. Your career will move right on. You will take that job in Denmark. I will look after our kids."

Dottie's eyes widened. "We're moving to Denmark?"

"Yeah. We're gonna sell everything here and we'll move to Europe. Right away."

A hectic flush rose to Dottie's cheeks. "What, even these chairs? But I just bought us this furniture."

"Honey, Europe is well known for its furniture. These are European chairs."

"What about *your* career, Derek?"

"I know what I'm doing. Honey, it is senseless for intelligent people not to have children. Why would I want to vote against the future? What we need is a good strategy. And I've got one for us. You will work. I will stay home with the children."

"Really?"

"Yes."

"You'd make that sacrifice for us?"

"What sacrifice? I love the idea of two kids. I need this. It'll be broadening for me. Am I nailed here in Washington, for any reason? I can hit a RETURN key anywhere in the world."

Though it was his birthday, Dottie needed consoling. He lavished some on her. That worked. Dottie was still weeping in happiness as they lay in bed together. Van stared silently at the ceiling.

It was a very good move for him to get out of Washington. A lateral move, very Liddell-Hart, very Sun Tzu. When power avoided you, a counteravoidance move lured power back in.

His wife didn't need to know this, but the Administration had way too many people like himself, wandering loose. Now that Van had learned, by startling counterexamples, something about sound and competent governance, he was very aware that the Terror was just the Bubble by another name. It was just as wild, just as turbulent, and just as unlikely to last. No government that was not desperate and totally winging it ever, ever would have asked Dr. Derek Vandeveer to become a warrior.

And yet he had done just that. Odder yet, he had grown to understand the war. He had the scars to prove it. He had become the kind of person who could shift a world's destiny through acts of organized violence.

He had become a professional. And his profession was always going to be something that didn't quite exist. The profession of cyberwarrior was always mostly going to be about lying low. The indirect approach, as Liddell-Hart liked to put it. The leak. The putsch within darkness. The patient stalking. The compilation of databases. The cybernetic awareness. The brief and devastating strike. And the silent exfiltration. And the wait.

The Terror was merely an overexcited phase, and like the Bubble, it was going to burst of its own hype. And when it did pop, it would be a rather good thing not to be visibly holding the bag. To be, say, a low-key house husband living in distant Europe. Raising two little kids.

Two days later, as he was watching the bidding for his possessions on eBay, Van's phone rang.

"Vandeveer."

The voice on the phone was distant and laggy. "Van? Kind of a blast from the past here. This is Jimmie Matson! You remember me? We used to work together!"

Van paused. He could place the voice before the memory came. Of course. Jimmie Matson at Mondiale. His top lab exec. Why hadn't Jimmie from Mondiale just said "It's me, Jimmie from Mondiale"? Of course, Van realized, Jimmie had his reasons not to say such things. Nobody from Mondiale ever said "Mondiale" now.

"Of course I remember you, Jimmie. What's up?"

"So, I just saw on your Web log that you're thinking of moving to Denmark! Well, I'm here in Switzerland."

"How come?"

"I got a post here, a kind of liaison committee . . . The WIPO and the World Telecommunications Union . . . plus some WTO people . . . Well, it's hard to explain in a few words, Van, but policy here is a major mess."

"Try me."

Jimmie sighed into the phone. "Van, I so wish I'd gotten that great post you wanted for me at the CCIAB. But the feds weren't having any of me, for security reasons I guess . . . Anyway, it is just so impossibly bad up here on the global level . . . You would never believe what is going on behind the scenes here in Geneva . . . The French and Germans really get it about the American hyperpower thing, they are all over our case diplomatically . . . All the delegates here hate each other, Van. They hate each other, they can't speak the same language, and they are crooked. Plus they have no idea what they are trying to do, technically. That is the worst part. They've got nobody to fill this job of technical director."

"Right."

"I thought of you for that job, somehow. I mean, it's an international bureaucracy job, not much for a guy of your caliber, but there's health insurance and a nice subsidized apartment . . . Beautiful headquarters building right on the lake. Really pretty. You've got to hand 'em that."

"They need someone there to knock heads," Van said.

"Uh, yeah. Officially, this post calls for an executive with advanced technical skills who has had private-sector international telecom experience and has also served in an advanced capacity in a major government. There's just one hitch. There is no such guy. And if there was . . . Well, no guy in the world who had done all those things would ever want to come and get involved in this. This is like trench warfare."

"I just did all that. I'm used to it."

"I gotta warn you, Van, this scene feels pretty hopeless!"

"Hope is not a feeling, Jimmie. Hope is not the belief that things will turn out well, but the conviction that what we are doing makes sense, no matter how things turn out."

Jimmie said nothing for a long moment. Then he spoke in a new voice. "Van, how long have you been reading Vaclav Havel?"

"Oh, President Havel has been a favorite of mine for some time now," said Van.

"Could you fly over here right away, please? I mean, like, *right away.*"

"I'll be doing a lot of commuting to Denmark."

"They've got great trains in Europe," Jimmie said.

"Fine. You make arrangements. I'll be bringing a small child with me, so book me two seats."

"All right. Can you take the next plane?"